ILLARIA

BOOK TWO OF THE PARADISE SERIES

IVANA L. TRUGLIO

JONQUIL
PRESS

First published in Australia in 2015
by Jonquil Press
ABN: 99871403756

National Library of Australia Cataloguing-in-Publication data:
Author: Truglio, Ivana L.
Title: Illaria/Ivana L. Truglio
ISBN: 9780992565466 (paperback)
Series: Truglio, Ivana L. Paradise series; bk Two
Subjects: Fantasy fiction
Dewey Number: A823.4

Cover illustration by Les Petersen

Typeset in Minion Pro 9.5pt/11.4pt

For my father,
Nicola Truglio

ABOUT THE AUTHOR

Ivana lives in Sydney, Australia working as a senior editor for a multinational publishing company. She devotes most, if not all, of her spare time to writing the Paradise Series.

At various times, she has studied aviation, archaeology and ancient history at university. She currently holds a private pilot licence and rides a motorbike.

She has also been known to play the flute, dance ballet and play fencing (although not all at the same time). During her studies, it was rumoured that she lived in the university library.

Ivana is married and has two young children who reap the benefits of having a mother with a wild imagination. She has been writing since she was a child and the characters in the Paradise Series have been living in her head for around 15 years.

ACKNOWLEDGEMENTS

My first thanks go to my test readers, Patrick Harper and Carol Ballantine, for their encouragment when I felt disillusioned and their fantastic ability to be sounding boards for my ideas. I know *Illaria* wouldn't have found its way without you.

To my wonderful team of editors Zehra Bharucha, Shannon Kelly and Liz Gandy, thank you all for willingly giving up your time to help me perfect this book and make it a more enjoyable read for everyone.

For two of my biggest kickstarter supporters Nicole Jay and Keiran Jones, the characters Dorian, Elwood, Lord Kynon and Vaughn were named as you requested as part of your reward. Thanks again for your support!

To Catherine Y and Kylie Abbenhues, my friends and biggest fans, thank you for all your help to nudge my books along. I can't tell you how much I appreciate your support in this adventure! I particularly liked *Rilla*'s appearance at a book week parade.

To my husband, who never complains when he hears the furious typing he now associates with my stories, thanks for everything – I could never have done this without you.

Lastly, to everyone who bought a copy of *Rilla* and particularly those who shared with me certain characters or scenes that you liked, thank you so very much. Without you, I may not have continued writing the series so thank you a thousand times over for your enthusiasm!

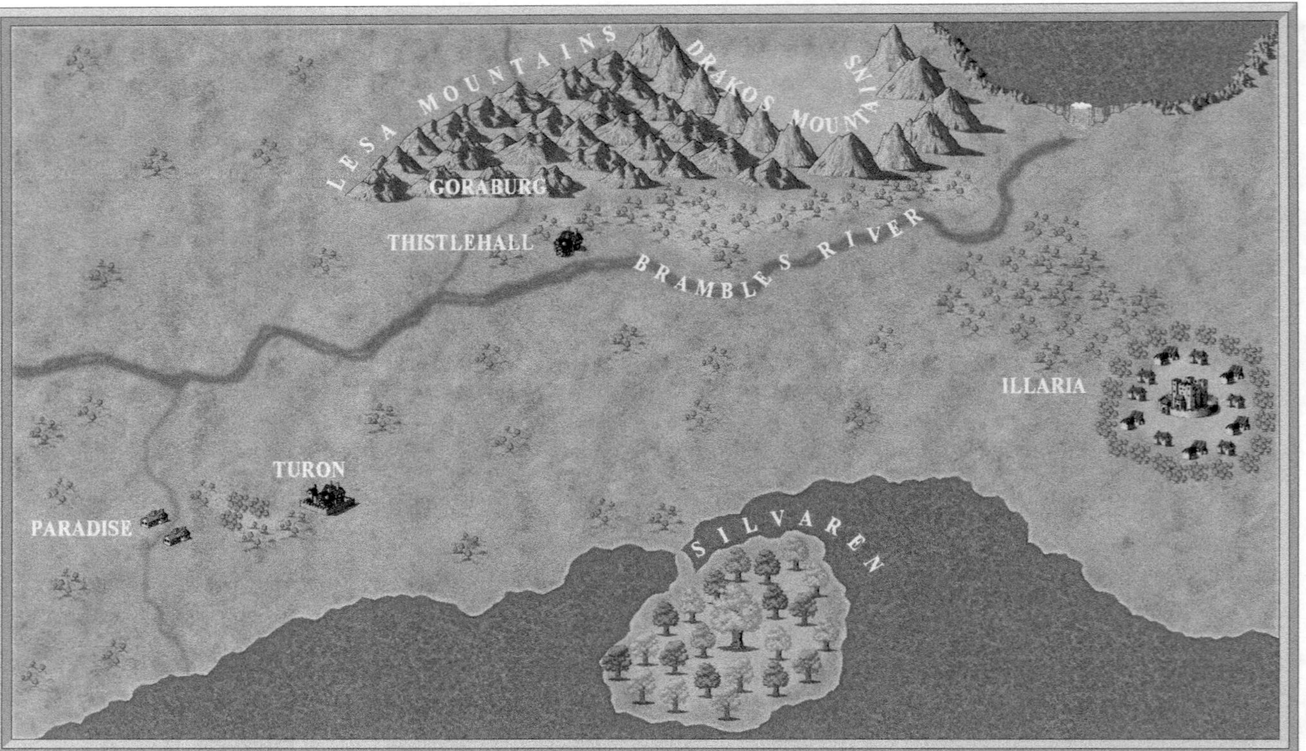

LESA MOUNTAINS
DRAKOS MOUNTAINS
GORABURG
THISTLEHALL
BRAMBLES RIVER
ILLARIA
TURON
PARADISE
SILVAREN

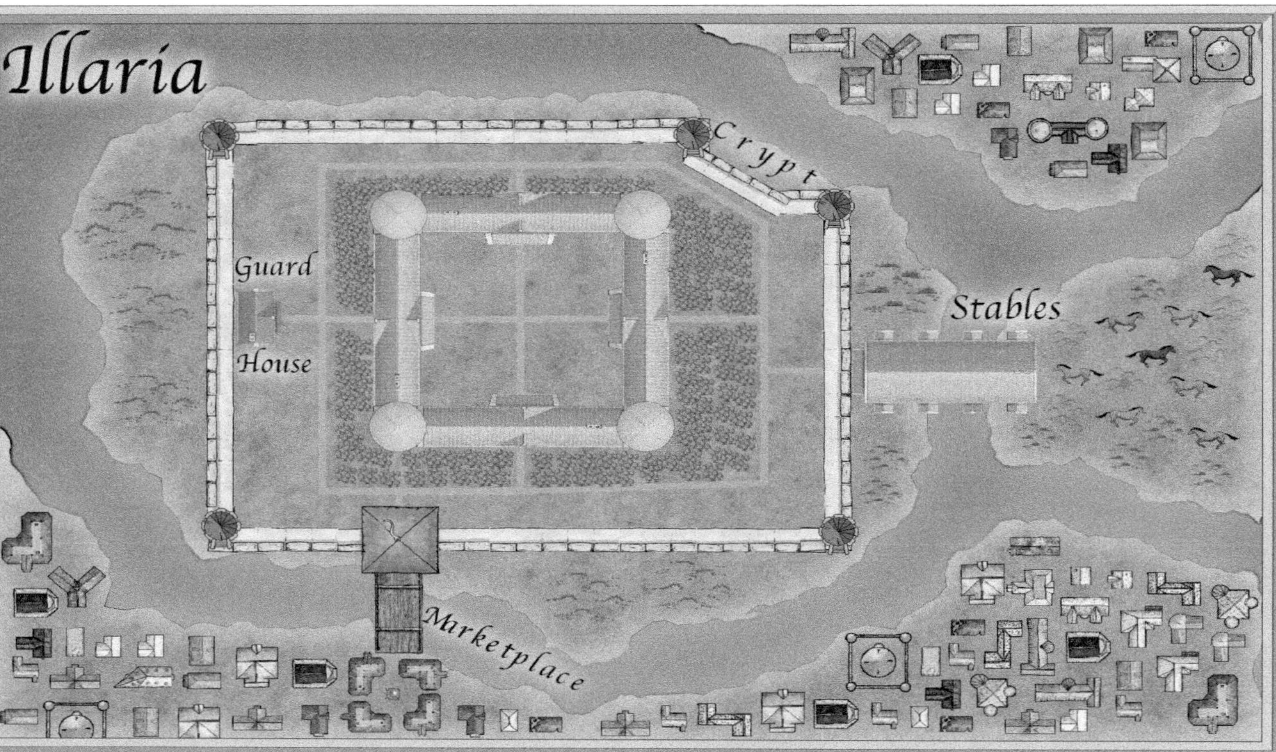

Illaria
Crypt
Guard
House
Stables
Marketplace

Chapter One – Illaria

"Stupid, stupid Nyssa," Lishe muttered angrily, for the hundredth time. Shuut listened to her, curled up in a tight ball. She was cold, hungry and tired, but that was just on the surface. She shielded her thoughts as best she could from the powerful lintep. As far as she had pieced the facts together, Lishe and Nyssa had known each other when they were younger – more than that, they had been the best of friends. It seemed as though they had completely parted ways when Nyssa had left Illaria to find Kora. Lishe knew about Rilla being Nyssa's daughter, but it was entirely possible she had no idea that Shuut was as well.

"Were they going to Illaria?" Shuut looked up at the intrusion to her thoughts. Would it make a difference if she told her? How much pain would Lishe be able to inflict on her without killing her? It was a question that plagued the Banwep. Lishe hadn't tried to hurt Shuut since she'd been inflicted with Nyssa's power. Why not?

Think, Shuut, think. A strange look flashed in the pale blue eyes.

"Whatever you're trying to plan, don't bother. I will kill you as soon as you've served your purpose and Nyssa's power will finally be mine."

"Why don't you just kill me now?" Shuut unfurled herself with no small amount of effort. "Then you can have her power straight away."

"Nothing would please me more, but I need you to lure that little brat away from the elf."

"I mean nothing to her," Shuut replied, hoping the lintep didn't know the truth. "What makes you think you'd be able to lure her away with me?"

Lishe studied her intently. "Someone taught you to hide your thoughts well. Too bad for you, I know the whole group of them could have left you behind when I attacked you, but they didn't. That means they're loyal enough to you to want to save you if they can. My only problem is the elf. He must be more powerful than most."

Shuut made no reply. There was no use arguing the point. They both knew it was true. The only advantage Shuut had was that Lishe didn't know Rilla was her sister and Plyke was her cousin. In fact, if she knew about Plyke, it could all be so much worse.

Annoyed by the banwep's silence, Lishe tested the limits of her control on Nyssa's power. She relaxed her grip from around the girl's body. Almost instantly, Nyssa's power fought for freedom. The Banwep howled in pain, curling into a ball yet again. Lishe sighed angrily. If she had to constantly keep Nyssa's power contained, she wouldn't be able to use much of her own power herself, not to mention the fact that she would be unable to sleep or even rest.

She had two choices before her – get to Rilla, lure her away from the others and kill both girls before she collapsed from exhaustion or take some time to teach the banwep how to build a wall around Nyssa's power so that it couldn't escape her. Much as she wanted to just kill the brat and steal Nyssa's power, she knew that rushing into things would not benefit her in the long run. If she took a day or two to get the banwep to build a wall around Nyssa's power, she would be able to focus more on the task at hand with at least a few days before the wall crumbled.

When they were studying together in Illaria, Lishe had been so angry with Nyssa for not even trying to control her power as well as the rest of them. Just because she was more powerful and could perform the tasks more easily, she didn't bother honing her skills the same way her friends did. Now, it made for the perfect revenge. Lishe would soon be able to steal Nyssa's power exactly because she had lacked the skill to defend herself. It was only a minor delay to have the power transferred to the banwep first – minor, but incredibly inconvenient.

* * *

A faceless woman calmly walked into view. Shuut was pinned up against a tree. Nyssa stood as though frozen, sobbing. The woman twirled her black hair between her fingers while asking questions that Nyssa and Shuut refused to answer.

Fire shot from Nyssa's mouth to the other woman but the flames stopped short of her in a ball. The woman turned the ball back to Nyssa and started burning her arms and legs. Nyssa screamed. Shuut yelled at the torturer.

Eventually, the woman turned to Shuut. Nyssa stopped screaming and Shuut began to gag. The woman howled in anger as Nyssa fell lifeless to the floor.

Images from his dream flashed over and over in Arishen's mind. He knew it was real, but how could he convince the others? They didn't understand or believe him. Nyssa was certainly dead and Shuut was in danger. Who was that woman? If only he could have seen her face. Why were the faces always a blur? Arishen was so preoccupied with his thoughts that he didn't notice Rilla's eyes on him.

Rilla heard his thoughts without wanting to. Since her power had started to peak, she couldn't control what she could and couldn't do with it. She actively tried not to, but she was fairly certain that with just a little effort, she would actually be able to see Arishen's dreams. Would it help if the other lintep could see it? Maybe they would be able to tell if it was real, or who the other woman was.

She bounced the thought to Eliséo through Elessa, being careful to close her eyes for the moment it took to pass to them. Eliséo glanced over to her and nodded almost imperceptibly before turning to the older lintep.

"Master Aurelius," the old lintep turned his grey head towards Eliséo, "I wonder if it would be possible to have a master of the mind help with Arishen's vision. I know there are many masters who excel in this area. Perhaps they would be able to actually see the seer's vision for themselves."

"Hmm, I do understand what you are suggesting, Ambassador Eliséo, but I don't see how it would change matters," Aurelius shook his head ever so slightly.

"Perhaps if someone could identify the unknown person, it might give them more incentive to help our remaining companions, assuming either of them are still alive and in danger."

The Paradisians remained silent during the conversation. They had travelled with Eliséo for long enough now to understand when he was using diplomacy to get his way.

The lintep master looked over at Arishen, eventually shrugging his shoulders. "They could certainly try it. I make no promises as my area of expertise does not lie there."

"What's your area of expertise?" Tika asked, eager to keep the conversation about magic alive.

"As a master, I am quite skilled in all areas of lintep powers. That being said, I've always liked the more practical aspect of things," he smiled at the look of confusion on the human's face, though his smile quickly turned to a frown when he saw the confusion on Rilla and Plyke's faces as well.

"Ambassador, am I correct in assuming these young lintep are not overly familiar with the varied uses of lintep power, even though they are the offspring of Lady Nyssa and Lady Kora?"

He watched as Rilla and Plyke missed a step and shared a wild glance. "I see they have not yet understood who they really are or what they are capable of. Well, children, there will be plenty of time to deal with that once we have your powers safely under control."

"Is there only one master for each area?" Tika asked, unwilling to let the subject of magic drop.

"Well, no, not always," Aurelius answered, "It simply depends on each individual lintep, as to whether they are skilled enough to become a master and where their powers lie."

"Does that mean that most lintep aren't skilled in all areas?"

"All lintep have at least a small amount of skill in each area, but it is quite rare for any to excel in more than one or two of these areas. I might add that those areas are usually similar to one another."

"How many different areas are there?"

"Is he always like this?" the old lintep looked over to Eliséo, almost willing him to stop the stream of questions.

"There is no force in the Outworld capable of stopping him." Eliséo stifled a laugh.

"Well, I suppose strictly speaking there are a number of areas, but as I mentioned, most are linked with at least one other area. In fact, they could broadly be grouped into three areas – mind, practical and communication."

"But …" Tika looked over at Rilla and Plyke and bit off his reply. Master Aurelius looked at him expectantly. When Tika didn't continue, he looked over at the two young lintep.

"Is it possible that the two of you have already displayed such skills? And with some degree of power and control?"

They didn't answer.

"I told you that I'm skilled in all the areas. Just because I prefer the practical side of things doesn't mean I can't easily read your minds if I choose too."

"Actually, it does mean that," Eliséo told him flatly. "You may be able to, but only with a great deal of effort. Apparently both of them have learnt to build strong walls to protect themselves."

Aurelius tried to hide his surprise at the information. "Well, your lessons should prove to be quite interesting." With that, he dropped the subject. Tika took the hint and stopped asking questions. Rilla and Plyke exchanged worried glances before turning to Eliséo, who simply shook his head at them.

Eliséo cursed inwardly. He would have to stay at least for their testing with the masters. They, particularly Plyke, didn't exactly understand the extent of their powers. Rilla had been freely using them her whole life, without realising it and then actively using them when she realised what she was. She could do things most trained lintep had never even dreamt of before. Plyke had held his power back so fiercely that when he did try to do anything, it rushed out and tried to escape him, but before that was always a moment, a brief spark, where he could do amazing things with it – things no untrained lintep should be able to do.

The odd company walked on in silence, each lost in their own thoughts. Eventually, the Paradisians were jolted out of their musings by the sight of the lintep stronghold. They stood and stared at the enormous expanse of Illaria. From the boundary of the stronghold they had walked past a rapidly thinning forest, through a multitude of farms and orchards. Finally, the fields had given way to a town, larger than any they'd come across in the Outworld.

Initially, the streets they walked on were dirt, compacted down from years of people, animals and wagons travelling down them. Towards the higher buildings and denser part of town the streets were paved with cobblestones to compensate for the amount of traffic on the major thoroughfares.

As with Turon, they came to a large market square. They took in the vast array of colourful materials and trinkets then their eyes strayed to the most amazing variety of fruits, grains, vegetables, bread and meat they had ever seen. However, their attention was quickly diverted by the majestic castle that stood before them.

Across from the market was a moat, much wider than the stream that had flowed through their Paradise. It was fed by a stream to the north, which was split by the castle and joined up again to flow away to the south. A cobbled bridge spanned most of the way across the moat until it was met by a wooden drawbridge. They listened as Master Aurelius explained that it was lowered each sunrise and raised each evening, leaving the castle protected by the moat and portcullis.

As they neared the drawbridge, they looked up to see guards standing watch at their posts along the sandstone wall that encompassed the castle grounds. They took no notice of the travellers being escorted in by the familiar master lintep. The Paradisians walked in stunned silence across the bridge.

As they neared the gate, the castle disappeared from their view completely. Tika gripped Plyke's hand excitedly. Together, they walked across the moat, following close in the footsteps of Eliséo, Master Aurelius and Rilla into the massive courtyard on the other side of the fortified walls.

Once they had passed through the gateway, they stopped and stared at the perfectly manicured gardens. They'd never seen a place where the gardens were for purely ornamental purposes. The only garden in their Paradise had been the herb garden behind the healers' house. There hadn't been any ornamental gardens in the small towns they'd passed through in the Outworld and though Silvaren was made of beautiful and magnificently large trees there hadn't been a flower garden in sight. This garden had walkways cutting through the flowers and grass with stone benches at irregular intervals. On occasion, the benches were set in pairs with matching stone tables between them, but all had one thing in common – they faced the brilliant golden hued sandstone castle.

It loomed above them, four levels high with towers in each corner. On the lower levels, the windows were thin slits, large enough for arrows to be shot out of them and nothing more. At the higher levels, the windows became progressively larger until the top level where the stained glass windows were as wide as a person was tall, with elaborate designs carved into the sandstone all around them.

At the top of the castle were intricate railings behind which they could see more guards standing at attention. Below the railings was a line of gargoyles, varying from grotesque to angelic faces, peering down at them. It was only when Tika turned to share his amazement at the sight with Arishen that he noticed the seer was missing.

"Where's Arishen?" At the note of panic in his voice, the others turned. "He was right behind us when we got to the walkway." Tika turned to run back across the bridge but bounced off something hard and invisible at the portcullis before falling to the floor.

"Well," said Aurelius, with a hint of amusement in his voice, "it's good to know the old wards still work."

"What old wards?" Tika asked as he got to his feet, rubbing his rapidly bruising elbow.

"The ones we put up around the stronghold to make sure humans couldn't easily attack us," the old lintep master answered. "Your partner must have led you in by the hand, if I'm not mistaken. Rilla, why don't you run back and bring your seer past the wards?"

Rilla walked back across the wooden drawbridge and onto the cobbled walkway, only breaking into a run when she was close enough to see Arishen frantically beating his fists against thin air. The ward was completely invisible, but not sound proof. As she neared the seer, she could hear him shouting out for someone to let him in and cursing that he'd been left behind.

"Keep your voice down, Arishen!" Rilla reprimanded him as soon as she was on the other side of the ward, glancing up as a guard turned his head at the commotion. "Every lintep within hearing will know you're a human with all that yelling and cursing."

"Well, so what if they do?" replied the seer angrily. "Just you make sure no one leaves me behind any other of these magical wards."

"So what if they do?" Rilla repeated incredulously. "You *do* realise that it's against the first rule of Illaria that you're even here, don't you? Master Aurelius has bent that rule to keep me and Plyke safe, but word cannot have spread yet to every lintep in this place. Can you imagine what they would do to you if they discovered a human in their stronghold?"

Arishen quietened down and had the sense to look chastened as Rilla glanced, yet again, at the guards on top of the wall. She took him by the hand and tugged him across the bridge, not noticing his face redden at her touch. As soon as they had joined the others, she dropped his hand and stormed over to Eliséo.

"Honestly, you'd think he wasn't grateful that we got him into Illaria, the way he's acting," Rilla muttered under her breath to Eliséo.

She would have much preferred talking through Elessa right now but had been warned enough by both her tree and the elf not to do anything so stupid. The only comfort he could give her was a hand placed gently on her arm to calm her. She understood the last thing they needed was a scene in front of Master Aurelius. He had risked quite a lot by allowing Tika and Arishen entry into Illaria. It would not do to have him regret the decision so soon.

"I suggest you don't walk at the rear of our company, young seer," the old lintep advised Arishen. "We don't want to leave you behind again. Many of the lintep living in Illaria are somewhat less than impressed with humans and may use their powers in a ways you'd rather never feel."

Arishen shivered as Rilla's words were confirmed by the master lintep. He nodded his head and moved to walk beside Plyke. They walked on through the extensive grounds of the castle. Tika turned his head at the sound of a horse neighing, but Plyke pulled him straight ahead, following the others.

As they passed through the main entrance to the internal castle grounds, the young lintep cousins drew in their breath and came to a halt. The entire inner courtyard was divided into grass quadrants, with sandstone pathways to each side of the castle, where an arch opened up into the covered hall which wound its way around the entire inner courtyard. Along the hall were smaller archways where lintep were perched, either watching students in the quadrants or talking to each other. A very few of them were sitting back against the arches, reading from scrolls or leather-bound books.

What had caught Rilla and Plyke's attention were the lintep in each quadrangle, practicing with their powers. In one quadrant, students were using the same small white stones Nyssa had shown them, but what they were doing with the stones was far beyond what Rilla's mother had asked of them. In the next quadrant, lintep were sparring with each other using wooden weapons, the way Rilla and Plyke had once sparred. The third quadrant had lintep fighting each other with just their power and the miscellaneous objects that were lying around.

The last quadrant, however, was the one Rilla was most excited by – it seemed as though lintep were experimenting in whatever way they wanted. Some were disappearing, others were playing with water and fire, heat and cold. They were all things she had already experimented with in the most dangerous of ways and she was overwhelmed by the fact that she wasn't going to be held back by Nyssa's lack of experience any more.

"How soon will we start our training?" Rilla asked, her eyes fixed on the last quadrant.

"Little one, it will probably be months, perhaps even years, before you are allowed into *that* quadrant."

Rilla flinched at the term "little one". It was what Rhanya had called her when no one else would even talk to her. To have another person calling her that without understanding the first thing about her was almost unbearable.

"Which quadrant will they be allowed in first?" Tika asked.

"The one with the stones," Master Aurelius answered promptly. "Every lintep begins their practical studies there. In that area they learn the basic skills and control they will need for the other areas. But even before that, each Outworld lintep undergoes a series of tests to ascertain what level they are at and where their strengths lie."

"When will that happen for Plyke and Rilla?" Tika asked, barely waiting for his previous question to be answered.

Aurelius coughed uncomfortably. "They will first need to convince the

Council of Masters to allow their human friends to remain in Illaria. If they do not agree to that condition, Rilla and Plyke will have to decide whether or not they want to stay here."

"Uh … when will that happen?" the young human asked hesitantly.

"Immediately."

Master Aurelius turned and led them along the covered pathway to a magnificent open stairwell that twisted and curled its way up into the distance. As they walked up the stairs, they noticed openings wide enough to poke their heads through so, being curious Paradisians in a lintep stronghold, they each did just that and were startled to see the openings spaced evenly all the way to the top of the stairwell where streams of sunlight shone down. Before they could be left behind, the four of them hurried to catch up with Eliséo and Master Aurelius as they were led to the Council of Masters.

Chapter Two – The Council of Masters

"Can't you walk any faster than that?" Lishe asked impatiently. "I need to get to that little brat before they start training her."

"I'm sorry to delay your plans," Shuut replied sarcastically, knowing now that the deranged lintep wouldn't kill her until Rilla was within her reach. "But if you would just let me build this wall without walking, I think we'd both be better off."

"Stupid Nyssa," Lishe muttered yet again.

"No matter how many times you call her stupid, it's not going to change the fact that she outwitted you with all your power," Shuut goaded her. If she was going to have to travel with this lintep, better to push her limits now to know what might help her later.

"She did *not* outwit me, she simply killed herself to buy her daughter a few extra days."

"You were going to kill her anyway," Shuut pointed out unhelpfully, careful to avoid the fact that she was Nyssa's daughter as well.

"Yes, well, she killed herself faster than I was going to kill her," Lishe replied testily. "*That* makes her stupid."

"No, not really," Shuut was enjoying this game. "Some would say it makes her quite clever because she avoided more torture and she denied you her power which, let's face it, was what you were after in the first place."

Suddenly she couldn't breathe. Her feet were dangling a few inches off the ground. Her throat was being crushed by an unseen force. Her lungs were burning.

"I have more than enough power without Nyssa's to add to it and as soon as I have that brat, I'm going to snap your pretty little neck. Are we clear?"

Shuut struggled to nod her head through Lishe's hold on her body. Lishe withdrew her power and the banwep crumpled to the floor, gasping for breath, tears streaming from the corners of her eyes. At least she'd confirmed that the thing Lishe wanted the most was Nyssa's power. Rilla was important to Lishe too, but only because she wanted to stop the prophecy. Now all Shuut had to figure out was why.

* * *

Master Aurelius led the newcomers up the twisting stairwell and down a long hallway. The stone floor had been worn smooth by years of use. There were wooden doors on one side, separated by unlit lanterns and tapestries that depicted images from battles and magnificent feats of magic. The other side of the hall had windows facing the internal courtyard so they could still see all the training lintep.

The grey haired lintep stopped at a door with a simple design carved on the wood, behind which was the Council of Masters. Marilisa and Tommaso had alerted the masters and mistresses that a meeting of the council was required immediately so, when Aurelius opened the doors, they were already waiting for him.

Master Aurelius felt the Paradisians peer around him as he took off his outer robe, revealing an elaborate blue tattoo on his left arm, similar to the carving on the door. The other twenty-five members of the council were seated around a large wooden oval table, each with a blue tattoo of their own. The designs varied slightly from one to another. The more elaborate ones with bands around their arm, exactly like the design on the door, were seated together at one end of the room, close to where Aurelius himself usually sat, with the simpler ones at the other end.

As he led the newcomers in, Aurelius heard a sharp intake of breath behind him. He could hear Rilla's thoughts swirling past her mental walls. Convincing a handful of lintep would have been much easier than an entire room of them. Aurelius took a step away from the situation to look at things from the girl's point of view. Given what was facing them, he was impressed Rilla and Plyke were so calm on the surface.

Without much effort, he gently nudged Rilla with his powers and she immediately withdrew her thoughts back behind her walls, where he was certain she would keep them for the remainder of the meeting.

The old Master caught Mistress Kayte's eye, her bright golden hair making her easy to find. She raised a worried brow at him. Marilisa had told them the gist of what had happened and she didn't hold much hope that these new lintep would be allowed to remain with their human companions.

"I see we have a full council today," Master Aurelius said as he looked over to Marilisa. "You forgot to call King Lukys. Why don't you run along and do that now? Take Tommaso with you. He can find Lord Aaron, as it will interest both of them to hear this session of the Masters."

"Should I not then get Lord Kynon too? I think it would greatly interest *him* as well," Marilisa asked, flicking her straight black shoulder-length hair off her face.

"Lord Aaron will find him. You and Tommaso get back to patrolling the borders," the older lintep told her in a voice that brooked no argument. She left the room in silence with Tommaso, sneering at Rilla and Plyke as she passed them.

"Aurelius, it is most unusual to involve the royal family in matters of the council," a lintep with severely cut black hair began once the doors had closed behind Marilisa and Tommaso. "Is there really such a need for a matter as simple as this?"

"There is nothing simple about this matter, Jorg," replied Aurelius. "Or did Marilisa not tell you everything?"

"She told us you allowed two humans to enter Illaria," an older lintep replied curtly. Sitting beside Jorg, her soft, wavy brown hair made her look no less severe than he.

"Yes, well, she did leave out the most important part of the matter, Vika," Aurelius attempted to hide his annoyance with Marilisa. Royal or not, sometimes the girl was too arrogant to tolerate. "The two new lintep refused entry without their companions. I thought it best, given who they are, to allow temporary access to the humans until we, including the royal family, decide what the best course of action is."

"We don't need the royal family for that," Master Jorg maintained. "Our rules are few and simple – the main one being that we *do not* allow humans into Illaria. I suggest you take them back to the border before anything unfortunate happens to them."

Aurelius felt a commotion behind him. Rilla was trying to push forward, presumably to defend her friends, but Eliséo was keeping her as hidden as possible behind the master lintep. They might not recognise her instantly, but her red hair would soon jog a few memories and they would begin to figure out who she was. It would be better if the king and his cousins were here before then. Aurelius didn't know how much longer he could stall the discovery.

"Nothing unfortunate will happen to them in this council, Master Jorg," a much younger lintep made herself heard. "Humans may not exactly be my cup of tea, but I will not see any harmed when they haven't wronged us."

"Isis, you are the newest member of the council and should sit in silence while you learn how things are done here," Vika replied icily. Aurelius rolled his eyes as he noticed the older mistress reposition herself so that her elaborate blue tattoo could not be missed by the young mistress. Though he understood the need for masters and mistresses to have tattoos clearly marking their skill level, he always hated how the more senior members of the council used them to treat the younger ones as inferior. Isis had the simplest design of the entire council – a naked flame with a single band around her arm.

"I do not believe Mistress Isis spoke out of turn," Mistress Kayte spoke loudly and clearly, her short blonde hair bobbing around her face as she turned towards Vika. "No matter when they joined the council, or where they sit, each master or mistress has equal rights to an opinion. I agree with Isis that no harm should come to these two humans while they are in Illaria. If we choose to deny them access, then they should be safely escorted back to the Outworld."

Aurelius could feel the discomfort of the humans. This close to their unprotected minds, he could feel everything, hear every thought. They were quite justified in being so afraid of the lintep, though they didn't know the half of what could be done to them.

The doors opened again and in walked the three lintep Aurelius had been waiting for. King Lukys, a thin circlet of gold around his curly light brown hair was followed by his cousins, Lord Aaron and Lord Kynon. The lords had the same light brown hair, but their curls faded into waves. The similarities ended there. Whereas the Lukys had brown eyes, Aaron and Kynon shared the lighters colours more common in their family. It had been one of the reasons Aurelius had tried to hide Rilla and Plyke from the council. Their eyes would soon have given them away as part of the royal family if nothing else had.

Master Aurelius returned a slight nod from Lukys as the king passed him. The three lintep approached the end of the room to take the last remaining chairs.

"Master Aurelius, I trust there is sufficient reason behind this sudden summoning of the Council of Masters and the inclusion of the royal family?"

"King Lukys, I do believe this particular matter would be of interest both to the Council and your family," he turned to finally bring both Rilla and Plyke into view. "These two young lintep refused to enter Illaria without their human companions."

"Why should that concern us?" Kynon asked snidely.

"Lord Kynon, it may interest you to know that both are in the final stages of their power peaking and would quite possibly have died had I refused them entry."

"That doesn't answer my question," the younger lord replied, irritably twisting a strand of his wavy brown hair.

"This is Rilla, daughter of Lady Nyssa and this is Plyke, son of Lady Kora." There was a sharp intake of breath all around as Aurelius pulled the two young lintep in front of him. "I felt that Lord Aaron would want to meet his grandchildren, including the prophecy child, preferably alive."

On the other side of King Lukys, Lord Aaron sat straighter at the mention of his daughters' names. Every lintep in Illaria knew that the girls had left over twenty years ago and never returned. Beside him, he saw Rilla and Plyke start at the statement.

"My grandchildren?" Aaron whispered, barely audibly. "I have two grandchildren?"

"If I might have permission to speak?" Eliséo waited for King Lukys to nod before continuing. "Lord Aaron, you have *three* grandchildren. Your oldest granddaughter is on her way to Illaria as we speak."

"Three grandchildren?" Lord Aaron was visibly surprised by the news. "What of my daughters? Where are they?"

Aurelius looked over to the silent Paradisians as they shuffled their feet, avoiding the gaze of every lintep in the room.

"Would someone please explain why Lady Nyssa and Lady Kora have not accompanied their children to Illaria?" King Lukys' voice echoed through the silent chamber, his brown eyes boring into each of the newcomers. "Ambassador Eliséo, you must have at least an idea where they are if you travelled here with their children."

"In truth, King Lukys, I met young Plyke when he had already left his mother behind in their Paradise. I did not know who he was until a few short weeks ago." Eliséo answered evasively.

"What of my Nyssa?" Lord Aaron found his voice again.

"We found her living with the crystal dragons, Lord Aaron," the elf informed him. "When it became apparent that her oldest daughter, who was injured at the time, and herself were slowing the rest of us, we parted ways to allow us to reach Illaria in time for Rilla and Plyke."

"But they are following close behind you?" Aaron sounded so hopeful at the thought. Aurelius saw his brow furrow as the Paradisians and the elf remained silent. "They *are* following close behind you, Ambassador, are they not?"

"It is possible they are not," Aurelius came to his rescue, pulling Arishen in front of him. "Young Arishen here is a human seer. He had quite a violent vision as we passed through the barrier into Illaria. If his vision is to be believed, it is possible something may have happened to them."

"What *may* have happened to them?" King Lukys asked the seer.

"I … I can only tell you what I saw, King Lukys," Arishen stammered, avoiding the king's gaze.

"And what is that?" Lukys asked. Aurelius watched him impatiently rapping his fingers on the table and wondered how they were ever going to achieve their goal for this meeting.

"They were attacked by a woman. Nyssa is dead and Shuut is in grave danger." The seer's answer caused an immediate uproar in the chamber. Lord Aaron was speechless, staring blankly at the tall human. The members of the council were instantly at odds with each other. Vika claimed it must have been a false vision brought on by the magical barrier. Isis and Kayte insisted they should find out if it was real. Jorg claimed that the boy had made up the vision as a reason for him to stay in Illaria.

"Silence!" Lukys' voice thundered through the chamber. Aurelius marvelled at his control over the council without the use of his powers. The Masters and Mistresses quietened within seconds. "Master Reuben, you shall look into this human's mind to see if he did indeed see what he claims and if there is any more detail to it than that."

Master Jorg raised his hand in application to speak. He barely waited for the king to look his way before objecting, making sure to display his extensive blue tattoos. "I have more experience with powers of the mind than Master Reuben. I believe *I* should be the one to delve into the human's mind."

"Master Jorg, there is no doubt in my mind that you are more skilled than Master Reuben," the king began with a stony smile. "However, your views towards humans are quite well known and I don't trust you to treat this seer's mind with care."

Aurelius felt Arishen panic at those words. His thoughts flew around his mind. *What am I doing here? I'm in a city full of people who can read my thoughts, or worse!* The poor boy barely noticed Master Reuben rise from his seat and walk around the table until he was standing in front of Arishen. He did not make a display of showing his blue tattoo, but Aurelius watched the Paradisians' eyes as they noticed the similarity to Master Jorg's tattoo. The only difference between the two mind masters was that Reuben had fewer bands around his arm than Jorg.

"Peace, young human, I will do you no harm." Reuben reached out a hand to place on the seer's shoulder. At his touch, Arishen visibly calmed. "If you will allow me, I will simply take a look in your mind for your vision. If you wish to help me find it, simply close your eyes and recall the vision yourself and I will see it as you do."

Aurelius noticed the seer glance over to Eliséo, who nodded reassuringly. The elf's relationship with these Paradisians intrigued Aurelius, but he had little time to dwell on the matter as Reuben delved into Arishen's mind. Aurelius recalled the seer's description of the vision and wondered how Reuben would see it.

"Young human, are you projecting faces on those you call Shuut and Nyssa? Were they as faceless as the other woman in your original vision?" Reuben asked the boy. Arishen nodded.

"Have you ever had a vision of any of these people before?" The seer shook his head.

"Yes, you have," Rilla nudged him. "It was when you still slept through your visions. Remember, the dreams of Shuut rubbing her goosebumps?"

"That's right," Tika whispered. "She was furious because she thought Rilla had told you she was …"

Aurelius notice Eliséo swiftly use his elbow to stop Tika from saying more. The elf knew more about lintep than any other outsider. Whatever he was stopping the Paradisians from saying would have some significance they couldn't possibly understand.

"Were these dreams of Shuut accurate?" Reuben brought the conversation back to the point. The Paradisians nodded as one. "They're calling you a seer, so I assume that means you've had many accurate dreams? More than can be explained away by mere coincidence?"

"Yes," Arishen finally found his voice.

"And, from what young Rilla says, you have had some waking visions?" Reuben patiently led the boy through the questions he needed answers to, rather than digging for them in his mind.

"A few," the seer admitted hesitantly.

"But they were important ones that saved our lives more than once," Rilla pointed out with an annoyed look at the seer. Master Reuben acknowledged her statement with a kind look.

"The people in your visions, are they always faceless?" Another nod from the tall human boy. "But if you know the person in the vision, you can always tell who it is?"

Arishen smiled suddenly. The mind master returned his smile, whispering so Aurelius could barely hear him. "I've known many seers in my time. You're not the only one with faceless dreams."

Reuben placed a reassuring hand on Arishen's shoulder before turning to face the Council. "I believe the boy's vision was indeed a true vision. What I can't determine is whether it was a past, present or future vision. No matter which it is, I believe Lady Nyssa and her oldest daughter, Shuut, are or will soon be in very grave danger. I would suggest sending out a scouting party for them with some of our most skilled lintep, as whoever attacked them has more skill than I have seen since Lishe. The only difference between them is *this* lintep has more power."

At the mention of that name, there was a sharp intake of breath in the room. Lishe was well known to most of them and even a little feared.

"Could you tell if it was indeed Lishe from the vision?" Lord Aaron asked in a trembling voice.

"I could not hear them talking, but Lady Nyssa knew she was defeated from the beginning." Aurelius caught the apologetic look in his eyes. "Those of us who grew up with Nyssa were well aware that she was powerful beyond our wildest dreams, but did not tend to her studies to increase her skills.

"Lishe was particularly envious of her power and increased her skill to try to make up for that. If Nyssa was afraid of this lintep from the beginning, it wouldn't be much of a stretch to assume who it was. She had long black hair, but other than that, I cannot tell you more."

"Do you think any lintep we send out there, as skilled as they may be, will be safe if it's Lishe?" Mistress Kayte asked. "If it's true what is said about her stealing power from other lintep …"

Aurelius knew the thought was on everyone's mind. Lishe had left Illaria a number of years ago, having been refused the status of a mistress because of the way she used her power and, since that time, rumours had reached Illaria from lintep in the Outworld that someone was stealing other lintep's powers. It was an unimaginable scenario – another lintep's power would always feel wrong and be unpredictable at best.

"From what I saw in the vision, it would appear as though the unknown woman was indeed after Lady Nyssa's power," Master Reuben answered quietly. "I think Lady Nyssa may have given her daughter her power with her dying breath to avoid letting it slip into the other lintep's grasp."

Silence descended around them. The thought of a lintep stealing power was horrifying, but at least they made the decision themselves. To have that power thrust on you without your consent would be unimaginable agony, especially power as great as Nyssa's. It would take a master or mistress to control that amount of extra power.

"Can you be certain that's what happened?" King Lukys asked the mind master.

"I'm as certain as I can be without having been there myself. Nyssa fell limp just as Shuut began gagging. It would appear as though she somehow transferred her power into her daughter through her mouth, though how she knew how to do that is beyond me," he spread his hand helplessly. "The Nyssa we knew would not know how to do that and would never experiment with her powers to that extent."

Rilla had been quietly listening to their conversation, trying to understand what they were talking about. At the idea of Nyssa experimenting with her power, she shifted uncomfortably. She was the one who had made Nyssa start to experiment in the first place. *If my mother really is dead, could it possibly have been my fault? Would she still be alive if she hadn't given Shuut her power? Would this Lishe really have killed her to steal her power?* Rilla closed her eyes. She wanted to fade away into nothing. If she faded away, maybe it wouldn't all be real, maybe Nyssa and Shuut would arrive in Illaria in just a few days and Arishen's dream wouldn't actually have been a vision – if she just faded away.

"Where's Rilla?" At Lord Aaron's worried voice, Eliséo looked beside him. Without eyes on her, Rilla had managed to disappear completely from view. What was she doing showing her skills so openly to the entire council? He reached out to where he thought her arm was and brushed past her long, wavy red hair to pinch her skin. If she had gone invisible absently, she would not be reached by a gentle touch.

"Ouch." He heard her voice before she appeared, looking at him angrily and rubbing her arm. "What was that for?"

All he had to do was raise his eyebrows towards the Council for her to realise that all eyes were on her. She'd done it again – used her powers without even thinking about it. If the circumstances had been different, he might have congratulated her on being able to use her powers again so effortlessly after building her walls, but this was not the time. He was furious with her for showing her powers so freely, without understanding the consequences of doing so.

"Well, I would like to settle this matter of whether Rilla and Plyke will remain in Illaria as I am now quite anxious to test them both," Master Aurelius announced.

Eliséo hid a smile. Aurelius had managed to simultaneously bring them back to the matter at hand and be the first to claim access to the new lintep's training. They would be safer with him than Master Jorg or Mistress Vika.

"They are free to stay, Aurelius. It's their human companions we don't want," Jorg was quick to voice his opinion. "Humans are not allowed in Illaria."

"If they go, I go," Rilla replied hotly.

"Me too," Plyke stood by Tika and gripped his hand tightly. "No one is taking my Partner away from me."

"What you say is true, Jorg," old Master Graham spoke out in a soft, clear voice. "Humans are not allowed in Illaria. However, that rule was created for the humans who fear magic and wish to do us harm. These two humans are certainly not here to threaten us and both have traces of magic in their lives. A human seer is a rare find, to be treasured and nurtured. And who has ever known a human to choose a lintep as a Partner? There is magic in the Partnership that no lintep can deny. I vote we allow the humans to remain in Illaria."

"I agree with Master Graham," Mistress Kayte immediately voiced her support.

"All in favour of allowing the humans to remain in Illaria, raise your hands," King Lukys stood and counted seventeen hands, Mistress Isis, Master Reuben and Master Aurelius among them.

"All against allowing the humans to remain in Illaria, raise your hands." Mistress Vika and Master Jorg were only joined by another seven hands. Eliséo knew they were furious at the thought that humans were to be allowed to remain in Illaria. He would need to secure their safety before he left.

"Young humans," King Lukys addressed Arishen and Tika directly, "you may remain in Illaria as long as Rilla and Plyke do. I suggest you remain close by them until word spreads that you are not to be harmed. Do you understand?"

The two humans nodded, speechless.

"Mistress Kayte and Master Reuben, I need you to organise a search party for Lady Nyssa and her oldest daughter. Try to find volunteers before forcing anyone against their will. The Council is now dismissed."

With these final words, King Lukys stood from his chair and walked quickly out of the room, Lord Kynon close on his heels.

Eliséo stood aside with Master Aurelius and the Paradisians until the masters and mistresses had left the room. They were about to leave the room when they realised Lord Aaron was still there.

Understanding that he wished to speak with his grandchildren, Eliséo ushered Arishen and Tika towards the arrow slit windows, leaving Rilla and Plyke behind.

Rilla waited uncomfortably as Lord Aaron walked over to them. She wasn't certain what to make of him with his downcast eyes and slumped shoulders.

"I never thought to meet my grandchildren this way," he raised his head to look them both in the eye. Plyke gasped suddenly beside her. She followed his gaze to Lord Aaron's eyes – they were the exact same green and brown as Plyke's.

"To be honest, Lord Aaron, we never expected to meet any of our family," Plyke told his grandfather, once he'd recovered from the shock. "In our Paradise, we weren't even meant to know who our parents were. Kora only told me she was my mother to keep me safe from the Paradise leader."

"Ah, my Kora," the old lintep sighed, "at least she is alive and well, yes?"

"Well," Plyke scratched the back of his head, "she was when we left her."

"What he means to tell you is that Arishen dreamt that she was threatened and fled the Paradise sometime after we left. We have no idea where she is or if she is actually safe." Rilla replied bluntly.

"Rilla!" Plyke scolded her softly.

"He was bound to find out sooner or later," she shrugged. "What's the point of letting him think either of his daughters are safe when we don't know that they are?"

Three dead, another possibly dead and the last missing.

"I didn't say three dead," Rilla said in confusion. "Shuut isn't dead and neither is Kora, as far as we know."

"Who said anything about three dead?" Plyke turned to her in surprise.

Not again! Rilla closed her eyes and screamed inside.

Eliséo turned at the commotion in his mind. With his heightened hearing, he could just barely overhear what was being said. Rilla didn't know about Nyssa's brothers and youngest sister. She had no idea how she was torturing Aaron with her words.

"Are you reading my thoughts, young Rilla?" Lord Aaron asked her sternly.

She tapped her teeth together. "Not on purpose. Sometimes I hear thoughts without meaning to."

"I see." Aaron looked over her shoulder and motioned Master Aurelius to join them. "I suggest you test them as soon as possible, Aurelius. I do not want my entire family to die because we don't teach them well enough or in time."

Eliséo watched as Master Aurelius nodded and put a hand on each of their shoulders protectively.

"They will be safe with me, I promise you."

The old lintep looked at his grandchildren again before shaking his head sadly and walking out of the door.

"What was that about?" Rilla asked in confusion.

"I take it your mother never mentioned the rest of her family?" Aurelius asked. Rilla shook her head.

"And yours?" he asked, turning to Plyke to see him shake his head.

"Families weren't really spoken about in our Paradise." Plyke tried to explain.

"Even if your mother didn't abandon you in one." Rilla added, crossing her arms angrily.

"Eliséo?" Aurelius turned to him for an explanation.

"It appears as though Nyssa left Rilla in the care of her father once they'd arrived in the Paradise before she knew that Kora was there. Kora had no reason to tell Plyke anything because the more he knew about his family, the more danger he would be in from the Paradise leader.

"Rilla was only reunited with her mother a week or two ago and had no time to ask her about their family while they were training to keep their powers under control and fending off attacks in the Outworld. They know nothing of their family other than their mothers are sisters and now they have family in Illaria. They barely even know the history of Princess Rilla and the war with humans."

Through his bond with Elessa, Eliséo could hear bitter thoughts flowing through Rilla's mind, but there was little he could do to stop them.

Why should I care anyway? Why should I care about a family who clearly never cared about me? I was invisible to both of them.

He tried not to shake his head as he watched her fade from view.

"Rilla!" Plyke called out.

"What?" She looked over to Plyke in annoyance, reappearing just as easily as she'd disappeared.

"You did it again," he told her in a softer voice.

"I think it's time I test you both. Follow me," Master Aurelius took control of the situation. Eliséo brought up the rear as they left the council chambers.

Chapter Three – Testing

Eliséo watched Aurelius shoulder his robe, concealing his elaborate tattoos, as he led them out of the council chambers. He was one of the few masters who didn't feel the need to show his rank at every available opportunity. It was one of the things Eliséo liked most about him.

The elf admired the small tapestries adorning the walls as they walked down a long hallway past two of the twisting stairwells. He knew they were heading to the most secluded training room in the castle. It was a wise decision – they did not want anyone watching and making the two young lintep more nervous than they already were.

She's not nervous, Elessa's voice sounded softly in his mind. *She's reverting back to her ways from the Paradise. If she's not careful, she will become as alienated here as she was there.*

There's nothing I can do about that, Eliséo told her as his eyes glowed softly.

You could tell Aurelius, she suggested. Eliséo faltered at the comment.

Well, you could, she repeated unflinchingly. *What would happen if Rilla slips up, uses her bond powers and someone here notices her eyes glow? She doesn't even know the difference between those and her lintep power. Aurelius could teach her in safety if you let him.*

Eliséo was lost in thought after that. It *was* getting more dangerous for them and would continue to do so while Rilla learnt to use her powers. There were so many things that could go wrong. Someone could realise that she was bound to an elf's tree or, worse than that, if they realised how powerful she was through that bond, they would soon realise that it must be a royal elf's tree. He had kept his identity so well hidden for hundreds of years. The Paradisians knew the only tree she had touched was the one that made a branch and flowers for her. Luckily, they hadn't realised it was his tree. If they found out and told anyone, then his secret would be out and both he and Liessa would be in danger.

"Ambassador?" Aurelius' voice brought him out of his thoughts. "We're as safe as we can be here, but under the circumstances, I would rather have all four of them inside the room with me. Will that be a problem?"

Eliséo understood what he was actively not asking. Testing a lintep's power properly required them to be able to focus completely on the task at hand. If they felt anxious, he wouldn't be able to get a true measure of their power. He knew Plyke would be jealous of Rilla's power and they should both already feel at least a little nervous, but it would be so much worse with them all together.

"That will be fine, Master Aurelius," Eliséo finally decided on what he thought would be the safest, albeit the worst, scenario.

Tell him! Elessa urged, making the elf's eyes blaze silver. He brushed aside her demand as Aurelius opened the first and second set of wooden doors, both with carvings of a mouth and musical notes on them. The Paradisians followed him in with Eliséo only a step behind. Aurelius closed the doors behind the elf before turning to face him.

"It would seem your tree has something to say, Ambassador." Eliséo was glad they were behind double doors but still cursed Elessa for forcing his hand. It would not necessarily be any safer for the lintep to know the situation.

It would be better than for someone to realise when you've already left, she chided him.

"I think you should begin with Plyke," Eliséo told him abruptly. "What I have to say can wait until later."

"Very well," Aurelius raised a dubious eyebrow, but walked over to Plyke without another word to the elf.

Unlike the more austere masters, Aurelius firmly believed that a lintep undergoing testing should be as comfortable and relaxed as possible so that he could get a true reading of their skill and power.

"Choose your area, little one," the master lintep swept the room with his arm. "We can sit wherever you like. It may take some time to test you."

He waited for the boy to survey the room. It was long and rectangular with three arrow slit windows along the outer sandstone wall. The sun shone on Plyke as he walked closer to them. Aurelius watched as the boy closed his eyes, basking in the sunlight before seating himself comfortably on a cushioned chaise beneath a window closest to a corner of the room. There were a number of chaises scattered throughout the room, each with a small table and wooden chair in front of them. In the corners of the room stood small chests of drawers with an oil lantern on top of each one. None of them were lit this early in the afternoon.

Aurelius motioned for Eliséo to take the others to the furthest chaise from Plyke. Once he was certain they would not be a further distraction, the master lintep walked over to the wooden chair in front of the chaise that Plyke had chosen and seated himself.

"Shall we begin?" Aurelius asked Plyke, softly. The boy nodded anxiously. "You need not fear that your powers will escape you here, young Plyke. I have tested many a lintep these long years and kept them all safe and alive."

A small smile escaped Plyke's lips as he tucked his hair behind his ears. Aurelius seized the change in demeanour to begin.

"A few questions to start with. Did you first discover your powers on your own or did someone tell you about them?"

"Well, I think Kora must have noticed something when I was quite young. I don't particularly remember using my power before she taught me anything. I couldn't have been more than three or four years old at the time."

"Very well, and what sorts of things did she teach you?" Aurelius kept the momentum going. He didn't want any unnecessary memories clouding the boy's mind.

"The first thing she taught me was to build a wall around my power," his eyes unfocused as he remembered. "She told me it wasn't safe to show people what I was and that I had to do my best to hide everything from them."

"I see," Aurelius stalled, thinking how best to proceed under the circumstances. "Did she, by any chance, teach you how to control your power if it ever escaped your wall?"

Plyke shook his head. Aurelius fought the urge to groan at the stupidity of this situation. Kora knew better than to do this to her own son. Half her family had died because they weren't trained properly.

"Have you ever used your powers through your wall?"

"Yes, but I haven't done it often and I'm not very good at it." Plyke offered up his answer as an apology.

Aurelius silenced him gently with a wave of his hand. "I will be the judge of your skills, little one. Now tell me what you've managed to do with your power so far. Don't leave anything out if you can remember it. I need to know as much as possible before testing you." He sat back in the wooden chair and waited for Plyke to begin.

"I can feel what people are feeling, and sometimes hear what they're thinking, but only if I'm touching them." He shook his head. "Actually, it's more that I can't stop myself from doing all of that if there's any skin contact. I don't ever do it on purpose."

"Go on," Aurelius encouraged him when he saw the boy hesitate. "You don't need to apologise for anything in this room. You haven't been trained properly so whatever you've done or haven't done will not be judged by anyone."

Plyke took courage from his words. "Once, when I was sparring with Rilla, I let my power out of my walls just a little bit, to cover my axe. That's what it looked like she had done with her swords and I couldn't get an advantage. Well, anyway, it was the first time that I felt comfortable with my axe and could finally hold my own against her. But then, when we stopped, I couldn't control my power. It was escaping from me."

Aurelius could see him panicking at the memory and brought him back. "But it didn't escape you, and you're safe now." Plyke looked into his pale blue eyes and instantly calmed down. "Is there anything else you've done?"

"I'm not sure exactly what I did, but there was one time when I sort of cast out my senses to see if I could figure out where the danger was coming from. I couldn't see anything, but I could hear something and I could feel … bad magic," he hesitated. "I can't explain it any better than that."

Aurelius nodded, knowingly, and motioned for him to continue.

"Well, the only other thing I've done is talk to Shuut, sort of, with my mind.

She … well, she'd been attacked by someone or something and we didn't
know what had happened and so I tried to talk to her, to calm her down, to
tell her not to fight against the cage around her mind."

"Did you say a cage around her mind?" Aurelius interrupted, straightening
up in the chair. Plyke nodded, coming out of the memory. "Can you describe
anything about the cage?"

"Uh, all I remember is that it was sapping her strength. I didn't want to
touch it. Any time Shuut's mind crashed against it, it took more of her energy.
It would have killed her if she hadn't stopped, but she kept doing it because
she didn't know we were going to help her. She only stopped after I promised
we would help her if she would just stop fighting."

"She figured it out," Aurelius whispered to himself. In a louder voice, he
continued the testing. "Did you find a way to free Shuut's mind?"

"Yes, but … I didn't free her myself." Aurelius followed Plyke's gaze to
Eliséo, his brow furrowing at the deception he knew was taking place. There
would be time to clarify all of this later. For now, he turned his attention back
to the boy in front of him.

"Is there anything else you've done?"

"Oh, Nyssa's stones," Plyke smiled suddenly. "Nyssa gave us one of her
white stones each and taught us how to lift them and move them around."

Aurelius smiled. "So Nyssa still has all her stones then?"

"Well, no," Plyke hesitated, risking a quick glance towards his cousin. "Rilla
lost one of them and Nyssa was furious with her."

"Yes," Aurelius laughed, "she would have been. She was always so very
proud to be the only lintep ever not to lose a single stone. Much good it did
her when she …" he stopped abruptly when he realised he was rambling.
"Very good, young Plyke. We shall start your testing now. Let's start with
your wall," Master Aurelius decided. "It's what you were first taught, so I
assume you're more comfortable with that than any other aspect. With your
permission, I will try to breach your wall."

"What?" Plyke panicked. "No!"

"Fear not, young Plyke," the old lintep reached out and placed a hand
on Plyke's arm. "I will not search for anything. I just need to see if you can
already protect yourself from others who would not restrain themselves or if I
must teach you that skill."

Aurelius smiled as Plyke grudgingly nodded his head. The boy had no idea
that he had calmed down so quickly and accepted the task at hand because of
their skin contact. The old master had exuded as much calm and reassurance
as he could muster when placing his hand on Plyke's arm, knowing that he
could calm and reassure the boy simply with his touch.

He removed his hand from Plyke's arm and leaned back into his wooden
chair with a sigh. It was so much easier with lintep born and raised in Illaria.
Those that came in from the Outworld were always so defensive, so terrified

of being hurt. He closed his eyes to help him focus. He was a master, so could breach amateur walls without any effort, but he disliked looking the lintep in the eye when doing so.

Sending a tendril of power out of his mind, Aurelius searched for Plyke's mind. What he found there shocked him – walls within walls! He must have been terrified in his Paradise to try to protect himself so vigorously. It was more like a maze than a proper fortification, but it was certainly doing a marvellous job of keeping out intruders. He saw that surface thoughts were allowed out of the maze and followed their path back inside to the first wall Plyke had ever created. It was a child's idea of a wall made with stones of all colours, patched over in many places by grey stones, presumably later in life.

He smiled to himself as he marvelled that a child so young could create something so effective. His smile vanished as he remembered it was created so effectively to protect him from the leader of their Paradise. Not wasting any more time, he poked and probed around the wall, searching for a way in. Not finding one, he drew his power back into his own body and opened his eyes.

"Your wall is amazing, young Plyke," the master lintep acknowledged readily. "I have never seen such fortifications as you have created. I was able to follow your thoughts to your inner wall, but could not find a single entrance to your mind. Kora taught you well."

Aurelius' eyes sparkled at the way his words gave the young lintep confidence. Before Plyke could get carried away with his thoughts, Aurelius brought him back to the task at hand. "You say your mind powers are stronger with skin contact. Have you had any experience without skin contact?" Plyke shook his head. "Very well, we shall see if that was through lack of trying or lack of skill. What I want you to do is think of a colour. Any colour at all and try pushing that colour into my head. Can you do that for me?"

Plyke began to shake his head, then caught the excitement in Tika's face from the corner of his eye. Instead of irking him, it finally gave him the courage he needed to try embracing the power his partner was so envious of. He closed his eyes and then thought of Tika's hazel eyes. He focused on the colour, opened his eyes, looked straight into Master Aurelius' eyes and thought as hard as he could about the colour. He had no idea what he was doing, or if it was even working until he noticed the smile on the old lintep's face.

"I believe your Partner has hazel eyes, with dark brown streaks through them and a light green ring around the edges?" Seeing Plyke's grin, he nodded with satisfaction. "You know, most lintep simply think of a plain colour when I test them like this, especially if they have as little skill as you claim to have. Those lintep barely manage to get a single shade through to me and you have given me an exact picture of young Tika's eyes."

"I didn't know if it would work," Plyke was protested. "I've never even tried that before."

"Well, you do come from one of the most powerful families in Illaria," Aurelius told him candidly. "Now let us try the other way around. I'm going to think of a colour, a plain one, and I want you to read my mind to find it. I will not be projecting it out to you."

"I … don't know how to do that," Plyke hesitated. "Kora was quite insistent that I never try doing anything of the sort."

"Young Plyke, Kora only said that because you were surrounded by humans and she held a firm belief that lintep should not use their powers on defenceless humans. I am a lintep, giving you full permission to read my mind."

"No, you don't understand," Plyke shook his head. "I'm not saying I don't want to try. I don't even know where to start with that sort of task, not unless I'm touching you."

Aurelius was shocked into silence. For one whose power lay so clearly in the mind, he couldn't fathom Kora not even teaching him the basics.

"How did you use the stone that Nyssa gave you?" He questioned a confused Plyke.

"Nyssa told me to just let out a tiny tendril of power to surround the stone and move it around."

"It's the same principle," he assured the boy. "Just send out a tendril of your power into my mind to find the colour I'm thinking of."

Aurelius watched as Plyke closed his eyes and struggled to let out a single tendril of his power. He waited to feel the touch of power on his mind, but was left completely untouched by it. Looking closely, he noticed beads of sweat on Plyke's brow. This simple task was more difficult for him than for any other lintep he'd ever tested. Most had at least experimented with their power before reaching Illaria. But then, none of them had lived in a Paradise as dangerous as Plyke's. He reached out a hand to arouse Plyke from his task. The boy's eyes flew open as soon as there was skin contact.

"Blue!" he shouted triumphantly, not realising that the master's hand was on his arm. His face fell when he followed the master's pale blue gaze down to his arm. "Oh."

"You can't be perfect at everything the first time you try it, little one," Aurelius tried to comfort him. "Especially if you weren't taught anything other than how to build a wall and hide your powers."

"What's next?" Plyke asked him, dejectedly.

"Let's take a little break from testing your power." Aurelius did not need to exert his skills to understand how Plyke was feeling. "All I want you to do is listen."

Aurelius sat back in his chair and motioned for Plyke to relax into his chaise. He started to whistle a soft tune. The goosebumps on the boy's arms alerted him to the fact that it was at least loud enough for him to hear it but the lack of expression on his face told him that he wasn't listening for it. Plyke absently started rubbing his arms where the goosebumps had appeared but nothing more than that.

"You withdrew your power back into your wall, didn't you?" Aurelius asked him, knowing the answer before Plyke's nod confirmed it. "Well, that would be why Eliséo couldn't tell if you were a full lintep or not. I can safely tell you that you are, but the fear of your power escaping your hold has made you lock it in your walls so tightly, I doubt any but a master lintep could have told you."

Master Aurelius stood and walked over to the nearest chest of drawers. He opened the bottom drawer and took out a small green felt pouch. From the top drawer, he picked out ten white stones and placed them in the pouch as he walked back to his chair. Sitting down, he handed the pouch to Plyke.

"These are your white stones. Treat them with care. If you lose them all, you will need to convince a master or mistress to give you a new set and most aren't easily persuaded.

"Now, you told me Nyssa taught you how to wrap your power around a stone and lift it. Show me." He folded his arms and leaned back in his chair, waiting for Plyke to make a move.

"We only did it for a few nights and it's been over a week since then."

Plyke's lack of confidence was going to be one of the most difficult hurdles to overcome in his training.

"Plyke, I'm not here to judge you," Aurelius tried to reassure him. "I am assessing your skill levels so that your training can commence with the right people. Just try and show me what you can already do."

Plyke took a deep breath and thought back to his first lesson with Nyssa. He took a stone from his pouch and placed it on the table between them. Carefully, he let out a tendril of power towards the stone. Once he had reached it, he wrapped his power around the stone and lifted it just barely above the table, moving it closer to Aurelius.

"Very good, Plyke," the master reassured him. "Now, let out a little more of your power to lift your stone up higher."

Bolstered by the words of encouragement, Plyke let out more of his power to follow the initial tendril. It was enough to allow him to lift the stone to eye level. Grinning, he looked over to Tika to see the excitement in his eyes, but at that moment, he lost all concentration. His power started to escape his control and more of it poured out past his walls. Panicking, he tried to pull it back inside, but it was flowing away from him too quickly. He shut his eyes and curled up into a ball, his power flooding the room, forcing him to hear

Tika and Arishen's thoughts. His head felt like it was about to explode and he screamed out in pain.

Suddenly, the pain went away. He couldn't hear any thoughts but his own. Tentatively uncurling himself and wiping tears from his eyes, he looked up at Master Aurelius in confusion.

"I promised your grandfather you'd be safe with me," he said with a twinkle in his eye, then leaned forward to whisper to the frightened boy. "You're not the first lintep to lose control of their power, nor will you be the last. Go, join your Partner and send Rilla over to me." Plyke smiled his thanks to the old master lintep and walked over to his companions, relieved that his testing was over.

As Plyke walked over to them Eliséo's heart began to race. He still hadn't decided what to do.

You must tell him, Elessa voiced her opinion yet again. *Imagine what will happen if he doesn't know.*

If I tell him, I have to tell all of them, Eliséo tried to reason with her. *Imagine what will happen if one of them lets it slip or, worse still, purposely tells someone in a moment of spite.*

I don't see you have much choice. If you don't tell him, she'll slip up and he'll know anyway, but what if we're already gone by then? Better tell him now and let him teach her the difference between her powers so that she can hide it from the other masters. Imagine what would happen if the rest of them find out.

Elessa's argument made up his mind, but he was still worried about telling the Paradisians. *You don't have to tell them. Call up your mist around just the three of you and they won't know.*

He won't be able to test her with them in the room at that point. Eliséo tried to reason through the problem with her and was caught completely off guard when he heard Master Aurelius' voice right in front of him.

"Are you going to tell me what ails you or are you going to force me to read your mind?" The tapping of his foot was the only hint of his irritation. "Rilla can't concentrate on her test when she's watching your glowing eyes the whole time."

Still undecided, Eliséo quickly called up a thick mist barrier around the two of them. He knew Rilla had seen through Eléna's thinner mist in Silvaren and wasn't certain he wanted her listening in on this conversation.

"Something happened to Rilla in Silvaren. I did not realise it would impact her in Illaria and did not discuss what I should do about it with Lady Eléna."

"I take it her companions are not aware of this event."

Eliséo shook his head.

"I see. Assuming you have decided to tell me about it, are you certain you want to keep the others in the dark?"

"The fewer people who know, the better, but I don't know if we can hide it from them." Eliséo didn't voice his fear that if they didn't tell them and one of them found out by accident, they might be so angry as to betray her.

"Why don't you tell me what happened and we can decide from there."

"One of the trees in Silvaren bound herself to Rilla," he breathed the words out so softly that the lintep almost didn't hear him.

"Are you certain?"

It wasn't a surprise the master questioned his statement. Such a thing had never been known to happen before. Eliséo didn't trust his voice, so only nodded his head.

"Whose tree was it?"

Tell him! Eliséo's eyes shone a bright silver with Elessa's voice resounding in his mind.

"Mine."

Aurelius stared in shock. Not for the first time that day, he was completely speechless. He looked at Rilla through the mist, his thoughts swirling so quickly he could barely keep up with them.

"That will … make training her an interesting challenge."

"Will you be able to keep this from her other teachers?" Eliséo's voice betrayed his fear.

"I honestly don't know," Aurelius held up his hands, helplessly. "What I do know is that I will need to test her rigorously and there is no chance that her companions won't discover the truth. You don't have to tell them it was your tree, but you should tell them what happened. There is little chance they won't notice her eyes glowing."

"Can't I take them out of the room?" Eliséo pleaded. "Then they won't see and you can teach her how to tell the difference between her powers."

"You ask a great deal of me, Eliséo. Are you certain you don't want to trust them?" When he saw the determined look in the elf's eyes, he relented. "Very well, dissipate your mist and take them to your room – it should be prepared for you by now. I will bring Rilla there myself when I am finished with her."

"Thank you Aurelius," Eliséo breathed out a sigh of relief. Aurelius simply shook his head, not knowing if his decision was a sensible one. Once the mist had dissipated, the master lintep returned to a fuming Rilla. She had been purposely excluded from a conversation she knew was about her and could say nothing.

"Patience, little one," he said in a soft voice. "We will begin your testing once your companions have left."

Rilla glared at him angrily. She knew they'd been talking about her but Elessa had blocked her out and Eliséo had created a thick enough mist to ensure she couldn't see or hear through it. Aside from that, she was irrationally irritated that he continually called her "little one". That term had ever been reserved in her heart for Rhanya alone. She waited in silent fury while Eliséo explained the situation to the boys.

"It appears as though Rilla's testing may take a while longer than Plyke's. I have my own private chamber in the castle. I'll take you there now and Master Aurelius will bring Rilla once her testing is complete."

Master Aurelius waited in silence for the four of them to vacate the room. What Eliséo had told them would quite probably be the case, but it wasn't the actual reason he was leading them away. He wondered if he would even be able to get a true reading of Rilla's skill and strength without including her new elf powers.

"Well, little one," he turned from the closing door to see her flinch, "there is no reason to be afraid. Shall we begin?"

"I'm not afraid," Rilla told him bluntly. "I just don't like you calling me that."

"I've never had a complaint before now. Is there a particular reason you don't like it?" He saw Rilla's eyes glaze over at some memory. She was silent for such a long time that he thought she wouldn't answer.

"My best friend in our Paradise used to call me that," Rilla finally opened up. "He died to protect Shuut and to give me a chance to protect the boys."

"If that was the case, did he not then also die to protect you?" The question was asked gently.

"No, I was safe enough in the Paradise. Rhanya pushed me to win freedom from my father, the Paradise leader. Erton arranged the murder of many people he suspected were touched by magic, but he would never have dared do that to me because everyone knew I was his daughter and so would have realised that he was touched by magic too."

"I see," Aurelius began to piece the story together. "So that's why Plyke was taught to hide his powers from such an early age and you weren't."

"No, it's worse than that. I don't remember anything from before the Paradise. Once we were there, I was only three years old … my mother left me and soon afterwards Erton became the Paradise leader. I don't even know how. Anyway, it was already a well-known fact that magic was not accepted in Paradises, so Erton hid who he was and never bothered telling me who, or I should say what, I was."

"You mean to say you didn't know you were a lintep?" Aurelius asked incredulously.

"I had no idea," Rilla shrugged uncomfortably. "Not until well after Shuut took us away from our Paradise. I pieced it together before we reached Turon and then, when we met a full lintep, I made sure to ask some questions that confirmed what I strongly suspected."

Aurelius listened to her story in complete disbelief that Nyssa could be as uncaring as to leave her daughter in someone else's care and not train her in even the basics before doing so. The sisters seemed to be one worse than the other when it came to their children.

"I suppose this means that your experience with your power will be a shorter story than Plyke's."

"I doubt it," Rilla replied quietly. "I'd apparently been using my powers the entire time I was in the Paradise without realising it. People used to ignore me, mainly because Erton had forbidden anyone from calling me by name, so I felt like I was invisible to everyone. I must have actually become invisible sometimes, because people didn't see me when I went into houses or rooms where I shouldn't really have been, but I honestly thought they were just ignoring me. I didn't realise what I was doing.

"The only time anyone noticed me when I was trying not to be seen was just before we left the Paradise and Kora found me after looking past me a few times. I don't think she knew who I really was, or at least she didn't realise that Nyssa was my mother."

"Interesting. Is that the only time you used your powers in the Paradise?" Aurelius barely knew where to begin with her. He'd never tested a lintep who had grown up not knowing what they were.

"Well," Rilla hesitated, "there was one time when I thought I heard someone say something, but no one else heard it. I think I *may* have heard his thoughts."

Aurelius' lips curled up into a smile despite his best efforts to stop them. "Did you not think this a little, shall we say, odd?"

Rilla was getting flustered by the memories of Rhanya. "I was distracted. Arishen had had a dream of Rhanya and knew he was dead, but when I asked if anyone had seen him, no one answered. Arishen finally said 'he's not coming', but just after he said that, I could have sworn I heard him say 'he's dead', but no one else reacted to that. I knew he was dead. As soon as he didn't come to the eating hall that morning, I knew."

She stopped talking and stared blankly ahead, fighting off the tears that threatened to stream down her face. Instinctively, one hand went to clutch her tree pendant and the other to find the note Rhanya had written for her before he died. She still kept it in her pocket, as close to her as possible.

Rilla, he didn't want you to be sad for him. Elessa's voice suddenly came through to her. *Remember that everything he did was to win your freedom. He was happy to do that for you.*

Tears flooded her eyes and burned down her cheeks. She looked up to Aurelius and then froze when she saw the expression on his face. Elessa had just spoken to her – her eyes must be glowing bright green. After all they'd done to keep their secret hidden, the tree had just slipped up and ruined everything.

"I didn't really believe him," Aurelius shook his head in wonder. "There's no denying it now."

"What are you talking about?" Rilla asked him cautiously, trying to remember how to block Elessa out of her mind.

We told him, Rilla. Elessa told her quickly, before the girl managed to block her out. *He had to know before he started testing you. There has to be at least one master who will try to protect you and teach you when Eliséo leaves.*

"Has he told you now?" Aurelius asked her, curiously.

"No, his tree did."

"From my understanding, she's your tree now too." Aurelius straightened out the wrinkles in his brow with his long bony fingers. "If only you had learnt to properly use your lintep powers before that happened, it might not be so difficult to keep your secret. It is no matter now. Let's just continue with your story."

He waved the issue aside. "I need to know all the times you've used your power purposely, accidentally and without even realising it until later. Everything you've done is important for the initial test. There are no repercussions in this room. Especially considering the circumstances, I won't be angry with you or judge you for any use of your power, however reckless it was."

"Well, I don't think anything else happened in our Paradise," Rilla started hesitantly. "The next time anything happened wasn't actually anything I did."

"Everything you think is related to magic of any sort is important, so don't leave anything out, no matter how irrelevant you think it is." Aurelius reassured her once again.

"Well, when we were travelling with Shuut, before we reached Turon, she kept trying to read our minds. I don't know how successful she was with the boys, but whenever she turned her mind to me, I instantly felt what she was doing and told her to stop."

"Did you try to block her out?"

"No, I can't remember if that was before or after I realised what I was," Rilla replied with a shrug. "The first time I tried to actively do something was in Turon after talking to Ratchin."

"She still lives there, does she?" Aurelius asked with a small smile. "Did she know you were a lintep when you were talking to her?"

"No, I was still trying to convince myself that I really was a lintep. So I asked her lots of questions and then tried something just to see if I could do it." She stopped abruptly, caught in the memory of the scolding she'd received for it.

"I gather she wasn't impressed when she saw what you did?" Aurelius prompted her gently.

"She was furious," Rilla guiltily lifted her eyes, "but she didn't warn me what could happen."

"So what happened?" he asked her curiously.

"Well, she said that she could make her mind travel anywhere she had been before or that she could follow a person somewhere. But she didn't say it was dangerous!" Rilla blurted it all out.

"*You* did that?" Aurelius was incredulous. "Without any training whatsoever, you managed to do that?"

"Yes." Her soft voice betrayed her insecurities.

"Exactly how did you accomplish that?"

"There was a fringa and his kryti travelling with us. The same one you met outside the boundary of Illaria. Anyway, I followed the fringa out of the room down to the end of the hall and heard what he said before he came back." She smiled at the memory. "He didn't believe that I hadn't followed him or that I didn't actually hear him from the room, so he went downstairs, through the inn until he stumbled upon Ratchin." She scratched the back of her head, stalling for a moment. "Ratchin realised someone was with the fringa, but when she realised it was me she was so angry. She yelled at me so much."

"She was scared for you, Rilla." Aurelius was quick to placate her. "You have no idea how many lintep Ratchin has tried to save over the years. Sometimes she manages and sends them on their way to Illaria, or even brings them here herself if there is no other choice. But she's seen enough lintep die by doing even simpler things that. She was probably terrified of what would happen to you."

"Oh," Rilla's small voice was lost in the huge room. "I didn't realise that."

"It's no matter now," Aurelius brushed the issue aside. "Did Ratchin teach you anything after that?"

"Not exactly," Rilla shifted uncomfortably. "She took me with her when she went to heal a farmer's son. She told me to get past the gatekeeper without him seeing me, so I had to blend into the background while she even stopped to talk to him."

"That was the first time you did that intentionally?"

Rilla nodded before continuing. "When we were at the farmer's house, she just let me watch how she healed his son, warning me that she might need to use me at some point, but she never did. I felt a bit useless just standing there, so I drained heat out of their teacups before giving it to the farmer and his wife to drink."

"Did Ratchin show you how to do that?" Aurelius was leaning back in his chair, trying not to show Rilla how intrigued he was with her story.

"No," the young girl shook her head. "Not exactly. She did the opposite back at the inn by warming the bath water a little, I just assumed it would work the same if I tried it the other way around.

"There wasn't really anything else that Ratchin showed me. I just sort of watched what she did and tried or modified that. She left me with a warning to be careful because no one would be around if I made a mistake and I would likely kill myself."

"Well, at least she told you that." Aurelius' brow furrowed momentarily. "Very well, and is that the extent of what you've done?" He leaned forward, expecting to begin her test but was surprised when she continued.

"No, I healed the fringa's wing after we left Turon. After that, Ensil was the first person I healed, but since then I've had to heal most of my companions. Sometimes I injured myself quite badly and other times I managed to spread the pain out through my body. Once or twice I used Eliséo and spread the pain out through him as well."

Aurelius was speechless, but motioned for her to continue her story, not trusting his voice.

"I think there are only a few other things, at least things that I'm fairly certain were my lintep power and not elf magic anyway," she tapped her teeth together. "I asked Plyke to tell me how to build a wall because Kora had taught him. So I tried to do that one day and seem to have been relatively successful with that. It took a while to reach my power as quickly as I used to but I think I'm getting the hang of it again.

"Then there was the time that Eliséo was in danger so I sent a tendril of power out to his attacker and then got the heat from my torch to run through my power to burn him. I don't even really know how I did it, but it needed to happen, so it did."

Aurelius nodded, a perfect picture of understanding, all the while screaming on the inside that she was too reckless and was going to kill herself one day.

"I think, aside from the stones that Nyssa made us practice with, the only other times I did anything were after we crossed the river on our way here. Arishen and I were being attacked and he told me to burn them with fire from my fingers like we had seen Nyssa do in the Drakos Mountains."

She stilled at the memory. Aurelius coughed to break her concentration.

"I can't really remember much of what happened after that, but by the time I was aware of anything, everyone else had crossed the river and fire had spread across the grasslands and into the forest. So we had to find a way to get through the forest."

"Nyssa was with you then?" the master lintep finally found his voice.

"Yes, she's the one who saved me from whatever happened with the fire. Then I had to teach her how to mould her power into something that could hold water so we could douse the fire in the forest as we walked through it."

"You taught Nyssa?" His eyebrows shot up in amazement.

"Well, yes, but she was quite angry that I was making her experiment when she had just yelled at me for doing the same thing."

"Oh, young Rilla," Aurelius almost laughed, "that's not the reason she was angry. Can you imagine how she felt being taught by her daughter rather than a master? She was always so powerful that she could manage any task they set her without bothering to hone her skills. You have managed probably more than she has without ever having the benefit of a master's teaching. It is no matter. If that is all, then we shall begin your testing."

"Well," Rilla hesitated, "There's one more thing but I don't really know what it was …"

"Would this have anything to do with what happened in Silvaren." Rilla nodded. "Then you had better tell me so we can see what it was."

"Eliséo does this thing, well you saw it just before, where he creates a mist all around you. We had to do that for our first river crossing because we went under the river, or through the river. I mean, we walked along the riverbed and kept the water out with the mist.

"I had to make one of my leaves from Silvaren burst into flames, which I actually did just accidentally. Then Eliséo needed to borrow some of my strength. I'm fairly certain he did that through Elessa actually, and then I had to borrow some from Plyke. I don't really know how to explain it other than I sent out a tendril of my power through my hand into his hand until I felt his power and tied a knot with the two tendrils and then pulled and, well, it worked."

"That does indeed sound like a combination of the powers, but you are right to think that it was your lintep power pulling Plyke's power. I know that an elf's power doesn't work like that." He rubbed the stubble on his chin and looked at the fading light in the sky. "If that is all, I think we should begin."

The master lintep stood and went to the same chest of drawers as before. Again, he opened the bottom drawer and took out another small green felt pouch. He counted ten white stones from the top drawer and placed them in the pouch. However, before walking back to his chair, he picked up the unlit lantern on top of the chest of drawers and took it with him. He placed the lantern on the small table between them, concentrated for a moment until the wick was alight and then handed the pouch of stones to Rilla as he sat down once more.

"Your skills are certainly well developed on the practical side of things, so we may begin there. Take one of your stones and place it on the table." He waited for Rilla to do so before continuing. "I want you to raise the stone to your eye level and then lower it back down."

Rilla let out a tiny tendril of her power, remembering the catastrophic lesson with Nyssa where she had lost one of her mother's precious stones. She surrounded the white stone with her power and gently lifted it to her eye level before placing it back on the table.

Aurelius continued to dictate a number of things she should do with the stone, including moving it to different parts of the room and handling multiple stones at a time. Rilla complied with his initial requests as though she had done these things all her life, rather than only a few times before. It was only when she was handling more than a few stones that she wavered and lost concentration.

"Well done, young Rilla," he congratulated the lintep with a sad smile. "You're certainly your mother's child."

"I most certainly hope not!" Rilla exclaimed, vehemently. "If she really had so much power and never learnt to use it properly, I don't want to be anything like her. From the sounds of it, she could have been a mistress had she tried."

"Indeed. If you've already gathered that, you may yet be a better student than she was. But you're going to have an interesting time of it because of your mother's legacy." He didn't elaborate any further. Rilla watched as he placed one of her stones on top of the lantern then took a small knife from the folds of his robe and opened a small gash across his left forearm. "Heal me."

Rilla took a deep, calming breath and placed her hand gently over Master Aurelius' arm. She focussed on the torn skin and proceeded to stitch it together in her mind. There wasn't too much pain for such a small gash, but she made sure to spread the pain out through her body, rather than to injure her arm. When she took her hand away, she smiled at the sight. It was as though he had never cut himself in the first place.

"I gather the injuries you healed in the Outworld were more significant than this?" He looked at her with an odd expression, but Rilla couldn't read anything into it. She nodded without offering any more information. She didn't want to tell him how close she'd come to killing herself when she'd healed Ensil after he attacked her.

"I think we may leave the rest of your healing test for another day when we have another subject for you to work on. Mistress Kayte will be most interested to see what you can do and, with any luck, make sure that you never injure yourself again when healing someone."

Rilla watched as Aurelius turned his attention to the stone on top of the lantern. Once he had lifted it with his power and placed it on the table, he gave her a new task.

"Take the heat out of this stone so that I can touch it with my bare hand."

Rilla hadn't taken heat out of anything and into herself since that one night in Turon. She remembered not being able to take much of the heat out but couldn't think of what else to do. Instead of touching the stone, she placed a finger just above the stone and felt the heat radiating out of it. She quested out toward that heat with her power and then took it inside herself, spreading it out until she began sweating and then stopped.

Aurelius leant over to touch the stone. Rilla knew there was still enough heat to warm his fingers, but not enough to burn him.

"Why did you keep the heat in you?"

"I don't know," Rilla replied uncertainly. "I didn't know where else to put it."

"Take out the rest of your stones and transfer the heat evenly into each of them. Mind you don't use any of your own heat for it."

Rilla did as he told her. After three stones, she felt a slight chill and stopped. "I don't think I can do the rest, not without using my own heat."

Aurelius' smile surprised her. "At least you've learnt that you have a limit there. Well done."

He picked up the lantern, extinguished the flame and walked back over to the chest of drawers to replace it.

"Now, you may recall that Marilisa went to attack Eliséo outside the border. I'm not sure if someone taught you or if it was instinctive, but you used your power to counteract her actions. We need to see if you can do that every time or not."

Before she had time to take in what he had just said, Rilla saw sparks flying towards her from the master's pale blue eyes. Without thinking, she leapt up and pushed out her power, driving the sparks to the floor. They immediately flew back into the air and attacked her from all angles. She managed to fend off some of them, but others were getting through. Panicking, she let through even more.

Help me! She called out to Elessa, eyes glowing bright green. *What are the words for your mist?*

Seconds later, Aurelius saw the beginnings of Eliséo's same thick mist drawing around Rilla. His sparks could not break through it. Calmly, he drew all of his remaining sparks back within himself, not willing to lose more heat than necessary for this test.

"If you can hear me, you're safe now." He held his arms wide open with the palms of his hands facing upwards. "I won't throw any more sparks your way." He waited patiently for the mist to dissipate, revealing the smouldering lintep inside.

"You could have warned me!"

"That would have defeated the purpose. I had to see if you would be able to react the same way every time and see what you would do when more pressure was placed on you. Now that I know you would call on your tree for help, I believe we'll need to train you in different ways to defend yourself."

"You surprised me!" Rilla retaliated. "I wouldn't have asked Elessa for help if you didn't know about her."

"You can't be certain of that, little one." He tried, unsuccessfully to lead her back to her chaise. "I will do my best to help you hide this bond, but I may need to push you more than you'd like to see when you would instinctively use it. Otherwise, how am I to know how to help you?"

Rilla grudgingly returned to her chaise. "What next?"

"Now to the mind," he replied easily. "We'll do the same exercises I did with Plyke. First, I'd like you to let me into your mind without resistance. I need to look at the wall you've created and see if I can find a way in."

Aurelius sent out a tendril of his power into the young lintep's mind. From what he'd seen of Plyke's wall and the fact that he'd taught Rilla how to build her wall, he was surprised by what he saw. They were as different as two walls could be. Whereas Plyke's started as a child's creation and became labyrinthine, Rilla's was a deliberate and pure fortification. There were no child's coloured blocks, only sturdy bricks and mortar. It looked like they had painstakingly been placed perfectly, not leaving a single gap anywhere and it was so high. It must have taken her weeks to build such an imposing tower.

He sent his tendril of power as high up as the tower went, almost afraid to go all the way to the top for fear of losing his way back to his own mind. Half way to the top, it was evident that the tower had been rearranged at some point. Instead of double bricking, it became a single brick fortification. Eventually, he reached the top which had a surprisingly simple contraption to close it – a wooden cover, bolted from the inside.

Without wanting to try it, he wondered if he could actually burn the door or if it was just an illusion. He probed around with his tendril to see if there were any weak spots around the entrance only to find himself repelled by the weight of Rilla's power seeping through the door to chase him away. Respectfully, he retreated from her mind to find her staring angrily at him.

"So you think you can just burn my wall down?" She spoke fiercely. "I'd like to see you try it."

"Control your temper, little one," the master lintep chided his student. "I have no wish to actually breach your wall and I have no doubt that it would be difficult for anyone to do so. I simply wondered why you had taken such trouble to create a brick tower only to close it off with a wooden door."

Her eyes flashed bright green for a moment. "Elessa and Eliséo didn't know I was building a wall that day and I almost closed myself off from them."

"That *day*?" Aurelius queried, almost whispering.

"Yes," Rilla replied offhandedly. "Plyke told me how he built his wall and I built one the same day to protect myself before we reached the karliki and crystal dragons."

"I see," Aurelius faltered.

"If I had closed the wall off with bricks, I didn't know how to open myself up to them if I needed to. It took a while to learn how to access my power properly from within the wall, but I think I've got it now and it's such a small opening at the top that I can defend it with my power if I need to."

The old lintep rubbed his forehead between his eyes, trying to think how to proceed. Mistress Vika or Master Jorg would try to claim her as a mind student and things would only go from bad to worse. He would have to find a reasonable excuse for Master Reuben to take her instead. Was there any way that he could hide the elf tree's bond from the mind master? His own area was more in the practical side of things so Lord Aaron would never agree to let him teach his granddaughter the mind powers.

"Master Aurelius?" Rilla's voice jolted him out of his thoughts. He heard a bell tolling to signal the end of the afternoon lessons in the castle and looked past the girl to see the sun had almost set.

"Let's just quickly finish your test so I can take you back to your companions. I need you to think of a colour, any colour, and send that thought into my mind."

Rilla thought of the silver tree pendant Lady Eléna had given to her on her first visit to Silvaren. She focussed on the colour and pushed the image out towards the Master. Feeling a slight resistance, she pushed harder only to find the resistance grow.

"Rilla, you don't need to be so forceful," Aurelius admonished her. "The lightest of touches is all you need for such a simple task."

"I'm tired," Rilla closed her eyes and fell back into the chaise. "Can we finish the test tomorrow?"

"That would not be advisable. Your training will begin tomorrow morning."

"But we just got here, and we've been travelling non-stop for weeks." Rilla heard the whining note in her voice and stopped short. "I'm sorry. I'm just tired. What else do you need me to do tonight?"

"I will think of a colour and you will attempt to read my mind to see it."

For an instant, Aurelius saw the images in Rilla's mind of her travels the past few weeks and all he saw was blood. Red, running blood.

"Red." Rilla's voice brought him back to himself. Her weariness was affecting him too deeply.

"Good," he sighed. "Now I'm going to do the same as your little fringa friend. I will leave the room. You need to follow me with your mind until I return and then give me a full description of what you saw or heard."

"I only ever did that once," she protested.

"Yes, and I need to see if you can do it again," he told her once more. He stood and gave her little time to think what to do next.

Rilla watched his retreating back before quickly closing her eyes and focussing on the image of his body in her mind. She followed the image in her mind, not knowing if she was really following him or not. He opened the only door to the room and stepped outside, being sure to lock the door before looking both ways down the empty hallway. None of the lanterns had been lit along the walls, thought it was already getting quite dark. It was a secluded part of the castle, where no private chambers were located. He picked up one lantern and used some of his body heat to create a small flame. Once the flame was burning brightly, he turned to his right and walked a few paces down that way before shaking his head and turning back down the way he'd come and past the door again. Turning the corner, he came to another wooden door, traced the image of a flame that was carved on it and walked back to the room where Rilla waited for him. He unlocked it, stepped back inside and walked over to his chair, placing the lantern on the small table. Rilla opened her eyes once he was seated again.

"Well?" he asked, stifling a yawn.

"You locked the door behind you, lit a lantern and turned right before going back to the left. You traced a flame that was carved on a wooden door and came back."

"Interesting," he muttered under his breath. In a louder voice he questioned her further. "Do you know how you followed me?"

A shake of her head.

"Did you only see me or did you see the surroundings?"

"I … don't think I saw you at all, except your hand when you reached it out in front of you. I saw the empty hallway with lanterns on the walls and the wooden doors. That's all."

"And you don't know how you followed me?" He needed as much detail from her as he could get and she didn't even know how she was using her power.

"I just closed my eyes, pictured you before you left the room and sort of followed you." By this point, she was holding her head in her hands. "My head hurts now, but not as badly as it did in Turon. I guess you didn't go as far away from me as the fringa did."

"I'm going to have to work a small miracle to get Master Reuben to be your mind master," he muttered once more.

"Is he the one who saw Arishen's dream?" Rilla asked.

"Yes. He's also one of the younger masters so it may be quite difficult to insist upon." He waved the issue aside. "Never mind that for now. The last thing we need to test is your communication skills."

Rilla waited for him to continue but he didn't. Instead, she heard a high pitched whistle and goosebumps immediately raised the flesh on her arms. It took only a moment for her to realise what was happening. She strained to understand anything about the whistle. It sounded like a tune rather than anything with meaning.

"I can hear it, but it just sounds like you're whistling a tune," she told the master once he had stopped.

"I think that's enough for today. I shall petition to be your practical master. Master Graham will be your communication master. There won't be any objection to Kayte as your healing mistress and I *may* be able to get you Mistress Isis for fire." He patted her arm gently as he got to his feet. "Follow me. I'll take you to Eliséo's room where they will no doubt be awaiting you impatiently."

Chapter Four – Eliséo's Room

Eliséo didn't risk looking at Rilla as he ushered the boys out of the testing room. He knew she would be furious with him for excluding her from his conversation with Aurelius. He only hoped the old lintep would be able to calm her down enough to get a true reading of her power and skill level and, hopefully, untangle her lintep power from her elf magic.

He knew Plyke had shown both his power and lack of skill when his power had flooded the room. Thankfully, being an elf, Eliséo had his own mind wall and Elessa's power to shield his thoughts and feelings, otherwise the boy could not have helped but realise why he was so concerned about their testing – at least, Rilla's testing.

He could tell that Plyke was too weary and still absorbed by the details of his test to notice or care that Rilla was being allowed to take her test in private. Before Arishen or Tika could think to point it out, he quickly led them away from the testing room, towards the stairwell closest to his chambers.

"Do you have your own room in Goraburg too?" Tika asked him after a few moments of silence.

"No, not one that is permanently set aside for me," Eliséo turned to look at the small hazel-eyed boy. "I don't have occasion to visit Goraburg in an official capacity as often as I do Illaria. I am always offered a private room, but generally I stay in the guest quarters closest to Ilya's room."

"Why do you have more reason to visit Illaria?"

The questions kept coming as they walked up an open, twisting stairwell into yet another hallway. This one was more lavishly decorated with long rugs running along the length of the hall. The tapestries were larger and the doors spaced further apart. A number of statues were situation against the windowed wall. Eliséo knew these halls so well he could walk them blindfolded.

"There are many similarities between the lintep and elves, more so than the karliki and elves. Whereas the karliki have lost all their magic powers, the elves and lintep still retain theirs, which means both races have similar problems with humans." Eliséo paused and looked back at Tika and Arishen with a smile. "That is to say, *most* humans. Aside from that, both races live above ground, so are more vulnerable to attacks. Although Illaria has a unique set of defences with its magical barriers, Silvaren's only defence is the elves and the trees, which means it is attacked more frequently than Illaria."

"Why doesn't Silvaren have magical barriers like Illaria?" Eliséo wasn't surprised that this question came from Arishen.

"Elf and lintep powers work differently. Elves can't create barriers like those we had to pass through with a lintep holding our hand."

"But we've seen you call up your mist so many times since leaving Silvaren," Arishen persisted. "Why can't you just leave a mist permanently in place?"

Eliséo tried not to react to the suggestion. How could he possibly explain away the mist in a reasonable way? Very few elves, other than the royal family, had enough power to do things like that. He had done it each time out of necessity, even with Master Aurelius. That was a mistake he couldn't take back. He was becoming reckless now that Rilla was involved in his life.

Don't blame the girl for your actions, Elessa chided him. *Just tell the boy that elf magic doesn't work the same way and you can't permanently leave a mist barrier in place.*

"As I said, the two powers work differently. Elves can't create anything permanent with our magic unless trees are involved."

"Then why not plant a barrier of trees on the edge of Silvaren?" Tika asked him.

"For one thing, elf trees take years to reach their full potential so that would only ever be possible as a long-term solution," Eliséo answered patiently. "But what it really comes down to is that these are matters for the elves, namely the ambassador and the queen, to discuss with King Lukys, not for humans and training lintep to discuss with anyone. Are we understood?"

Tika and Arishen nodded silently.

I've placed Liessa in trouble, Eliséo guiltily admitted to Elessa, *and the worst part is she has no idea there could be any trouble in her life.*

You give her too little credit, Elessa scoffed at him. *She must have at least some idea that things are not quite as they should be. Otherwise, why would Lady Eléna abdicate for her?*

"Do all elves talk as much with their tree as you do?" Tika asked. Eliséo knew the boy had been watching his eyes glow. "I don't remember seeing many eyes glowing in Silvaren."

"You only saw a glimpse of life in Silvaren," Eliséo replied dismissively. "Most elves are not away from their tree as often, or for as long, as I am. They are able to talk to their trees using direct contact, rather than with their mind over great distances. Our eyes don't glow if we have direct contact with our trees."

He stopped suddenly at the end of a hall, just before another stairwell, at a door with a tree carved on it and took a small key out of his pocket. "These are my chambers," he said as he unlocked the door and pushed it open for the boys. He heard their gasps as they stepped inside.

Silvaren was spectacular in its earthy beauty with leaves and flowers of all different colours and shimmering vines hanging down as their version of doorways. The beds and tables had been moulded by the trees themselves.

Goraburg was no less impressive with its hundreds of caverns and tunnels with stalagmites, stalactites and shimmering underground lakes. In contrast, everything there had been carved of stone or crystal. The only light that came in was reflected off the water or crystallised stones.

Illaria was completely different. The imposing sandstone castle was among the largest structures in the Outworld that Eliséo had ever seen. He was often still overwhelmed by the sumptuous rooms, some decorated even more lavishly than his own.

His antechamber had a square wooden table with four matching chairs in the middle. To both sides were similar chaises to the ones in the testing room. Just above one of the chaises was a rope with a small silver handle hanging from the end of it. The wall facing the hall had a doorway to the bed chamber.

Eliséo walked in, followed by the Paradisians. He dropped his rucksack on the floor and watched as they admired the ornate, stained glass window facing them. He noted that fresh sheets of parchment and a full inkwell had been placed on his elaborately carved wooden desk.

The stone fireplace beside his window was unlit. He would need to see to that before night fell. These sandstone walls were efficient at keeping the heat out in summer but, on these cooler nights, he wished himself back in his cosy rooms with Elessa.

As the boys looked around, Eliséo walked over to another silver handle, hanging by his bed, and pulled twice. He saw the Paradisians eyeing the bed. It was larger than four of their sleeping mats laid out side by side and higher than the desk. The pillows were piled so high, he often had to throw them off for fear of suffocating.

"What's the silver handle for?" Tika asked him.

"I thought you might be hungry after our last week in the Outworld," Eliséo replied with a smile. "If I pull that silver handle twice, the servants in the kitchen will bring up food and drink." At the unasked question in the air, he added, "They know I came with guests and so will bring enough for all of you."

"What happens if you only pull on it once?"

"For one ring, a runner will be sent up to the room to take a message or do a task for me," Eliséo explained the simple system. "Three rings indicate I need a skilled lintep to warm the bathwater for me."

"Bathwater?" all three boys asked at the same time. Eliséo smiled at their simple thoughts and opened the last door, off to their left. A bath, full of steaming water greeted him. He laughed as the boys sighed with longing at the sight.

"How do they warm the bath water?" Plyke asked.

"I take it you missed the fireplace in the bathroom?" At their surprised look, he pointed and continued. "A skilled lintep would use a small spark of their heat to light the fireplace and then take the heat from that larger fire to warm the water."

"I suggest each of you have a bath tonight. I need to leave in the morning and all three of you will have a busy day ahead of you," Eliséo knew he couldn't hold off the truth much longer. He had hoped they would have assumed he would be leaving, but the crestfallen look on their faces proved otherwise.

"Why are you leaving so soon?" Tika asked in a crushed voice.

"To begin with, I was only charged with bringing Rilla and Plyke safely to Illaria. I was always meant to return after that," he was determined to tell them as much of the truth as possible. "Had things gone smoothly, I may have had the luxury to stay and help the four of you settle in, but as the situation with the karliki has become quite dangerous, I need to inform my queen so that she can decide how best the elves can assist them."

"Will the lintep be able to help them?" Plyke asked.

"I will tell King Lukys the turn of events, but with a dangerous lintep possibly on the way here, he may decide that the protection of his own people is more important."

"Will we be … safe here?" Tika asked, worriedly. "I mean, without you to look out for us and Plyke and Rilla in training, will Arishen and I be safe? With or without this dangerous lintep around?"

Eliséo considered things from the young human's point of view. In the Paradise, each of them would have contributed to their society with their chosen trade. If they had stayed in Turon, they would have attempted to find apprenticeships to earn money to keep them alive. In Illaria, their options were even more limited. How many lintep would be happy to take on a human apprentice?

It hadn't been discussed yet, but Lord Aaron would undoubtedly insist that Rilla and Plyke stay in the castle, at his expense, as was their birthright. But what of Arishen and Tika? All of these thoughts flew through his mind in a matter of seconds.

"If I can arrange it before I leave, would you both be happy for me to find you an apprenticeship?" He saw their eyes light up at the suggestion. "Tika in the stables and Arishen with a carpenter, yes?"

"The stables in the castle grounds?" Arishen spoke for the first time since entering the room.

"Most likely," Eliséo nodded. "It's possible I could find stables in the farming areas, but most likely they would want farmers rather than stablehands. Why do you ask?"

"I'm assuming there aren't any carpenters within the castle grounds. I'll be stuck out in the town somewhere, unable to get to the castle to see the others without a lintep to escort me past the barrier." Eliséo did not miss the bitter edge to the seer's voice.

"We'll come and see you every day," Plyke insisted.

"Maybe for the first few weeks," Arishen said, "but then you'll make friends with other lintep and forget about me. Then once that happens, the lintep will be able to remove me from Illaria with little objection and I'll be in the same situation as I was before."

Listening closely, Eliséo felt a pang of guilt for feeling more justified in not confiding Elessa's bond with Rilla to the boys. It was exactly this type of situation which could have Arishen betraying Rilla out of spite or jealousy. He would now have to do as much as he could to mitigate any damage before it occurred.

"Master Reuben seemed happy enough to work with you earlier today and Tommaso was excited to find a human seer. Perhaps I could talk to them about training you in the castle," his mind was racing to find solutions that sounded plausible. "Even if you live out in the town with a carpenter, if you are being trained by Master Reuben, he is sure to want to keep you in Illaria, even if your relationship with Rilla and Plyke deteriorates the way you imagine it will, not that I believe it will."

"Do you really think Master Reuben would train me? Would he even be allowed?" Arishen smiled at the idea.

"I'm not sure, Arishen," Eliséo answered truthfully. "This entire situation is unprecedented. Humans have not been allowed in Illaria for so many years that there has never been a question of whether they are allowed to be trained by master lintep. Once Rilla has returned and you are all shown to your rooms for the evening, I will enquire about both the training and apprenticeships. But for now, I hear our food approaching."

A few moments later, a servant boy knocked at the door bearing a tray laden with food. Word had already started to spread that two humans had accompanied the great grandchildren of Princess Rilla to Illaria.

Eliséo noticed him peek from under lowered eyes before closing the door behind the departing boy. At least there was no malice in those eyes. Perhaps not all of the younger generation were against humans. Rubbing his forehead with his long, slender fingers, he tried to sort through all the problems that faced him.

"Eat your fill," he told the boys. "I can always request more food if necessary. I need to make myself presentable before speaking with King Lukys, Lord Aaron and Master Reuben."

They didn't need to be told twice. Before he had even shut the door to his bed chamber, they had already seated themselves and started eating from the tray.

By the time Eliséo returned from his bath, he found Tika and Arishen with their heads on the table, fast asleep. So much for getting them to wash themselves that night. His eyes skirted the room until he noticed Plyke perched on the windowsill, looking out at the enormous expanse of Illaria through the fading orange light of the setting sun.

Clean from his bath, Eliséo no longer had streaks of dirt all over his skin. His black hair was no longer matted with mud and sweat, but was the same glossy black as all the other elves in Silvaren. The wardrobe in his bedchamber had been full of clothes. He had changed into light and dark blue clothes, fitted to his slender figure.

"You've changed," Plyke smiled at him. "It's a wonder the masters recognised you when we arrived."

"Well, I rarely have such interesting journeys on my way here," Eliséo returned the smile, "but I find it best to attire myself as an ambassador should when addressing the royal family and the masters if at all possible."

"I've been wondering …" Plyke hesitated. "Well, you mentioned about Tika working in the stables and Arishen with a carpenter. I assume they'll live with other people in their trade, like in our Paradise? But what will happen with me and Rilla? Will we learn a trade at the same time as our training? Where will we live?"

"That's one of the things I need to discuss with Lord Aaron," Eliséo answered easily. When he saw that didn't mean anything to Plyke, he continued, "If you had come here with Kora, and Rilla with Nyssa, it may have been more apparent to you what usually happens. Actually, I should say, if you hadn't lived in a Paradise your entire life, the answer would be clear to you. Generally, in the Outworld, children live with their parents, or any other family they have."

"So …" Plyke answered uncertainly.

"Lord Aaron is your grandfather," Eliséo reminded him gently. "Most likely, he will insist you and Rilla stay in the castle. The entire royal family lives here."

Plyke's jaw dropped at the information. Eliséo saw his eyes flicker over towards his Partner and a sombre look came over him. "What if I want to stay with Tika? He *is* my Partner after all."

"That's true, Plyke, but Partners have to live their own lives," Eliséo tried to reason with him. "If I succeed in finding him an apprenticeship, the stable master may not agree for Tika to live elsewhere, even if Lord Aaron is willing to have him in the castle itself."

Plyke nodded, glumly. "Can we pull the cord for clean bath water?"

"No need," Eliséo answered with a smile. "Elves can clean water with just a few words. The bath is still hot and ready for you to use."

Plyke returned his smile and immediately left the room.

Chapter Five – Royal Audience

Eliséo knew Rilla's test would last past sunset. With Tika and Arishen already asleep and Plyke presumably to join them soon after his bath, it would be best to seek an audience with King Lukys and Lord Aaron before it became too late in the evening. He could always talk to Master Reuben in the morning, assuming he wasn't one of the lintep going to Nyssa and Shadow's aid. It was probably best to try to sort out all of that before the morrow so that he could still leave as early as he'd planned.

He walked over to the cord and pulled down on the silver handle a single time. It was only a matter of minutes before he heard a runner arrive outside his door. He opened it even before the knock sounded, so as not to disturb the sleeping boys.

"I need you to find King Lukys, Lord Aaron and Master Reuben," he told the young girl as soon as she'd caught her breath. "Tell them I need an audience at their earliest convenience – tonight if possible."

The runner girl nodded and turned to deliver his message, long brown hair streaming out behind her. Eliséo looked after her with a twinge of doubt. Would he be able to secure all the things he needed to before leaving?

Help me! Eliséo's eyes glowed a soft silver as he heard Rilla's sudden plea. *What are the words for your mist?*

Without any effort, he watched Rilla's test through their link with Elessa. He thanked their good fortune that Master Aurelius had managed to secure the testing of Rilla for himself. He doubted he could have trusted many other masters with the secret he had revealed. It was clear that Aurelius was doing his best to see what situations would push Rilla to reveal her bond in a moment of weakness. So far, there had only been that one instance. Eliséo was certain he would have been aware of any others.

Wearily, he kept watching the lesson while waiting for the runner girl to return. He was so distracted by it that he barely heard Plyke return from his bath until the boy was next to him.

"I've been wondering," the young lintep sounded thoughtful. "If Lady Eléna knew who I was because she knew my entire family, does that mean that she's met Kora before?"

"Yes," Eliséo answered, taking his attention completely away from Rilla's test. "Their entire family visited Silvaren when they were just children."

"Yes, but do you know if Kora ever visited after that time?" He ran his fingers through his brown hair, betraying his sense of unease. "What I mean is, if Arishen's vision was true and Kora fled our Paradise, do you think there's any way that she could have found her way to Silvaren, as a sort of safe haven for a while?"

"I see." Eliséo considered the scenario for a moment, piecing together the question that Plyke was too afraid to ask. "It's entirely possible that she could have done that. I will ask after her on my return and if she happens to be there, I will be certain to tell her that you have arrived safely in Illaria."

"Do you think she would come?" Eliséo could hear the doubt in his voice. By now, the boy had understood the fact that Kora had disagreed with many things in Illaria and left years ago for that very reason.

"There's no way to know what Kora will do if she discovers you're here. The best thing you can do is concentrate on your training and not forget the most important thing that she taught you."

"All she taught me was how to build a wall," Plyke pointed out dejectedly.

"Really?" Eliséo raised an eyebrow at him. "I thought she taught you that your powers, especially your mind powers, shouldn't be used against humans.

"Get some sleep, Plyke. It's going to be a long day for you tomorrow."

Plyke had fallen asleep on one of the chaises by the time the runner girl returned. Eliséo's audience with King Lukys, Lord Aaron and Master Reuben was to be held in the King's private chambers immediately.

The elf cursed under his breath. He knew Rilla's test was done and she was on her way back with Aurelius. He wanted to talk with the old master to see if he had any plans yet for who might train the newly arrived lintep, but did not have time before the audience.

"Master Aurelius will soon escort Rilla to my chambers. Let him know that I wish to speak with him." Almost as an afterthought, he added, "I don't mind if he waits here until I return."

Eliséo hoped the old master knew him well enough to understand that he wanted someone to watch over the Paradisians until he'd returned. With little ceremony, he took a lantern off the wall outside his room, lit it from the lantern in the runner's hand and walked off in the direction of King Lukys' private chambers.

Not wanting to collide with Rilla and Master Aurelius, he took the stairwell next to his chambers up to the next level. At this time of night, the pale moonlight barely reached from the centre of the stairwell to light the way. He followed the long hallway, down a thick carpet, to the King's chambers. Thankfully, he'd been to Illaria, and stayed long enough each time, to know his way around the entire castle without getting lost. It was more than he could boast with Goraburg.

Often, as he walked this way, he took the time to study the many portraits of the royal family along the wall. This time, he was in too much of a hurry. Along the way, he thought of all he would need to secure in this audience. There was too much at stake. His only advantage was that he would at least be in Lord Aaron's good graces for safely bringing him two grandchildren. Aside from that, he only brought bad news of the Outworld and more requests than he knew would be granted to him.

It was with much trepidation that he finally knocked at the wooden door with a crown carved on it. It was opened by Master Reuben, who quickly looked down the hallway before admitting him in. Eliséo said nothing, but raised a questioning eyebrow as he entered the room. He was greeted silently until the door had been closed behind him.

"Your arrival with humans caused quite a stir amongst the council," Master Reuben explained to him, "and with Nyssa's attacker possibly on her way here, we are all on our guard."

"So you believe his vision then?" Eliséo asked, hoping against hope that his first request would be easily granted.

"I've worked with enough seers to know a vision when I see it," he nodded his head. "The problem with most of them is that you can never tell if it's already happened, is going to happen or is currently happening."

"If it's any help, it seems as though he usually dreams things as they are happening and only rarely dreams of the future," Eliséo offered up the information freely.

"Yes, I had gathered as much from what his companions said. He's a very interesting case. I'd love to know more about his dreams. They could certainly come in useful if we can train him to focus his visions."

With Master Reuben getting carried away about Arishen's vision, Eliséo decided to push his luck.

"Would you consider taking the boy under your wing?" he asked. "Young Tommaso seemed quite excited at the idea of a human seer. He may be an eager helper in your endeavour."

"Me?" the brown haired lintep replied in surprise. "Surely one of the more skilled masters would be better suited to the task."

"Come now, Reuben," King Lukys spoke up. "We all know that you are more tolerant of humans than the other mind masters. Who better than yourself to train him, if that's what you'd like to do."

"Will the council permit it?" he asked, his voice betraying both his hope and fear.

"The council deals with matters pertaining to *lintep* training," King Lukys reminded him. "I have decreed that the humans may remain in Illaria but any training accorded to them is of no concern to the entire council. If you wish to train him, you may do so, in your own time. Just be aware of the reaction it may cause from other members of the council if they discover what you're doing."

Eliséo hid a smile at the excited spark in Master Reuben's brown eyes. He had already secured one item on his list without much effort. Arishen would now either have regular visits to the castle or would at least have constant contact with a master. Now to see what he could do about the rest of his requests.

"Much as I'm glad we've dealt with this matter, Arishen's training was not actually the reason I requested this audience," Eliséo hastened to turn the conversation to other matters. "There are a number of other problems facing us at the moment, both with the newcomers to Illaria and in the Outworld itself."

"Let us talk of the Outworld first," King Luyks waved Eliséo to take a seat. Similar to his own chambers, there were a number of chairs around a table in the middle of the room. He seated himself next to Lord Aaron, while Master Reuben resumed his seat beside his king.

"I bring ill tidings from Goraburg," he began with a heavy heart. "Vladimir Mikhailovic has been charged with treason for trying to usurp his father's position. He, and all his followers, were sentenced to death but a number of them, including Vladimir himself, managed to escape. Ilya Mikhailovic has been named the heir and now has the heavy burden of helping his father find his brother and the rest of the traitors to put them to death before they can cause any sort of uprising in Goraburg."

Shocked silence greeted the news. Lintep and karliki generally had little dealings with each other, but King Lukys had met the clan leader and his children a handful of times. In all the time that Eliséo had been the ambassador, these two leaders had probably had more in common than any other lintep king and karlik lord.

"I realise that with a dangerous lintep possibly on her way to Illaria, you may not be able to assist the karliki in this time of conflict, but its best you know of the situation as early as possible."

"Has Queen Eléna been alerted to the situation?" The king finally found his voice.

"*Lady* Eléna is currently unaware of the situation," Eliséo corrected him. "I will be leaving as early as I can tomorrow to alert Queen Liessa to all current events."

"Why would Eléna abdicate for her daughter?" The question was asked aloud, though Eliséo was unsure if Luyks intended for him to answer it.

"We do not question our queen's actions, but trust that she has good reasons for them and accept them as we must."

It was the only answer he could give. He knew full well the reason Eléna had abdicated in favour of her daughter and thought her decision to do so was a foolish one. It would only attract such questions from everyone and possibly draw attention to the fact that she had another child somewhere. He was the only foundling in Silvaren so it wouldn't take long for people to figure it out. Had Eléna jeopardised his freedom in trying to secure stability for her people?

"Very well, then under the circumstances, I suggest you take a horse of your choice from our stables." King Lukys did not part with his horses willingly, so Eliséo knew he understood the gravity of the situation. "Keep us well informed of the situation both in Goraburg and Silvaren. If Eléna's reason for abdicating becomes common knowledge, I do not want to be the last person to find out. All I can hope is that she is not ill and hoping to groom her daughter before her death."

"I believe Lady Eléna is in good health, but I shall keep you informed of any developments in that area. With Goraburg, I hope that my queen will allow me leave to assist the karliki as it was partially through my actions that the incident occurred."

King Lukys' fixed him with his questioning brown eyes. Eliséo weighed up his options of how much he could actually tell the lintep king without giving away the secret of the crystal heart belonging to the karliki.

"Had we not arrived in Goraburg when we did, it's quite possible that Vladimir would have succeeded in overthrowing his father without Mikhail realising what was happening until it was too late.

"If we'd had the luxury to stay and help in the first place, the situation might have been averted. As it was, Shadow, or as the others call her, Shuut, had been struck down by a lintep and Rilla and Plyke needed to get to Illaria – as Master Aurelius will tell you, we barely made it in time for them."

"Yes, you mentioned an attack by a lintep in the council," Lukys immediately latched onto the morsel of information dangled in front of him. "Would you mind explaining exactly what happened?"

Eliséo knew they needed to talk about it, but didn't know how to go about it. Celtan obviously knew of the existence of the crystal heart, but it might not be common knowledge to the lintep.

"It appears as though a lintep, a very powerful and skilful one, was hunting us down. We're fairly certain that they were sending out groups of mercenaries to attack us but we're not certain who the target was. The worst thing that happened was that Shadow, Lady Nyssa's oldest daughter, was struck down with some sort of cage around her mind.

"Plyke will be able to tell you more about it but, from what he told me, it was a type of mind snare that sapped her strength if she fought against it. We had no way to help her ourselves, so we asked for safe passage through Goraburg to reach the Drakos Mountains in time to save her."

"So the crystal dragons got rid of the mind snare?" At the mention of his daughter's name, Lord Aaron had finally sat up straight in his chair and begun to listen attentively.

"Not exactly," Eliséo wavered. It was really only Vladimir and his followers who shouldn't know who had the crystal, and that was only if they realised what had happened with Shadow. If anything, the lintep would be just as anxious to protect this secret as the karliki were.

"She was healed in Goraburg, by means of an ancient gift the crystal dragons bestowed upon the karliki many years ago."

King Lukys and Lord Aaron each drew in a quick breath. Only Reuben looked puzzled. Eliséo immediately understood that at least the royal family knew of the existence of the crystal heart.

"I think it would be best if we talk about that with Kynon as well," Lukys'
brown eyes went unfocussed. Eliséo had seen lintep working their magic
often enough to understand that Lukys had just summoned his younger
cousin with his mind.

"Until he arrives, there is another matter I wish to discuss with you," Eliséo
decided there would be no better time to talk about the apprenticeships
if he was to depart early in the morning. "Plyke's Partner, Tika, was to be
apprenticed to the stable master in his Paradise had circumstances permitted
him to remain there. As such, I thought you might see your way to ensuring
he could work in your own stables. He would be happy to lodge there and
Plyke should not be too distressed as his Partner would still be within the
castle grounds and he could visit him whenever he desired."

"I think that would be an excellent idea," Lord Aaron agreed. "I will see to it
that Rilla and Plyke stay in the castle, in the rooms that my own dear children
occupied when they were all still alive. If Plyke becomes too distressed at the
distance from his Partner, we could see if there is an alternative for him."

"What of the seer?" Master Reuben asked, hesitantly.

"Young Arishen was to be apprenticed to a carpenter in his Paradise,"
Eliséo answered easily. "It only stands to reason that we find him a similar
apprenticeship here where they understand the condition is that he be
allowed time to carry out his training with you."

"I'm not certain it would be wise to have the human living unprotected in
the city," King Lukys interrupted. "There are some quick tempered lintep who
may not be overly enthused by the idea of a human living among them and
any trade master would only be in danger with him lodging there."

"Could he work with a carpenter and live in the servants' quarters in the
castle?" King Lukys was already shaking his head before Reuben finished the
question.

"No, Reuben. I fear the only solution is that he lodge in your own house
with your servants. It will be easier to keep an eye on him there and no one
would dare attack a master's home.

"If you are happy to be responsible for the boy, I suggest you take on the
task of finding him an appropriate apprenticeship as it may take more time
than Ambassador Eliséo has to spare."

Eliséo smiled gratefully at the king. He couldn't believe the success he'd had
in securing so many things for his young companions. All he had to do now
was survive the meeting when Lord Kynon arrived. Eliséo had never been
overly fond of that side of the royal family. Perhaps it was because they were
the least tolerant of humans and weren't content to merely ignore them but
actively sought to use their power against them whenever the opportunity
arose. Did he really want Kynon to know he had the crystal heart with him?

A knock at the door brought him out of his thoughts. Master Reuben bid the three of them a quick farewell before opening the door for Kynon and departing when the lord entered.

"What's the meaning of this?" He asked irritably, still rubbing the sleep from his hazel eyes. "Do you know what time it is?"

"Kynon, you should be more concerned about political matters than your nightly routines," Aaron chided him instantly. It was no secret the two of them didn't get along very well. After all, Aaron's side of the family was the most accepting of humans, so they were often bickering over how their magic should or should not be used in the Outworld, should any of them ever venture out there.

"If you had managed to keep your entire family safe in the Outworld, perhaps you'd be less concerned with external political matters than you are," Kynon tried to bait him.

"I did not summon you here to bicker," Lukys replied icily. "These *external political matters*, as you call them, may very soon have an impact on your life in Illaria, Kynon, so perhaps you'd like to pay attention to them."

Silenced by his king, Kynon sat down in the chair recently vacated by Reuben and folded his arms sulkily.

"Ambassador, if you would like to elaborate?" It was more of an order than a question, but Eliséo obliged King Lukys.

"It has recently come to my attention that a gift from the crystal dragons to the karliki can be used to dissipate any magical mind snare placed on a person," Eliséo paused momentarily. Kynon's reaction mirrored his cousins' exactly. "Even amongst the karliki themselves, knowledge of the existence of this artefact is merely a legend and the power that the gift holds is not well known.

"With the treasonous actions of Vladimir, it is imperative that the gift remain a thing of legend. The only reason I tell you is because it was used to cure Nyssa's daughter. If the person who cast the mind snare on her is the lady in Arishen's vision and she is on her way to Illaria then you may need to make sure you have a number of masters ready to dissipate the magic without the aid we had in Goraburg."

The three cousins listened in silence to Eliséo's words. Even with their walls, Eliséo couldn't help but hear their surface thoughts running amok with the idea that they might have such a powerful and dangerous lintep on the way to Illaria with no experience in how to protect themselves against such magic.

Lintep were a fairly peaceful race. They'd never battled amongst themselves and therefore had only needed to learn certain skills. How to create and dissipate powerful mind snares was something only masters had ever contemplated, but more to pass on the knowledge rather than to use it.

"We'll need to ask Jorg to work with Plyke during his training," Luyks announced. It was what Eliséo had been trying to avoid, but there was no way around it. Plyke's only chance to not be a sitting duck with Jorg was to employ the only skill Kora had taught him – block out the master with his walls. They were from opposite sides of the human debate with Plyke going so far as to have a human Partner from a Paradise. Eliséo knew that Jorg was the best mind master on the Council so he would have the best chance of finding a way to dissipate the mind snare if Plyke could describe it to him well enough.

"Lukys, if you would permit it, I would request permission to sit in on the lessons," Aaron spoke softly but determinedly. "It seems as though most of my remaining family were targeted by this rogue lintep and my mind skills aren't quite as poor as it might please some people to think. If I can assist or simply watch and learn during these sessions, I would very much like to do so."

"I will talk to Jorg about it," Lukys acquiesced easily. "Eliséo, is there anything else you need to discuss before leaving in the morning?"

"I should probably mention that the crystal dragons have no idea that their prophecy child walked right through their mountains and is now in Illaria," he admitted. "I'm certain they will discover it sooner or later, as we're bound to send word to them of Nyssa and Shadow once we find out what has happened to them. They may not be very impressed by that and could quite possibly try to demand access to her."

"The crystal dragons? My Nyssa was living with *them*?" Aaron asked vehemently. "If I'd known that they were manipulating my daughter, I would have stopped them instantly."

"Then you should probably know that they had control of Shadow until only a few weeks ago," Eliséo told him calmly. "She and Nyssa had been told that the other was dead in order that the dragons could manipulate the prophecy. Now that they've been reunited, the dragons' hold over them is broken."

"Are there any races you managed not to disturb on your travels here?" Luyks asked him with a hint of humour. Eliséo smiled, but omitted to tell them of Elessa's bond with Rilla.

"I won't let them control another member of my family," Lord Aaron spoke quietly. It sounded like a promise to himself.

"I think that's all the news I can relate to you on this short visit," the elf effectively wrapped up the audience. "I will take my leave of you now to rest before my early departure."

Lukys waved his hand in easy dismissal and Eliséo left the room to return to his own chambers, happy in the knowledge that he'd secured the most agreeable solutions he could for the Paradisians and not revealed too many of his secrets to the lintep.

Chapter Six – Departure

"Where have you been?" Aurelius asked in a tired voice as soon as the door closed behind Eliséo. "I returned with the girl to find you had vanished and requested me to mind the Paradisians in your absence."

"My apologies, Aurelius," Eliséo slumped down on the only chaise in the room not already occupied by his companions. "I must leave in the morning and had to organise a few things before then. How did her test go?"

"She's powerful," the master admitted with a sigh, "and skilful in the most unusual ways. Unfortunately, because she wasn't taught anything, she's too reckless and most of the time doesn't even realise it."

"It could be because she wasn't taught anything that she is skilful in an unusual way," Eliséo was quick to point out to him.

"I think we both know she would be unusual even if it weren't for that. She was too tired for me to get a completely accurate reading, but I think there would be more than one situation where she would instinctively call on help from … other sources."

"Do you think things would go more smoothly if I make it clear to other sources that assistance should not be given if it's asked for in future lessons? Though I doubt she knows of any other assistance that could be afforded to her and the damage is now done with that one instance."

"So you saw that," Aurelius mused aloud. "I did wonder if you would be aware of it."

"She asked for help so loudly, even had I been blocking her out, she would probably have broken through my walls," the elf grimaced at the memory of the time she had yelled out to him when they had left the Drakos Mountains. He'd ended up on his knees, cradling his head in his hands.

"I will see if I can secure Reuben to teach her the mind skills," Aurelius nodded to himself. "I don't want Jorg anywhere near her. Perhaps I can secure her practical skills myself, though Vika may fight me on that. For healing, I would prefer Mistress Kayte, but there are a few others superior to her in power, though not in skill. She needs to be taught how to communicate with other lintep, but at least *she* can hear the whistle. I should be able to get Master Graham to help with that."

Eliséo allowed him to think aloud, happy to hear the plans for Rilla's training, but he knew Aurelius would have little choice with at least one of Plyke's masters. "Master Jorg will be training Plyke in his mind skills."

"No!" It was a strangled cry. Everyone knew that, of all the masters and mistresses in Illaria, Jorg was the most unforgiving in his lessons. The fact that he was the most skilled and possibly the most powerful in mind magic did not make him the best teacher.

"I'm sorry, Aurelius," Eliséo sympathised with him. "I had no choice in the matter. Plyke is the only one who saw what the mind snare on Shadow looked and felt like. If the lintep are to stand a chance against this person, whether it's Lishe or not, Jorg really is the best hope you have. At least there is one positive result in all of this – Lord Aaron will be present at all of those lessons in an effort to learn and assist in any way he can."

A beautiful and serene smile bloomed on the lintep's face as he closed his eyes and breathed deeply.

"At last! It's taken over thirty years for him to come out of his shell. Lord Aaron is one of the most skilled lintep I know in terms of mind magic, quite possibly more so than Jorg. In fact, he may be more skilled than I am in practical magic, but he stopped trying when his family was killed and completely withdrew when his daughters left Illaria. He's been a shadow of himself since that time."

"His grandchildren have rekindled his fire," Eliséo bit his lip. "They don't know what happened to his family. I'm not sure if you'll have a chance to tell them anytime soon, but if there is an opportunity, perhaps you could.

"Rilla has a habit of alienating herself everywhere she goes without realising what she's doing. She's already put up a wall of resistance to Aaron. In fact, when Rilla and Plyke discovered they were cousins, the boy was overjoyed to have found part of his family. Rilla was completely indifferent. I have a feeling that her parents have harmed her in more ways than one – abandoned by her mother and ignored and mistreated by her father. She can't understand how Aaron feels right now. She may ruin their relationship before it even begins."

"You ask quite a lot of me," Aurelius chided him. "Why don't *you* stay in Illaria to keep an eye on her and *I'll* go to Silvaren to carry out your duties."

"Don't worry, I'll be keeping an eye on her, but she doesn't always listen to me," Eliséo told him plainly. "She's still just a child, really. A child thrown down a waterfall and told to swim."

"Well, at least she's in Illaria now. We'll keep her safe and teach her well," Aurelius said. "She's determined to learn everything she can and thoroughly master the skills. In that, at least, she is unlike her mother. It's a good sign, Eliséo. She could very well become the mistress we all knew Nyssa could have been had she simply tried."

"I've often wondered about that," the elf took the chance to ask what he'd never been certain of. "Are members of the royal family allowed to sit on the council?"

"You ask a complicated question," Aurelius rubbed his stubbly chin. "It's not a question of if they are allowed to or not, but more a matter of if they have time for it. A master or mistress of the council is expected to be available to teach and test all day, every day if necessary, and to attend all council meetings. A member of the royal family may not have the luxury of time to do this, depending on their other duties.

"King Lukys would never have time for the council. We're quite fortunate that he managed, at such short notice, to attend our meeting today. Lord Aaron would possibly have time for it if he wished, but as I said, he lost his fire with his family. Lord Kynon, well, he would certainly have time but can't be bothered with it."

"What of Princess Aislen?" Eliséo knew King Lukys only had one child. In the lintep world, that was seen as a dangerous thing. Whereas elves saw a single heir as a way to avoid conflicts for the crown, the lintep preferred to have an abundance of heirs should anything happen to some of them. Attacks from humans were not uncommon in the Outworld, as Lord Aaron had discovered for himself.

"Yes, Princess Aislen could easily sit on the Council, but she actually prefers to shadow her father. She will make a good queen when it is her time."

"Well, it will be quite a few years before we see if either of them manage to master the skills required to even consider sitting on the council," Eliséo looked over at Rilla and Plyke.

"Mistress Isis is the youngest member of our council and she is quite a rarity at thirty-six years of age," Aurelius reminded him. "She was born and grew up in Illaria. We were amazed at her natural skill before her lessons even began. I know your Rilla and Plyke are powerful, but it may take them many years to hone their skills to the level required. Neither has been taught even the basics and they are both sixteen now. We have years of catching up to do with them."

"At least they are finally safe enough here to do that," Eliséo replied.

"One of them is safe enough," Aurelius countered. "What are we do to if the other source is discovered? If it slips out somehow? The most I can do is make sure no one is aware of the involvement of any one person, but that may not be enough."

Eliséo paled at the thought. He knew it was a distinct possibility that Rilla would somehow lose her focus in a lesson and try to rely on Elessa's bond. How soon would people realise whose tree she had bonded with? How soon before they then made the link that the power she could access was too great to belong to anyone other than a royal elf? Then he and Liessa would be in grave danger of either losing their lives or having their future completely changed.

Stop thinking these thoughts, Elessa chided him for the hundredth time. *You can't change the future by constantly thinking about it.*

If you had only considered the future for a moment before you created a bond with Rilla, we wouldn't be in this mess, Eliséo replied angrily, making sure to block his thoughts from Rilla. He did not want her dreaming about this conversation.

Eliséo noticed Master Aurelius staring at his eyes. Undoubtedly, they were softly shining silver instead of remaining a dull grey. He broke off his conversation with Elessa. There wasn't much more he could say to the master. They both knew the danger both he and Rilla were in because of their bond. Their only hope was that she completely understood that she could *not* use that power except under the most extreme circumstances – being attacked in a lesson did not count.

"We should both get some rest," he said, dismissing all other thoughts. "I need to leave early in the morning and when you awaken, you will need to petition for their masters. Thank you for watching over them while I was away."

"One last thing before I leave," Aurelius hesitated. "How will the humans stay safe when you leave them? Rilla and Plyke won't be able to watch over them."

"Tika will work in the castle stables," Eliséo informed him. "He'll be close enough to Plyke there that no one should dare to harm him. Arishen is to live with Master Reuben and hopefully gain an apprenticeship in the city. If everyone knows he is living with a master, there should be little trouble. They can stay here tonight and then Lord Aaron and Master Reuben will organise the rest tomorrow."

Aurelius bobbed his head up and down in agreement. Eliséo opened the door and waited for the lintep to take one of the lanterns off the wall and light it before bidding him farewell and closing the door behind him.

Knowing there wouldn't be a problem from anyone in the castle, Eliséo should have felt safe. If he were alone, he would have, but with the four Paradisians fast asleep in the room, he didn't quite trust to their safety that night.

Muttering a few words under his breath, he thickened the air around the doorway to the point where no one would be able to pass through it until he dissipated the spell. Happy in the knowledge that Rilla had not witnessed that bit of magic, he went to his bedroom, and climbed onto the large, comfortable bed. In a matter of minutes, he was asleep.

* * *

It was her first night in captivity. Shuut had spent most of the day trying to build a wall, which Lishe had explained to her in such an offhand way that she barely understood what she was doing. Lishe had been pushing her almost non-stop in the same direction that Nyssa had been leading her before they were attacked. Shuut knew that meant they were still travelling towards Illaria, though she had no idea how far away they were from the lintep stronghold.

"Do you actually have a plan yet?" Shuut asked the power-hungry lintep out of curiosity. Lishe glared at her with pale blue eyes.

"Find the brat and kill her."

"Yes, you've already said that," Shuut replied evenly. "But *how* do you intend to find her? You don't even know where she is."

"She has to be in Illaria by now or she's already dead," Lishe reasoned. "So we go to Illaria and kill her."

"You're going to just waltz into the lintep stronghold and kill someone?" Shuut asked incredulously. "You would *never* reach her before someone realised who or what you are."

Lishe laughed cooly. "I won't even have to reach the city before twisting someone's thoughts to make the girl come to me."

"She's not stupid," Shuut's temper rose with the lintep's laughter. "If you threaten to kill me unless she comes out, she's bound to tell someone else that you're there, even if you tell her not to."

"That makes your existence a little useless then, doesn't it?"

Shuut immediately went silent. She wanted to save her little sister's life, but that didn't mean that she wanted to hasten her own death. All she had to do was figure out exactly what this lintep intended to do before they reached Illaria.

"How long until we get there?"

"Two, maybe three days," the lintep replied. "It all depends on how quickly you build your wall. Speaking of which – it's time to test how far you've come."

Shuut suddenly felt Nyssa's power flowing out of her body and panicked. She had no idea how to stop it. A few moments later, before the pain began again, she felt all the power being forced back into her body and shoved roughly into her hastily built wall. There was no more pain.

"That will do," Lishe nodded. "Just close it off at the top, so that the power can't escape again. Do that and we'll both be able to get some sleep tonight."

* * *

Dawn found the Paradisians and Eliséo still sleeping. Since the attack on Shuut on this side of the Bramble River, Eliséo had not had more than a night of sleep in a row. If he hadn't been an elf, he would have collapsed from exhaustion long ago. The Paradisians had slept, but never soundly.

Tika woke first and looked around to find Arishen still asleep with his head on the table and Rilla and Plyke curled up on a chaise. The door to Eliséo's room was open. He stretched and walked over to the window next to the elf's bed. The sun was only just beginning to rise, casting orange rays into the rooms.

"You're going to just waltz into the lintep stronghold and kill someone?" Tika turned to see Arishen's lips moving. "You would never reach her before someone realised who or what you are."

He looked to Plyke and Rilla to see if they had woken up yet but then his eyes swivelled back to Arishen when the seer started sleep talking again.

"She's not stupid. If you threaten to kill me unless she comes out, she's bound to tell someone else that you're there, even if you tell her not to."

"Who are you talking to?" Tika asked the sleeping seer, close to his face, hoping to get more out of him. There was no answer. Arishen slowly started to stir and nearly fell off his chair when he saw Tika's hazel eyes staring at him.

"What are you doing?" he asked Tika in annoyance.

"Trying to see who you were talking to in your sleep," Tika answered without backing down. "You were talking about someone coming into Illaria and killing someone."

Arishen narrowed his eyes. "You heard that?"

"Well, you said it," he replied uncertainly.

"I had another dream about Shuut and the person who attacked her," Arishen answered, eyes cast down. "They're on their way here and the other person wants to kill someone. I think she's after Rilla."

"Why would anyone want to kill Rilla?" Tika asked in confusion. A noise behind him made him stop and turn to find Eliséo standing in the doorway to his bedroom.

"Because she is named in a prophecy," Eliséo answered calmly. "If anyone doesn't want the prophecy to pass, all they would need to do is kill Rilla."

"I don't understand why anyone would want to stop a prophecy that would destroy Paradises," Tika persisted. "If I could destroy them all right now, I would."

"Not everyone shares your views, Tika," Eliséo cautioned him. "There are many who still wish to find a Paradise to live in because they believe it must be better than the Outworld."

"Ours wasn't," Tika mumbled.

Eliséo crossed the room and placed a hand on the boy's shoulder. "Most people in the Outworld have no idea that some Paradises may have become dangerous places to live. They still cling to the idea that they really are paradises to live in. If I hadn't met you and heard your stories, I might still be one of those people. But now we understand why the prophecy is so important. We need to destroy them otherwise other people will be in danger, just like people in your Paradise are."

"But if it's so important that Rilla fulfils the prophecy, why are you leaving us so soon?" he asked, upset. "What if this person really is on their way here to kill Rilla?"

"There are plenty of lintep here to protect her," Eliséo answered, feeling absurdly guilty for leaving them now. "I've done as much as I could for the four of you before leaving. You will work in the castle stables and be near Plyke."

Turning to the seer, he continued. "Arishen, you will live with Master Reuben. He has agreed to help you learn more about your skills and to find an apprenticeship for you in the town. No lintep, even those against humans, would dare attack you if they know you are under his roof and his protection."

Arishen half smiled at the news. "Does Master Reuben live in the castle too?"

"No, Arishen," Eliséo shook his head. "He lives in the city outside the castle walls, but I'm certain he will escort you into the castle any time you are free from your apprentice duties."

Plyke and Rilla had finally awoken with the conversation in the room. Eliséo watched them walk over to join the conversation.

"What about us?" Plyke asked. "Where will we stay and what apprenticeships will we have?"

"Well, Illaria is different from your Paradise. Here, lintep children live with their parents until they choose what they want to do with their lives. Their parents generally pay for everything, including their lodging, meals and lessons." Eliséo didn't know how to continue. He didn't know if Lord Aaron wanted to tell them himself and he didn't know how the two young lintep would react to the news.

"But our parents aren't here," Rilla pointed out. "If Tika lives in the stables where he will be apprenticed and Arishen lives with Master Reuben, where are we going to live?"

There was a knock at the door, saving Eliséo from answering her. The elf quickly muttered a few words under his breath, dissipating the air lock he'd put on the door the night before, hoping Rilla didn't notice, before opening the door. Lord Aaron himself was on the other side.

"Good morning, Ambassador Eliséo," he greeted the elf amiably, green and brown eyes sparkling brightly. "I believe you must depart early this morning so I've taken the liberty of passing by the kitchens to request a meal to break your fast before your journey."

"Lord Aaron, that is too kind of you," Eliséo answered in genuine surprise. In all the time he'd spent in Illaria in the last thirty years, Lord Aaron had never come up to see him in his room nor had he ever looked so full of life.

"I thought you might like to say a quick farewell to your young companions and then I can escort them to their new homes," he added by way of explanation. "The castle is a large place and I didn't want them to get lost trying to find their way around without you."

Tika ran over to Eliséo and nearly knocked him over with the force of his hug. Eliséo was quick to get over his shock and embrace the young boy. "I'll be counting on you to keep Plyke focussed on his studies," he whispered in the small human's ear before disentangling himself. He saw a small tear trickle down Tika's face as he nodded to the elf and stood aside.

Arishen was the next to walk over. "Thank you, for not dismissing my dreams like most people," he said, scratching the hair behind his ear. "And I'm sure you had at least something to do with Master Reuben taking me in, so thank you for that too."

"You're a gifted seer, Arishen. If you pay attention to Master Reuben and take your apprenticeship seriously, you will gain more skills in Illaria than you will ever need to survive the Outworld on your own, should it come to that."

Eliséo knew there was no point insisting that the situation would never occur because he understood the likelihood of it all too well. He simply hoped that Arishen would never be in a position to betray Rilla before or after that event.

"I'm sorry I ever thought you were only protecting Rilla," Plyke spoke softly, once he was standing next to Eliséo. "I don't know how you did it, but I'm glad you managed to get me to use my power in the Outworld and actually help me with that. If nothing else, I thank you for letting us know that Rilla and Shuut are my cousins. That means … so very much to me." The boy choked back tears as he said his last few words. Without allowing Eliséo a chance to reply, he walked away from him and went to grip his Partner's hand.

Rilla refused to move, refused to look at him. She didn't want to say goodbye to him. She'd already had to say goodbye to too many people. First Rhanya, which still made her heart ache, then Ratchin, whom she'd only known for a day but who had taught her so much. The elves were a collective loss for her because they knew so much about her entire family. But to her surprise, even more than the elves, she regretted having to part ways with Shuut and their mother. She'd only known Nyssa for such a short amount of time and had found out Shuut was her sister on the same day she was reunited with her mother. Watching Eliséo leave was more than she could bear now, even if Arishen's vision of Nyssa and Shuut was wrong.

Plyke noticed the look on Rilla's face and shared a look with Tika. "Lord Aaron, perhaps we can wait with you in the hall while Rilla says her farewell to Eliséo?"

Aaron looked surprised at the suggestion, but shrugged his shoulders and held the door open for the three boys to exit. They all shouldered their rucksacks, strapped on their weapons and followed him out of the room.

Eliséo thanked Plyke with a nod and waited until the door had closed behind them before walking over to Rilla.

"I can't do this," she walked away from him to the window. "I can't say goodbye to you."

"You know I don't have a choice, Rilla," he told her softly as he walked to her side. "Even had I not had another reason to ride swiftly back to Lady Eléna, the situation with the karliki and Nyssa's possible death are more than serious enough to bring to the attention of Queen Liessa."

"I know," she mumbled, staring out at the rising sun, "but I don't know how I'm going to survive in this place without you. There are masters who will hate me just because of Nyssa. I've a grandfather I didn't even know was still alive and hadn't really thought of before. I don't have anyone looking out for me. I'm all alone."

I still have secrets to hide and if I don't manage it, I'll put you and Liessa in danger, probably myself as well.

With no one else in the room to see her eyes glow, Rilla turned and talked to Eliséo and Elessa through their bond. *I know you must have seen at least part of my test yesterday. What if something like that happens again? What will I do?*

The most you can try to do is pretend that you don't have extra powers and not call on Elessa during your lessons, Eliséo replied, his eyes glowing a soft silver. *If your life is ever in danger, don't think twice about the danger you'd put any of us in. Use all the magic you can to save yourself. If it really comes to it, we'd rather keep you alive than keep a secret that causes your death.*

"You only say that because I'm the prophecy child," Rilla shied away, reverting to her old tactic.

Eliséo drew her in for a long embrace, stroking her long fiery curls. "I don't care that you're the prophecy child. You're a part of my life now and I don't want to lose you. I don't want anyone to hurt you and I want you to master every lintep skill you possibly can. Show any who doubt your worth how wrong they are about you – that you're nothing like your mother when it comes to your power.

"Most importantly, try not to still feel responsible for the boys. You've brought them to the safest place they could be aside from Silvaren. Your duty to Rhanya is fulfilled now so please let it go and let someone look after you for a change. Your grandfather is desperate to keep the rest of his family safe so if anyone dares threaten you, he will come to your aid."

And you will never be alone as long as you are open to us, Elessa added warmly.

Rilla was crying by the time they'd finished talking. She clung to Eliséo for another minute before stepping away and wiping the tears from her face. Without another word, she stood up on her toes, kissed the elf on the cheek and walked swiftly to the door, picking up her rucksack and swords without a backward glance.

Eliséo stood still for a moment, looking at the closed door. His chest felt constricted, like it did the day he was banished from Goraburg. It amazed him that a girl he'd known for only a few weeks was already as dear to him as his best friend in the Outworld.

Shaking his head to clear his thoughts, he went back to his bed chamber to change into his travel clothes. Thankfully, he had a spare set in Illaria that were always ready for him if he needed to leave in a hurry. He left his mud-caked clothes on the floor for the servants. They would undoubtedly be clean and ready for him on his next visit.

By the time he was ready to leave, a servant from the kitchen had arrived with a tray of food he could easily pack in his rucksack for the journey to Silvaren. He carefully placed most of the food in his pack before shouldering it and starting to eat an apple as he left his room to walk two levels down the twisting stairwell, through the inner courtyard and out to the external courtyard.

Once there, he made his way over to the stables. To greet him there were Master Reuben, Mistress Kayte and three other lintep he didn't recognise all in riding garb. His mind raced back through the events of the previous day. He'd forgotten King Lukys had requested a search party to find Lady Nyssa.

"Ambassador Eliséo," Kayte greeted him, "if you would allow the five of us to accompany you into the Outworld, perhaps you would be able to point us in the right direction to search for Nyssa."

"Of course," Eliséo replied easily. "I can show you where we came in and where we were coming from. But if the seer's vision was accurate, I fear you may only be leading yourselves into danger."

"Thank you for your concern, but we are all skilled lintep," Reuben reassured him. "Even if the vision was accurate and it was indeed Lishe, she would think twice before attacking five fully trained lintep while trying to contain Nyssa's power in another person."

Eliséo took the hint not to offer further advice but proceeded to walk through the stables, touching each horse on the nose before settling on a chestnut mare. The stable master himself came to saddle the horse for the elf, while his stable hands saddled horses for the five lintep to accompany him.

In a matter of minutes they were mounted and ready to go. Eliséo resisted the urge to look up at the castle in case any of his recent companions were watching and sensed his unease at leaving them. He trotted his mare out across the bridge into the city. The five lintep followed closely behind him.

Heads turned at the sound of the horses on the cobblestones. It would be unusual for such a large group of people to ride out of the castle so early in the morning.

Before long, they were galloping through the farmlands to the outskirts of Illaria. Eliséo steered them towards the place where he and the Paradisians had entered the day before. Once they had passed through the boundary, the elf reined in his horse and waited for the others to join him.

"You'll be able to follow our path for at least a few hours," he told them as he pointed to the broken branches and crushed leaves that the kryti had damaged in their haste to bring Rilla and Plyke safely to Illaria. At their confused looks, he added. "My companions made some unusual alliances in the Outworld. We came from the Bramble River, so once you lose the krytis' trail, keep heading in that direction and you should come across Nyssa and Shadow. I wish you all the best in bringing them both back safe and alive to Illaria."

"Thank you, Eliséo," Kayte gripped his hand in fond farewell. "We will send word to Silvaren once we return to Illaria. Ride safely."

"Ride safely," the elf returned her farewell and nodded to Master Reuben before turning his horse towards his own home and urging his horse into a trot.

Chapter Seven – Mistress Isis

Rilla closed the door behind her, gently touching the tree carving on it, strapped her swords to her sides and looked over at the faces of the boys she had sworn to protect. Was Eliséo right? Had she fulfilled her obligation to Rhanya yet? They probably were as safe here as they could possibly be anywhere in the Outworld. Her eyes strayed to Lord Aaron. What had Eliséo said? My grandfather is desperate to keep the rest of his family safe. I know that includes me, but what does he mean by the rest of his family? Has something happened to some of them?

"You must take care, Rilla, that your surface thoughts are limited to general musings rather than such deep matters," Lord Aaron told her gently. "There will be time for that tale to be told. For now, keep your thoughts to yourself or any lintep worth their training will be able to see them, whether they try to or not."

Rilla instantly pulled all her thoughts into her wall, leaving nothing on the outside. It surprised her that she wasn't angry with Lord Aaron for seeing her thoughts. Perhaps it was because she knew she was distracted and he was right, or perhaps it was because he wasn't trying to read her thoughts but to protect her before they met any other lintep.

"That's better," he smiled warmly, "now let me take you to your rooms."

"Our rooms?" Plyke asked him immediately. "What do you mean?"

"Did Eliséo not tell you?" Aaron asked in surprise. "You and Rilla will live here in the castle, in the rooms that belonged to my children. After all, once you come of age, you will be a lord and lady yourselves. We can't have you living in the city."

Rilla shared a startled look with Plyke. She hadn't even considered living in the castle, let alone the fact that she would become a lady and Plyke a lord.

"But what about Arishen and Tika?"Plyke asked in a panic.

"Don't worry, Plyke," Tika reassured him. "Eliséo said I'm to be a stablehand in the castle stables so I'll still be here."

"But you won't be in the castle, in my room. I've never spent that much time away from you before."

"It would have happened even in our Paradise. I would have worked in the stables and you would have had your own apprenticeship. We would only have seen each other at meals and after a long day's work. It won't be much different here. I'll work in the stables and you'll concentrate on your lessons. I'm certain we'll see each other every day." Tika looked over to Lord Aaron for confirmation.

"I can arrange for Tika to join us for our evening meals, so that at the very least you see him once a day," the old lintep was quick to provide easy contact for the Partners.

"Wait, what about Arishen?" Rilla asked suddenly. "Eliséo said he would live with Master Reuben out in the city. How are we meant to see him when he can't cross the bridge alone?"

"Yes, I was wondering that myself," her grandfather said with a slow nod. "In any case, Master Reuben is riding out this morning in search of Nyssa and Shuut. The servants in his house won't know to expect a human so it may be safer, until he returns, for young Arishen to stay within the castle grounds. I shall request for you to work in the stables alongside Tika until Master Reuben returns and we can sort out the other details later."

"Thank you, Lord Aaron. I would very much like to stay near my friends until Master Reuben returns," Arishen replied carefully, though Rilla knew from their time in the Paradise that Arishen had stayed as far away from the farms as possible – he had never been very good with animals.

The old lintep smiled and motioned for the four companions to follow him. He led them to the twisting stairwell nearest Eliséo's room. The morning sun had risen enough for light to flood the stairs from the central light shaft. At the top of the stairs they alighted into a well-lit hall. Along the walls hung portraits of his ancestors, most long dead. Some of them bore some similarity to himself.

"Who are all these people?" Plyke asked curiously.

"They are your ancestors. Every person in our family as far back as can be remembered. They line this entire level of the castle and in more recent years have extended into some areas of the level below us," he replied as he came to a stop between the two wooden doors both with carvings of a bed. "These two rooms once belonged to my children. They are your rooms now. You may come and go as you please. If you need me, my room is the first one around the corner on your left hand side." He fought the urge to drown himself in the memories threatening to flood his mind and instead handed a key to each of his grandchildren.

Rilla hesitantly took the heavy bronze key offered to her. Even in their Paradise, she would never have had a room to herself, aside from the Isolation hut. Much as she had treated it like her own hut, there was always the possibility that she would be taken out at any moment for another Paradisian's punishment. To have a real room all to herself permanently, one that she could lock at will, was a completely foreign concept.

"How will we earn our keep for these rooms?" Eliséo had explained that things worked differently in Illaria, but she couldn't believe that Lord Aaron would simply pay for them to live there for nothing in return. The old lintep looked at her in confusion.

"You are my grandchildren," he replied unhesitatingly. "Until you finish your studies and choose how best to serve Illaria, I will look after you. That includes housing, feeding and clothing you. It will also include all of your lessons. As part of the royal family, you are entitled to private lessons should you wish them."

"Does anyone else have private lessons?" Tika asked the question. Rilla was too stunned to do so.

"At the moment, there are only three other young royal lintep in lessons. They are all grandchildren of Lord Kynon and he has them in group lessons." The old lintep paused for a moment. "It's just about the only thing we ever agreed on – that our family should not be taught differently to any other lintep in Illaria."

"Then group lessons for the two of them, yes?" Tika confirmed. Rilla couldn't help but smile at Tika's easy acceptance of their change in circumstances.

"It would be best to have private lessons, just until it has been decided which levels to put them in, but yes, I think group lessons are the best way to go."

"It's settled then," Tika smiled amiably. "What's next? Are we going to the stables or are their lessons starting this morning?"

"Breakfast!" Plyke said hurriedly. "What about something to eat before our lessons or a visit to the stables?"

"I think we can arrange that," Lord Aaron replied. "If you would like to leave your belongings in your rooms, we can go to the dining hall. There is bound to be food there. The earliest risers of the castle must be up by now."

Rilla looked at their key then at Plyke, hesitatingly. After a nod from Lord Aaron, she placed the key in the door and turned it. She pushed open the door and peered inside. Her rooms were just as lavish as Eliséo's, but even bigger.

Arishen followed Rilla as she walked through her chambers. Rilla hadn't been through Eliséo's room like the boys had so wasn't certain what to expect. She walked through the antechamber, where tables, chairs and extra chaises were scattered, into her bedroom. She stopped in amazement at what she saw inside. Arishen almost crashed into her as she silently observed the room.

The wall facing her had a window almost from the ceiling all the way down to the floor. In front of the window, with heavy blue material hanging from four posts around it, was the largest bed she had ever seen. She wondered why anyone would ever need a bed so large and so high. From the looks of it, the blue drapes could be closed on all sides, shutting out every ray of sunlight.

Next to her bed was a massive stone fireplace, large enough to warm the entire room and ante chamber. The wall to her right had an elaborately carved desk with plenty of sheets of parchment, new quills and fresh ink. Beside that was a ridiculously large wooden cabinet. She knew there couldn't possibly be clothes in there but wondered why she would ever need a cabinet so large to fit her clothes when all she had were her travel clothes and a dress from Silvaren and whatever she'd managed to take with her from their Paradise.

Arishen pointed out another door to her left and she walked over to open it, wondering what else she could possibly need in her chambers. She couldn't believe the bath and fireplace she saw within. Instantly, she thought of Ratchin and how she warmed their bath water.

"Lord Aaron, will we be allowed to light the fires and heat the water from there ourselves?" she called out to her grandfather in excitement. The old lintep followed her voice through to the bathroom and smiled at her.

"All in good time, young Rilla," he reassured her. "Until your masters have approved you to do that, you can rely on the servants with your silver handle like the rest of us."

"My silver handle?" she asked curiously.

"Oh yes," Arishen was quick to enlighten her. "Eliséo told us you pull once for a servant, twice for food and drink and three times for a skilled lintep to warm the bathwater. But … well, he didn't mention what happens when you're done with your bath. How do you get rid of the water?"

"That would be because elves can clean water with their magic," Lord Aaron replied. "His room is not set up the same way as all other rooms in the castle. This bath and every other one in the castle is located against the wall so that they can access pipes. A skilled lintep will deliver the water to your bath through these pipes and when you are done, you simply pull the plug out for the water to drain out through those same pipes."

"That's amazing," Rilla exclaimed. "How do the lintep get the water through the pipes?"

"I can see the masters are going to enjoy teaching you," her grandfather patted her on the shoulder, not answering her question, as he led her back to her bedroom. "I would suggest you leave both your bags and weapons here. Lintep do not take kindly to people walking armed around the castle grounds."

Rilla followed his suggestion and disarmed herself, leaving her weapons with her rucksack. Arishen was quick to follow suit.

"Will we be having lessons with a weapons master?" Plyke asked as he and Tika joined them.

"I suppose that could be arranged, but it is a little unusual for the royal family to have such lessons," Lord Aaron replied, rubbing his stubbly chin. "I will see what I can do about that. In the meantime, let me take you to the dining hall."

"Wait," Rilla called out. "I can't do this."

"What do you mean?" Lord Aaron asked in confusion. "What can't you do?"

"It's not fair that we get to stay in these large and … well, just magnificent rooms, when we know that Tika and Arishen will be sleeping somewhere in or around the stables. At least Arishen will eventually live with Master Reuben, but even that can't be as nice as this."

"We'll be fine, Rilla, really," Arishen tried to calm her. "Think about it from their point of view – we're humans, so we're lucky to be here in the first place and you're both royalty, so you couldn't possibly live anywhere other than the castle.

"If we stayed here too, it would be a slap in the face to every other lintep in Illaria because they'd see themselves as better than us and even they don't get to live here."

Rilla looked at the seer in shock. She'd never expected him to accept the differences people imposed on them now that they were finally in Illaria. If anyone, she might have expected it from Tika, but certainly not Arishen.

"Let me put it this way. We're all still alive because of you, Rilla," Arishen pointed to her. "If our payment for that is to watch you finally being treated the way we wish we could treat you, then we're happy for that."

She looked at the three boys, Plyke and Tika nodding their heads in agreement with Arishen, and smiled with tears stinging her eyes. She felt Lord Aaron's eyes on her, but carefully guarded her thoughts from him. He didn't know about her past and she didn't want him to find out everything about her until she was ready to tell him.

"Alright then, to the dining hall," Rilla blinked back her tears and looked to her grandfather for directions.

"I'll take you to the common dining hall," he told them as he led them back down the same hall they had come by and down three flights of stairs. "It's easiest to use that one of a morning as you'll get hot food straight from the kitchen for a few hours so it doesn't matter what time you emerge from your chambers.

"For the midday meal, you will most likely go to the dining hall as well, unless you are in a particularly intense lesson where food will be brought out to the classes. The evening meal will usually be in my private dining room, with Tika and Arishen joining us if you wish it. It's possible King Lukys or his daughter, Aislen, will invite us to dine with them on occasion in their dining room, and on evenings of celebration everyone will eat in the common dining hall together."

Rilla's head swam with all this information. In their Paradise, every meal had been in the eating hall and in the Outworld, meals had been whenever they needed a break, wherever they found a convenient place to rest. Her heart sank with the thought of how many other rules or guidelines were going to be imposed on them before the end of the day. She looked over at Plyke to see the same thoughts mirrored on his face and rolled her eyes. He stifled a laugh and moved to walk beside her.

On the bottom level of the castle, Lord Aaron led them towards the common dining hall. Tika could hear voices raised in hearty conversation well before the smells of freshly baked bread, boiled potatoes and roast meats reached his nose. No one even glanced their way as they entered through the double doorway. There were people constantly coming and going.

He took everything in as Lord Aaron ushered them inside. It was a long rectangular room with elaborately carved chairs at the far end and wooden benches all around the edges with long tables running between them. In the centre of the room were a number of tables laden with the bread he had already smelt, roast meats, boiled potatoes, fruits, jugs of various drinks.

He followed Lord Aaron's lead as the lord went to one of the tables, picked up a clay plate and started to fill it with food from the tables. Tika was quick to follow his lead. He was still ravenous. After filling a polished wooden cup with crushed apple juice, he joined the others at a table close to the elaborate chairs.

Noticing that everyone else in the dining hall was already eating, he looked hesitantly at Plyke before taking his first bites. In their eating hall back in their Paradise no one was permitted to eat until Erton began the meal. Here, it seemed as though everyone could come and go as they pleased, eating whatever foods they wanted and go back for more if they were still hungry. It was like nothing he had ever known before.

"Who are all these people?" Tika asked Lord Aaron, between mouthfuls of his steaming hot bread.

"Some of them are castle servants, the ones further down that end of the hall," he pointed towards the double doorway they had entered through. "Others are members of the royal family or members of the Council of Masters. Many are students, getting ready for an early start with their lessons."

"How many lintep are there in Illaria? Do they all learn here in the castle at some point?" Tika was burning with curiosity. "Do some of the masters live in the castle?"

"You'll need to excuse Tika," Plyke said. Tika looked over to see the bewildered look on Lord Aaron's face. "We've learned to just let him ask all the questions because there's no way of stopping him."

"I see," Lord Aaron recovered. "There are thousands of lintep in Illaria. I'm certain you passed through some of the farmlands and part of the city on your way here. Both the city and the farms surround the castle and stretch all the way to the boundaries on all sides.

"There are other lintep in the Outworld who choose not to live in Illaria, but send their children here for lessons because they know it is the best place to learn. Those children stay in boarding rooms on the ground level of the castle, alongside any masters who don't own their own homes in the city."

"How many masters and mistresses are there?" Tika continued barely giving the old lintep a chance to catch his breath. "Were they all in the council yesterday, or do they not all need to attend meetings?"

"For such an important meeting, all the masters and mistresses were present," Lord Aaron replied gravely, making Tika remember his place as a human in the lintep stronghold. "There are currently twenty-six members of the council, but their number is only limited by the strict level of skill and power needed to pass the council test."

Tika ate the rest of his meal in silence. Together with his friends, he watched all the lintep in the dining hall, trying to distinguish the students from the servants and the council members from the royal family. When he had finished, a servant came to take his empty plate and cup. He noticed other servants doing likewise for everyone else as they began to rise from the benches.

Wordlessly, Tika and the other Paradisians followed Lord Aaron as he walked back out through the double doorway, down a busy hallway and out through a tunnel into the outer courtyard of the castle grounds. As they walked along pebble paths through well-tended gardens, Tika heard the familiar sound of horses. His curiosity instantly piqued, he gripped Plyke's hand tightly until they came to the stables. Plyke squeezed his hand in return and smiled.

The royal stables of Illaria were more than triple the size of the ones in their Paradise. There were stalls for at least twenty horses that Tika could see, all lined up on two sides of the stable, with openings on both ends – one to the outer courtyard and another out to the extensive gardens and paddock at the rear of the castle, still on the island, surrounded by the moat they had crossed the day before.

He stared in amazement at all the stablehands going about their work, making sure that the horses were well cared for and their tack kept clean and oiled. Lord Aaron told them to wait as he walked inside to find the stable master. In a matter of minutes, one of the stablehands had fetched the stable master.

"Lord Aaron," the stout man greeted him warmly as the morning bell tolled through the castle grounds, "it's been a long while since I've seen your face in the stables. To what do I owe the pleasure?"

"Edric, my old friend, I come to ask you a favour," Aaron paused, not quite knowing how to phrase the request. "King Lukys and I would see it as a personal favour if you were to take on an extra stable hand, two for a few days, but one to stay for the foreseeable future."

"Why do I smell horse manure in that request somewhere?" Edric replied warily.

"It may have come to your attention that two humans were granted leave to remain in Illaria so long as their lintep companions do," Lord Aaron watched

Edric nod hesitantly. "Well, one of these humans is the human Partner of my grandson and I would be eternally grateful if you would take him on as a stable hand and keep your eye on him. The other is a seer who will lodge with Master Reuben ..."

"... but Master Reuben has ridden out this morning so you need me to watch him until the master returns." Edric finished the sentence, already shaking his head. In a low voice he asked, "Do you have any idea how much trouble this could cause in my stables?"

"Tika won't be any trouble," Plyke retorted before Lord Aaron could stop him. "He's very good with animals of all sorts. They just seem to trust him instantly. You won't be sorry to have him as a stablehand, I can assure you."

"Edric, this is my grandson, Plyke," Lord Aaron hurried to introduce him. "Tika is his Partner and was to be apprenticed in the stables in their Paradise before their departure. I will be personally responsible for anything that occurs during his apprenticeship with you."

"I will agree to a two week trial," Edric rubbed his face with his calloused hands. "If the other stablehands don't take to him by the end of that time, you'll have to find him a new apprenticeship. Agreed?"

"Agreed," Lord Aaron shook his hand to seal the bargain, "and you take the seer until Master Reuben returns."

Edric sighed heavily and simply nodded his head.

"Tika, Arishen, this is Edric. He is the stable master," Lord Aaron introduced them. "You will heed his word and follow all of his commands immediately. I do not want to hear that either of you have been complaining about mucking out stalls all day when that's what you may be asked to do. Am I understood?"

Lord Aaron's tone of voice brooked no argument. He had suddenly changed from the gentle old grandfather he knew they were beginning to see him as to a stern lord who was not to be trifled with. The children nodded instantly, said a quick farewell to their friends and followed Edric into the stables.

"Where to now?" Plyke asked.

"Your first lessons," Lord Aaron replied, already walking back towards the castle. "Your teachers will already be waiting for you by now. The bell you heard before signals the beginning of the morning lessons.

"Rilla, I'm not certain who Master Aurelius has assigned to you today, but Plyke, you'll be with Master Jorg."

"Isn't he the one who didn't want to let us stay?" the young lintep asked hesitantly.

"Master Jorg indeed has less favourable opinions of humans than most lintep in Illaria but he is, without doubt, the best mind master currently teaching," the old lintep reassured them. "Aside from teaching you how to better control your skills, he will need to work with you to find a solution to the mind snare you saw on Shuut."

"How can I possibly do that when I don't even know what I'm doing yet?" Plyke instantly panicked. "He'll be expecting too much from me."

"Calm yourself, young Plyke," Aaron reached out a hand to place on Plyke's arm, exuding as much calm and stability as he could. "I will be present at every one of your lessons with Master Jorg. I am somewhat skilled with mind powers and would like to help find a way to heal other lintep from this foul magic, should it be used on anyone else."

Plyke inhaled deeply, not understanding what his grandfather had just done to calm his nerves. Rilla watched it all, silently. She knew Plyke's powers were strongest when it came to empathy and mind skills. It only stood to reason that the same power could be used for or against him without his knowledge if he wasn't trained properly. She wondered if she would realise if it was ever used on her.

"How long will we have private lessons before we join in the classes?" Rilla asked in an effort to distract herself from the thought.

"Most lintep start group lessons when they're quite young and progress all together through their classes with the exceptional few progressing through faster than the rest of them. A fair few of these exceptions go on to become masters and mistresses, but not all of them.

"According to Master Aurelius, you both have strong skills in certain areas and are quite lacking in others. It will be up to your teachers when they think you can join the group lessons without slowing down the other students."

Aaron led them back through to the inner courtyard to one of the winding staircases. They went up one level and down a hallway, past five other doors before reaching the one with three waves carved in a circle to meet each other in the middle. Here he paused and knocked, waiting for an "Enter" from within before opening the door. Masters Jorg and Aurelius were waiting for them.

"Good morning, students," Aurelius stood to greet them. "Plyke, you will begin your lessons with Master Jorg this morning. He will teach you to bring your powers out of your wall without losing control of them. Once he is satisfied you can do that safely, you will work with him to describe the mind snare on Shuut and how to dissipate it. In this rare exception, Lord Aaron will join you for these lessons in an attempt to assist with the mind snare issue."

Master Jorg bridled at the mention of Lord Aaron sitting in on the lessons. Rilla and Plyke shared a wary look before Master Aureilus continued.

"This afternoon you will have a joint lesson with Master Graham who will teach you both more about the lintep whistle, where you both lack skill. Rilla, follow me now."

Without giving her a moment to say farewell to the others, Master Aurelius led her back out the door and straight into an identical room save for the image of a flame on the door. Rilla remembered it as the symbol Master

Aurelius had traced on a door the night before. Once inside, she immediately recognised the youngest member of the council, her short brown hair framing her face and making her look even younger than she was.

"Mistress Isis, here is your student for the morning," Aurelius announced as Isis stood to greet them. "Rilla, this will be one of your most important lessons. Heed Mistress Isis well for I do not want to hear of you injuring yourself again with heat or cold after this."

Rilla's face flushed as she watched the master walk out of the door. She stood there for a moment not knowing what to do. Eventually, she turned to face Mistress Isis.

"Come, sit down." The young mistress sat on one end of a chaise, a leg curled up under her, patting the other end with her hand. Rilla hesitantly went to sit next to her. "Master Aurelius has told me things from his perspective but I want to hear them from you so I can better understand how and what to teach you." She looked at Rilla with big brown eyes. Rilla raised her eyebrows at the mistress.

"I don't know even know where to start," she shrugged helplessly.

"Of course," Mistress Isis nodded her head, "let me explain. My particular area of expertise lies in the balance of fire and ice. I'm quite skilled in the practical side of things. It would possibly have been best for you to have your first lesson with Mistress Kayte, for healing, but she has led a search party to find Nyssa.

"I will do what I can to teach you how to recognise your limits in all areas concerning balance so that you don't injure yourself in your lessons. So if you will tell me of any times you experimented with heat or cold, that will be a marvellous beginning."

Rilla listened to her words carefully. From this point of view, she must have sounded just like her mother – more power than sense or skill. She didn't want to tell Mistress Isis anything because she knew she would simply be reprimanded for her actions.

"Rilla, I know you weren't taught much in the Outworld," Isis tried, unsuccessfully, to reassure her.

"I wasn't taught anything until I met Nyssa and she only got me to use her stones and that was just a few weeks ago," Rilla retorted hotly.

"That's exactly why you were in danger so often, from what I hear," the young mistress tried to placate her. "I won't get angry at anything you tell me. Master Aurelius has been quite clear in telling me you were forced to experiment to keep your friends alive and that you didn't realise the danger it posed to either you or them when you experimented."

Rilla took a deep breath. "The first time I tried anything with heat was when I cooled down some cups of tea."

Isis instantly followed up on the nugget of information. "Had you been shown how to do this by someone?" Rilla shook her head. "Did you know it was possible?" Another shake of the head. Mistress Isis reached out a hand to touch Rilla only to find the girl backing away from her.

"Please, don't do that," Rilla told her quietly.

"Don't do what?" Isis thought she knew what had just happened, but couldn't believe that Rilla had already understood what she was about to do.

"I've seen two people do that with Plyke already," the girl replied, eyes downcast. "I don't want anyone to reassure me with their touch. I don't want anyone using their powers on me like that."

Isis smiled to herself. "You're a clever girl, Rilla. Most of the students don't realise that's happening for at least the first few months. Even Plyke probably hasn't realised it. I doubt your other teachers will be happy to know you've discovered that trick. I promise not to do it to you, but I really do need you to tell me everything: how you discovered you could do certain things and whether you were taught them or not. Agreed?"

Isis could barely contain her excitement. She was pleased to see Rilla smiling – perhaps she could set her at ease just like that, without swaying her feelings with a touch.

"Ratchin warmed bath water, using her own heat, so I just assumed it would work the other way and took the heat from the cups into myself. I didn't even think at the time that I could get rid of the heat. It was only the first time I'd done something like that," Rilla finally began to open up.

"Have you since tried moving heat around rather than just keeping it within yourself?" Isis led her on.

"Yes, there was the time that I had to heal Tika's leg, but mostly it was just hot and swollen by that point. I took as much heat into myself as I could and then heated a cup of water to make tea."

"That was very clever of you to even realise you could take heat out of another person. It's a clever and dangerous thing, not necessarily for you, but for the person you're taking it from," Isis was quick to clarify herself. "I mean that it can be used against you rather than in an act of healing. Someone could drain the heat out of your body, leaving you dead, if they know how to get rid of the extra heat from their own body."

"I would never have done that to Tika!"

"No, but it could be done to you if you don't realise what's happening in time," Isis warned her, not attempting to try soothing the horror from the young lintep. "Let's move on. When else have you done something with fire or water?"

"When Eliséo and Ilya Mikhailovich were in danger. Another karlik had them at knifepoint. I knew I had to get the karlik to drop the knife at Eliséo's back for him to save Ilya's life, so I did the only thing I could think of. I sent out a tendril of my power all the way back to him, to the knife, and then took the heat from the torch I was holding, passed it through the tendril and then pushed it as hard as I could into the knife so that it became too hot for the karlik to hold."

"Rilla, that's amazing!" Isis clapped her hands in glee. "Extraordinarily dangerous without training, but just amazing that someone with as little experience as you could even think to do that. Had you ever sent out tendrils of your power before or know that it was possible?"

Rilla shook her head, smiling shyly. "Nyssa taught Plyke to do it a few weeks ago, but I had already figured it out by then."

"Is that the last time you experimented with fire?" Isis asked, bursting with curiosity.

"No, the last time was the worst, but I didn't have a choice. Arishen and I were on this side of the Bramble River with everyone else on the other side, waiting to come over. We were attacked by four huge men and there was no way we could last until the others arrived.

"Arishen had a vision of fire burning the men and remembered Nyssa had shot fire from her fingers for a moment in the Drakos Mountains. He told me to do that and we knew it was our only hope. So I gathered as much heat as I could into my hands and then shot fire from them. I was a bit shocked that it worked and couldn't move, so Arishen dragged me in a circle to burn all the men.

"Oh wait, that reminds me, I made one of my leaves burst into flames without knowing how, just before we crossed the Bramble River the first time."

"One of your leaves?" Isis was bemused by her story and then abrupt change. "What do you mean, one of your leaves?"

"Lady Eléna, well I suppose she was still Queen Eléna then, gave me some leaves from her tree when I passed through Silvaren on my way to the Paradise when I was little," Rilla explained. "Eliséo told me each leaf would burn for as long as a branch so I had to light one. He didn't explain how, but just expected me to do it. I was so angry with him that when I was holding the leaf, it just burst into flames."

"It was clever of him to make you so angry," Isis smiled knowingly. "He must have known that anger can be turned into heat and that excess heat could be used to light your leaf. But right now I'm actually a bit more interested in the other story, where you shot fire from your hands. What happened straight after that?"

"Arishen told me to stop when the men were all burning and then I don't really remember much. I think Nyssa must have crossed over the river next and healed me. I don't really know what happened, but the next thing I remember is sitting in front of a fire, with everyone around me."

"I can guess what happened, but it would be easier if you let me take a look at your memory of it," Isis told her, hoping the girl would agree.

"I don't know how to let you do that without letting you inside my wall, and I refuse to do that," Rilla replied firmly.

"Very well," Isis had understood not to push her just yet but was disappointed by the hurdle. "I assume you used up too much of your body heat when lighting that fire and Nyssa had to warm you up, probably using the heat of the fire you created, to save your life. And that's the reason why these lessons will be your most important. I will teach you to understand what your limits are so that you don't injure yourself like that again.

"I understand your experience with healing has had similar consequences, so I'll help you with that as much as I can until Mistress Kayte returns. Although I have a feeling that you won't need to heal your friends in the next few days."

Rilla watched as Isis stood up and dragged a small wooden table in front of their chaise. She then went to a small tap in the corner of the room that Rilla hadn't noticed before, took two glasses from a nearby chest of drawers, filled them with water from the tap and brought them back to the table. Next, she chose two lanterns from the top of another chest of drawers and brought them back to the table, finally sitting down next to Rilla again.

"Considering your lack of training, I'm just going to assume you don't know anything," Isis told her plainly. "I'm not assuming you're not clever enough to figure things out yourself. It's just a few things all lintep should be taught before they start using the practical side of their magic."

"That's fair," Rilla agreed, finding herself trusting her new teacher more and more.

"First, most lintep magic is based on balance, as you may have discovered on your own. This doesn't just have to be heat and cold. It extends to healing as well. Take these few items here," she motioned towards the table. "We have an unlit lantern and cold water. There isn't really much we can do with them without adding some of our own heat to the lantern to create a fire.

"Essentially, the spark of heat from your body is transferred to the wick of the lantern, leaving you just that little bit colder. You don't need to use much heat to start a fire, but you do need to concentrate the small amount of heat to a single point in your body and transfer it quickly enough to light a flame. If you try to transfer it too slowly, the heat will disperse and all you will have done is lost some of your own precious heat for no reason."

"So when I was holding my leaf and Eliséo made me angry, he just hoped I would be holding the leaf tightly enough that the anger would transfer as heat through my fingers into the leaf?" Rilla asked, trying to understand the concept.

"Yes, but now I want you to do something similar without the element of anger," she held up a finger. "Watch first and then do."

Rilla watched as Isis explained how she was pooling a small amount of heat into her fingertips and then quickly pushing that heat into the wick. Every time she did that, she took back a bit of heat from the fire before blowing it out completely. Eventually, she motioned for Rilla to try at the same time as her, again explaining the steps in excruciating detail.

Rilla mimicked Mistress Isis' actions and placed a finger lightly on the wick. She called some heat to her fingers and quickly pushed it into the wick. A flame rose so high that it touched the top of the lantern's frame. In comparison, her teacher's lantern started with a tiny flame that eventually spread to the rest of the wick.

"That wasn't bad for your first try," Isis reassured her. "Now hold your hand close to the flame and take back the heat you lost, without taking too much or burning yourself."

Rilla placed her hand near her lantern. There was less heat there than she'd spent as the flame had dwindled down to the normal size of the wick. She drew in small bits of heat at a time so as not to extinguish the flame, making sure to spread the warmth around her body so that she wouldn't burn her fingers. When she was fairly certain she'd restored the balance, she blew out the flame as Mistress Isis had done each time.

"This time, I want you to use much less heat," the young lintep instructed her. "Remember, you only need a single spark to start a fire. Let the spark build on itself around the wick to create a proper flame."

"How will I know how much heat I need for that?" Rilla asked, feeling a little lost in her first lesson.

"Practice," Isis smiled at her, "and lots of it. We've got all morning together for you to learn exactly how much heat you need to start a fire. If you manage to learn that, and prove to me you can do it time and again, we might start on the water."

"What will we do with the water?" Rilla asked curiosity getting the better of her.

"Now that is a fun skill to learn. We will take the heat out of the water leaving it as cold as you left yourself after you shot fire out of your hands."

"But the water isn't warm. How can we take any heat out of it?"

"Ah," Mistress Isis held up a finger, "now you're not thinking it through. Just because the water isn't as warm as the flame doesn't mean it has no heat in it. That simply means it has less heat than a fire. We can still gather all of that heat up, leaving a glass of solid ice, and transfer that heat, without using any of our own heat, to light the lanterns."

Rilla's eyes went wide at the thought. There were so many things she would learn to do with her powers that she hadn't even known were possible. She couldn't believe how lucky she was to be here in Illaria, with nothing else to do all day but learn how to do it all.

Chapter Eight – Master Jorg and Master Graham

Plyke didn't take his eyes off Master Jorg as Rilla and Master Aurelius left the room. Had it not been for the presence of his grandfather he would have felt trapped.

In my lessons, you will learn to control the powers of your mind. Plyke heard a voice in his mind and withdrew completely behind his walls, not allowing anyone to break through, though he could feel battering on the outside of them.

So focussed was he on protecting himself that he was taken by surprise when Master Jorg grabbed his arms and started shaking him.

"Let me go!" yelled the startled boy, wrenching himself free from the grasp.

"You were not responding to me," Master Jorg's said icily. "In my lessons, you must always be open to hear my words."

"Then why don't you try speaking to me before jumping into my mind?" Plyke asked him, more calmly than he felt.

"The boy has a point," Lord Aaron voice his opinion. Plyke caught his eye and smiled gratefully.

"If it were up to me, you wouldn't be allowed in this room during the boy's lessons," the Master replied stonily. "As it is, I would appreciate it if you would observe rather than interfere. Are we clear?"

"I think not." Lord Aaron lifted his chin. "The only reason you have your Master's tattoo and I don't is because I would not have had time for the duties, not because I wasn't skilled enough to pass the test. Don't think that I can't easily decide to teach my grandson myself until I think he is ready to join the group lessons."

The young student listened to the conversation with burning ears. Had he just understood that his grandfather could have been a master if he'd wanted to? He wondered if Rilla knew that. Hopefully, they would have time later in the day to discuss their lessons. Shaking his head, he brought himself back to the room.

"As I understand it, your goals for this morning are to teach Plyke to bring his power out of his wall without losing control, so that in his afternoon lesson with Master Graham, he can at least hear the lintep whistle. Only if you have time after that are you to find out as much as you can about the mind snare so that together we can try to find a solution to it." Lord Aaron kept his eyes firmly locked on Jorg's until the Master turned away.

"Sit down," Jorg instructed Plyke without preamble. "Let your power out so I can see what happens."

Plyke hesitated and looked to Lord Aaron who nodded, encouragingly. He went and sat on the wooden chair Master Jorg had pointed out to him as the master sat on the more comfortable chaise opposite it. He closed his eyes to concentrate and brought just a little of his power outside his walls. He held onto it tightly to avoid a repetition of the previous afternoon.

"Bring more of it out," Jorg instructed him. Plyke momentarily wondered how the master could tell how much power he had pulled out in the first place but was soon absorbed with bringing out more of his power and trying to hold onto it as well.

"Do you have more power inside your walls?" Master Jorg asked, arching an eyebrow as Plyke nodded. "Let's just work with this for now. Let go of your grip on it."

Plyke shook his head, sweat already beading on his forehead with the effort of not letting his power slip away from him.

"I can't teach you to control your power if you don't show me what happens when you let go," Jorg relented a little. He'd never come across a lintep with as much power as fear. When the young lintep didn't respond, Jorg looked over to Aaron.

"Plyke, what are you so afraid of?" His grandfather's voice soothed him.

"If I let it go, it will slip away and I'll die," he answered through clenched teeth.

"We won't let that happen, will we Master Jorg?" Aaron shot Jorg a meaningful look.

"That's right," Jorg hoped he understood what Aaron was playing at. "We'll both surround you with our power so that it can't possibly escape from you."

The student looked between him and his grandfather and nodded. Jorg only had a moment to prepare before Plyke's power crashed against him. Together with Lord Aaron, he just barely managed to contain it safely around the boy.

"Pull your power back in now," he instructed the young lintep with a strained voice.

"I don't know how," Plyke told him.

"Just pretend you've only let a bit of your power out and pull that in. Then keep doing it until it's all back inside your walls." Jorg had never come across a lintep with so little skill in his life. It was a dangerous position to be in. He would need to be extremely careful with this one. If he did not teach him to control his power, he was certain that more than Plyke's life would be at stake. He would instantly be removed from his position in the Council and, if Lord Aaron had anything to do with it, quite possibly be banished from Illaria altogether.

It took the better part of an hour for Plyke to pull his power back inside him all by himself. Every other time his power had pulled free from him, he'd been helped by someone else to put it back. This time, Master Jorg and Lord Aaron weren't helping him, they were only making sure that it wouldn't flee him completely.

"Will that ever get easier?" Plyke asked them when he was done. He was already exhausted and was certain the lesson was far from over.

"In time," Jorg answered him. "I think what we should do is work on it progressively. This time just pull out a single tendril, let it go and then pull it back."

Plyke did as he was told. He barely let go of the tendril before catching hold of it again and pulling it back in.

"Good," Jorg encouraging him. "This time, let out the same amount and try picking up one of your white stones with it before pulling it back in."

Plyke pulled the small felt pouch out of his pocket and took a smooth stone from it, placing both the stone and the pouch on the floor in front of him. He pulled out a tendril, like Nyssa had taught him to, and wrapped it around the stone, lifting it to the level of his eyes before placing it back on the floor and withdrawing his power back into him.

"Excellent," Jorg congratulated him. "That was much better control. Now I want you to progressively try pulling out more and more tendrils and pulling them back in. Lord Aaron and I will immediately notice if you need our assistance, so don't worry about that."

Plyke spent the rest of the morning pulling his power out from behind his wall and placing it safely back within it. He didn't get any faster at it, but at least he could pull out more than a few tendrils now without fear that they would immediately escape him.

* * *

Rilla waited impatiently for Plyke to arrive in the dining hall. That morning had been the most fun she'd ever had in her life. Mistress Isis had let her play with fire magic! It had been amazing. Even though she wasn't completely certain of where her limits lay, she now knew enough to understand when she was close to her limits and what she could do to minimise the damage she had caused.

They hadn't progressed to the water side of things yet, but Isis had promised that they would get there very soon, quite possibly even in their next lesson together. She had been fairly certain that Rilla would be admitted to a more advanced class than was usual for her age when she had grasped the basics of her lessons.

Finally, she saw Plyke entering the room with Lord Aaron. Far from being excited, Plyke looked exhausted. Rilla took care not to show too much enthusiasm as he walked over. If she had spared a thought for him, she would have realised that Plyke would have had more trouble than she did in the lessons.

"How did it go?" she asked amiably as Plyke sat across from her with a plate full of food. Rilla had already eaten half her plate by the time he'd arrived.

"Well, much as I hate to admit it, Master Jorg was probably the right choice for my mind master," Plyke answered with a grimace. "Kora didn't teach me anything other than to hide my powers away and Nyssa only taught us how to move stones around. Neither of them really knew how to teach me anything so Master Jorg had to start right at the beginning. It must have been quite a challenge for him."

"You did very well, Plyke," his grandfather reassured him with a pat on the back. "You've improved tremendously even from the start of the lesson. I'm certain you'll be able to work with Master Graham this afternoon."

Rilla sat in silence. She knew that Plyke's skill was nowhere near as great as hers, but she had just assumed that in a few days he would be able to do everything she could do. It hadn't even occurred to her that learning to take control over his power might be a long and slow process.

"How did your lesson go?" Plyke asked, breaking her train of thought. "Who did you have?"

"I had Mistress Isis," Rilla answered, bursting into a smile. "Remember the youngest member of the Council, with the fewest tattoos? That was her."

"So what did you do with her?" Plyke asked.

"Well," Rilla bit her lip, hesitantly, "you know how I had a bit of trouble in the Outworld sometimes?"

"You mean where you used your power in a way that almost killed you a few times?" Plyke smiled mischievously at her but Rilla was no longer looking at him. Her eyes were filled with trepidation as she saw Lord Aaron's eyes widen in shock.

"Yes, well, Master Aurelius thought it best that Mistress Isis teach me how to recognise my limits so that nothing like that ever happens again … hopefully," Rilla told him uncomfortably. "She taught me to light a flame and recover the heat I lost in doing that, both without losing too much heat or burning myself while trying to recover it."

"That's … quite an advanced lesson," Lord Aaron ventured eventually. "Had you ever done anything like that before?" Rilla shifted uncomfortably under his stare. She nodded her head, refusing to elaborate.

"Rilla shot fire from her fingers to save herself and Arishen from some attackers in the Outworld," Plyke said as Rilla glared at him. "We were attacked quite a few times after leaving Silvaren. Most of the time, Rilla had to heal at least one of us and then the last time, she and Arishen were on the other side of the river and there was no one there to help them, so they had to do something. Arishen had a vision of Rilla shooting fire through her fingers, so that's what she ended up doing."

"I see," Lord Aaron said softly. "Well, at least you are safe here and Mistress Isis will make sure you learn how to stay that way. It's the very least my family should be taught."

Rilla was burning with curiosity. She wanted to know what had happened to her family. Three dead – that's what he'd said. Who was dead and how had that even happened? She knew it had to do with their magic somehow, but no one had explained anything about it. She resolved to ask him about it later. He seemed to get along better with Plyke so maybe she could convince him to ask for her.

Lord Aaron waited for his grandchildren to finish their meal before escorting them back up the winding stairwell to their classroom. He led them to a room with musical symbols carved on a wooden door.

"Isn't this the same room Master Aurelius tested us in last night?" his granddaughter asked.

"Quite probably," he replied. "The lintep whistle can be quite distracting to others if the students don't know what they're doing and try to communicate too loudly. Until you are both competent in this area, your lessons with Master Graham will take place in this room."

He opened the door outwards, knocked on the second door behind it and waited for Master Graham to open it.

"Good afternoon, young lintep, Lord Aaron," the old lintep greeted them in a soft, but strong, voice. "Will you be joining us this afternoon, my lord?"

"Not today, old friend," Lord Aaron answered affectionately. "I'm sure you'll have your hands full with these two without the added distraction of a doddering old man around."

"Doddering old man indeed!" Master Graham scoffed at him. "You're almost thirty years my junior and finally look more alert than I've seen you in many a year. I trust these two are the reason for that."

Aaron patted his old friend on the arm and looked back over to his grandchildren.

"After your lesson, feel free to visit your friends in the stables and bring them up to dine with us in my chambers," Lord Aaron told them before he turned to leave, having noticed their sidelong glances at him with Graham's comment. "We will certainly have much to discuss."

"Come in, come in children," Master Graham waved them through the doorway once their grandfather had departed and leaned his entire body weight to close the door behind him. "From what I've been told, we have much to do in our lesson this afternoon. Now Plyke, how did you go this morning with Master Jorg? Can you keep even a bit of your power out of your wall now for an extended period of time?"

"We, uh, didn't really try that," Plyke mumbled. "Master Jorg just got me to take my powers out from behind my wall and put it back again, all morning."

"I see," Graham rubbed his stubbly chin. "Well, you're going to have to keep some of your power out for at least a few minutes at a time this afternoon. Do you think you can try that?"

Plyke looked hesitantly at him.

"I'm sure Master Graham can help contain your magic, like that time Nyssa and I helped you in the Outworld," Rilla suggested.

"Master Jorg has already had to do that once today, with Lord Aaron's help," Plyke confessed. Master Graham's eyebrows shot up in surprise.

"Master Jorg couldn't contain your power by himself?" Graham rubbed his stubbly chin again as Plyke shook his head. "And Rilla, you've helped contain Plyke's power before?"

"Well, yes," she hesitated, "but I only did exactly what Nyssa told me to do because Plyke's power was quite a bit stronger than she'd anticipated."

"Yes, but do you remember how you did it?" he waved aside her hesitation. She nodded. "Good. Then if Plyke needs help, you can help him first and I will help him second."

"Why?" asked Rilla curiously.

"Did Nyssa explain what you had actually done when she asked you to help her? He saw her eyes grow wide with understanding. Plyke looked puzzled. "If I ask Rilla to close her power over mine, she could technically have control over me."

"But she would never do that!"

"I would never do that!"

Master Graham almost laughed at the immediate reaction of the cousins.

"How obvious you both make it for everyone to know you grew up in the Outworld, let alone a Paradise. No lintep from Illaria would ever give another lintep the chance to ensnare their power like that, because the temptation could always arise.

"How do you think Lishe began on her terrible journey to collect other peoples' power for herself? One of her Masters must have taught her that in a lesson without realising what she would one day be capable of. These days, it is forbidden to even talk about that with students until they are quite disciplined and we are certain of their views on how their power should be used." Rilla and Plyke listened to him in stunned silence.

"So why are you saying that I can do it with Plyke?" Rilla asked in a hushed voice. He could feel her trying to hide her sudden fear.

"If Plyke trusts you, as it appears he does, and he has as much power as it sounds like, he may need both of our help," Master Graham tried to explain. "I won't allow you to cover me with your power, so the only way to do this is if you cover him first, in that extreme situation."

"And then you cover me and have complete control over me?" Rilla's voice rose as she started to panic. "No!"

Graham watched as the girl began to disappear in front of his very eyes. He stared at the young lintep in shock. None of his students had ever dared raise their voice at him or argue against his methods. Admittedly, none of his lessons had ever taken such a strange turn before. He shouldn't even be discussing such topics with lintep as young and unskilled as these two. Not knowing where else to turn, he did the only thing he could think of.

Aurelius, I need you in the communication class room. He whistled the message out as loudly as he could. It wasn't the most discreet way of calling Aurelius, but he didn't have time to find him with his mind to send a direct message to him.

He watched the two young lintep intently as Plyke began to rub the goosebumps that had suddenly appeared on his arms and Rilla, distracted by the sound, became visible again.

"Was that you?" she asked him warily.

"It was indeed," Master Graham answered her levelly.

"I didn't hear anything," Plyke said.

"That's because you still have your power tightly locked in your wall, young one," Master Graham answered calmly. "I know Master Aurelius thought we should be able to train you in the lintep whistle together, but it appears as though he may have been mistaken in that."

A few moments later Master Aurelius arrived, red faced and out of breath. He opened the door without knocking and shut it quickly behind him.

"What's wrong?" he asked, taking in the looks on Rilla and Plyke's faces as he did so.

"It would appear that young Rilla, at the hands of her mother, was taught how to control another lintep," Graham waved the girl to silence as she went to protest. The look on Aurelius' face told him that his old friend was unaware of the circumstances.

"She did what?" Aurelius cried out in horror. "Why would she do that?"

"She threatened to do it to me in the first place," Rilla defended herself. "She told me she could stop me from using my power at all if I didn't listen to her instructions, but it wasn't fair because her lessons were so boring."

"Yes and then when I let out my power because she told me it would be fine, she couldn't contain it herself," Plyke continued. "So she told Rilla to do the same over her power and just start squeezing in slowly until she told her to stop."

Graham stared in shock at Plyke. "She told you too? How could she be so reckless?"

"It stands to reason," Aurelius sighed heavily. "Nyssa and Lishe were taught by the same practical master. They had more advanced lessons than other lintep in their age group because Nyssa had so much power and Lishe was so skilled. I think their master must have told them theoretically how it worked but Nyssa never employed the technique …"

"… and Lishe employed it all too often." Master Graham finished his thought. "Were the two of them alone in that class? Are there any other lintep we need to be wary of?"

"Kora might have been in that class, as she was certainly powerful and skilled enough, but she was a few years younger than Nyssa and Lishe, so more than likely she wasn't," Master Aurelius massaged his temples with his long, bony fingers. "I can't for the life of me remember who taught them."

"It was over thirty years ago," Graham reminded him gently, "none of us have memories that go so far back."

"We need those memories now," Aurelius told him. "If Lishe is on her way back, we need all the lintep who know of such ways to use their power to help us against her. I will call a Council session for tonight."

"That will take too much planning for possibly very little gain," Graham interrupted him. "What you need to do is sit in on this lesson. If Plyke is as powerful as I am beginning to understand, I may not be able to help him alone. He already told me that Aaron had to help Jorg this morning. I'm not allowing Rilla to help me and she refuses to let me help her. If you've managed to help him by yourself, I will ask you to stay in case we need you."

Aurelius looked over to Rilla whose defences were letting her down. He could sense that she was angry and scared at the same time. He reached out a hand to place on her arm in an attempt to calm her. She recoiled instantly and screamed.

"Don't touch me!"

"Peace, Rilla," Aurelius tried to soothe her with his voice, "I was merely trying to calm you down."

"Yes, I've seen you and Lord Aaron calm Plyke down the same way and I've already told Mistress Isis I don't want anyone to do the same thing to me," she replied hotly.

"What do you mean?" Plyke asked her in confusion. Clearly, the boy had no idea what she was talking about.

"Not now, Plyke," Master Aurelius silenced him. "Rilla, take care not to disrupt too many of our traditions before you've even been here a full day."

"But I ..."

"That's enough," his voice low and commanding.

Rilla instantly stopped herself from protesting. She was so frustrated. After having such a fantastic lesson with Mistress Isis in the morning, she was devastated at how badly this one was going before it even began. She felt a pinch on her arm and looked angrily at Plyke as she rubbed the small patch of red skin.

"What was that for?" she snapped.

"Stop going invisible," he told her in an exasperated voice. "That's the second time you've done it just in this lesson."

Hot tears started streaming down her cheeks as she thought of all the restrictions facing her. She had to stop fading away. She had to stop using her power in ways she already knew she could, yet allow others to do the exact same thing to her. She had to stop disrupting traditions she didn't even know existed. And worst of all, she couldn't just crawl into the comforting embrace of Elessa. It was all she wanted to do right now and the last thing she could.

She squeezed her eyelids shut as she reached out for her tree, knowing she could only feel her embrace for a moment or two. Elessa was instantly there for her, soothing her gently, but quickly, and promising her as much contact as she wanted once she was in her own room.

A moment after her tree had broken contact with her, Rilla opened her eyes, knowing that they wouldn't still be glowing. She wiped the tears from her face and held her head up high.

"I'm ready for our lesson now," she told them quietly. "I will listen to Master Graham as long as neither of you touch me. I won't do anything if Plyke's power escapes him and I promise you my power won't escape me so neither of you need to worry about containing my power yourself."

Graham shared a worried look with Aurelius. He'd never had a student as powerful, skilful, untrained and stubborn as Rilla before. Understanding this was probably the most she could offer them for now, he nodded.

"Let's begin then," he said as he slowly eased himself down into a chair, leaning on his old knees with his hands. Perhaps he was getting too old to be an active master anymore. Aurelius sat beside him and clapped him on the back. If Graham didn't know better, he'd have thought his old friend had just read his mind, but the fact was that they knew each other so well, Aurelius would probably have been able to read the thoughts on Graham's face.

"Plyke, make sure you let out at least some of your power, or this lesson will be wasted on you," Graham told the boy. He waited patiently until Plyke was ready and then started the lesson. He whistled a quiet, simple tune.

"I heard that!" Plyke cried out excitedly. "I mean, it was really soft, but I heard it."

"Well done, Plyke," Master Graham congratulated him. "Rilla, was it soft for you too?"

"It was much softer than when you whistled before," she replied uncertainly, "but was quite loud enough to hear properly."

"Could you understand it?" he asked them both. The cousins shook their heads simultaneously. "Very well. Plyke, pull out a bit more of your power so you don't have to strain to hear me. Master Aurelius will help you if you need it, so try not to cloud your mind with those thoughts."

He waited for the boy to do as he asked before whistling the exact same tune again. It was always the first one he taught. It was the simplest and most important tune any lintep could learn.

"I can almost make it out," Plyke's brow was furrowed with concentration as he listened to the tune.

"I can't make out anything," Rilla pouted. She closed her eyes and shook her head. "Oh, you were angry with me."

She froze as she realised she'd said the words aloud. The three lintep were all looking at her in confusion. She sighed, knowing she would have to explain herself now.

"When you taught me to build a wall and I did it that day," she turned to face Plyke. "I didn't realise you were angry with me until just now. Kora had been teaching you how to build a wall from when you could remember and it would have taken you such a long time to do that when you were a child. You were angry with me because I did it in a day and you were jealous of that."

"You really didn't spend much time with other people in our Paradise, did you?" he asked her. She shrugged her shoulders helplessly.

It took another seven times listening to the same tune before Plyke finally understood what it meant.

"Help!" he cried out excitedly. "You're whistling for help."

His excitement quickly faded as the power tried to break free of his grasp in his moment of distraction. In his panic, he forgot to pull in his power as Master Jorg had told him earlier that day.

An instant after the pain started, it was gone. Plyke looked up to see a look of concentration on Master Aurelius' face.

"Thank you," Plyke sighed, upset that his moment of triumph had turned into one of weakness. He carefully tucked away his power so that it wouldn't escape him again.

"Young Plyke, I will organise for you to have lessons with Master Jorg every morning for the next few days," Aurelius told with a hint of resignation. "If you do not learn to control your power, you will be of no use to anyone in your lessons and we will not be able to keep you safe. Lord Aaron will continue to join these lessons. I may ask him to take you for lessons in the afternoon as well so that we can start the process to understand the mind snare that you saw on Shuut."

"Mind snare?" Graham asked him in confusion.

"Not now, Graham," Aurelius hushed him. "I'll explain later. For now, just see if you can get Rilla understanding the whistle."

She doesn't appear to have much aptitude for it. Aurelius heard Graham's thoughts in his mind.

That would be the only thing then, he replied directly. She has entirely too much aptitude in everything else as far as I can see. It's quite possible she'll either turn into Nyssa or Lishe if we aren't careful with her.

"I'm not my mother," Rilla said quietly. She hadn't meant to, but she'd heard every word the Masters had said to each other. "If I have aptitude for most areas, I will train as hard as I can to increase my skill in them. If I don't have an aptitude for communication, then I will try until I can at least understand the most basic of tunes."

"Rilla, you shouldn't listen in on other people's conversations," Master Aurelius chided her gently.

"Well you shouldn't secretly talk about people right in front of them," Rilla replied, hurt and angry. "It's not my fault that I can hear your thoughts to each other if you think them so loudly."

"They were whispered, Rilla," Aurelius explained. "Most lintep would have to strain themselves to even hear a shout that wasn't directed at them. You shouldn't have been able to hear that."

"Well, maybe I'm better at that because I can't understand the whistle," she retorted hotly, though inwardly she wondered if Elessa's powers were working through her automatically. Would it be possible, if elves hear better, for her to be able to hear thoughts more easily now too? It had happened more often since Elessa had bound them together.

"Master Graham, are you happy to end your lesson here for today?" Aurelius turned suddenly to the old Master. "I think it best that Rilla and I have a short lesson ourselves."

His old friend sighed and nodded. "Plyke, you've done very well for today. I'd be happy for you to join a group communication lesson as soon as you have your powers under better control." Plyke grinned from ear to ear at the news.

"Very well, Plyke, you have the rest of the afternoon free," Aurelius told him. "I trust you know your way around enough to find either your room or the stables?"

Plyke nodded and eagerly left to find his Partner, promising to meet Rilla in Lord Aaron's rooms later that evening.

"Rilla, will you allow Master Graham to join us in this lesson?" Aurelius could feel the girl's erratic feelings. He had to try to keep her focussed before she made a mistake that only he could prevent her from making.

Drawn back by the sound of her name, Rilla looked from one old Master to the other and nodded her head, almost in defeat. How could the day have soured so much since that morning's lesson with Isis? Things had gone so well there. Maybe she wasn't as skilled in anything else as she thought she was.

"Rilla," Aurelius drew her back again. "I need you to stay focussed, in this room with us."

"Sorry," she mumbled, "I was distracted. It won't happen again."

"Unfortunately, Rilla, it will," Aurelius told her. "What we need to do is teach you how to control your power even when you are unfocussed. I think that's probably one of the most important things you'll need to learn. But before that, we need to teach you how to protect yourself, and others, by not even accidentally listening to their thoughts."

"I can do that?" Rilla asked, intrigued despite her anger and hurt.

"If we teach you well enough, then yes," Master Graham answered her. "I think Master Jorg would be the best master for you in that regard, but as he has his hands full with Plyke and Master Reuben is away for the time being, it seems it's down to the two of us to help you."

"Well, I'm ready," Rilla said, eager to prove that her powers were not lacking in any other area than communication. "What do you want me to do?"

First, we start here, Aurelius pushed the thought into her mind. Without thinking, Rilla immediately blocked him out.

"And that's where our first problem is," he sighed, his bony fingers rubbing his temples. "You're too defensive, and most of the time you don't even realise what you're doing."

"Rilla, for the moment, assume that you've known us all your life and you trust us implicitly," Graham instructed her. "Do you have anyone like that in your life, who you trust completely?"

Rilla thought back through the short list of people she counted as friends. Of all of them, only Eliséo knew all her secrets, but she still tried to keep some things hidden from him. Rhanya would have understood. She probably could have told him, if he were still alive. The thought brought tears to her eyes. She blinked them back quickly and looked at Master Graham.

"There was one person I trusted completely," she answered quietly. "Do you mean for me to pretend that you are that person so that you can talk directly to my mind?"

"Close your eyes, Rilla," Master Graham instructed her. "Think of this person and let everything else fade away. When you hear a voice in your mind, pretend that it's coming from your friend and that you are safe."

At his instruction, Rilla closed her eyes and pictured Rhanya – his wrinkled old face, his steady hands, his warm embrace and ready smile.

Aurelius watched as she did as she was told. He waited until she was at peace and smiling before he tried anything, signalling to Graham that he would talk to her first. He was fairly certain he knew who she was thinking of. If he could get the phrasing right, it would make all the difference.

Little one, you are safe here with me. He knew calling her "little one" would either win her over or make things worse, but he had to push his luck. Not feeling any resistance to his thoughts, he carried on. Tell me how your lesson with Mistress Isis went this morning.

It was amazing! Rilla replied, the smile coming through in her thoughts. I learned so much from her and I think I'm much safer now, at least with fire anyhow.

Well done, little one, Aurelius continued. I'm certain Mistress Isis had more fun with you than she's had with any of her students so far. All we have to do now is see if we can get the same result with the rest of your teachers.

"Open your eyes now, little one," Aurelius said aloud. He waited until she had done so to continue. "That was well done, Rilla. You opened yourself up to my mind. Now I need you to open your mind to Master Graham, with your eyes open and not thinking of your friend."

Rilla nodded, determinedly. She felt a strange voice in her mind and began to recoil. Immediately, she saw the disappointment in his eyes and stopped, concentrating on his hazel eyes. They were kind and gentle. They were the eyes of someone she should be able to trust. She brought some of her power back outside her wall and listened to his words.

I only want to help you, Rilla, he told her gently. Will you work with me to that end?

Yes, she answered with her mind. I'll try my best.

"Good," he patted her hand for a moment before she slowly drew it away. "Now that we've established you can certainly hear thoughts directed towards you and can project your own thoughts, time to work on the other side of the spectrum."

"Do you think it's a matter of her power?" Aurelius asked suddenly. "If she constantly keeps some of it outside her wall, perhaps it automatically goes questing around to find things without her realising it."

Rilla watched as Graham shrugged. "It's a possibility of course, but how can we test that?"

"I've no idea." Aurelius replied. "I have never come across someone like this before. Have you?"

Rilla listened intently to the conversation and watched as it ended with Master Graham shaking his head.

"What if I just ask my power not to do that?" Rilla ventured a suggestion. The Masters stared at her blankly.

"What do you mean 'ask' your power not to do that?" Master Graham questioned her. "It doesn't work like that."

"Why not?" Rilla was thoroughly confused. That's how she always worked with her power – asked it to do things for and with her. Why shouldn't it work for something that wasn't practical? "Can I at least try it?"

"Anything is worth a try," Aurelius nodded, motioning for Master Graham not to interrupt. "Go ahead, Rilla, and tell us when you're done."

Rilla smiled and nodded. She closed her eyes and imagined she could see tiny tendrils of her power floating all around her body. She called out to it and saw all the tendrils turn towards her mind. Without knowing if it would work or not, she explained that she wanted it to stay near her and not go over to the Masters, not listen to their conversation. She couldn't tell if there was a difference or not, but she opened her eyes and raised her eyebrows in hope.

"Okay, well, I think I've done it," she told them, "but I won't know until you try to talk to each other again."

This is ridiculous, Master Graham immediately sent the thought hurtling towards the younger Master. Lintep power does not work that way. She can't simply "ask" it to do or not to do something.

Rilla's power is quite unique, Graham, Aurelius explain. She grew up thinking she was a human and didn't even know she had power until a few months ago. I believe many of the things she can already do are as a result of her not being told certain things are or aren't possible and just trying whatever she could imagine doing.

Rilla looked from one Master to the other. She could tell that they were talking to each other with their minds, but she couldn't hear their thoughts.

"It worked!" she exclaimed excitedly.

"It worked?" Master Graham asked incredulously. "What do you mean it worked?"

"Well, you were talking to each other just now, weren't you?" She waited for the masters to nod before grinning. "I didn't hear a word of it."

Master Aurelius beamed at her, proudly. "Well done, little one."

Rilla smiled back, surprised that she now didn't mind him calling her that. Her face fell when she glanced over at Master Graham. He wasn't even smiling. He was simply staring at her, a look of intense concentration on his face.

"What's wrong?" she asked him, almost timidly.

"I think I know why you can't understand the lintep whistle," he rubbed his chin thoughtfully. "You've never had to work hard for anything to do with your power. If you always just ask it to do something or work with it, then you don't really know what it is to work hard."

"I've done plenty of difficult things," Rilla protested hotly.

"So I've heard, but only because you imagined you could and so you did," the old Master told her. "But the lintep whistle has very little to do with the practical or mind side of lintep magic. It's the only skill where working with your magic doesn't help a bit. It's a new language for you to learn. Some lintep are simply better at it than others. I think all I can do is teach you set whistles and their meanings, but that may be all."

Rilla slumped back into her chaise, completely deflated. She had assumed she would be good at any skill they could throw at her, as long as she worked hard enough. To be told, right from the beginning, that she would almost certainly not be able to ever understand much of the lintep whistle was like being struck by a physical blow.

"Graham, I told you she can only do the things she can because no one ever told her she couldn't," Aurelius chided him softly. "Now look what you've done."

Rilla heard him talking, but the words were empty to her. She sat in her chaise and stared blankly in front of her. Could he possibly be right? Was there really a skill she wouldn't be able to master – ever?

"Rilla, child, listen to me," Master Aurelius patted her knee gently to bring her out of her thoughts. "You can work on it. Lintep children are taught to understand the whistle at the same time as they learn to talk, so there aren't really beginner classes we can put you in. But I'm certain Master Graham will be happy to work with you a few times a week and see what happens." Master Graham nodded enthusiastically.

"Yes, of course. We can have short lessons every evening, after your other classes have finished. It will just take more time for you, but it can be done." Rilla looked at him skeptically, but decided to accept his offer.

"Right, now we just have one more problem to sort out," Master Aurelius clapped his hands together softly. "You disappear unintentionally quite often. It's good that you know how to do that and are so very adept at it, but we need to make sure you only do it when you mean to do it. So what I want you to do is describe to me what was going on the times you've done it accidentally."

"I don't know," Rilla shrugged her shoulders. She was upset about Graham's comments and didn't feel like talking to them anymore. "I suppose most of the time, I was just wishing people wouldn't see me."

"Is that all?" Master Graham looked at her sceptically. Rilla hung her head low and avoided his gaze. "Out with it, girl. What else?"

"It happens when I wish I could fade away, or when I wish people couldn't see me or …" she hesitated, "or when I just think people don't see me in the first place and treat me like I'm invisible or I don't exist."

Master Graham looked at her carefully, leaning back in his chair.

"You're power is quite unique, Rilla. It seems to instinctively know what you want and makes sure to help you achieve that goal, most of the time without you even realising that's what happening. I'm not even sure how to go about changing that without placing restrictions on you, which I don't want to do because I want to see what else you could be capable of."

"Yes, it appears as though we could actually learn quite a bit from you, if we manage to keep you alive long enough for that to happen," Master Aurelius chimed in. "But your safety is, of course, our main concern as it is with all lintep when their power peaks. So we will have to carefully tread the line of keeping you safe and placing minor restrictions on you."

Rilla listened to the two of them intently. She had already realised that she was a little odd when it came to her power, but she had thought the masters in Illaria would have seen more people like her.

"Was anyone else in my family like this?" she asked suddenly, not even knowing why – family had never been important to her since she arrived in the Paradise.

"That's a difficult question to answer, Rilla," Master Graham answered her. "I knew more of them than Master Aurelius, but even then all of your family were born and raised in Illaria. You and Plyke are the first to be born and raised in the Outworld, in a Paradise no less!

"Even so, I can tell you that your family has always been among the most powerful in Illaria. That's not to say that other families don't exhibit great power or that every member of your family is very powerful, because there are always exceptions. But it is safe to say that the greatest in skill and power have almost always come from your family."

"Is that why they're the royal family then?" she asked curiously. She knew that the royal family in Silvaren had the most power and wondered if it worked the same way here. "I mean, if another family becomes more powerful somehow, will they be the royal family instead?"

"That's possibly how it started," ventured Aurelius, "but these days, it's more about general politics and the people are happy with King Lukys. Princess Aislen shadows his every move so we are all assured that she will be just as good a ruler as her father.

"It's getting late now. For tomorrow, I'll organise your morning lesson with Mistress Isis again and perhaps in the afternoon you can have a lesson with me for your practical magic. Then make sure to find Master Graham in this room before you finish for the day. That will be all now."

Aurelius dismissed Rilla with a wave of his hand and waited for her to close both doors behind her before turning his attention to Master Graham.

"She could become quite dangerous if we don't keep our eyes on her," Graham said, finally. "She's too powerful for her own good and with a mother like Nyssa, well, it could all just go to her head and she could just breeze through her lessons."

"There are a lot of possibilities, Graham, but that she will become like Nyssa is the least likely of them all," Aurelius assured the older master and related the short story of Rilla's life being abandoned by her mother and then not quite seeing eye to eye with her when they finally met.

"Well, that's one thing in her favour then," Graham admitted, grudgingly. "But she could still turn out like Lishe, who had more skill than power."

"Graham, the girl grew up in a Paradise where her father murdered anyone who stepped out of line. From the sounds of it, she hated him just as much as the others did. I very much doubt we'll have another Lishe on our hands," Aurelius found himself defending the girl. "Give her a chance to just be herself and show you who she is before you decide who you think she is."

Chapter Nine – Lord Aaron

Lord Aaron stood at the window in the hallway, looking down onto the courtyard. He watched a group of young lintep training, just as every other lintep in Illaria had done since the castle was first built over a thousand years ago. He'd lived in the castle his entire life, just as his family had always done. His daughters, and now his grandchildren, were the only exceptions to that.

He wondered, for the hundredth time if they would both still be here if the rest of their family hadn't died – if Kora had stayed, Nyssa would have had no reason to follow her. The thoughts distracted him for the better part of the afternoon, as they quite often did.

As the sun began to set and the courtyard lost light, his mind came back to the present. His grandchildren and their friends would be joining him for the evening meal and he was certain they would have just as many questions for him as he had for them. All he had to do was handle them all carefully. He didn't want a mere slip of the tongue to drive away the rest of his family before he knew they could look after themselves with all their power.

He walked back to his room and looked around. It was still a lord's room, despite the changes in his life. There was a tapestry hanging on one wall and portraits of his immediate family on the others. A magnificent oval rug lay behind the door. He smiled as he remembered complaining of the cold sandstone floor in his youth. Lukys had given the rug to him after that, as a gift for completing his training at such a high level. His cousin had encouraged him to take the test to become a master, knowing that he could pass it. Aaron had declined, thinking that he could better serve Illaria in a political role.

There was a large rectangular table in the middle of the room. He'd purchased it himself when his family had grown larger than his previous table could seat. It had now been many years since the table had seen more than himself and an old friend or two. He'd already alerted the kitchen staff of the change to his evening arrangements so that when he pulled the silver handle, he knew there would be enough food for all of them.

He set about lighting the lanterns that hung on the walls of his antechamber and closed the door to his bedchamber. Soon there would be no light from the large window beside his bed and it was still warm enough not to need the fireplace, so there was no point in leaving it open. It wouldn't be long before the children arrived.

When they arrived, he opened the door to welcome in the boys, looking behind them for the missing Rilla.

"She wasn't in her room when we passed by," Plyke told him as the three of them entered. "I'm sure she'll come as soon as she finishes her lesson with Master Graham."

"Indeed," Aaron agreed softly, as he closed the door behind them. "How was your day in the stables? You look fresher than I imagined you would after your first day. Or should I say you *smell* fresher than I expected."

The smaller human, his grandson's partner, grinned from ear to ear, looking sideways at taller one's scowl. "It was fantastic! We mucked out stalls and cleaned tack all day. Plyke couldn't stand the smell of us when we left, so he made us bathe in his room before coming here."

"You've never smelt so bad in all your life!" Plyke protested immediately.

"I think you're going to have to get used to that," Tika replied mischievously. "I'm going to be living in a room above the stables. There surely won't be baths up there."

"You can't come into the castle smelling like *that*," Plyke insisted.

"Then you'll just have to come and visit me in the stables more often," Tika retorted.

"How long until Master Reuben returns?" Arishen stalled the argument that was about to break out.

"I'm not sure, young Arishen," Lord Aaron replied with a weight on his shoulders. "It depends on how long it takes the search party to find Nyssa and return."

"You mean Nyssa and Shuut," the seer corrected him. Aaron looked at him sadly, not knowing how to answer him.

"I fear that may depend on what they find. If they find the two of them alive, they will escort them back to Illaria," he sighed heavily. "However, if they find my daughter … well, they would bring her back … and warn us of the danger we could all be in."

Plyke elbowed Arishen in the ribs. The seer glared at him angrily but said nothing. Aaron knew his grandson was trying to protect his feelings, which was quite admirable of the boy, but it was to no avail.

Eventually, a knock sounded at the door. He went to open it himself and found Rilla waiting on the other side.

"Sorry, I'm late," she said as she stepped lightly into the room, avoiding his gaze. "It was an … interesting lesson."

"You mean you finally couldn't master something with the greatest ease imaginable?" Plyke choked back his laugh with a warning look from Tika. "Rilla, honestly, it's not the worst thing ever that you couldn't understand the whistle straight away. Look at how good you already are at *everything* else. This is probably the only area you're going to struggle in at all and here I am just struggling to keep my power from escaping my grasp every time I try to use it."

"Yes, I know," Rilla replied quietly, eyes downcast. "I suppose I'm just not used to things being so difficult."

Lord Aaron pulled the silver handle at the door twice and walked back to Rilla, gently placing a hand on her back. He felt her flinch at his touch and immediately took a step away from her, not quite understanding her reaction but not wanting to push her away.

"Our food will be arriving shortly," he told them all, motioning to the table, careful not to touch Rilla again. "Please be seated."

The four children waited for him to sit before doing likewise. Aaron noticed their apparent discomfort with the situation and did his best to diffuse the tension.

"I understand you've had quite an interesting journey since leaving your Paradise. Perhaps one of you would like to tell me about it?"

All eyes immediately settled on Tika as he smiled broadly and immediately began to relay their story. He barely stopped for breath, even when the servants arrived to lay their table with food.

Lord Aaron was careful not to interrupt often during the story. He sat back, picking slowly at the food in front of him, watching the reactions of the other three children as certain parts of the story were told.

It was obvious, from the stolen glances and harsh stares, that there were certain things some of them wanted to avoid sharing with him. It surprised him that it wasn't just Rilla shooting warning looks at Tika. He knew he could simply send a tendril out to Tika's mind, to watch his thoughts as he recounted their journey, but his grandchildren would never trust him if he did that. In fact, it seemed to be the only thing that Kora had really instilled in Plyke, which wasn't at all surprising considering her views on the matter.

Knowing how Rilla could often accidentally hear and project thoughts, Aaron was being careful not to let any of his thoughts stray out from his walls. He didn't want to scare off the girl before he got to know her. From what Tika was being very careful not to say in his story, Aaron could tell that it would be all too easy to alienate his granddaughter without even realising it.

They had finished eating by the time Tika had recounted their last adventure with the Kryti bringing them to the walls of Illaria and how Rilla had forced Master Aurelius' hand to let him and Arishen into the stronghold in the first place.

"And that's about it," Tika finally sat back in his chair, crossing his arms proudly across his chest. "Now we just have to hope that we can stay in Illaria long enough to learn a trade and look after ourselves in the Outworld when we finally have to go back."

"I will see to it that you will both be taught a trade for as long as you remain here," Lord Aaron reassured the humans. "It's the least I can do to thank you for helping to bring my grandchildren safely to me."

He saw the look pass between Rilla and Plyke. He knew what was coming. They'd both been wanting to know about it since Rilla had overheard his thoughts the day before. Everyone else in his life already knew what had happened. If he didn't tell them, they were bound to find out anyway.

"And now I suppose it's my turn now," he ventured. "I don't know how much

Nyssa and Kora told you about our family."

"Nothing," Rilla and Plyke answered simultaneously. The old lintep nodded sadly and was silent for a long time.

"I don't really know where to begin," he told them at a loss. "I suppose I should tell you that Nyssa is my oldest daughter, with Kora born just a few years later. After the two of them, we had two sons, Vaughn and Fredryck, then one more little girl, my precious Adina.

"My wife, Graesyn, and I decided to take the children for a trip to Silvaren when they were all quite young. Nyssa's power had already peaked, Kora's powers had only just started to peak and the little ones were still a few years away from it all.

"It was a foolish decision. We should never have left Illaria until all five of them were fully trained, but we innocently thought nothing could possibly go wrong if we were there with them. How wrong we were.

"The children were all so excited to see Silvaren and meet the elves. Queen Eléna was just as excited to meet them all. She had been a great friend of Princess Rilla, my mother, and was elated to meet her grandchildren. From Tika's story, it sounds as though she tried to keep an eye on my entire family even after that final visit I made to her.

"It was on our way back from Silvaren that it happened," he paused, lost in thought, unable to go on.

"What happened?" Plyke asked him in a gentle voice. Lord Aaron looked at him with haunted eyes for a moment before blinking back the memories.

"We passed through a town, Hedgefall, on the way back home and stayed overnight in an inn. I don't know what we did to give ourselves away. Perhaps we were talking about my mother and some humans overheard us. The war had ended years ago, when I was still a child, but humans have long memories when it comes to grudges. They must have realised that we were somehow related to the same Princess Rilla who had started the war in the first place and tracked us down once we left Hedgefall the next day.

"Vaughn and Fredryck had spied a small forest and wanted to run ahead, to pretend they were elves. Graesyn took Adina and the boys with her to the forest while Nyssa, Kora and I lagged behind. I was making sure they kept up with their practical skills while we were away from Silvaren. I didn't want them falling behind in their classes.

"I gave the humans exactly what they were waiting for – an opportunity to attack the younger ones with only one adult nearby. I don't even know what happened, but as soon as we heard the screams we ran towards them. By the time we got there, Adina and Fredryck were already dead. Graesyn was trying to heal Vaughn, but she told me he had used too much of his power trying to save Fredryck and she was doing exactly the same thing with him.

"It was too late for me to do anything. They were both so close to death that if I tried to save either of them, I would have died as well leaving Nyssa and Kora to try to find their way safely back to Illaria. I couldn't do it, so I watched as Graesyn and Vaughn died in each others' arms."

He fell silent, staring blankly ahead of him. The four children were speechless. He knew they could not have imagined the truth. He could barely believe it himself as it was happening to him. Three of his children and his wife, dead simply because they were related to Princess Rilla.

"That's why I heard you say three dead, another possibly dead and the last missing," Rilla said quietly. "You were talking about all of your children."

Lord Aaron looked over at her and nodded.

"And that's why you want us to be trained properly," Plyke continued. "So we can defend ourselves and know our limits in the Outworld."

It was a sad smile, but it was the best Lord Aaron could muster under the circumstances.

"I don't understand, then," Plyke continued in confusion. "If Kora saw all of that and knew why it happened, why didn't she teach me to better control my powers? She made it almost impossible for me to survive once my power peaked. How could she do that?"

"Maybe she hoped you wouldn't be too powerful," Tika suggested with a shrug.

"All I can think is that she hoped blocking off your power with a wall would be enough to control it," Lord Aaron answered. "She barely finished her training before she left Illaria. She couldn't have known that would never have worked."

"Why did she leave if she knew the Outworld could be so dangerous?" Plyke asked. Aaron could feel the anger with his daughter bubble within him.

"I don't know Plyke." Aaron shrugged, helplessly. "She spent most of her spare time in the library. She wouldn't tell anyone she what was researching. Then once she'd decided to leave, no one could change her mind, not even Nyssa."

"Then Nyssa left to find Kora, which is why she dragged Shuut halfway round the Outworld searching for her," Plyke finished off the story. "Shuut told me before we parted ways that she'd spent most of her youth travelling around, looking for Aunt Kora."

"Well, at least Kora didn't abandon you in our Paradise like Nyssa did with me." Rilla's voice had a bitter edge to it. "She could have tried to protect you when your power peaked. My mother wouldn't have even been around when my power peaked. I would have died with no one but my father knowing why and he probably would have been happy about it because I wouldn't have been a thorn in his side anymore."

"I can't believe either of my daughters were so careless with their children's powers," Lord Aaron swiftly took control of the situation. "I will rectify their mistakes. You will both have the best teachers I can secure for you and all the resources you need to complete your training in a safe environment. I will make certain that neither of you are put in the same situation as my own children."

Chapter Ten – Search for Nyssa

Kayte turned to face Reuben and the other three members of the search party. Maelynda, Amry and Derryn had studied alongside Nyssa and were probably the closest thing she had to friends in Illaria. Kayte was glad they had volunteered for the mission. She didn't have the stomach to force people to do something like this against their will.

If the seer's vision was accurate, Nyssa had created this mess herself and didn't deserve to be saved by anyone. No lintep worth their power should ever be caught off guard in the Outworld to the extent that another lintep could completely control them. Knowing she would need all her concentration for the task ahead, she put her disappointment with Nyssa aside.

"We ride fast, but carefully," she told the rest of them as she turned to gallop in the tracks of the Kryti.

The sun had reached its peak by the time the kryti tracks ended. There was a muddle of tracks all around one particular clump of trees. The kryti had clearly come from a different direction to the travellers at great speed. Kayte dismounted from her horse to study the pattern. One set of footprints was much heavier than the others, which meant either Rilla or Plyke must have been carried by one of the others for some distance. There were three other footprints nearby, one of dragging feet – that must have been the other of the two lintep. Kayte shook her head in annoyance. They had certainly been cutting their time finely to reach Illaria before their power peaked.

"This way," she motioned in the direction of the Bramble River. "We follow these tracks back towards the river. With any luck, we'll come across Nyssa and her older daughter without incident. Keep your ears and senses sharp. If there is a rogue lintep around, I do not want to be caught unawares."

Her four companions nodded and waited for Kayte to remount her horse before they headed off in the indicated direction.

It was late the next evening when they finally found her. Nyssa's body was lying slumped against a tree with her head hanging down. Kayte was already dismounting as she heard Maelynda retch from the top of her horse. As Amry and Derryn went to Maelynda's aid, Kayte motioned Reuben over to take a closer look at the body with her.

Nyssa's arms had singe marks along the length of both of them. Small bugs were crawling in and out of her open mouth and she could see where vultures and owls had been ripping off her flesh and eating her insides.

"You saw the boy's vision," Kayte turned to Reuben with raised eyebrows. "Does this look anything like it?"

"The marks on her arms are consistent with a lintep using a ball of fire to drag up Nyssa's arms. Aside from that detail, Arishen's vision ended when Nyssa threw her power out from her mouth and then slumped down to the ground, lifeless. So her mouth should be open," Reuben confirmed her fears.

"So it's possible his vision was true," Kayte closed her eyes to steel her nerves.

"More than possible, Kayte," Reuben answered her grimly as he touched the body. "She's gone soft again so the timeframe fits with the vision. I think we need to prepare for the worst. We should assume the lintep responsible for this was Lishe. Even with Nyssa's skill not developed as much as it should have been, her amount of power would have saved her from anyone else. Lishe is the only one we know who took the test to become a mistress and wasn't granted the status even though she was skilled enough. The masters were afraid of what she could become and inadvertently sent her away to achieve that very end."

"You think the rumours are true then?" Maelynda asked in a trembling voice. "Lishe has been killing other lintep to steal their power?"

"It would appear so," Kayte replied in disgust. "Even skimming through her studies, Nyssa would have been able to best Lishe because her power was always so much greater. Lishe was always more skilful so if she only gained a bit more power, she could have bested Nyssa without a fight."

"And she was always so jealous of Nyssa's power." Amry mused aloud.

"We *all* were jealous of her power," Derryn corrected, "and we knew it was wasted on her because she never bothered to hone her skills."

"It does no good to talk ill of the dead," Reuben hushed them. "Let's just bring her back to Illaria so Lord Aaron can bid farewell to yet another member of his family."

Kayte went to her saddlebag and took out a long length of white silk. Carefully, she began wrapping the body tightly, with help from the others, so that no part of her damaged flesh could be seen. Even through her outrage at the situation, Kayte felt a prickle of sympathy for Nyssa. Even she, as a mistress, would probably find it difficult to best Lishe if the rumours about her were true. She mounted her horse again and waited as the other four lifted the body to place it in front of her. She would have to ride more carefully now.

"Be on your guard," she told them as they mounted their steads. "It makes no sense for Lishe to be around here for no reason. If the seer's vision was accurate, she was torturing people to get information out of them and Nyssa gave her power to her daughter to prevent Lishe from getting it. We don't know what information she was after and we don't know if she was headed to Illaria. If we passed her on the way here, then she will see us on the way back and know that we suspect foul play."

* * *

"Quiet," Lishe hissed as a group of riders galloped past them for a second time. Shuut knew better than to disobey her captor. The past few days had taught her exactly how much pain she could be made to endure before sweet oblivion saved her. She wasn't keen to feel that much pain again any time soon.

"They must have been from Illaria," the lintep said in a hushed voice once the sound of horses had faded away. "No one else would have bothered looking for Nyssa and bringing her back with them. How did they know she was out here?" A boot to Shuut's side told her the question wasn't rhetorical.

"I don't know," she wheezed. "Maybe they were expecting her and went to find her when she didn't arrive." Shuut had realised that Lishe knew practically nothing about their travelling party. She didn't know Arishen was a seer or that Plyke and Rilla were cousins. Thankfully, she also still didn't know that Rilla was her sister and Nyssa was her mother. She intended to keep all of this information to herself.

If a riding party was sent out so soon, she reasoned within herself, *Arishen must have had a vision of Nyssa's death and told them about it. That means they've reached Illaria alive.* She struggled to keep the smile off her face.

"They can only know Nyssa was on her way to them if the brat told them, which means she's in Illaria," Lishe thought aloud.

"So you won't be able to get to her now," Shuut smiled smugly before Lishe slapped her across the face.

"Of course I will," the lintep retorted. "It just changes *how* I get to her. That's all."

Shuut tried to keep her growing sense of unease away from her surface thoughts. It was all she could do to hope the lintep in Illaria were preparing their defences for when they inevitably arrived.

* * *

The search party galloped into Illaria, three mornings after they had left. The wooden drawbridge was lowered to the cobble bridge for them earlier than usual as the guards heard and then saw the party approaching through the cobbled streets of the city. The guards rang the warning bell to wake everyone in the castle.

By the time the five riders had reached the stables, Edric was waiting for them and yelling at Tika and Arishen to wake up. He knew they were connected with the search party somehow.

"Arishen, go and find Lord Aaron," the weathered stablemaster ordered the boy. He hadn't proved to be very useful in the stables, making the horses skittish with his nerves. Better to get him out of the way when five tired horses needed urgent tending had left, Edric called out to his stablehands, "Water, feed and clean these horses before they collapse."

Mistress Kayte dismounted as two stablehands held the silk wrapped body in place. Maelynda and Reuben helped her slide the body off the horse as Amry and Derryn came around to hold the feet.

"Is that Nyssa?" Tika asked him in a hushed voice. Edric looked at the boy, puzzled. He turned questioningly to Reuben and Kayte. He hadn't been told the nature of their mission when they'd left. From the grave look on their faces, he knew the answer.

"Can I go to Plyke when the horses have been tended to?" the small human had tears in his eyes. "He and Rilla will be devastated by the news."

Edric nodded, wordlessly, as he watched the procession leave the stables and head to the castle. He hadn't known Nyssa well, but Lord Aaron was one of his oldest friends. They'd grown up together. He'd seen the change in him when Graesyn and their children had died and then again when Kora and finally Nyssa had left Illaria. His grandchildren had finally boosted his spirits again. He dreaded to think what Nyssa's death would do to him.

Lord Aaron woke with a start. The warning bell was ringing. It could only mean one of two things – either Lishe had arrived in Illaria or the search party had returned. He got up and dressed in a hurry. Just as he was opening the door, someone started knocking on the other side.

"Lord Aaron!" He recognised Arishen's voice shouting, loud enough to wake the dead. Aaron opened the door and motioned him to silence, but it did little good. The boy was too agitated to notice anything around him.

"Five riders arrived at the stables. Edric told me to find you."

So, the search party had arrived. Rilla and Plyke soon turned the corner of the hallway. Aaron had barely got his bearings before they arrived.

"Did they find Nyssa?" Rilla asked.

"I didn't see her," Arishen replied, his brow furrowed. "But Edric sent me to find Lord Aaron before I really had a chance to look."

"What's all this racket about?" Kynon emerged from his room and walked over in his usual gruff manner. "Some of us are trying to sleep."

"The search party has returned," Aaron told his cousin, shortly. "Get Lukys and meet us in the inner courtyard."

Kynon nodded grimly and headed down the long hall that would bring him to his cousin's rooms. Aaron headed for the staircase next to his chambers and led the three children down to the inner courtyard.

When they emerged from the staircase, Lord Aaron stopped dead in his tracks. The search party had indeed arrived. Mistress Kayte and Master Reuben were holding a silk wrapped body. He stared at the silk sheets. He knew it was Nyssa – it had to be her. Yet he couldn't find the words to ask. He heard Rilla asking about her sister, but she was far from his thoughts.

Kayte was watching Lord Aaron like a hawk. Sending a quick thought to Reuben's mind, she handed over Nyssa's body to him and approached the older lintep. She knew what a fragile state he would be in and her skills might be more useful that the mind master's.

"Lord Aaron," Kayte walked slowly over to the older lintep, "we found your daughter by following the tracks of your grandchildren. There was nothing we could do for her by the time we got there."

"Was the young seer's vision accurate?" Lord Aaron asked, without taking his eyes off the silk-wrapped body. "Had she been tortured before the end?"

"Yes," Kayte answered softly. She looked past Lord Aaron to the seer as he drew in a quick breath. "We assume it was Lishe. We did not find your other granddaughter, but that does not mean we didn't pass them on our travels. With all the power Lishe must have gathered by now, she would easily have been able to hide from us."

A sudden commotion in the courtyard caused everyone to turn towards Tika as he ran towards them.

"The dream …" he puffed out, tired after rubbing down the horses and sprinting to find his friends. "They're on their way here … I heard Arishen talking … in his sleep …"

"What are you talking about?" Arishen asked as all eyes turned to him. Tika rested his hands on his knees, doubled over, trying to catch his breath.

"Remember, it was the morning … the morning after we arrived. It sounded like it was about them … You were talking in your sleep about someone coming to Illaria and killing someone."

"I can barely remember it and I didn't have time to write it down," Arishen told him, eyes cast down. "All I can remember is that they're on their way here and the other person wants to kill someone."

"Master Reuben, can you look at his dream?" Tika turned to the mind master. "Like you did the day we arrived?"

"That's not as easy as you may think, young human," Master Reuben told him. "Last time it was possible because the seer remembered the vision and could bring it to the front of his thoughts. If he can't fully recall this dream, I will have a good deal of trouble finding it."

"*You* might have trouble finding it," all eyes turned to Lord Aaron as he spoke, "but I won't. Arishen, do you trust me?"

The seer instinctively took a step back. Aaron saw him look wildly at all the eyes on him until his gaze settled on Rilla's hopeful face. He felt the seer's fear melt away.

Aaron placed his left hand on Arishen's forehead to create ease of access to his mind. There was no point doing things the difficult way when time was

of the essence. He searched back through the seer's memories until he found
the right day. It had to have been just before he had knocked on Ambassador
Eliséo's door. He dismissed the discussions they were having – there was no
point eavesdropping on them. Finally he found it!

Two faceless women stood in the forest.
"Do you actually have a plan yet?" The younger one asked.
"Find the brat and kill her."
"Yes, you've already said that," the first one replied. "But how do you intend to
find her. You don't even know where she is."
"She has to be in Illaria by now or she's already dead," the second one
reasoned. "So we go to Illaria and kill her."
"You're going to just waltz into the lintep stronghold and kill someone?" the
first woman asked. "You would never reach her before someone realised who or
what you are."
The second woman laughed. "I won't even have to reach the city before
twisting someone's thoughts to make the girl come to me."
"She's not stupid," the first woman's temper rose with the laughter. "If you
threaten to kill me unless she comes out, she's bound to tell someone else that
you're there, even if you tell her not to."
"That makes your existence a little useless then, doesn't it?" The second
woman replied coldly.
The first woman remained silent for a moment and then asked "How long
until we get there?"

The dream ended. Lord Aaron removed himself from the seer's mind. As
he opened his eyes, he saw Kynon and Lukys had joined them.

"Tika is correct," he told them all. "Lishe, if that's who we're assuming it is,
is on her way here with another woman."

"Shuut!" Rilla cried out softly. Lord Aaron spared her a glance before
continuing.

"They're on their way here so that Lishe can kill a girl, but I don't know
who."

"It's Rilla," Plyke told him. "We were attacked a number of times after
leaving Silvaren. We think they might have been after Rilla because that's
when we found out who she was. We thought they might have been after
Shuut at first, but Rilla and Arishen were by themselves on the other side of
the river when they were attacked. There would have been no point to that if
Shuut was the intended target."

"Besides, if Shuut *was* the intended target, she'd be dead by now," Tika
pointed out.

"It sounds like Lishe is going to use Shuut as a lure to get her target out of
the castle," Lord Aaron told them. "She said she wouldn't need to be inside

the castle walls for her to twist someone's thoughts. How can that even be possible?"

"It depends if she really has stolen other lintep's powers," King Lukys replied in a heavy voice. "We can only send thoughts out as far as our power extends. For most lintep, that's probably no more than a hundred feet. If she has gathered power from multiple lintep, she could extend that reach significantly.

"So, Rilla, be on your guard. Do not allow any thoughts into your mind, or if you can't help it, make sure you don't listen to any of them. Your teachers will need to just use runners to send for you until we know you're safe."

Rilla stood frozen in place. *If Lishe has Shuut, she'll kill her as soon as she gets me out of the castle. I can't lose my mother and my sister to the same person. I wouldn't let that happen.*

Lukys overheard her thoughts and quickly spoke her name to drag her out of them. "Rilla, did you hear me?" He only waited for her to nod before addressing his cousin. "Aaron, I presume you want Nyssa to join the rest of your family in the crypt?"

"It would seem only fitting," Aaron replied sadly. "Her mother and siblings would want her there with them."

"Very well, I will arrange for that to occur tomorrow morning," Lukys placed a gentle hand on his cousin's shoulder. "I'm sorry, Aaron. The most I can do is provide her a sound resting place."

"I'll help you." The offer came from Lord Kynon. "Braedan and Nyssa were quite close when they were young. He will be sorry to hear what has become of his cousin."

Aaron thanked him with tears in his eyes. Mistress Kayte led him away as the other members of the search party took his daughter to the embalmers with Kynon. There was much to be done to prepare her body for the crypt before the next morning.

Chapter Eleven – Mistress Kayte

Rilla watched helplessly as Nyssa was taken away. She hadn't even seen her face through the soft white silk, but she knew it was her. She missed the look that passed between Arishen and Tika, and didn't notice when Tika put his arm around his Partner's shoulders. If she'd noticed that, she might not have flung away Arishen's hand as he tried to comfort her.

"Don't touch me," she told him in a low voice. Out of the corner of her eye, she saw King Lukys turn towards her.

"Rilla, he was only trying to comfort you," Tika defended the seer.

"I don't need comforting," Rilla told them all. "Nyssa only bore me to help fulfil a prophecy for Kora. Then she abandoned me in a Paradise with a father who came to hate me and murdered anyone with a hint of power.

"When we were finally reunited, she was more excited to see Shuut and was more interested in teaching Plyke to control his powers than she was in me. Most of our conversations ended with her yelling at me. I do *not* need comforting over a mother like *that*. She should have been protecting her daughters rather than abandoning them."

The boys stared at her in shock. She didn't care. She felt numb. *Just like when Rhanya was killed.* Closing her mind against the thought, she looked up to see King Lukys approach them.

"Boys, I'm sure Edric will be expecting you back at the stables. Plyke, Master Jorg and Lord Aaron will be ready for you shortly. With Lishe on her way here, it's more important than ever to unravel the mystery of the mind snare and your lessons cannot be interrupted at this early stage or you could still easily lose control of your power."

His tone brooked no argument. Arishen and Tika took the hint and hurried off across the empty courtyard to the stables. Plyke turned the opposite direction and began the climb up to Master Jorg's classroom.

"I know," Rilla said before Lukys could instruct her, "Mistress Isis will be ready for me shortly."

"She will indeed, but not before I'm done with you," Lukys looked down at her with stony grey eyes. With a pang, Rilla realised they were just like Nyssa and Shuut's eyes. "You may not have heard what happened to your grandfather's family, but you should be able to see how difficult Nyssa's death is on him. Don't make it any worse by proclaiming what a bad mother you think she was, even if it's perfectly true."

"He told us a few nights ago," Rilla mumbled, chastened by the king's words. "I didn't think about that. I was just worried about Shuut. If Lishe is using her as bait to get me, then it will work. I *can't* let her kill my sister."

"We'll deal with that when we have to, Rilla," Lukys said, softened by her fear. "If Lishe brings Shuut to Illaria, we will try our best to keep both of you alive. Now off you go to your lesson."

"Thank you," Rilla offered a shy smile as she turned towards the nearest stairwell. She met Plyke in the hall outside their classrooms. Master Jorg and Mistress Isis had not arrived yet.

"I know you're scared, Rilla," Plyke broke the awkward silence, after a minute or two. "Nyssa was powerful and it looks like Lishe bested her with little effort. She's got your sister now and isn't afraid to kill both of you. You might fool the others that you're just angry with Nyssa, but I saw how angry you were with Eliséo for keeping his knowledge about her secret. I know you wanted to get to know her and now that you've lost her you're just plain scared you might be next."

Rilla didn't answer. She simply stared out of the window onto the empty courtyard, silent tears streaming down her face. Plyke put his arm around her shoulders and held her close. He didn't need their skin contact to know exactly how she was feeling.

Plyke watched as the quiet courtyard began to bustle into activity, envying those students of their carefree lives and wishing he could join them for the day. He turned at the sound of footsteps behind him. Master Jorg, Mistress Isis, Mistress Kayte and Lord Aaron were emerging from the twisting stairwell. With his arm still around Rilla, he felt her heart skip a beat as she realised the new teacher might be there for her lesson.

"Plyke, we have a lot of work to do," Master Jorg told him as he opened the door to the classroom. "Your other lessons for today have been cancelled."

Plyke gave Rilla's arm a quick squeeze and followed the master and the lord into the classroom. He barely had time to sit down before they started to question him again.

"So far, you've told us that the mind snare was specifically put on just one person. Do you know if Lishe tried to put it on anyone else?"

Plyke shook his head. "Even if she did, it wouldn't have worked because of Eliséo's mist. He summoned it around the six of us after Shuut collapsed."

"What I'm still unclear on is how it was taken off her in the first place," the master thought aloud, shaking his head.

"It had nothing to do with lintep power," Aurelius reassured him. Plyke looked at him oddly, wondering how he knew that. "It's not something that can help us. What we need to do is figure out exactly how the snare was placed on her mind in the first place. Did it weaken her or did she weaken herself by fighting against it?"

"I can't remember," Plyke told them in frustration. "All I remember is that I couldn't hear her through the snare, but she could hear, or at least feel, me there. She stopped fighting against it because I told her we would get help for her but that she had to last long enough for that to happen."

"Let's then assume, for the moment, that the snare itself wasn't harming her," Master Jorg hypothesised. "What was the snare made of?"

"If it was a lintep creating a snare, it can't have been anything other than lintep power," Lord Aaron answered.

Plyke sat there quietly, listening to the two older lintep theorising between themselves. He tried to remember more about the snare. It had felt quite solid, like the barriers around their Paradise and the barriers around Illaria.

"What if it was actually part of her own power?" he found himself asking. The older lintep looked at him in confusion. "What if she detached part of her power and sort of contained Shuut's mind with her power, the same way that everyone has done to me to contain my power when it goes out of control. Would that work?"

"What sort of lintep would give up some of their power like that?" Master Jorg asked in horror.

"But if she's been stealing other lintep's power, she could easily part with some of that, couldn't she?" Plyke persisted with his theory.

"The boy could be right, Jorg," Lord Aaron pointed out. "Lishe is no ordinary lintep. After all, what sort of lintep would steal power from another lintep in the first place? Surely, to that type of person, parting with that same stolen power would not be a great step."

"But how are we to find a way to get rid of the snare if that's what it is?"

"I don't know," Lord Aaron told him, "but we need to try. In the worst case scenario, Lishe will try to kill my granddaughters. Failing that, she may try to ensnare their minds in the hopes that they will die soon afterwards."

"Would it help if I let you see that memory?" Plyke asked, almost hating himself for doing so. He'd avoided it for the past two days, through all of their questions, but if Lishe really was coming to kill Rilla, he'd never forgive himself for standing in the way of Master Jorg and Lord Aaron being able to help her.

"If you can see what I saw, it might help. I'm not sure how that side of our power works, if you'd be able to do more than just see it."

"That would help tremendously, Plyke," his grandfather smiled for the first time that day. "If you'll permit me, Jorg, I'd be happy to try it."

Plyke and Master Jorg both knew it was just a courtesy that Lord Aaron had asked permission to use mind powers in his mind class. He really had no choice in the matter.

"Alright then," Plyke nodded, stealing himself against the mental invasion. "What do I do?"

"It would be easiest if you recall the memory," his grandfather placed a hand on his arm to calm him. "Bring the memory out of your walls, to the surface area. From there, I should be able to see it and walk around in it, so to speak."

Plyke closed his eyes and thought back to the river crossing. He'd been exhausted by the end of it – they all had. Eliséo had let them all sleep while he watched over them. In the morning, he'd woken Plyke up before the others to ask him the impossible. Plyke recalled the memory with a bitter taste.

"She's trapped," he told the elf, averting his eyes from the banwep. "There's some sort of lock on her mind. She scared me when I went in there. I don't even know if she realised I was there, but her mind is jumping all over the place, trying to free itself."

"You have to go back in there." Eliséo's voice made it clear that there was no choice in the matter. "If what you're saying is true, she will only weaken herself faster by fighting against the lock. We need as much time as she can give us or she won't survive. You need to tell her that."

"I…I've never done that before." Plyke lowered his eyes, almost in shame. "I was only taught to listen, not to speak."

Eliséo looked at him in surprise. "From what I saw during my time in Illaria, all you need to do is think about something without letting anything else distract you and the rest should take care of itself. All you can do is try, Plyke."

Plyke shivered in the morning chill, rubbing his arms with his hands distractedly. He didn't want to do this. He'd been furious with Shuut for doing the same to him. How could he now do it to her? His only comfort was that he had no other choice. She might very well die otherwise.

Bracing himself for the chaos within her, Plyke placed a hand on Shuut's forehead again. He flinched at the intensity of her fear and frustration, but didn't pull back this time. In his mind he called her name over and over, eventually noticing it was having a calming effect on the trapped banwep. He hoped that meant she could actually hear his thoughts.

You need to stop fighting. He couldn't hear any reply, but his strength had always lain more in empathy. She was confused and frightened. He knew it was difficult for her to trust anyone, even the innocent Paradisians she had rescued.

We're going to find help for you, but you need to stop fighting or you won't last long enough. There was less confusion but her fear was still there, held back by sheer force of will.

Plyke took his hand away from her forehead and sighed with relief. "I think she won't fight anymore."

"Did she say anything?" Eliséo asked anxiously. Plyke shook his head. "Well done, Plyke. That was a brave thing you just did. Hopefully you have given us enough time to save her. Now, wake the boys."

Lord Aaron gently shook Plyke's arm to bring him out of his memory. He looked over to Master Jorg, fear flashing in his eyes. Knowing there was nothing else to be done, he projected the entire memory to the mind master. The shocked look on Jorg's face told him what he'd always suspected, that the masters didn't think he was capable of such magnificent feats of the mind.

"I … didn't think that was possible," Jorg found himself talking without meaning to.

"You mean you didn't think it was possible for anyone but you," Aaron corrected him. "I think we've finally put that debate to rest. I've shown you the memory, now what are we going to do about it?"

* * *

Mistress Isis wasted no time in opening the door to her classroom and ushering Rilla and Mistress Kayte inside. Rilla had spent enough time learning balance with fire and water. She now needed to learn more about the healing side of balance. It would save time if she could explain to Kayte how this young lintep worked.

"Do you know if Shuut is alive?" Rilla asked Mistress Kayte hesitantly, once the door was closed. "Did you see anything that would show if Lishe killed her too?"

"I don't know, Rilla," Kayte replied honestly, "but Nyssa wasn't killed by Lishe – she killed herself."

"What do you mean?" Rilla's brow instantly creased. Isis watched her carefully. She knew how volatile the girl's emotions could be. Kayte could easily push her too far without realising it.

"If the seer's vision was accurate, which is looking more and more likely," she admitted, "Nyssa was tortured by Lishe and then shot her power into Shuut. Essentially, she killed herself by giving up her power. For a lintep as powerful as Nyssa, giving up her power, voluntarily or otherwise, would cause instant death."

"Why would she do that?" the question was whispered so softly that Isis barely heard it. She caught Kayte's eye, wondering the same thing.

"Time for your lesson, Rilla," Mistress Isis turned the conversation before Rilla had too much time to dwell on the recent events. "You've been doing very well in learning your limits with fire and water, but just as important as that is the healing side of things. I think you should begin by telling Mistress Kayte all the times you've healed anyone quite quickly now."

She clapped her hands together, hurrying Rilla to a chaise. The young lintep was quick to take her seat. She proceeded to tell the Kayte about her experiences in healing, from the Fringa's broken wing to Master Ensil's sword wound and all the times she healed her companions between Silvaren and Illaria.

Kayte's eyes grew wider with the information. Once Rilla had finished, she looked over to Mistress Isis, questioningly.

"Was she the same with fire?"

"Even worse!" Isis told her with a grin. "Ask her how she knew to try it in the first place?" Mistress Kayte looked over to Rilla quite hesitantly. The girl didn't bother waiting for the question.

"A lintep took me with her when she went to heal a boy who had been gored by a bull. She knew I would watch everything she did and made me promise to be careful when I tried it myself."

"Her warning appears to have fallen on deaf ears," the older mistress chided her. "What were you thinking to risk your life and your companions' lives so many times?"

"I didn't ever risk my companions' lives." Rilla shook her head in confusion. Isis didn't have time to warn Kayte not to reprimand her so roughly.

"Not intentionally, no, but you could just as easily have hurt them as healed them," Mistress Isis watched Rilla's reaction as closely as Mistress Kayte. She saw her eyes grow wide and knew there was something, some part of the story Rilla hadn't told them yet.

"What happened? What did you just remember?" she asked, before Kayte could ruin it.

"It was an accident. I didn't mean to do it! I didn't even know I was doing it." Rilla's voice had faded to a whisper by the end. "I fixed it as soon as they stopped me."

"Rilla, you're safe now," Mistress Isis attempted to calm her down, without touching the girl. She shot a warning look at Kayte to stop her from making matters worse. "Whatever happened in the Outworld was *not* your fault. You weren't taught how dangerous your power could be. We simply need to know what happened so we can teach you how to avoid situations like that again."

Isis held Rilla's gaze firmly, but gently. She knew Kayte would be furious that she'd been overridden in her own lesson. Rilla shook her head and closed her eyes and started to disappear in front of their eyes.

"What is she doing?" Kayte hissed to Isis.

"Rilla, don't be afraid," Mistress Isis pleaded with the young lintep. "You don't need to fade away from us. Mistress Kayte doesn't know your story. She doesn't know how much danger you were in and that you saved everyone's life so many times."

Isis knew she should have explained everything to Kayte beforehand, but they hadn't had time. All she could hope was that the older mistress follow her lead. Kayte didn't disappoint her.

"That's right ... I'm sorry Rilla. If you explain to me what happened, then I will understand why you had to do what you did. Mistress Isis is correct – you weren't taught by anyone in the Outworld so it's amazing you could do any of these things in the first place. You couldn't possibly know how much danger they could put you in."

"I didn't mean to do it," Rilla repeated, quietly, as she slowly reappeared. "I needed to borrow some of Plyke's strength when we crossed under the Bramble River. Eliséo tried to explained how to do it and it worked, just a little bit too well."

"I think I know what you mean," Mistress Kayte told her, "but I need you to tell me exactly what you did."

"Eliséo told me to sort of link my power to Plyke's, so I sent out a tendril and tied it around one of his tendrils. Then I pulled."

Rilla paused, tears streaming down her cheeks. "I felt so much power. It … felt wonderful. I didn't know I was pulling the power out of him and making him weaker. Eliséo had to snap me out of it before I saw what I was doing. He'd fallen on the floor and looked so very pale."

Isis pulled a handkerchief from the pocket of her dress and went to sit next to the terrified girl. She wiped away her tears and risked everything by putting an arm around the girl and pulling her into an embrace. With a wordless warning to Kayte to stay silent, she rocked the girl back and forth muttering soft comforting sounds until she stopped shaking.

"You're safe now, Rilla," Isis stroked her long fiery curls. "Plyke is safe too and he isn't angry with you. He knows you didn't know what you were doing and you only did it to save all of your lives."

"He was so shaken," Rilla whispered into her shoulder.

"But he let you take his power without a struggle," Isis persisted, "and he let you continue to use his power through the river."

"Only until I realised he couldn't give me any more strength," the young lintep sat up straighter, disentangling herself from Isis. "I asked him to take a leaf out of my pocket and light it from the one that was almost spent. His fingers were shaking so much that I had to give him his power back."

Kayte finally smiled.

"That was very well done, Rilla. A lot of lintep would not have realised when they were pushing someone else's limits too far."

"But then he was angry with me for making that decision for him," Rilla told them, lost in her memories. "He was so very angry with me."

"He was just worried about you," Kayte reassured her. "He didn't want you to have to take on so much of the burden yourself."

What were they doing? Kayte projected the question to Isis. *How were they crossing the river that made Rilla need so much of Plyke's power?*

I don't know, Isis replied with her mind. *This has nothing to do with fire. She didn't tell me about it.*

Distracted as she was, Rilla couldn't stop her power from overhearing their conversation. How much was she allowed to tell them? She closed her eyes and reached out to Elessa and Eliséo.

Can I tell them about the river crossing? she asked.

Eliséo saw that she was in a lesson with Mistress Kayte and Mistress Isis and didn't want her eyes to shine bright green in front of them. He risked a quick reply before cutting the contact.

As long as you make sure they know that you were lending your power to me because I shouldn't be able to do that.

Rilla opened her eyes once she felt the connection disappear. She knew her eyes were their normal shade of green when the older lintep looked at her.

"Eliséo created a sort of mist bubble. If it had enough power, it could safely take us under the Bramble River, away from our attacker. He asked to borrow some of my power, but it wasn't quite enough. Well, not to cross the entire river anyway. So I borrowed some power from Plyke to give to Eliséo. But when he couldn't give anymore, I cut that connection and just gave as much of my own power as I could until we reached the other side."

Rilla blurted out the story – as much of it as she could tell them anyway – and held her breath while she waited for one of them to reply.

The silence was unending. Rilla let out her breath slowly, feeling the hot air pass over her lips. She couldn't hear what they were thinking. They were blocking their thoughts too well.

"It was just after Shuut was attacked with the mind snare," she tried to explain. Perhaps they thought Eliséo had made a reckless decision to go under the river instead of over it. The Mistresses remained silent, staring at her in disbelief. "We didn't have a choice."

"Does anyone else know about this?" Mistress Kayte finally found her voice.

"Master Aurelius," Rilla answered cautiously, "Eliséo and the boys."

"Let's keep it that way," the Mistress told her in a voice that chilled her to the bone. "You have a unique gift for getting your power to do anything you can think of. It's something I don't want *any* of our other students to know about. If word spreads that things like this are possible, we might have more than just Lishe to deal with."

"But surely no one would do something like that on purpose, to take someone's power like that," Isis protested.

"I had not even attempted to think of how such a thing could be possible," Kayte replied, "and I think we are lucky that others haven't thought about it either. If we keep students believing they can only do the things we teach them because that's all that's possible, we might be safe.

"If they realise, like Rilla, that their power can potentially do anything they ask of it, we'll be in a lot more trouble than we are now. Bad enough that some advanced students, long ago, were taught things that only masters should know. If they were all taught things like this, I fear we'd have a small army of lintep to contend with."

Rilla and Isis shivered.

"Let's get back to the lesson then," Isis replied in a brittle voice. "Rilla needs to learn her limits when it comes to healing. Hopefully she doesn't need to employ those powers while she's here but, with her history, I think it's safest if we just teach her as much as we can now."

Chapter Twelve - Return to Silvaren

Eliséo rode hard and fast, only slowing down on occasion to water and feed his horse. He could not afford for Fleuris to die on the way, nor did he want the blood of the gentle chestnut mare on his hands. He had seen too much blood spilt in the past few weeks – more than he should have. As he travelled towards Silvaren, mainly along the coast, he had purposely ridden away from human towns and villages. His swift mode of travel always stirred up an air of unrest in the humans. He did not want that now of all times. The elves, karliki and lintep had enough to deal with on their own without adding humans into the mix.

It was still early on the fifth day after leaving Illaria when he finally saw the magnificent trees of Silvaren rise up out of the horizon. The sight always made his heart ache with joy. Even though he had been born in the Outworld and spent most of his time with other races, he still called Silvaren home and the sight of those trees was all he needed to feel completely at peace.

Knowing it would still take hours to reach his home, he urged Fleuris into a faster gait, desperate to reach Elessa and his mother. There were so many things he had to discuss with Lady Eléna. He wondered if any of their discussions would extend to the new queen. With a bitter taste in his mouth, the thought turned towards the weaponsmaster. Would Ensil be a party to the conversations or would Eléna tell him select bits of information afterwards?

Eliséo had known Eléna was his mother for hundreds of years. She had told him as early as she could without risking that his youthful exuberance would lead him to tell other elves. From that day onwards, she'd been teaching him to use his magic but keeping from him the fact that he could do it all without the aid of her crown.

It had come as quite a shock for him to find out who his father was. Even more so that his father had known all along who he was and never mentioned it to him.

At least that means he knows how to keep a secret, Elessa told him firmly. *Now that you know, it can't possibly hurt to ask his opinion alongside Eléna's about Rilla and her bond.*

He may yet have his own agenda, Eliséo replied warily. *He's the oldest elf in Silvaren. He started the story about the crown. He's been cleverly shaping the way the elves think for thousands of years. Whether he did that for the good of the elves or for his own reasons is yet to be determined.*

You are too willing to think the worst of every situation, she chided him gently. *Just hurry home to me. I've missed you.* With that, their conversation ended. Eliséo knew she was still there with him, but she was waiting for him to reach her before they spoke again.

It was nearing dusk when the Fleuris slowly found her footing down the steep hill to the thin strip of sand that connected Silvaren to the mainland. They were just in time for low tide, when the water would be low enough for her to safely cross to the island.

Eliséo kept the chestnut mare to a slow and steady walk. He was home now and there was no point alerting every elf who saw him as to the state of affairs in the Outworld by recklessly galloping towards Silva. There weren't any other horses in Silvaren, so he directed Fleuris to the lake below Silva to water her and give her a good rub down after her tireless days of service.

Once he arrived there, he spied Raeslin swimming in the lake and called her out to help him. Leaving her with strict instructions to feed, water and rub down the horse, he left to find his mother.

Being careful, as always, to avoid directly touching Silva with his bare skin, he ascended the levels until he was close to the top. He walked the long and winding path up to Liessa's room, assuming that to be the best place to find them both in the evening. There, he found the golden-eyed Farrow standing to attention outside the glittering vines that stood in place of a door. With a single glance, he knew Farrow could tell he'd ridden hard to reach the elven stronghold. It was no secret that Eliséo's loyalty lay with Lady Eléna. She was the one who had requested him to go on his journey with the Paradisians in the first place.

"Wait here," Farrow told him in his raspy voice as he silently slipped between the glittering vines to the queen's chamber. A few moments later, he reappeared and held the vines aside. Eliséo entered with a quick inclination of his head.

"We were expecting your arrival much sooner," Liessa announced as soon as Eliséo was inside. He flourished a short bow towards her with a cocked eyebrow.

"What the queen means to say is that we hoped your errand would be carried out quite quickly and easily," Lady Eléna said.

Eliséo tried not to smirk as Lady Eléna tried to smooth over her daughter's abrupt manner.

"We encountered a number of difficulties along the way, my Lady," Eliséo replied evenly. He did not know how much they were to share with the queen – that decision was entirely up to his mother. She held her secrets close to her heart and most of them for good reason.

"Has Rilla been safely escorted to Illaria?" Queen Liessa asked him bluntly.

"She has, my queen," Eliséo replied. "All four of the Paradisians have been granted entry into the lintep stronghold, at least for as long as Rilla and Plyke decide to remain there."

"Plyke?" Liessa asked with a start. "Why do they care about him?"

"It would appear as though young Plyke is also a lintep, my queen," Eliséo explained the bare minimum, knowing that Eléna would be able to fill in the blanks for herself.

"I see," Liessa missed the hidden meaning in his announcement, "and did Shadow not wish to remain in Illaria as well?"

"Shadow was not with us by the time we reached Illaria," Eliséo avoided saying anything he didn't expressly need to. However, as the queen, Liessa would need to know of two other bits of information. "I bring ill tidings from the karliki and the lintep."

"The karliki? Why in the Outworld would you have news from there? I thought you were exiled from Goraburg fifty years ago," Liessa exclaimed with raised eyebrows.

"Lord Mikhail has seen fit to revoke his previous ruling on that matter," Eliséo answered easily. "His eldest son, Vladimir, has been trying to usurp his position for these past fifty years. Vladimir's plans were revealed to Lord Mikhail while we were there and he ruled that Vladimir Mikhailovich and all his supporters should be immediately put to death. He named Ilya Mikhailovich as his heir."

"He didn't," Liessa gasped.

"One of Vladimir's supporters overheard the decree before they were all rounded up and helped the rebel escape with at least a handful of karliki before the rest of them were put to death," Eliséo continued. "We do not know where he has gone or what he plans to do, but all of Goraburg is now on high alert. I believe any assistance we provide would be most welcome to the karliki."

Silence filled the room as the implications of Vladimir and Mikhail's actions sank in. Eliséo watched as Liessa's face changed from horror to panic. She hadn't been the queen for long and hadn't yet had to deal with any situation similar to this.

"Before you decide whether you wish to help the karliki and how you might do that, there is a possibility that a dangerous lintep is on the way to Illaria," Eliséo was toeing a thin line. He didn't know how much he could reveal to them. He knew, from Rilla's thoughts, that Nyssa's body had been found and returned to Illaria. He saw Lord Aaron reach the conclusion that it was Lishe and she was on her way to their stronghold, probably to kill Rilla and then Shadow.

"Arishen had a vision when we arrived in Illaria that Shadow and Nyssa had been attacked by another lintep. From what he saw, it may be possible that Shadow has been taken hostage and Nyssa is dead."

"No!" Eléna cried out, her knees almost giving way beneath her. Eliséo ran to steady her. It had been foolish of him not to realise what her reaction would be. "Do you know if his vision was true?"

"I left Illaria the same day as the search party, my lady," he replied, catching her eye and nodding imperceptibly. "They promised to sent word once they returned."

"I thought the rumour was that she had died years ago." Liessa was clearly confused by the news.

"Yes, many people were under that impression," Eliséo clarified. "The crystal dragons themselves spread the rumour to further manipulate their precious prophecy. Lady Nyssa has been living with them these past twelve years under the impression that her daughter, Shadow, was dead.

"They were reunited once we reached the Drakos Mountains and travelled with us towards Illaria. We had to part ways because Rilla and Plyke were running out of time. Nyssa and Shadow were meant to meet us in Illaria no more than a week later, but then Arishen had his vision. I didn't have time to stay to find out what had happened to them. I thought it was more important to get the information about both the karliki and the lintep to you as soon as possible. Forgive me if I was wrong."

"No, you did the right thing," Liessa reassured him. "I will discuss with my advisers what our options are to assist both the karliki and the lintep without weakening our own home."

"By your leave, might I escort Lady Eléna to her room?" Eliséo hoped his tone was smooth enough to persuade Liessa. A distracted wave of her hand granted him his request. He walked over to his mother, placed a strong arm around her waist and led her out of the room.

In silence, she leaned heavily on his shoulder as he escorted her as quickly as he could to her room. Once inside, he sat her down by the hole in the trunk that served as her window and fetched her a glass of water from the ever ready pedestal bowl in the middle of the room. He mumbled the words for the mist and waited until they were completely hidden from view before talking.

"They found her," Eliséo hated being the bearer of such ill tidings, but steeled himself against such thoughts. "The search party returned this morning with Nyssa's body wrapped in white silk. No trace of Shadow was found, but Lord Aaron watched one of Arishen's visions to see that she is being held captive by the same person who attacked the two of them. Presumably it's the same person that began attacking us only a few short days after we left Silvaren. It seems so long ago now."

His eyes clouded over with the memory of the first dawn attack. The Paradisians had learnt so much since that time. Rilla's healing skills had progressed magnificently and all of their fighting skills had come along by leaps and bounds.

"Can you be certain?" Elessa asked him, without a shred of hope.

"I saw it all through Rilla's eyes," he told her gently, as he sat on the floor at her feet. "They will inter her in the crypt with her mother, brothers and sister on the morrow. Lord Aaron is shaken, but I'm certain he will hold himself together for his grandchildren."

"Dear Aaron," Elessa sighed with a sob, "what horrors he has has to endure in his lifetime. I cannot imagine a worse fate for a father, or for a sister. We will have to tell Kora. She is here now."

Eliséo stared at her uncomprehendingly. He must have heard her incorrectly.

"You heard me correctly," Eléna told him, patting his arm. "Kora arrived over a week ago. She had to leave the Paradise where she had been living. It seems as though Rilla's father has been making life miserable for many of its inhabitants. With Rilla and Plyke gone, he wanted Kora out of the way. She decided to leave after the first attempt on her life."

"Does she know Plyke passed through here?" he asked, knowing the answer before he'd finished the question. "And you told her he was on his way to Illaria when he left."

Elessa nodded. "She refuses to return."

"If we tell her that Lishe is on her way there and may try to hurt her son, she may change her mind," he tried to find a way to persuade her.

"We all know that if Lishe is aiming to hurt anyone, Plyke is far from being her target," Elessa pointed out.

"At the very least, she should go there to make sure her son isn't swayed by the general lintep way of thinking," Eliséo dug his heels into the argument. "They were barely willing to keep Tika in their stronghold and the boy is his Partner. What if they turn Plyke into exactly the type of person Kora was trying not to let him become?"

"Kora chose her path long ago, my son," Elessa said as she lent her weary head back onto Silva's smooth trunk and closed her eyes. Eliséo watched as Silva's colours swirled around her. He kept his silence until she spoke again.

"I know there is something else troubling you, something you've kept secret from your queen. Are you ready to tell me now?"

"We have a problem," Eliséo sighed. "Rilla cannot keep her link with Elessa a secret for much longer. Already we had to tell Master Aurelius so that he could protect her and try to keep her from revealing her bond, but that arrangement cannot last forever.

"She has seen too much of my power – things I should not have shown her. We were in so much danger in the Outworld. She has already asked Elessa how to create this very mist to protect herself. The foolish tree told her. Any time she wants to talk to me, her eyes glow bright green. At least she now knows to close her eyes when she does that, but she might not think to do it every time. She may slip up and I need to know what to tell her to do when that happens."

"The harm doesn't come in other people knowing," Elessa thought aloud. "It comes from them understanding how much power the elf bound to that tree has. They may assume that the two powers work together so that her own strength makes the elven spells stronger, but if any realise that isn't actually the case, they will understand that there is another eligible heir to the throne. I gather you told Aurelius it was your tree?"

Eliséo nodded, unable to think through the problem.

"I think we need to talk to Ensil," Eléna's eyes turned from a dull slate grey to a bright, shining silver. "He will be here soon."

At a word from Eliséo, the mist around them dissipated. Together, they waited in silence, lost in their thoughts. Eventually, they were interrupted by the arrival of the old weaponsmaster.

"Forgive an old elf for keeping you waiting," Ensil puffed as he pushed his way through the vines in the entrance to Eléna's room. "My body is not what it used to be and I have not needed to climb the height of this tree in a long time."

"Ensil," Eléna smiled, "you are always welcome, even if you falsely complain of your old body."

Eliséo tried to keep his composure as he called up the mist. He listened on in silence as Lady Eléna told the old elf their problem.

"How difficult would it be to tell Elessa she can't help Rilla anymore? Not unless her life is in danger," Ensil asked. "Would she listen to you?"

"I've already told Elessa and Rilla not to do things like that again," Eliséo told him. "What I'm concerned about is that Rilla will slip up and use what she already knows. We don't know what to do when that happens. The lintep masters and her friends all know what the glowing eyes mean. Some of them have already seen her eyes glow but she managed to dismiss it as reflection from firelight. They won't believe her a second time."

Ensil rubbed his lip with his forefinger. "Would any of the boys remember it was your tree she touched?"

"No," Eliséo shook his head, "they didn't know it was Elessa."

"Then the next time it happens, it may be best for her to simply admit what happened," Ensil told them. "Unless she admits to having knowledge she could only get from you, then you should still be safe."

Eléna stared at him in shock. "Surely it would be wiser to keep it a secret."

"Eliséo is right," the old weaponsmaster told her. "They can't keep it a secret much longer. The most we can hope is to keep the tree and elf's identity secret for as long as we can and hope Liessa is accepted as queen before people put the pieces together to understand he must be your son."

"Once it's revealed, Elessa should give her as much knowledge as she can about elf magic," Eliséo decided. "At that point, it can't hurt and will give her more of a chance to protect herself."

"That's probably the best idea," Eléna finally gave in, her shoulders sagging. "Go and get some rest now. Liessa should have a decision for you in the next day or two about the karliki and lintep situations."

Eliséo shook his head, remembering his other self-imposed task. "I need to speak to Kora first. Where is she?"

Eléna's eyes glowed a soft silver as she spoke. "She's resting by the lake under Silva, but she grows restless. You will only catch her if you hurry."

Eliséo half ran, half floated down the levels of Silva. His eyes glowed a soft silver as he convinced the air around him to speed his passage. Every elf could do it, but few were as gifted in their mastery of air as he was.

He reached the lake just as Kora was pulling her feet out of the water. There were no other elves around. It was already quite late in the evening and most of them would be nestled away, warm and content, in their trees. Eliséo longed to go to Elessa, but knew it was more urgent to speak with Kora.

"Lady Kora," he called out to her to delay her departure, "please wait. I have information about your son."

Kora froze at the words, eyes wide with fear. "How do you know who my son is?"

"Plyke came through Silvaren weeks ago, with Rilla and the others," Eliséo explained as he reached her side. "He kept his identity safely hidden until we were almost at Goraburg."

"Rilla? Goraburg?" her brow furrowed. "What are you talking about?"

Eliséo took a deep breath. He'd forgotten that Rilla's identity had been kept secret in their Paradise. "The nameless girl who led the others out of the Paradise. That was Rilla, daughter of Lady Nyssa. Shadow wanted to take her to the crystal dragons because they had sent her to find their prophecy child."

"Shadow? Nyssa's daughter?" Kora was shocked by the news. "But Nyssa didn't think humans were worth the effort of the prophecy. Why would she have a daughter and name her Rilla?"

"From what Shadow, your oldest niece, tells us, Lady Nyssa left Illaria soon after you did, to try to find you. She dragged her oldest daughter around the Outworld for years until she settled down with the crystal dragons," Eliséo watched as Kora's eyes narrowed at the mention of the dragons. "They convinced her that it would please you if she gave birth to the prophecy child to help destroy the Paradises."

"So she really did just have a child, a daughter, and named her Rilla to try to appease me?" Kora was incredulous. "Then why did she abandon her in that awful Paradise with her arrogant, evil, father?"

"That's something I think she regretted," Eliséo told her, wondering how she was going to take the news of her sister's death.

"She'll regret that until the day she dies if Rilla didn't reach Illaria in time," Kora noticed Eliséo avert his gaze. "Rilla and Plyke *did* reach Illaria, didn't they?"

"They did," Eliséo nodded his head, "and not a moment too soon. Both of them were in and out of consciousness by the time we reached the boundary. Master Aurelius met us there and brought them and their companions into Illaria."

"They let humans into Illaria?" Kora's voice rose to a high pitch. "How did that happen?"

Eliséo smiled at the memory. "Rilla told them she would refuse entry without her friends and Plyke stood firmly by her side. The two already knew they were cousins by then. Once Aurelius realised who they were, he brought them all before the Council of Masters, King Lukys, Lord Aaron and Lord Kynon. Your king agreed to let the humans remain as long as Rilla and Plyke remained."

"I never thought I'd live to see the day," Kora breathed out, barely louder than a whisper. "I suppose it's only fitting that my child would be one of the first to bring humans into the lintep stronghold. What did Nyssa say when she heard that?"

"Nyssa wasn't with us at the time," Eliséo knew he couldn't delay it any longer. "Arishen, did you know he's a seer? He had a vision of Nyssa and Shadow as he passed the boundary into Illaria. It's quite possible that your sister is dead. We think that Lishe might have been the other lintep in the vision, but Arishen doesn't know her, so he couldn't identify her."

"Lishe," Kora whispered the name in terror. "I was always scared of her in Illaria. The masters taught the three of us things that we shouldn't have been taught, all because Lishe wanted more and more knowledge. They should have known what kind of person she was by then. They shouldn't have taught us things like that."

"Things like what, Kora?" Eliséo asked her urgently. "We think Lishe is on her way to Illaria as we speak, to kill Rilla. What things were you taught? Could Lishe use any of it to kill Rilla?"

"Why would Lishe want to kill Rilla?" Kora avoided his question.

"She's been stealing other lintep's powers. Maybe she knows the prophecised Rilla would be powerful," Eliséo tried to find an explanation. "We know she wanted to steal Nyssa's power, but Nyssa gave her power to Shadow instead."

"She did what?" Kora stood up suddenly and started pacing. "Why would she do that? How did she even know to do something like that? She's never experimented with anything in her life."

"I think she may have been trying to save her daughter's life and keep Lishe from stealing her power, at least for a short time," Eliséo explained.

"But you got all of this from a seer's vision," Kora pointed out. She stopped pacing and turned to stare at Eliséo as he got to his feet. "You don't know if any of it's true."

"Arishen's visions are usually accurate," Eliséo told her, calmly. "He even dreamt about you leaving the Paradise. King Lukys sent out a search party for Nyssa and Shadow. They should have found them by now whether they are dead or alive. Mistress Kayte promised to send word as soon as they returned to Illaria."

"If Rilla and my Plyke are in Illaria, they're safe," Kora thought aloud. "The masters will keep them safe. My father will keep them safe."

"Not if they don't know what Lishe was taught all those years ago," Eliséo pointed out. "She intends to go into Illaria, kill Rilla, steal her power and then kill Shadow and take Nyssa's power. How can anyone keep her safe if they don't know what she is capable of? You need to go back there and help them."

"Go back there! I'm never going back there again. I swore I would never return when I couldn't convince anyone else that the Paradises should be destroyed."

"But your son, and your niece, are convinced the Paradises should be destroyed," Eliséo pleaded with her. "You already have the prophecy child on your side and your son willing to do anything to help her. They need your knowledge to stay alive so that they can help each other fulfil the prophecy."

"I can't do it," Kora told him, tears in her eyes. "If Lishe is on her way there, I'll only be in danger too. She knows I had just as much power as Nyssa, but I had more control of it."

"So you'll leave your son and your niece in Lishe's line of sight, while you stay tucked away safely in the trees of Silvaren?" Eliséo hated doing it to her, but if guilt was the only way to convince her, then so be it.

"You could have stayed there yourself to try to protect them," Kora told him stonily. "And yet here *you* are, tucked away safely in the trees of Silvaren."

"I am the Ambassador of the Elves," Eliséo drew himself up to his full height, towering over the lintep. "I came to inform Queen Liessa of the dangers both the lintep and karliki find themselves in, as is my duty. *You* abandoned your home and your family to live in a Paradise you had no business being in and now refuse to return to your home and father to protect your son and his cousin."

Kora's eyes turned from stone to water. Eliséo watched as she turned and fled from him, into the winding levels of Silva. He could only hope that she would change her mind and leave for Illaria as swiftly as possible.

He turned and headed back towards the outskirts of Silvaren, where he knew his tree would be waiting to greet him. Instead of rushing there as quickly as his feet would take him, Eliséo found himself walking slowly. His heart was heavy. What he had told Kora was true, but it didn't stop him from feeling miserable about having to leave Rilla and Plyke in so much danger. She'd brought his guilt to the surface.

Chapter Thirteen – Lishe

"How long until we get there?" Shuut asked yet again. She wasn't impatient to arrive. She only needed to know how much longer she had to come up with a plan – any plan. The banwep in her couldn't rest while she was held captive with no hope of escape or rescue.

"We should arrive tomorrow afternoon," Lishe answered distractedly. "Then I just need to get the brat out of the castle, kill you both and take your power." She smiled cruelly as she said the last words. After days of travelling together, that smile didn't chill Shuut as much as it first had.

"Why don't you just kill me now?" Shuut goaded her. "How do you know I won't warn Rilla when I see her?"

"Oh, I'll be certain to silence you before the brat reaches us," Lishe assured her. "I have more than enough power to do that and deal with her at the same time."

"How did you get so much power?" Shuut asked her, curiosity finally getting the better of her.

"I stole it from other lintep," Lishe answered blithely. "I started with weak lintep, with barely enough power to tell the difference between them and half-castes. Those ones didn't die, they just became empty shells of the people they used to be."

"Why would you do that?" Shuut cried out in horror.

"Nyssa had more power than me – more power than she knew what to do with and it was wasted on her," Lishe's voice turned bitter. "I didn't have anywhere near the amount of power as she did, but even with that, I practised hard every day to increase my skills to that of a mistress. Even after I took the test and performed every task perfectly, they refused to make me a mistress. So I gave myself the tattoos I deserved." She pulled up her left sleeve and showed Shuut an elaborate black tattoo. "Then I went out to get more power to be able to use all the skills I had acquired."

"But the power you really wanted was Nyssa's?" Shuut guessed.

"Nyssa and Kora's," Lishe corrected her, "but Kora tended to her studies more than her sister. She won't be so easy to catch off guard."

"You won't find her in Illaria," Shuut told her smugly. "She's not there."

"How do you know that?" Lishe's eyes narrowed. Shuut instantly regretted giving her that bit of information. Now she was one step closer to knowing that Plyke was Kora's son and had accompanied Rilla into Illaria. Had she just put her cousin in danger?

"Nyssa told us that she was looking for Kora in the Outworld," Shuut bluffed, hoping that Lishe didn't know much more about the sisters. "She said Kora left Illaria years ago and she was travelling the Outworld trying to find her."

"Well, after I have Nyssa's power, and that brat's, I will have more than enough power to be able to best any master or mistress they throw at me," Lishe balled her fists at her sides. "Even Kora won't stand a chance against me then."

Lishe was almost as angry now as she had been when Nyssa threw her power into Shuut. The banwep treasured that piece of information. It might be the key to her freedom, though she couldn't fathom how.

* * *

Rilla woke with a knot in her stomach. This morning they were going to inter her mother in the royal crypt with the rest of her family. She knew her mother was dead, but this seemed to make it more final, like an admission that she was gone and there was nothing any of them could do about it.

It hadn't been like that with Rhanya. She knew he was dead before she got to his room and knew there was nothing she could do about it. What had made it worse was that it was her own father who had ordered his death.

She wondered whether things would have been different if Nyssa had stayed. Would her father still have become the Paradise leader? Would Nyssa and Kora have reunited peacefully and taught their children to use their power and then safely escort them to Illaria together? Would the Paradise have remained true to its intended nature – a safe haven for humans from an Outworld full of magic and danger?

Little one, these thoughts will bring you no comfort. Elessa's voice was soft and gentle in her mind.

Has Eliséo returned to you yet? Rilla knew the tree was right, so she didn't bother arguing with Elessa and instead kept her thoughts to herself.

I arrived last night, Eliséo joined the conversation.

What aren't you telling me? Rilla asked him. She could sense his hesitation. *Has something else happened?*

There are some things it will be better for you not to know, Rilla, Eliséo explained. *Master Ensil and Lady Eléna have decided that the next time you slip up, you can admit to being bound to an elf's tree, but you can't let them know it's Elessa. For that to work, you can't know everything I know.*

Even if you're certain it's something I would want to know? Rilla asked him curtly.

Even then, Rilla, Eliséo replied. *Sometimes, you just need to trust me.*

I trust you, Rilla softened a little, *I just wish there was some way I could live without so many secrets surrounding me.*

She felt Eliséo embrace her with his mind, just as Elessa had done on so many occasions. She knew it was all he could do and, for the moment, it was enough.

Rilla met Plyke in the hall outside their rooms. All morning lessons had been cancelled for Nyssa's funeral. Everyone knew she was being interred in the crypt, but no one had bothered to tell either of them where that was or if they were expected to do anything that morning.

Together, they descended the winding staircase until they reached the empty inner courtyard, crossing it to reach the dining hall. Arishen and Tika were waiting for them at their usual table. They'd claimed it for their own in the mornings since their arrival. Any meal they shared in the dining hall was always there. Rilla and Plyke filled their plates with food and joined their friends.

They ate in silence, the cousins only picking at their food. Rather than feeling sad about Nyssa's death, they shared their guilt for not feeling as sad as they should. Neither of them had spent enough time with her for that.

Rilla remembered only images from her time with Nyssa before they entered the Paradise – her soft, shoulder-length brown hair, her misty grey eyes. After they were reunited, things hadn't gone smoothly for them. They fought more often than not and were silent with each other the rest of the time. The only time they'd worked well together was when Rilla had shown her how to mould her power into the shape they needed to get safely through the burning forest. Soon after that, they had to part ways.

Plyke's only interaction with her had been when she taught him to move her little white stones around. Other than that, she was only interested in him when he mentioned he was Kora's son. She had been more interested in Kora than she had been in the rest of them.

"What now?" Tika asked, when it was clear they weren't going to finish their food.

"I don't know," Plyke shrugged. "No one told us anything after they took Nyssa to be embalmed yesterday morning."

Suddenly, a whistling filled the air. It was loud and clear. Rilla and Plyke sat up straighter, while Arishen and Tika stared at them in confusion.

"It's going to begin soon," Plyke told them, confidently. "If we head out to the gardens outside the stables, we should see them as they pass by."

Rilla glowered unreasonably. She knew Plyke had a wonderful gift with the lintep whistle, and she truly was happy for him. That didn't stop her being envious of his apparent ease with the new language. She'd barely understood that the message was about Nyssa and hadn't even been certain that she'd understood that properly.

Rilla rose alongside her friends and followed a short line of people to the perfectly manicured gardens outside the stables and walked along the crushed pebble paths until she joined the crowd of lintep gathering around them. It appeared as though the entire castle was gathering for Nyssa's funeral.

In the far corner of the outer courtyard, stood a stone doorway at the top of three steps. She watched as lintep parted in front of her to create an easy pathway for King Lukys as he made his way towards the doorway. As he climbed the steps, his golden crown glinted in the sunlight. He turned to face his people and gravely raised his hands for silence.

Rilla's mind fled back to the Paradise when Erton had stood on the raised platform many times to announce things to his flock. But this wasn't the same. People didn't fear King Lukys – they respected him. She looked around her to find many lintep swallowing back their tears, others with wet cheeks. Again, she felt a pang of guilt that she had no tears to shed for Nyssa.

"My people, today we bid farewell to one of our own." The king's voice rang loud and clear through the courtyard. "Lady Nyssa was attacked by another lintep and died giving her oldest daughter a chance to live. Our hearts go out to her family and closest friends at this time of sorrow. Nyssa was well loved in her youth, before she left for the Outworld. She has been sorely missed these many years and our hearts are full of sadness that we will never see her smiling face again."

Rilla listened, frozen in place. She heard the gasps echo through the courtyard at the mention of an attack on her mother. King Lukys had been careful not to mention Lishe by name nor had he explained to them that Nyssa had thrown her power into Shuut. Was that part of the knowledge that the masters wanted to keep hidden from the people? Rilla was jolted out of these thoughts by Lord Aaron's voice.

"We thank you for your support at this time." His voice cracked as he choked back tears. "Nyssa was my oldest daughter. It seems unfair to have lost so many of my children, but that is the way of the world. I would ask only my family to join me in bringing Nyssa down into the crypt to rest with her mother, brothers and sister."

"That means you two," Tika hissed, shoving her forward with Plyke. She looked blankly at him and then at the expectant faces of the lintep who were now making way for her and Plyke to reach the entrance to the crypt.

Hand in hand, they walked towards their grandfather. There were a few other lintep making their way towards Lord Kynon, who was already standing by his cousin's side. It dawned on her that she had more family in Illaria than Lord Aaron and King Lukys, but she didn't know who they were. Rilla's face contorted into a scowl as she saw Marilisa standing next to Lord Kynon, her straight black hair brushed to a glossy sheen.

"What's *she* doing there?" she whispered to Plyke. He only shrugged in reply. Marilisa sneered at them, before an elbow in her side from Lord Kynon stopped her.

"Marilisa, they've lost their mother and aunt," he hissed at her. "Show some respect to your cousins."

Rilla stopped in her tracks, instantly pulled forward by Plyke. *Cousins?* She didn't realise they had more cousins in Illaria. How could any of their cousins be so prejudiced against humans? She would have to ask her grandfather later. It didn't seem possible.

As she took her place beside Lord Aaron, she noticed another lintep, only a little younger than her grandfather standing next to King Lukys. It had to be his daughter, Princess Aislen. She had the same wavy brown hair as the king, pulled back in a long plait, but her eyes were the same shade as Nyssa and Shuut's.

On the other side of Lord Kynon, she saw another two lintep around the same age as Princess Aislen, possibly the sons of Lord Kynon. They both had his brown hair but unlike Lord Kynon, they had the same grey eyes as the princess.

The younger one had his arm wrapped affectionately around the waist of a lady with blonde wavy hair and hazel eyes. In front of the couple were two much younger lintep, possibly even younger than she was. They were exact copies of one another, except the boy had grey eyes and the girl had hazel ones. Rilla raised her eyebrows at Plyke, but he only shrugged in reply.

Rilla waited alongside the rest of her family for a slow procession of pall bearers to bring a plain wooden coffin, holding Nyssa's embalmed and silk-wrapped body towards them. Once they had arrived at the opening to the crypt, the coffin was handed over to King Lukys, Lord Aaron, Lord Kynon, his sons and Princess Aislen. Together, the six of them turned to carry the coffin down the steps into the crypt below. Rilla found Plyke gripping her hand as they turned to follow the others into the crypt. She could feel his unease and consciously tried not to push any of her emotions through to him. The last thing she wanted on a day like today was to accidentally influence Plyke.

As they walked down the stairs, Rilla noticed all the lanterns on the wall had been lit in preparation. The air grew colder the further down they went. Eventually, the stairs ended and opened out into a massive cavern. There were statutes and coffins scattered all over. Rilla expected them to be covered in dust, but they all looked as though they had been placed there the day before.

She followed the small procession to one side of the cavern where she was horrified to see one coffin surrounded by three much smaller ones. Nyssa's coffin was placed next to them in a loving manner. Everyone stood back as Lord Aaron affectionately touched the five coffins, tears rolling slowly off his cheeks.

"Rilla, Plyke, go to your grandfather," King Lukys came over to whisper to them. "He needs your strength now."

Together, they walked over to Lord Aaron and stood one on each side of him, not knowing what to do. They'd never been in a situation like this before. All the funerals in their Paradise had been cremations of people they had known their whole lives. Even though Nyssa was so closely related to them, they'd barely known her at all.

Lord Aaron put and arm around each of them and drew them close. "I know you didn't know her well, and the little time you spent with her was full of trouble, arguments and danger, but she would have loved you both. I'm certain she was happy to be bringing you back to Illaria herself and would have been so proud of both of you once you started your training. Don't let the other things cloud your mind at the moment. Just think that she did what she thought was best and could not have known the consequences of her actions."

Rilla listened to his words with an empty heart. He had heard their story the evening after they'd arrived. Tika had told him almost everything – or at least everything that he knew anyway. Lord Aaron knew what Nyssa had done, or had not done, and was asking her to forgive those decisions now just because she was gone. She couldn't do it and she couldn't tell him that, so she said nothing.

* * *

It was late in the morning when Shuut finally arrived in Illaria. It was not how she had ever envisaged her arrival, but at least she was here. Lishe had urged her on relentlessly. She was aching all over, from the strange abuse from the lintep both of her mind and her body. The days had blurred into one another as she struggled to keep Nyssa's power within her and still walk at the pace that Lishe demanded of her.

"What are her friend's names?" Lishe asked suddenly.

"Why?" Shuut received a swift kick to the leg for her question. "I'm not telling you." She struggled to breathe as Lishe lifted her from the floor with her power, closing in on her throat as she did so.

"I ask the questions and you answer them. Are we clear?" Shuut struggled to move in her hold. Lishe was surprised when the banwep shook her head. "Tell me their names."

"No," Shuut gasped out as she fell in a crumpled heap on the floor. "If you're going to kill me either way, I'd rather not help you."

"Fine, then I'll just show her an image of me torturing you with instructions on how to find us," Lishe smiled viciously. "*That* will certainly get her attention."

"She won't come," Shuut insisted. "Or she'll bring an army of lintep with her."

"Oh, I doubt she'll do that when she thinks your life hangs in the balance if she disobeys me," Lishe told her in a sickly sweet tone.

Lishe pushed the banwep's body into the ground, holding her tightly while she sent her power out to find Rilla. She knew what the girl's mind felt like now. Even if it was just surface glances, she'd gathered that much from the banwep's memories. Besides, if Rilla was in Illaria, they would have taught her to conceal all but her surface thoughts by now.

It took almost all her stolen power linked together to reach inside the castle. She knew her way around it like the back of her hand. She'd grown up in the city around the stunning sandstone castle, but had attended classes inside the grounds as soon as her parents realised how skilled she was. They knew they could not teach her everything she would need to know themselves.

Lishe took a moment to think. At this time of day, Rilla was probably in the dining hall. Would she be able to single the girl out from all the others? Lishe briefly touched minds with a few lintep in the hall. It was going to be more difficult to find her than she'd anticipated.

Abruptly changing her mind, Lishe reached out to one of the younger minds she could find. It was bound to be a servant. If she could convince the servant that she was one of Rilla's teachers, it might just work. He was a guardian of the border so may have even greeted them when they arrived. Yes, she would go with that plan.

* * *

"Rilla?" a young servant boy walked up to her, hesitantly.

"Yes," she looked up at him, not recognising his face.

"Master Aurelius wants to see you, alone, outside the castle," the young boy told her.

"Where outside the castle?" Rilla asked, not entirely sure why Master Aurelius would want to meet her there and ask a servant to tell her.

"He didn't really say," the boy looked confused, "just outside the castle. Right after the midday meal."

Rilla thanked the boy and he hurried away. She looked after him thoughtfully.

"I don't like it," Plyke said instantly. "It could be the lintep we've been warned about. Master Aurelius has no reason to ask you to meet him outside the castle."

"We were told not to listen to any thought projections," Rilla reasoned. "They specifically told me that I would be sent messages with servants."

"But you aren't even meant to have a lesson with Master Aurelius this afternoon, are you?" Plyke asked.

"No," Rilla admitted, tapping her teeth together. "I was meant to have another lesson with Mistress Kayte before going to see Master Graham again. But maybe he just wants to show me something quickly before my lessons. I'll be back soon."

Before they could protest, Rilla hopped up from the bench and was heading towards the main door.

"I don't like it," Plyke insisted to Tika and Arishen. "She should be more careful. I'm going to find Lord Aaron. You two see if you can find any of the masters or mistresses. See if they can contact Master Aurelius to make sure the message really came from him."

The boys nodded and split up to find anyone they could to alert them to the situation. A sense of unease spread throughout Plyke. Something was very wrong with this situation. He hurried to find his grandfather.

* * *

Lishe kept part of her power surrounding the banwep, making sure that she couldn't even make a sound. Without a moment to lose, she ran through the city, keeping as much to the back streets as possible so as not to cause too much commotion. The banwep had no choice but to follow closely after her.

She knew it wouldn't take the brat long to go from the dining hall to the end of the bridge connecting the castle to the market place. For her plan to work, she had to get there before the girl. If her friends were around her when the servant gave her the message, they would surely alert the masters, maybe even Lord Aaron himself. She knew he'd lost a lot of his spirit when most of his family had died, but his granddaughter's arrival could have roused him from that state. He was one of the most powerful lintep she'd ever seen, which explained why all of his children had been so powerful, even if most of them had died before learning how to use their power.

Lishe pushed those thoughts to the back of her mind as she sprinted along the cobbled streets, dragging the banwep behind her. Just a little bit further and she would be there.

* * *

Rilla walked hurriedly across the perfect gardens towards the cobbled bridge. It annoyed her how protective the boys were being over her. After all, *she* was the one who had saved *them* so many times in the Outworld. Not the other way around. Besides, Master Aurelius was the only one who knew about her bond with Elessa. If he wanted to meet her outside the castle grounds, perhaps it was to discuss that in private, where no other masters or students could overhear them.

Once she reached the drawbridge, she slowed down. There would be no point making the guards on top of the watch tower suspicious. After struggling to keep herself to a relaxed stroll, Rilla finally found herself at the edge of the market place. She looked around for Master Aurelius but couldn't see him. The servant boy hadn't been specific on where to meet him.

Rilla stood still for a moment, trying to decide whether to stay and look

for the old master or return to the safety of the castle grounds. She began
to regret her rash decision. Maybe Plyke had been right. Master Aurelius
probably wouldn't have sent a runner to tell her to meet him outside the
castle. He had been one of the most vocal ones on how she should be kept
safe.

It was only when she turned to go back to the castle that she saw her – the
lady from Arishen's vision. What had they said? A pale lintep with long
straight black hair. Had they said anything about black tattoos on her arm?
They looked just like the tattoos the more senior members of the Council
had, but theirs were blue, not black. Rilla turned back, slowly, to take another
look. Could it really be her?

"Lishe?" she asked, almost in a whisper. The lintep was walking closer to
her, across the half-empty cobbled square. Rilla wanted to run away, but if
it really was her, she didn't want to turn her back on such a powerful and
dangerous lintep.

"I see my reputation precedes me," Lishe smiled icily. "Now don't make
a sound. I have your banwep with me and I won't hesitate to kill her if you
don't do exactly as I say."

Rilla watched in horrified silence as Lishe dragged a helpless Shuut out
from behind her and dumped her on the cobblestones. The remaining lintep
in the square quickly scattered away at this brutal display of power. There was
pleading in Shuut's eyes, but Rilla couldn't tell if it was for her to listen to the
lintep or to save herself.

"What do you want from me?" she found herself asking hoarsely.

"I want your power," Lishe replied, hungrily.

"Haven't you stolen enough as it is?" Rilla couldn't believe her ears. What
was she doing? It couldn't possibly help to goad this lintep.

"I can always use more," the black tattooed lintep replied dangerously.
"Now walk with me."

"No," Rilla remained where she was. "You're going to kill her whether I
listen to you or not, aren't you?"

"You're a clever brat, aren't you?" Lishe replied. "Being clever won't save
you from me."

Rilla watched in fascinated horror as a ball of fire came towards her.
Instinctively, she tried to drive the fire into the moat behind her, like she
had when Marilisa has shot sparks at Eliséo when they had first arrived. The
fire singed her as it flew past, but she managed to divert it enough to not
completely sear her skin. She drew the extra heat Lishe had burned her with
into a smaller ball of fire in front of her and shot it towards the lintep. She
screamed out in terror as Lishe deflected the small ball of fire towards Shuut.

The guards on the watch tower had noticed the commotion. They were
ringing the warning bells. Moments later, Lishe watched as Lord Aaron

himself came running across the bridge, with a much younger lintep and Masters Aurelius and Jorg close on his heels.

Within moments, the ball of fire burning the banwep was wrenched out of her control and flew into the moat, the water sizzling to quench it. She didn't know which of the lintep had just done that, but she wasn't taking any more chances with them.

"Enough," she shouted as she detached some of her stolen power and threw it around Rilla. She hated losing yet another bit of power, but she knew the lintep masters couldn't possibly know how to remove the mind snare and the brat would eventually die anyway. It irked her that she couldn't steal Rilla's power, but it was Nyssa's power she really wanted and she was not going to let them take the banwep away from her before she stole it once and for all.

As the brat crumpled to the cobblestones, Lishe turned to the burnt banwep. She was no use to Lishe anymore and would only slow her down as she tried to escape from Illaria. It only took a few moments for Lishe to smash through the rough wall in the banwep's mind to tie her power around Nyssa's power and start pulling it towards her. It was taking too long. She hadn't realised just how much power there was and Lord Aaron was approaching too quickly.

Seconds later, Lishe felt a wall of power close in around the banwep. She struggled to keep pulling Nyssa's power into herself, but couldn't do it. Lord Aaron's power was pulling his daughter's power and her power with it. She knew the old lintep was powerful, but she hadn't realised that his power matched her own so closely. The only advantage she had over him was that she could break off the power she had stolen from other lintep and leave that to do some damage as she fled.

In a moment of anger, she pushed through a tiny gap in the wall of power around the banwep with the least of the powers she had stolen, to put the mind snare on her once again. That done, she wrapped her own power around herself and disappeared from sight.

Chapter Fourteen – Mind Snare

Plyke ran to find Lord Aaron. If Rilla wouldn't listen to him and she really was walking into trouble, there was nothing else he could do to help her. It shouldn't be difficult to find Lord Aaron. He had returned to his chambers after the funeral. Plyke ran straight up the stairs, hoping he would still be there. Without pausing to knock, Plyke barged into the chambers to see Lord Aaron seated with his head resting on the table.

Aaron looked up angrily at the sudden intrusion. His irritation vanished as he saw the look on Plyke's face. Without asking permission, he quickly scanned the boy's mind to see what had happened. Instantly, he got to his feet and practically flew out the door, with Plyke only a few steps behind him.

Jorg, Aurelius, to the bridge NOW!

Lord Aaron whistled as loudly as he could, knowing it would only cover the grounds of the castle itself and no more, but that should be enough. Every master and mistress within hearing would feel the urgency behind the whistle and gather, even though he didn't name them. It was the best hope for his granddaughter.

The warning bells started ringing from the top of the watch towers as he ran into the outer courtyard. From the corner of his eye, he saw Aurelius and Jorg running towards the bridge, shadowed by Arishen and Tika. He barely spared them a glance as he charged ahead, across the bridge, as quickly as his old feet could take him. He was not going to let another member of his family die – not when he could save her!

In a moment of pure terror, he watched as Lishe did the unthinkable. A ball of fire soaring towards her was diverted to the defenceless banwep at her feet. Aaron wasted no time in sending out a thick tendril of his power to gather the ball of fire and throw it into the moat, where the heat couldn't be used against any of them.

He was half way across the bridge when he saw Rilla crumple to the ground. Lishe then turned her attention to the burnt banwep at her feet. Without thinking, he cast his power out to protect the banwep once again. If this was Nyssa's oldest daughter, then Lishe would be trying to steal her power and kill her at the same time. He couldn't let that happen.

He closed his power around the banwep, feeling a gap around her head where Lishe was trying to pull Nyssa's power out. When he tried to close the gap, he felt a smaller tendril of power slip past the gap, towards the banwep and then Lishe withdrew her power, allowing the gap to close.

In his distraction, Aaron did not focus on Lishe enough to stop her from disappearing in front of his eyes. By that time, all the masters and mistresses that had been within the castle grounds when the bells had started ringing and his whistle had been heard were all crossing the bridge at a run.

"She's disappeared into the city," he shouted at them. "Find her!"

Masters Jorg and Aurelius were the only two to stay behind. The others fanned out immediately to infiltrate the streets of the city, trying to find the rogue lintep. "What happened?" Jorg asked, as he knelt down beside him.

"What we feared might happen," Aaron replied, stonily. "Both of them have the same mind snare on them as young Plyke saw on Shuut."

"Shuut!" Tika yelled as Plyke brought him through the barrier. Aaron turned to find the three boys running towards them.

"Rilla," Arishen whispered at the same time, falling to his knees at her side. "Is she alive?"

Aaron looked at the three boys questioningly.

"You know this banwep?"

"This is Shuut, Lord Aaron," Plyke informed him. "My cousin, your oldest granddaughter. Eliséo probably called her Shadow if he mentioned her to you."

"I will not lose my granddaughters," Lord Aaron stood up straight and turned to Master Jorg. "I felt what Lishe did to Shuut so we can assume she did the same to Rilla. Let's bring them back to the castle. When Kayte returns, make sure she comes to Rilla's chamber. We may need her assistance in the end."

Aurelius quickly instructed the three boys to help them carry the injured sisters across the bridge, through the courtyard and up the stairs to Rilla's chambers. They set the girls down, side by side, on the lavish bed.

Without a second of hesitation, Lord Aaron set to work. Aurelius stood aside with Jorg and the boys as he took the heat out of Shuut's burns and directed them elsewhere. A flame instantly caught alight in the fireplace.

Without disturbing the lord, Aurelius instructed the three boys to get water from the bath in whatever they could find to carry it. By the time they returned, the fire was almost unbearably hot. They instantly doused the flame and went back to the bath to get more water. This went on for a few minutes, until Lord Aaron was satisfied that he had taken as much heat out of both Shuut and Rilla's burns as he could without hurting them.

"Aurelius, is Kayte on her way back yet?"

Aurelius shook his head.

"Do you think we can wait for her or do you want to try healing Shuut's burns yourself while Jorg and I work on their minds?"

"I think she can wait, Aaron," Aurelius was careful with his wording. "I would rather not leave the two of you unguarded while you work on such a difficult task."

Aaron understood what Aurelius was trying not to say. They all knew Lishe had disappeared and could be anywhere. They assumed, and hoped, that she had run off into the city towards the boundary of Illaria, but she could just as easily have slipped into the castle without anyone noticing.

"Very well," he nodded his head. He looked at the two girls in front of him and reached out a tendril of power to each of their minds. It only took him a few moments to confirm what he feared.

"Jorg, we were right about the mind snare. Lishe detached part of her power and wrapped it around their minds. But it wasn't her power. She used power from two different lintep, ones she clearly didn't mind detaching from herself, and completely ensnared them."

"Shall we work on one of them each then?" Jorg asked, willing to listen to directions for the first time in his life. Aurelius knew it was because of the display he'd seen on the bridge. Few lintep were as powerful as Aaron was. Lukys was probably the only one who still remembered the full extent of his skills. It was his cousin who had suggested he take the test to become a master all those years ago. Because of the decision not to do so, everyone underestimated Aaron's level of skill and power.

There was no way most lintep could have reached over such a distance to move a ball of fire like that, nor act quickly enough to prevent the black-tattooed Lishe from stealing Nyssa's power out of Shuut. They were in awe of him, but he cared nothing for that – he never had.

"Yes," Lord Aaron nodded. "You work on Rilla. If we manage to get the snares off, at least she knows how to contain her power. We don't know what condition Shuut is in with this extra power."

Plyke had been listening closely to their conversation. He knew they weren't saying everything, but trusting that the others knew what they were talking about. It was only at this last point that he realised they didn't know anything at all about Shuut.

"Um…"

The three older lintep turned at the sound from Plyke.

"Out with it boy," Aaron snapped at him, not unkindly.

"You should probably know that Shuut is a half-caste. I don't think she'd have much control over Nyssa's power at all, especially if it's as strong as you all remember it being."

"A half-caste?" Lord Aaron cried out angrily. "My daughter gave birth to a half-caste?"

Plyke stepped back involuntarily against the venom in his grandfather's voice. The outburst surprised the young boy. Lord Aaron had accepted Tika and Arishen into his life so readily. It took a moment for Plyke to remember how the rest of Lord Aaron's family had died. He must be furious with Nyssa for mating with a human. It suddenly dawned on Plyke that he would have only accepted Tika and Arishen because it meant keeping him and Rilla alive and safe in Illaria.

"Aaron, calm down," Jorg laid a hand on the Lord's arm. "You need to focus. Neither of us have done this before and we can't do it without a clear mind."

Plyke saw the immediate change in his grandfather. He started to piece it all together – why Rilla didn't want any of the Masters to touch her. They could change the way she felt with a single touch to her arm. He realised all his masters had already done that with him – probably even Lord Aaron had done it to him. He was disgusted that their power was used on each other so blithely – that it had been used on him without his knowledge. All four of them had been angry with Shuut for reading their surface thoughts. This was so much worse. Master Jorg wasn't reading Lord Aaron's thoughts, his was changing his feelings!

Moments later, a visibly calmer Lord Aaron went to sit on the bed next to Shuut as Master Jorg went to sit on the other side of the bed, next to Rilla. Master Aurelius stationed Tika and Arishen at the door to the antechamber, locking it so that they shouldn't be disturbed. Plyke was placed at the door to the bed chamber, with strict instructions to watch both his friends and the window behind the bed to make sure they weren't caught unawares by anyone.

Plyke watched as Master Aurelius settled himself at the foot of the bed, standing watch over the delicate proceedings at hand. The young lintep had no idea what Master Jorg and Lord Aaron were getting themselves into by plunging into the girls' minds, but he knew Master Aurelius was prepared to bring them back if they were in there for too long.

It was almost an hour later when Jorg pulled himself out of Rilla's mind. He looked over to Aurelius to see if there had been any change in Aaron. A shake of the head told him all he needed to know. He gently reached out with a tendril to the older lintep's mind and brought him back to the present moment.

"Are you having any sort of success?" Jorg asked when the Aaron finally focussed his eyes on him. "I keep trying to move the snare away, but it threatens to drag Rilla's power along with it."

"Yes, I noticed that. I've had some little success in creating a tear in the snare, but each time I do that, it begins to attach to my own power. Not in a snare, but as though it's afraid of not being attached to another power anymore."

"Can you bring the power into yourself, but keep it from encircling your mind, and then get rid of it somehow?" Aurelius asked from the foot of the bed. It was more a practical solution than a mind one, but that was his area of expertise.

"How would we get rid of it?" Jorg asked, not understanding his approach.

"Shoot it out." The tall boy, the seer, called out from the other room. He left his post to join them in the bed chamber.

"When Nyssa was giving her power to Shuut, it looked like she simply shot it out of her mouth and into Shuut. If you don't want the power to go into anyone, would it work to just shoot it into the sky or something?"

Jorg looked at the boy in in shock. *How did a human come up with a plausible idea?* It was almost the perfect solution, except for one thing. He didn't know what would happen when they shot it into the sky. Would it come back down and attach itself to an unsuspecting lintep?

"It could work," Aurelius stated, rubbing his stubbly chin. "I wouldn't shoot it into the sky. That could prove to be a bit too dangerous. But if we get a wooden box to contain it in until we figure out what to do with it, that might work."

"Can we put them together in that?" Jorg asked, pointing to the wooden chest at the foot of Rilla's bed.

"I can't see the harm in that," Aurelius looked at Aaron. "After all, we don't need to keep them separate. We just need to find a way to release them, the way that every lintep's power is released when they naturally die."

With a nod, Aaron moved to open the chest and started emptying the contents. They were his sons' clothes. Even years after his children died, their clothes were still in perfect condition. Removing himself from those thoughts, Aaron continued to empty the chest with the help of Arishen and Plyke. Together, the boys carried all of the clothes and placed them into the wooden wardrobe against the wall. Once that was done, the boys returned to the posts Aurelius had assigned to them and kept watch as best they could.

Aaron looked at Jorg and began with a nod. Lord Aaron took his time, delving carefully into Shuut's mind. He knew that, being a half-caste, she would have little, if any, control over her power. Carefully, he tore a rift in the mind snare. Before Nyssa's power had a chance to react, he pushed some of his own power through the rift to encircle her power himself. With the rest of his power, he carefully drew the mind snare in a long, steady stream towards the chest at the end of the bed.

Once he was done, he kept it at bay and opened his eyes to look over at Jorg. The mind master was struggling with the task. Beads of sweat were emerging on his forehead. Aaron made a rash decision and took a third part of his power and sent it towards Jorg, helping him to pull the mind snare away from Rilla's mind. It was a more powerful one than the one around Shuut, but it was no match for Aaron's own power, even if his was already split three ways.

Carefully, he and Jorg worked together to drain the rest of the mind snare into the chest and close it firmly before pulling away from it.

"It's done," Jorg said as he slumped onto a nearby chair.

"It's not," Aaron replied in frustration. "Every time I try to take my power away from the chest, I feel the two powers inside try to latch onto mine. I need a way to get them away from all people, even humans at this point, or they will latch onto the first person they come in contact with."

"Can you give that task to someone else while you tend to Shuut's mind?" Aurelius asked him gently. "You can't keep your power split like that for long and concentrate on both."

"Jorg?" Aaron looked over at him, hopefully.

"I can't do that," the master waved his hands and backed further into his chair.

"Can you contain Nyssa's power in her daughter?" Aurelius suggested an alternative.

"Is it stronger than Plyke's power?" Jorg asked, hesitantly.

"I don't know, but it's not as wild," Aaron told him. "She has a hastily built wall in there. If you can push it back in, I think you can manage it while Aurelius and I figure out what to do with the chest."

Jorg nodded in resignation and walked over to the banwep. Aaron began to withdraw his power as he felt Jorg's power coming in to replace his.

"What now?" Aaron looked at Aurelius. "Like you said, I can't split my power forever. I can't contain those powers in the chest forever. At the very least, at some point, I'll fall asleep whether I want to or not."

"I have an idea, but please don't dismiss it before thinking it through," Aurelius said, already half shying away from him.

Can Aurelius' suggestion truly be so terrible? Aaron kept silent, waiting to hear what he would say.

"We could bury it in the crypt. It doesn't have to be near your family. It doesn't even need to be near any of the coffins down there. We could bury it in the furthest corner, as deep down as we can and quickly cover it with dirt so that you can take your power away and leave the other two powers trapped," Aurelius finished in a rush.

"That's an abhorrent idea!" Aaron snarled.

"It would just be until we work out how to free it properly," Aurelius assured him. "There is no safer place to put it. King Lukys alone has the keys to the crypt. No lintep could accidentally come across it and no one other than the seven of us, including Lukys, would know about it."

Aaron bristled as he listened to the explanation. He knew Aurelius was right and couldn't think of any other alternative himself, which just went further to irritate him.

"Call him then," he said to the master in defeat. "Call him and tell him your suggestion. If, and only if, he agrees, will I agree to it as well."

Aurelius nodded and focused his mind. He searched for King Lukys and found him at the top of one of the watchtowers. With the same ease as though they were standing side by said, he sent his king a message.

"He'll be here in a few minutes," he looked at Aaron apologetically. "It will only be until we find another solution, I give you my word."

It took longer than Aurelius expected for King Lukys to knock on the door to Rilla's chambers. Hurriedly, he unlocked the door and was surprised to see not only King Lukys, but Mistress Kayte on the other side.

"The guards told me what happened to the two girls, so I called Kayte back to help with healing them," Lukys explained as they walked through the antechamber to the bed chamber.

Kayte immediately flew into action on Shuut's injuries. Lukys knew her skill was such that she could tell at a single glance the banwep was worse off than Rilla. It amused him to see Jorg shuffle out of her way as she worked on the banwep. The past few days had done a lot to shatter the master's air of superiority over others.

"Lord Aaron, you put the rest of us to shame," Kayte chided him. "You really ought to be a master yourself with all you are capable of."

"Not now Kayte," his cousin brushed the compliment aside. "Lukys, do you really think it's a wise idea?"

"I can't think of a better solution myself for the time being," Lukys replied uneasily. "I have an idea of what we could do, but I think we should safely get that chest out of the way before we speak about it."

It could be the crystal dragons are the key to helping us, Lukys elaborated directly to Aaron's mind. *Let's get this chest into the crypt and talk about it tonight.*

Aaron nodded and went to pick up the chest with Aurelius. Between the two of them, it was manageable. Lukys opened the door to the hallway and led the way for them down through the stairwells, across the inner courtyard and out to the manicured gardens. There was too much commotion at the front of the castle for anyone to take much notice of the three of them walking quickly and quietly towards the crypt.

Lukys took a heavy set of brass keys out of his pocket and fumbled through them to find the key to the crypt. Once he'd opened the door and let Aaron and Aurelius in, he quickly locked the door behind them. The three of them walked down the plain stone stairs to the crypt floor.

The lanterns, which had been lit for Nyssa's interment, were now extinguished. The only light was a soft blue glow from the luminescent bitter oyster mushrooms that grew in the crypt. Only the royal family and a select few of the masters knew the rare mushroom grew here. It was how they created the blue tattoos for masters and mistresses. The tattoos only glowed in the dark so most students had probably never even noticed it. This was one of the ways in which they could determine if a lintep had earned their tattoos or not – the bitter oyster was not found anywhere else in the Outworld that they knew of.

Lukys chose a corner of the vast room as far away from interred bodies as he could. As Aaron and Aurelius set the box down, he looked around for a shovel before noticing that the others were already using their power to dig up the dirt as quickly as they could. He joined them in their task and in less than a half hour, they'd dug a hole as deep as any grave.

He watched on as Aaron and Aurelius used their power to lower the chest into the hole. Now for the dangerous part. He hoped Aurelius' plan would indeed work.

"Once I take my power away, we'll only have a matter of seconds before the two powers in the chest try to reach out and cling to mine," Aaron warned them. "We'll have to work together to cover the chest with as much dirt as we can as quickly as we can. Are you ready?"

Aaron counted to three and jerked his power away from the chest. The three of them simultaneously used their power to shove the dirt back down the hole until it was full again. They looked at each other warily. Lukys hadn't felt the rogue powers attach to him and it wasn't likely they would have simply floated away.

"I think it worked," Aurelius ventured a guess.

"It was a good idea, Aurelius," Aaron admitted. "I just wish we'd had another option. We can't leave them down here permanently. What would happen if someone came across the box one day and opened it to find themselves burdened with another lintep's power or, worse still, in the same mind snare that my granddaughters had?"

"That day would be far away, Aaron," Lukys reassured him. "I have the only key to the crypt. The chest will be safe here until we can figure out how to release the power the way it should have been when it left its lintep's body."

"Speaking of your granddaughters, we should really get back to them," Aurelius suggested, shifting uneasily from one foot to the other. "If Jorg struggled to contain Plyke's power by himself, it's likely he won't be able to keep Nyssa's power at bay in Shuut's mind for much longer."

At the mention of his grandchildren, Aaron immediately swung into action. Lukys had to run to get ahead of him on the stairs to unlock the crypt door once more.

Chapter Fifteen – Trapdoor

Eliséo was sitting quietly in his nook with Elessa when Rilla was attacked. He had watched Nyssa's burial through Rilla's eyes that morning and was now whiling away his time reading a book until Queen Liessa called for him.

Elessa immediately grabbed his attention. Eliséo watched on in horror as he saw the black-tattooed lintep through the girl's eyes. Rilla barely had time to react and defend herself from the fire Lishe shot towards her before the mind snare was placed on her. Panicked, he turned to Elessa when he could no longer feel Rilla's mind.

She's withdrawn herself completely in her tower, Elessa told him. *She must have remembered what Plyke told them about the mind snare when it was placed on Shadow.*

Can you feel the mind snare around her? Eliséo asked in frustration. This wasn't the first time that he'd been blocked from Rilla's mind, however unlike the last time, he wasn't certain he could reach her if he tried.

I feel that she is trapped, but she's keeping herself locked tightly in her tower. She may not even be able to tell if her circumstances change, Elessa tried to explain. *I can feel hands on her body, lifting her up.*

Can you tell if it's Lishe? Eliséo demanded to know.

It's more than one person carrying her, Elessa answered uncertainly. *Unless Lishe had other people helping her, I doubt it's her. Besides, someone stopped the fire from burning Shuut.*

Eliséo watched as Elessa replayed the scene from Rilla's memory. There was anger in Lishe's eyes as she watched the fire move from Shuut to the moat. Only after that did Rilla collapse.

Lord Aaron! Eliséo exclaimed. *It could have been their grandfather.*

He hasn't used his powers in years, Elessa reminded him.

He thought he'd lost his entire family for years, Eliséo pointed out. *Can you tell what's happening now?*

I can only feel what she feels on her skin, Elessa told him. The elf waited patiently as she described to him what he could only imagine was someone placing her on a bed and then eventually heat being removed from her burns.

Eliséo sat stone still for hours as Elessa told him what was happening. He was oblivious to his own surroundings. Anyone could have happened upon him and taken him completely by surprise. Fortunately, it was only Kora who walked up to him and shook him by the shoulder. Instantly alert, he wildly pushed her away from him and went for his weapons only to realise they weren't strapped to him.

"Eliséo, it's just me," the lintep held out her hands and backed away.

"Kora, what are you doing here?" he asked irritably. She'd taken his concentration off Rilla, just when it appeared the mind snare was no longer on her. He wanted to get back to his link with her to see if she was coming out of her tower herself, or if the masters were helping her to know she was safe. Did she need him?

"I came to ask you about Plyke, but it seems I've interrupted you at a bad time," she hesitated and made to walk away. Eliséo was torn between trying to convince Kora to go to Illaria and watching over Rilla to see what was happening.

Talk to Kora, I will watch Rilla, Elessa reassured him.

"Kora, wait," Eliséo called out to the lintep before she left. "You're not interrupting me. What did you want to ask me?"

Kora stopped, but did not turn to face him. "Is Plyke angry with me?"

It was probably the only question Eliséo wasn't prepared for.

"That's not really something I think he'd want me to discuss with you," he tried to deflect.

"That's your diplomatic way of saying 'yes', isn't it?" she turned and faced him with puffy, red eyes. She'd clearly been crying. He hadn't realised he'd affected her so much with his words the previous night, even though he'd hoped he had.

"It's complicated, Kora," he motioned for her to sit down with him and waited until she had before he continued. "You know your entire family is more powerful than the rest of the lintep in Illaria. He's not angry with you for keeping his identity secret, or for teaching him to build such a magnificent wall – Master Aurelius commented on what a marvellous job he did right from when he was a young child." Eliséo caught the brief smile on Kora's face before it disappeared.

"But he's angry with me for not taking him to Illaria myself or teaching him more before his power peaked." It was more of a statement than a question. She knew it was true and she knew he had every right to be angry with her. Eliséo could feel her heart ache even with the distance between them. It was one of the few things that set him apart from other elves. Eléna had told him years ago that only elves in her line could feel things so keenly in those around them without skin contact.

"Mostly he's confused, Kora," Eliséo told her. "They all are. No one understands why you left and never came back. All Lord Aaron told me, years ago, is that you spent hours in the library for weeks on end before suddenly deciding to leave Illaria and not telling anyone what you had been researching or why you were going away." There was such a long moment of silence that Eliséo feared the lintep would not speak at all.

"I thought they would try to stop me if they knew what I was doing," Kora breathed out the words, barely louder than a whisper. Eliséo found himself leaning in closer to hear her.

"If they knew you were doing what?"

He'd never bothered thinking about the reason for Kora leaving Illaria.

She'd done it years ago without a word. Most people assumed it was simply because she didn't agree with many others in their opinions surrounding humans. From the sounds of it, there was a much greater reason than that.

"I found a mention of it one day in the library," she looked up at him scared, but defiant. "I just wanted to know more about my grandmother. Father barely knew her at all and Uncle Lukys was usually too busy to talk to me about her. But sometimes, just a few times really, he told me some wonderful stories about her and how she wanted to help the humans. He told me that she only fought against the humans who were afraid of magic and attacked Illaria out of cowardice. She strove to help other humans, ones who were afraid but didn't attack.

"That's how she died, you know," Kora pursed her lips. "She was trying to save some humans who'd been caught in the fight without wanting to and some rebel humans caught her off guard and killed her before any other lintep could save her."

"I thought she died in battle," Eliséo frowned. This wasn't the story he knew so well. He wondered whether even his mother knew the truth of it.

"So do most people," Kora nodded, knowingly, "but King Edmao, Uncle Luyks' father, told him what really happened. The story was changed over time because people wanted to see her as a heroine, dying in the heat of battle. They didn't want to know that she died while trying to save humans from the war she had accidentally started."

Eliséo stared at her, dumbfounded. It took a moment for his mind to start working again.

"What has that got to with what you were researching in the library?"

"When the war ended, Princess Ophélie, Rilla and Edmao's little sister, wrote down everything about the war and the events following it. She could see that the story was already being twisted and wanted to have the true events written down somewhere, even if no one but her family knew it was there."

"I don't understand," Eliséo interrupted her. "Why would Ophélie do that, preserve the true history of what happened, when it showed that not all humans are horrible people? I thought her side of the family hated humans more than most."

"That's what I asked Uncle Lukys when he first told me," Kora smiled sadly at him. "Ophélie adored Rilla and followed wherever she led. It was her idea to set up the Paradises once the war ended. She was trying to create a safe haven for humans who wanted to live away from the fight between those who had power and those who were scared or jealous of that power. She thought up the idea herself and they really were charming places that she designed. They were to be self-sufficient in every way so that the humans within would never want for anything but could also leave any time they wanted to."

"Does Lord Kynon know this?" Eliséo was struggling to believe her but was immediately rewarded with a withering look from the lintep.

"Of course he does, but he hates humans more than most because, in the end, Ophélie was also killed by humans, even after she helped create their Paradises. He thinks all humans are ungrateful savages who deserve to die."

"I still don't understand what any of this has to do with what you were doing in the library, or why you left Illaria," Eliséo came back to the same issue. He could tell she was trying to avoid actually telling him what she was doing but could not understand why.

"After mother, Vaugh, Fredryck and Adina died … well, I wanted to know more about everything – about the war, about the Paradises – everything. So I started to search through the library to find out all I could.

"I found Ophélie's journals about the war and the days following it. I found her plans for the Paradises and how she went about helping to create them. I read more about it than I had even heard rumours of and it astounded me. The way she used her power and convinced other lintep to use their power, well, it was something that only master lintep could dream of and carry out.

"She wrote about things that my teachers had never mentioned before, all to do with how to create the barriers so that humans could leave whenever they wanted to but only ever enter once in their life. It was amazing, even more intricate than the barriers put up in and around Illaria." Kora paused for a long while. Eliséo thought she wouldn't go on.

"Then I notice that some pages of her last journal had been torn out. After all of those pages, the prophecy was written out. It was the first time I'd seen it. I was still so young at the time, I hadn't even finished my training. But I had to know what had happened. Why there was a prophecy that seemed to talk of the destruction of Paradises in the very same journal that told of how idyllic they were created to be.

"I remember running to Uncle Lukys and asking him about the prophecy. He looked at me with such sad eyes as he told me all he knew. All of Ophélie's plans were ruined because of a few power hungry lintep."

"You mean Erton isn't the only one?" Eliséo asked, horrified to discover that King Lukys knew anything about the Paradises.

"No, all the Paradises were meant to have a single lintep stay on for a few weeks, to help with anything the humans needed, but they were meant to return to Illaria soon afterwards," Kora began to reveal what was missing from Ophélie's journals. "Uncle Lukys told me that Ophélie came back to Illaria to meet up with the others, but less than half of them returned. She waited a full year before going out in search of them, hoping that they had just been delayed but she knew the truth. They had stayed on to rule over the humans. As they were all masters or mistresses, it would not have been difficult at all to bend the humans to their will."

Eliséo's head fell into his hands as he tried to understand what had happened. The Paradises had been corrupted right from the beginning – not all of them, but most.

"So she went to try to persuade the lintep to leave the Paradises," Eliséo thought out loud. "But how could she enter any of them when she had already entered one?"

"That's what I wondered too," Kora said quietly.

"So you went into the Outworld, alone, to find them?" Eliséo asked incredulously.

"Ophélie had a map at the front of her last journal," Kora told him, guiltily. "I made a copy of it and set out to find them all. I didn't expect to be able to enter all of them. They must have just modified the barriers from the ones in Illaria to admit humans once and allow them to leave, but didn't have any effect whatsoever on lintep."

"How many did you find?" Eliséo barely knew which question to ask next.

"I found eleven of them before I …" Kora bit off the end of her sentence.

"Before you fell pregnant with Plyke and refused to abandon him in a Paradise or force him to follow you on your quest when he was still a baby," Eliséo ventured. Kora turned away from him, but he didn't need to look her in the eye to feel her anger and self-loathing.

"You have to tell him, Kora."

"I can't go back there," she shook her head, staring at her feet. "I can't. Not after all this time. Not after I failed."

"You failed nothing," the elf reached out a hand and lifted her chin to meet her eyes. "You set out to find out what Ophélie suspected. You now know firsthand why the prophecy came about and you know where to find them. All that remains is for you to return to Illaria …"

"And what?" Kora asked him angrily, tears stinging her eyes. "Convince the lintep to help me destroy the Paradises somehow? They couldn't care less about humans. In fact, I can think of quite a few of them who would be happy to know the situation. What I can't think of is a single lintep who would rally to my cause and help me find a way to destroy Ophélie's worst nightmare."

"Rilla will help you," Eliséo spoke quietly, "Plyke will too."

"Just because my sister was stupid enough to let the crystal dragons manipulate her into having a daughter and naming her Rilla, doesn't mean the poor young girl *is* the prophecy child, or that she's willing to help me."

"Whether she is the prophecy child or not, she *is* willing to help you and so is your son," Eliséo persisted. "They know better than most what Paradises have become."

"Even if they are, what use are two untrained Paradisian children going to be?" Kora asked him hopelessly. "I need a band of masters to help me and I'm certain they won't. I don't even know how to destroy the Paradises. I just know it needs to be done."

"Then imagine how Rilla feels," Eliséo tried one last time. "She didn't even know she was a lintep until a few months ago and had the prophecy thrust on her at the same time. Like you said, she's an untrained Paradisian. How is she meant to destroy the Paradises? Perhaps together, the two of you, with Plyke, can solve the problem."

She isn't waking, Elessa interrupted Eliséo's conversation with Kora. *I need you to help me with Rilla.*

Is she still safe? Eliséo instantly diverted his attention to the more urgent situation. *Has Lishe come back?*

She's safe, but if she doesn't wake up soon, the masters will try to breach her wall to get to her.

"What's going on?" Kora asked, alerted by both the glow and fear he knew she could see in his eyes.

"Promise me you'll leave for Illaria, first thing in the morning."

"What? No!" Kora shook her head emphatically. "I told you I'm never going back there, especially not with Lishe stealing power."

"Kora, *please*. Your son and your niece need you now more than ever. They are both in danger. They're frightened, confused and alone."

"My father will look after them," she insisted, turning away from him.

Eliséo, now. Elessa urged him.

"Kora, I don't have time to talk about this now. Go to Illaria or don't, I need to be alone right now," Eliséo stood and indicated that she should leave.

"No," she replied, refusing to stand. "What's going on with you and your tree? Why do you need to be alone and how can you possibly *know* that they're in danger?"

Someone is trying to get into her mind, Elessa warned him.

Can you get in without letting them know? he asked. *Did she ever bother to think of giving you a quick way in?*

No, but together, we can open her trapdoor before the lintep do, only if we hurry.

The urgency in her thoughts was not lost on Eliséo. If Kora wouldn't leave, then he would just help Elessa with her there and not say a word. He would have preferred to do this alone, but time was of the essence. Elessa couldn't tell which lintep was trying to breach her wall, but if it was anyone other than Master Aurelius, it could be the end of their secret.

Turning away from the lintep, Eliséo immediately joined Elessa at the top of Rilla's wall and together they started battering on the trapdoor, calling out her name as loudly as they could. It was not the best strategy, but Rilla had built such effective defences, she left them no other choice. All they could do was hope that the intruding lintep was still too far down her wall to hear their shouts.

* * *

Master Aurelius kept pace with Lord Aaron. He was more afraid for Rilla than for Master Jorg and Shuut. If anyone breached her wall, it could mean her bond with Eliséo's tree would be revealed. It would be best if he was the one to reach out to her, if he got the chance.

The two of them burst into Rilla's room with Lukys only a few steps behind. Aurelius took in the situation. Kayte was still sitting by the banwep's side, healing the burns as best she could. They were quite bad, but at least Lord Aaron had managed to remove all the heat from them. All that remained was for Kayte to fix the skin and any other damage that lay below the skin.

Jorg was slumped on the floor, his eyes closed in concentration with sweat beading down his forehead. He was so exhausted that he didn't even glance up at their intrusion.

"Aaron, Jorg needs your help," Kayte told them, looking up briefly from the banwep. "I'm healing the girl as best as I can, but he told me her wall was crumbling before he fell to the floor. I'm no mind master – he needs *you.*"

"You help him," Aurelius urged Lord Aaron. "I'll see if I can't help Rilla to wake up."

"What about me?" Lukys asked.

"You can heal Rilla's burns. They aren't as bad as her sister's so you should be fine, even if you are out of practice," Kayte smiled mischievously at him. Lukys raised an eyebrow at her, but sat down beside Rilla and set to work without a word.

Aurelius didn't know how attuned Lukys would be to her bond with the elf's tree, but he could only hope the king didn't notice anything amiss as Lukys worked on her burns. Aurelius took a deep, calming breath and placed his hand on her forehead. The old master didn't need the skin contact, but it made things just that little bit easier. At the moment, he needed all the help he could get.

Something wasn't right. He could instantly feel another presence. *What is that? Another lintep? No, Aaron has well and truly removed the mind snare from his granddaughters.*

Aurelius remembered Rilla's wall. She had built the tall tower with thicker walls at the bottom and thinner ones up the top with a wooden trapdoor to seal it off. Breathing deeply to steady his nerves for whatever he would find, Aurelius began the long climb to the top of her tower. In his haste, it took less time than he'd anticipated to reach the top of the tower. What he found there amazed him.

Eliséo, is that you? he asked timidly, hoping his thoughts would carry through to the elf as he and another entity shouted out Rilla's name over and over again.

Aurelius, what happened?

The elf's thoughts felt strange, different to lintep and human minds. Aurelius struggled to work with him.

Lishe attacked. Lord Aaron managed to get the mind snare off both girls, but the banwep's wall is crumbling and Rilla hasn't woken up yet. I need to get her out of her tower somehow.

That's what we're trying to do, another voice interrupted their conversation. Aurelius couldn't get past the alien voice. It wasn't a lintep, human or elf.

Elessa, keep calm, Eliséo reprimanded his tree. *We can all work together now. She can't seem to hear us from inside her tower. She must have completely withdrawn in there when the mind snare was placed on her and doesn't realise she's safe now.*

Have you found the lock? Aurelius asked them, trying to keep his wits in this extraordinary situation.

Elessa, you keep calling out to her. Aurelius and I will find the lock and try to open the door somehow.

Aurelius examined the wooden trapdoor to see how Rilla had created it. It was a rough wooden door with a keyhole and two hinges but no handle.

My skills do not extend to picking locks, he told the elf after a few moments of examination. *She's even thought to put the hinges on the other side of the door so they can't be unscrewed from the outside. That's one clever young girl.*

Yes, Eliséo agreed. *Though sometimes a little too clever for her own good.*

I see only two options before us then. We either try to burn the door, though I would rather leave that option to last, or one of us tries to push ourselves through the keyhole.

Let's try the keyhole, Eliséo instantly chose the safer option. *It will only work if you can get a tendril through. My powers are not the same as yours. With the door closed to me, I can't reach her.*

Aurelius recoiled at the idea that he would have to do it himself. As it was, Rilla barely trusted anyone in Illaria. It was possible that he was about to ruin that fragile relationship with her because of this unavoidable action.

He thinned out his power to the width of a thread of material – any thicker than that and he had no chance to get through, so small was the keyhole. Gathering his courage, the old lintep master attempted to invade his student's mind.

Slowly and carefully, he sent his thin tendril into the keyhole. To his surprise, it passed through without resistance. He waited until he had fed a good portion of his power through the keyhole and let it all pool together. Only then did he attempt to speak to the young lintep.

Rilla …

He barely finished saying her name before the girl reacted to the intrusion. In a panic, she opened her trapdoor and tried to force him to retreat from her mind without realising who he was. She was stretching his power too thinly through the keyhole. If she didn't release him, she could detach his power from his body, killing him.

Rilla, stop! Aurelius heard the elf cry out in alarm.

Eliséo? The girl asked in confusion.

Aurelius took the momentary lapse in concentration to stop his power snapping in two and quickly moved back up to her trapdoor while she was distracted. He was distantly aware of Lukys' uneasiness. If they didn't hurry, Rilla's secret bond with an elf's tree would be revealed in the worst possible way.

Let Aurelius out of your mind, the elf told her urgently. *He had to get in through your keyhole. You're pushing his power the wrong way. You could kill him if you don't stop.*

Aurelius? the girl asked in confusion. *I don't understand. What's happening? I thought it was Lishe.*

She opened her eyes and quickly took in the scene around her. She was back in her chambers with Shuut lying next to her. Aurelius was on his knees, head in his hands, screaming out in pain. Aaron, Kayte and Jorg were staring at him, horrified. To her consternation, Lukys was looking straight into her green eyes, glowing as brightly as an elf's.

Terrified, Rilla closed her eyes tightly and tried to help Aurelius push his power back out through the keyhole as Lukys swiftly climbed the height of her tower.

Eliséo, get out!

She felt Eliséo and Elessa retreat from her mind as Lukys neared the top of the tower. Aurelius finally pushed the last of his power out of the keyhole and Rilla slammed the trapdoor shut, leaving only a thin tendril of her power outside the tower.

Peace, Lukys, Aurelius soothed Lukys, reaching out a hand to his arm, actively seeking to calm him.

What is she doing to you? Lukys stopped his headlong rush to rescue him. Aurelius could feel his power pooling around the thin tendril Rilla had allowed to remain outside her tower.

It was a momentary misunderstanding is all, Aurelius reassured him. *She was simply trying to defend herself from my intrusion.*

She had you screaming in pain on the floor, Lukys' voice remained level and calm, though Aurelius could tell he was anything but calm.

Yes, she's quite a strong young lintep.

And her eyes were glowing, like an elf's.

Aurelius froze. Lukys had said it quite calmly, but their powers were all mingling in her mind. They could feel the king's anger and fear – he knew Rilla could too.

It was just the reflection from the fireplace, Rilla attempted to explain it away.

That fire was doused long ago, girl. Explain yourself now or I will breach your wall myself to find out what's happening.

Later, my king, Aurelius pleaded. *Might we explain it to you in your chambers once the others have left?*

I think not, replied the king stonily. *You can both come to my chambers now.*

Rilla opened her eyes as she felt the two older lintep's powers retreat from her mind. She avoided King Lukys' eyes and stared, terrified, at Aurelius who was heaving himself up off the floor beside her bed. Jorg and Kayte were helping him to his feet, while Aaron looked on helplessly. He wasn't struggling to contain his daughter's power in his granddaughter, but it left him free for little else.

"Aurelius, are you all right?" Lord Aaron asked.

"Yes, yes. Just marvelling at the damage an untrained lintep can do, even to a master as old as I am," Aurelius smiled through clenched teeth.

"Aaron, will you be able to work with Jorg and Kayte to help the banwep? I need to steal young Rilla and Aurelius for a while," Lukys refused to delay the conversation that Rilla was dreading.

"Yes, we'll be fine," her grandfather reassured him. "Just ring for food on your way out. The girls will need to regain their strength after this afternoon's ordeal. I fear the banwep may have been through much on her journey here."

Lukys only nodded as he motioned for Rilla and Aurelius to join him.

Chapter Sixteen – Bonds

"Explain yourself!"

Rilla squirmed away from King Lukys. He'd barely waited to shut the door to his chambers before rounding on her.

"And before you try to lie to me, understand that I will have no hesitation in breaching your mind as violently as I must to get to the truth."

She involuntarily took a step back from him, bumping into Aurelius as she did so. The master tried to place a calming hand on her arm only to have her flinch, wild eyed, away from him.

"Rilla, you don't have a choice," Aurelius held up his hands, trying to placate her. "He already saw your eyes. Just tell him."

She looked from one to the other, terrified. Eliséo had told her she could admit to a bond with a tree. All she had to do now was not let anyone know whose tree it was and most of all that it was a royal elf.

"There was an … incident in Silvaren," Rilla told him evasively, pushing the red curls out of her face.

"An incident," Lukys raised an eyebrow at her. "Would this incident have anything to do with why your eyes were glowing so brightly?"

"Yes," she whispered.

"I don't like being the last one to find things out. I assume Aurelius already knows at least some of the story, so you had better tell me everything."

"One of the trees bound herself to me."

Rilla supplied as little information as she thought she would get away with. She watched Lukys' reaction carefully. His face paled and his eyes widened, but he remained absolutely motionless. Rilla turned to Aurelius, helplessly.

"It appears she had no control over the situation," the master stepped in, trying to smooth over the revelation. "The tree decided of her own accord to create the bond and now that it's done, it cannot be undone."

"Whose tree is it?" Lukys asked the one question she couldn't answer. Rilla's heart started racing as she wiped her sweaty hands against her pants. Lukys didn't take his eyes off her.

"Don't force me to breach your mind, Rilla. You may have almost crippled Aurelius, but doubtless he tried to enter your tower more gently than I will."

"I can't tell you," Rilla shied away from him. "I promised I wouldn't. Don't make me go back on my word."

Aurelius tried to intervene on her behalf. "Lukys, don't force her hand. She has seen and done things none of us could dream of in our worst nightmares at her age. Please grant this favour she begs of you. She can and *will* answer any other question you have."

Rilla almost protested until she saw the pleading look the master gave her. She waited for endless moments as Lukys considered the proposal. Without a word, he walked from the more public audience room to his private, inner chambers. Rilla and Aurelius followed close on his heels.

Elessa! Rilla called out as soon as everyone's attention was averted from her eyes. *I'm in trouble. I need you and Eliséo to watch through my eyes and tell me what to say.*

What happened? It was Eliséo who answered her panicked plea.

Lukys has taken me and Master Aurelius to his chambers and is interrogating me, she replied as quickly as she could. *He saw my eyes glowing so I've already had to admit I'm bound to a tree but I told him I can't tell him whose tree it was.*

She cut the connection as soon as she saw Lukys slow down. He did not need to know that she was talking with them.

"Sit," he commanded. Rilla immediately obeyed, sitting close to Aurelius.

"Does anyone else know about this bond? Your companions, other elves, anyone?"

"My companions don't know," Rilla instantly replied.

"So at least one of the elves does," Lukys persisted. "I assume Eliséo knows, as Master Aurelius knew and tried to help you hide by going into your mind to wake you himself even though that is not his area of expertise. Would I be right to assume Queen Liessa knows?"

Rilla shook her head, not quite trusting herself to speak.

"No?" Lukys arched an eyebrow. "Then perhaps Lady Eléna was consulted about it before you left Silvaren?"

That's safe enough to admit, Eliséo told her, knowing her eyes would suddenly flash bright green.

"Lady Eléna knows," Rilla admitted, pointedly not mentioning that so did Master Ensil.

"Is your tree telling you what to say?" Lukys asked, suspiciously.

"I am being advised on what is safe to reveal," Rilla replied, crossing her arms defensively, not correcting him on his assumption that the tree was the one speaking.

"Does she have control over you?"

"It doesn't work like that," Rilla shook her head, disgusted by the idea.

"Then explain to me how it *does* work," Lukys replied more calmly than she knew he felt.

"Well, I can see what she sees and vice versa," Rilla began, cautiously, hoping Eliséo or Elessa would stop her if she was saying too much. "We can talk to each other."

"So if the elf who shares that tree is in Illaria, he or she can alert Queen Liessa about Lishe and Nyssa," Lukys interrupted, instantly seeing the advantages to the situation.

"Well, yes, but their queen doesn't know about the bond."

"But you could ask the elf to tell Lady Eléna, who could in turn tell the queen," Aurelius suggested.

She already knows, Eliséo told Rilla. *I told Liessa what I suspected and she awaits a message from Illaria to confirm it.*

"What did she just tell you?" Lukys asked as soon as he noticed her eyes glow.

"The elves are aware that there is a dangerous lintep who may have killed Nyssa," Rilla answered carefully. "They are waiting for a message to reach them to confirm or deny it."

"The message was sent yesterday," Lukys told her. "It will only arrive in a few days at the earliest. We should use your bond to communicate more easily with the elves."

"No!" Rilla cried out in a panic. "That would only increase the danger to the elf and possibly the tree. I won't do that to either of them."

"Even if I, as your king, command it?" Lukys demanded.

"I don't remember having sworn any fealty to you," Rilla replied quietly. The room suddenly chilled. Rilla could see flames sparking in Lukys' eyes and immediately called up the mist Eléna had shown her how to command, as thickly as she could.

"What just happened? Where has she gone?" Lukys asked Aurelius, without taking his eyes off the spot where Rilla had been sitting only moments before.

"She's probably still there, my king, but is protecting herself from you," Aurelius again tried to defuse the situation. "The flames before your eyes have probably scared her witless."

"She should be scared of more than flames. Make her come back," the king commanded angrily.

"I'm certain she can still hear you, my king. Perhaps you can persuade her yourself."

"*Persuade* her?" Lukys asked incredulously. "I grant her and her human companions asylum in Illaria to appease my cousin and you want me to *persuade* her to obey me?"

Rilla, what are you doing? Eliséo tried to reason with the girl. *This is not the best way to curry favour with your king.*

He's not my king. Rilla's reply sounded sulky even to her own mind. *Besides, he was threatening me.*

He only threatened you because you refused to cooperate with him. Tell him that the elf refuses to submit to the request as it will place them in danger. Before she could protest, he continued. *Then you tell him about your increased lifespan and the fact that you can use some elf magic, as he will plainly be able to see that by now.*

Are you sure? Rilla asked him hesitantly. Once she felt his reassurance, she dissipated the mist and sat straight backed, head held high, facing the two older lintep.

"The elf and my tree refuse to submit to your request to communicate with Queen Liessa as it will place them in danger." Her eyes had lost their glow, but she knew Eliséo would still be watching through their bond. "I have been told that I can safely tell you of the changes to my life if you would like me to."

The sparks of fire had left Lukys' eyes when her mist had dissipated. Unlike Aurelius, he hadn't understood that she had used her elf magic to disappear.

"What changes to your life could there be other than communication with the elf and the tree?"

"We aren't entirely certain, as I'm the first non-elf to be bound to an elf's tree, but there is a distinct possibility that my lifespan will be considerably increased due to the bond. Aside from that, I can use some elf magic. I'm not certain what magic the elves can do, but I already know I can do some of it, so it wouldn't be a stretch of the imagination to assume I could do whatever I'm given knowledge of."

Rilla watched Lukys and Aurelius carefully as she revealed these significant changes. Aurelius already knew she could call up the thickened air, but he hadn't made the link about her lifespan. He tried not to react to it, but she saw his eyes widen at the revelation.

Lukys sat very still as she related what she knew and suspected. He gave nothing away. Rilla wondered if she would be able to read his thoughts if she tried, but let the idea slip away before she caused herself any more trouble.

"Has the elf magic affected your lintep magic?" Lukys inquired after a time.

"I don't really know," Rilla replied truthfully. "I didn't even know I was a lintep until a few months ago and had barely tried to do anything with my own powers before I was bound to the tree. All I can think is that I might be less limited in what I can do than other lintep, but I don't think it's really had any sort of adverse effect."

"To be fair, you were already less limited than other lintep with how you use your power because of your lack of training," Aurelius ventured a suggestion. "I doubt it has much, if anything, to do with your elf tree bond."

"How does it put the elf in danger if we know their name?" Lukys persisted down the line of thought that Rilla had tried to steer him away from. "For that matter, I don't see that it puts *you* in any danger, so why have you kept silent on the incident?"

How do I answer that without giving you away? Rilla asked in a panic. *It only puts you in danger because no one can know you are Lady Eléna's son. I don't think any other elf would be in danger if the same had happened to their tree.*

Master Aurelius is probably wondering the same thing, Eliséo sighed, knowing the secret he had guarded closely for hundreds of years was in danger. *Just tell them that if people know who the elf is, they may try to harm you to harm the tree or vice versa, they may try to hurt me or Elessa to hurt you and stop the prophecy.*

Rilla saw the smouldering look on King Lukys' face and the confusion on Master Aurelius'. Why was she constantly forced into these positions?

"The elf, the tree and I could all be placed in danger if anyone knows the identity of the three of us," she tapped her teeth together, trying to decide how best to proceed. "An elf's tree dies if every person connected to it dies. It works the other way as well. If an elf's tree is destroyed, which I am led to believe is sufficiently difficult to do, then the people bound to it will die.

"However, as Lishe has already tried to kill me a number of times, it's reasonable to assume she would even attack a tree in Silvaren or capture and torture the elf involved, just as she did with Nyssa and Shuut, to get to me."

Well done, Rilla, Eliséo sent through a wave of gratitude and pride. She was quickly learning how to use words to her best advantage.

"That's a good reason, but it's not enough," Lukys crossed his arms and leaned back in his chair. If Rilla had known him better, she would have understood that he thought he had the upper hand and could relax.

"No one, other than the elves themselves, knows the identity of any of the trees. It can't possibly come to pass that someone finds out the identity of your tree and the elf and hurt you unless they get their hands on the elf and as no elf could ever be caught unawares by a human, lintep, karlik or crystal dragon, I do not think that would happen either.

"Then there's the small matter of my hearing you yell to Eliséo to get out of your mind before I reached the top of your tower. So exactly *what* are you trying to hide from me if I already know the identity of the elf?"

Frozen in terror, Rilla listened as the old lintep said those words aloud. Lukys was exactly right. Even if Lishe found out about Eliséo, she wouldn't have the first idea how to find his tree in Silvaren, if she even knew where to find the elven stronghold. At the most, she might be able to track Eliséo himself, but Rilla knew his mist alone was powerful enough to protect him should he be attacked.

Heart pounding in her ears. She didn't notice that Aurelius and Lukys were talking to each other. Thoughts were swirling around her mind but she couldn't tell if they were hers, Eliséo's or Elessa's.

"Rilla?" Aurelius shook her gently. She looked up at him with dull green eyes.

"Aurelius, go down to Lord Aaron and relieve him of his duties with his other granddaughter," Lukys instructed the old master. "Tell him to come here immediately. Between you, Jorg and Kayte, I want the children and the banwep to be kept safe. If there is any news of Lishe, send word to me immediately."

Aurelius stood hesitantly and patted Rilla reassuringly on the arm before obeying his King's command. Rilla wanted to beg him to stay. He was her only ally in this stronghold. but she was too terrified to say anything.

He knows! Rilla finally managed to think straight enough to talk to Eliséo and Elessa. *He knows and I think he's figured out who you really are, though I don't know how.*

Stay calm, Eliséo told her more calmly than he felt himself. *Kora is with me now. I will ask her to find Lady Eléna for us to avoid as much danger as possible.*

Rilla watched through his eyes. She couldn't understand why he hadn't already told her that Kora was there and safe but it was the least her of concerns.

* * *

Eliséo focussed his gaze on Kora. She was watching him intently and had been the entire time since he and Elessa had tried to reach Rilla behind her wall. All their conversations had taken place through Elessa so there was no chance she had heard any of them.

"What's going on?" Kora asked as soon as she saw his change in demeanour.

"I need you to get Lady Eléna, *now*," he laced his voice with command. He hated doing it, but knew she wouldn't listen to him otherwise. "Tell her she might need to bring Ensil with her."

He watched as she involuntarily stood and left his tree. He closed his eyes and tried to compose himself. How were they going to get out of this mess?

* * *

Rilla focussed herself back into the room with Lukys and saw him staring at her contemplatively. It didn't matter that he had seen her eyes glowing bright green again – he already knew most of the truth and suspected the rest. She didn't try to talk to him. Instead, they waited in silence until Lord Aaron arrived. Rilla fervently hoped it wouldn't be too long before Kora found Lady Eléna and Master Ensil. She didn't want to have this conversation without them.

It felt like an hour later, but in reality she knew it must have only been a matter of minutes before Lord Aaron walked through the door to find her locked in a staring match with his cousin.

"What's the meaning of this?" he asked as he crossed the room and pulled up a spare wooden chair to sit on. "Shuut is still in a fragile state."

"Has she woken up yet?" Rilla asked, finally looking away from the king.

"Yes, but Master Jorg is now teaching her to build a proper wall by herself," he replied testily. "Lukys, I should be there to help him. He isn't nearly as powerful as he presents himself to be."

"Jorg is the best mind Master in Illaria, Aaron," Lukys reminded him. "If he

157

needs help containing Nyssa's power, Aurelius and Kayte can help him. Your presence is needed here more than with them."

"Why? What else has happened?" Aaron asked as curiosity got the better of him.

"Young Rilla has been holding her secrets very close to her chest. In Silvaren, she was bound to Eliséo's tree and seems to think it could put him in danger if anyone knows of this, though Lady Eléna and Aurelius already know.

"Eliséo told us that Lady Eléna has abdicated in favour of her daughter. The only plausible reason I can see for this is if she has another child. Only if Eliséo is that child could his bond with Rilla put him in any danger."

Lukys stated everything so plainly that Rilla wondered how she had ever thought they could keep it a secret from anyone. Eliséo was right to question his mother's decision to abdicate. It really did bring more problems than it solved.

"How can that even be possible?" Aaron looked between the two of them in confusion. "Leaving aside whether the ambassador is also a prince, can a lintep actually be bound to an elf's tree?"

"I felt his presence in her mind and have seen her eyes glow like an elf's. There is little more she needs to do to prove it has happened."

"But there must have been hundreds of people visiting the elves over the years, possibly even thousands. Why has it never happened before if it were possible?" Aaron fumbled with the logic.

"Apparently, this particular tree is old and stubborn and wanted to help the prophecy child, if that's what I really am," Rilla voiced her opinion. She still doubted that she was indeed the prophecy child, but was heavily outnumbered in that belief.

"Getting back to the main point," Lukys redirected the conversation, which Rilla had been trying to avoid.

"I believe Lady Eléna, or Queen Eléna as she was at the time, may have been deceiving her people for centuries that she only had one child. If Eliséo is truly her son, that knowledge could still only hurt him if he had more power than his sister."

Rilla listened as King Lukys came to the right conclusion from all the threads of knowledge he had. In truth, she hadn't seen Liessa use her powers at all. It was possible that she had just as much power as Eliséo, but from all she had heard the queen barely had any power at all without the crown. Knowing even just a few things that Eliséo could do with his magic, Rilla was fairly certain it wasn't an exaggeration that he was much more powerful than his sister.

"Well, does he?" Aaron asked, turning to face Rilla.

"I don't know," she answered truthfully.

"So you *are* bound to the ambassador's tree then," Lukys let out a deep breath.

Rilla instantly cursed herself for so easily admitting that she was bound to Eliséo's tree. *How much trouble will this cause for all involved?*

"Rilla, this really is a fortunate thing if you could let us use that bond to our advantage. Imagine how much more easily we could communicate with the elves in this time of danger."

Eliséo, what's happening? Rilla heard Lady Eléna's voice through her bond with Elessa. She half listened as Eliséo explained the situation to his parents – Ensil was there too.

"Lady Eléna would like you to know that she will take severe and immediate action should you betray your knowledge to anyone," Rilla told the two older lintep, her eyes glowing bright green. Lord Aaron gasped at the sight.

"You can let her know that nothing is further from my mind," Lukys' voice was soft but clear. "I would never knowingly endanger an heir of Silvaren. All I wish is to be allowed to use this bond to our advantage if and when we need to."

"Your request is acknowledged, but you are warned to use this advantage sparingly, as it can only cause fear and jealousy amongst those who do not know the circumstances," Rilla spoke the words as she heard Eléna say them. Eliséo was telling both Eléna and Ensil what he heard through their link as she was doing with Lukys and Aaron.

"I don't believe it," Aaron said sceptically. "How do we know those are truly Lady Eléna's words. It could be that Eliséo, if that's who her bond is really with, is telling her what to say. He knows the former queen well enough to be able to word things as she would."

"Ask your elf what the last thing was that I said to him before he left my chambers the only night he was here."

It was a good test. Rilla had not been present at that audience and Eliséo would have had no reason to tell her such an insignificant detail even if he had told her any of the rest of the meeting. Without pause, Rilla replied.

"Are there any races you didn't manage to disturb on your travels here?"

"Are you satisfied that proves the elf is Eliséo?" Lukys asked Aaron.

"Indeed, but I am still uncertain that he is talking to Lady Eléna directly," Aaron replied gravely.

"Eléna said that she gave Graesyn something the last time you were in Silvaren, just before the terrible tragedy that befell your family," Rilla said as she pulled out her own necklace with the tree pendant. "It was the mother version of this one she gave me when I passed through before going to live in the Paradise."

Aaron leaned forward with tears in his eyes and took the pendant from Rilla's hands. He pressed it firmly to his forehead.

The plain pendant grew warm to Aaron's touch, drawing in the memories floating through his mind. When he released it back to her, Rilla saw those memories as though she had been there herself and smiled at the sight of her grandmother's delight with the gift when it had been bestowed upon her. The tiny gems scattered over the branches serving as shimmering leaves had left her breathless. She looked just like Kora, with Nyssa's grey eyes.

"I assume you're satisfied now with both the identity of the bound elf as Eliséo and the elf he's talking to as Lady Eléna?" Aaron nodded at Lukys' question. "Then I suggest we work with what we have to sort out our problems."

Not knowing if it would work, but hoping to avoid repetition of the conversation, Rilla suggested that Lukys and Aaron hold her hands and Eléna and Ensil do the same with Eliséo so that they could all talk to each other through Elessa.

Together, the six of them joined their minds in a place that was unfamiliar to most of them. Once they had pushed past the strangeness of it all, they spent the better part of the evening discussing the events which had taken place since the party had left Silvaren. Eliséo had not informed the lintep of everything that had happened on their travels and had not had a chance to inform the elves of the recent attack on the lintep stronghold.

It was hotly debated whether or not to involve Queen Liessa in the discussions as she was not privy to the knowledge of either the bond or the true identity of Eliséo.

"It can only cause her distress," Eléna insisted as Lukys refused to dismiss the argument. "No good can come of her knowing."

"Much good can come of it," Lukys insisted. "We would be able to involve the queen herself in these discussions at the very least. At the most, she will discover she has a brother who is powerful enough to help her in any endeavour she wishes to pursue."

"And what if other elves find out about it and decide that she shouldn't be their queen at all? What then, if her jealousy grows to unreasonable heights and my children's lives are put at risk because the elves are divided as to who should rule them? Will you hold yourself responsible for this and protect my children from a fate we can easily avoid by keeping this fact as secret as we have for hundreds of years?"

"I do not understand why the elves wouldn't still follow Liessa," Lukys insisted. "Edamo was not more powerful than Rilla and Ophélie, in fact, it's quite possible that Rilla had more power than the two of them combined, but that did not make any lintep insist that she be made our ruler instead of her older brother."

"Edamo and Ophélie still had more power than most other lintep," Eléna pointed out. "The difference in this case is that Liessa barely has more power than any other elf, whereas Eliséo has more control over the elements than any other elf excepting myself and Ensil. In a tight position, she would not be able to defend the elves with her power but Eliséo would."

Before he voiced the obvious solution, Lukys stopped himself and realised he was about to suggest exactly what they feared the other elves would – that Eliséo just be made the king.

"I see you have finally understood the root of the problem," Eléna said softly. "Liessa's life would be placed in danger and Eliséo's relative freedom would be jeopardised. And, much as I hate to imagine it of my own daughter, there is always the possibility that she would order Eliséo's death or exile to eliminate the threat to her life before other elves discovered the truth."

"My lady, I believe King Lukys has a point about involving Liessa in these conversations," Eliséo ventured to speak, continuing quickly before his mother had a chance to protest. "The best way for Liessa to prove herself in her role as the queen, and have the elves accept her before the truth is accidentally revealed, is to let her have access to all the information she needs to make good decisions for her people.

"Even with these conversations between ourselves, there is no way that Liessa can act on the information because none of us can just walk up to her and tell her we know these things without revealing how we know them. We don't have to tell her that I'm you're son or that I have so much more power than she does, but I do think it best that she be involved."

A brief but heated discussion amongst the three elves saw that Ensil would go to fetch Queen Liessa from her chambers.

"Wait," Rilla called out before he walked out of Eliséo's common room. "Can we let Kora know what happened with Lishe today?"

"Kora?" Aaron asked in confusion. "How can we tell her anything?"

"She's in Silvaren," Rilla answered, purposely avoiding Eliséo's attention. She didn't know if he would approve of her actions. "I saw her through Eliséo's eyes earlier today."

Everyone could feel the ache in his heart at those words.

"My little Kora is alive and well? When will she return to Illaria?" Without thinking of the reasons she had left in the first place, Aaron simply assumed that she would happily come home to him.

"I've been trying to convince her to do just that," Eliséo replied guardedly, "but she has been quite resistant to the idea."

"Why ever would she be resistant to the idea? Surely she would like to watch over her son while he learns to master his powers."

"I'm not certain she would like me to discuss that without her," Eliséo tried to avoid the topic. Rilla was beginning to understand why he hadn't immediately told Aaron about his daughter.

"Does this have anything to do with Ophélie?" Everyone turned their attention to Lukys in confusion when Eliséo concurred. "Then I assume she had some luck in her endeavours. Can you please let her know that I would be most interested to learn what she discovered and would appreciate it if she would do me the honour of calling on me in Illaria at her earliest possible convenience."

Gratitude exuded from Aaron. Lukys reached out, in the physical world, to embrace his cousin.

"It's the least I could do Aaron. After all, it was because of the information I gave her about our family that led her to leave Illaria in the first place."

Aaron knew well enough not to ask more questions of Lukys there and then. There would be plenty of time to talk to him before Kora arrived.

Ensil finally returned with Queen Liessa by his side. He had explained to her the unusual bond that was allowing them to talk with the lintep. Far from being outraged by what Elessa had done, she was most intrigued to see how the bond was currently being used.

The conversation between the lintep and elves lasted well into the early hours of the morning, long after Liessa had joined them. Rilla spent most of the time listening silently. She was too young and inexperienced in politics to have any meaningful input.

In truth, she was relieved when they came to a decision about each point and left her mind. Aaron and Lukys sent her off to bed while they remained and discussed the plans they now had to put in place.

She was so tired that she barely noticed the fact that her chambers were empty save for Shuut sleeping on one side of her large bed. Glad for the solitude, she removed all but one of the mountain of pillows and fell asleep almost as soon as she lay down.

Chapter Seventeen – Aftermath

The next morning, Rilla woke to find Shuut lying beside her, eyes open and watching her. Relief momentarily flashed in her sister's grey eyes.

"It took me so long to fix my wall so that it wouldn't fall apart again that I didn't have a chance to ask anyone what happened to you."

"Lord Aaron told me you'd finally woken up and he was helping you with your wall, but I didn't get a chance to ask him what else had happened to you."

Rilla lay beside Shuut, alone for the first time since discovering they were sisters. There were so many questions she wanted to ask, but the silence dragged on for minutes as they stared at each other. Eventually, Rilla broke the spell.

"I'm sorry about Nyssa. Arishen had a vision just as we passed through the boundary to Illaria. We convinced the lintep to send out a search party, but we already knew it was too late for her. Really, we were just hoping to be able to save you from Lishe."

"I've barely had time to think about Nyssa," Shuut shook her head. "Lishe was so intent on killing you, taking your power and stealing Nyssa's power from me that all I could think of was how to save you. I wasn't just going to let her kill my mother and my sister."

Rilla smiled at that, but quickly explained when she saw the look on Shuut's face. "Once I found out we were sisters and I was the reason the crystal dragons told you that Nyssa was dead in the first place, I thought you'd hate me. I guess it's just nice to know that you at least like me enough not to let Lishe kill me without a fight."

"I had a mother who dragged me all around the Outworld looking for Aunt Kora for years and a father who would have abandoned me but for the fact that the crystal dragons manipulated him into teaching me his banwep ways. As far as family goes, I thought that was it when I was eventually left to fend for myself in Turon.

"I never expected to find a cousin and a sister, but you both proved your worth to me long before I knew who you were. I would fight to the death to keep you both safe and alive."

Rilla couldn't believe her ears, but found herself returning the sudden and fierce embrace from Shuut. Whether it was relief or fear, they clung to each other, tears streaming onto their pillows until they heard a knock at the outer door. Wiping her eyes with her sleeve as Rilla walked to the door, the previous night's events rushed into her mind.

Would she be expected to do anything in particular now because her bond with Eliséo's tree had been discovered? Would she be allowed to resume her training as usual or would it be constantly interrupted for clandestine conversations with the elves? She tried to rid herself of these thoughts as she unlocked and opened the door. She was surprised to see her bleary eyed grandfather on the other side.

"Have you slept at all?" she asked, concern creeping into her voice. He shook his head, rubbing his eyes tiredly.

"I wanted to check on Shuut before resting. Is she awake?"

Rilla nodded and led him to her bed chamber, where the banwep was pulling back the curtains from around the bed to let in the morning light. At the sound of their approaching footsteps, she stopped and turned to meet them.

"You must be Lord Aaron," Shuut greeted him amiably. "Thank you for helping me yesterday. I know everyone was trying to save Rilla, but I'm not ignorant of the fact that you helped me when you didn't really need to."

The old lintep raised a questioning eyebrow and turned to Rilla for help. She tapped her teeth together, figuring out how best to explain the situation to her sister.

"Ah, Shuut, you know how you spent years searching for Kora in the Outworld with Nyssa, well, did you know that they had more family here in Illaria?" At a shake of her head, Rilla continued. "Nor did Plyke and I, but it seems as though we have quite a bit of family here. Lord Aaron is our grandfather."

Shuut took a step back and steadied herself by the bed. Rilla instantly rushed to her side, helping her to a chair with Lord Aaron. The confusion in Shuut's eyes was plain to see.

"Our grandfather? I don't understand. If Nyssa had family here, why didn't she bring me here herself, years ago? Why did she drag me all over the Outworld looking for Kora?"

Rilla shrugged her shoulders. She almost replied that Nyssa hadn't seemed to want either of her daughters very much with the way she treated them, but then remembered King Lukys' warning not to speak ill of Nyssa around Lord Aaron.

"What will happen today?" Rilla swiftly diverted the conversation. "Did anyone find Lishe yesterday? Will our lessons go ahead?"

"It would appear that Lishe evaded all lintep yesterday," Aaron answered with a deep sigh. "We know she isn't in the castle grounds because she would have taken any opportunity last night to kill the two of you and steal your power. All we can hope is that she doesn't return before you are both fully trained."

"Both?" Shuut latched onto the word as though it were a life line. "What do you mean both?"

"You're right, I should have said all three of you," Aaron corrected himself, misunderstanding her question. "Presumably, she didn't seek out Plyke because she has no idea who he is."

To ease the confusion she could see between them, Rilla attempted to clarify the situation without seeming to take control.

"Will Shuut and I share this room now?" Rilla asked as she shook her head slightly to silence the question on her sister's lips.

"Yes, I think that would be best for now," Aaron nodded, looking around the room. "I'll have another bed brought in by this evening. Of course, it would reduce my task list if you could show her around a bit. After last night, there are many things I need to help Lukys to organise."

"And the training?" Rilla prompted him.

"Master Aurelius has been most kind to already volunteer his services to carry out your testing and then I think your training can commence this afternoon," Aaron spoke as though Shuut knew everything about Illaria. "Rilla, Master Reuben would like to take you for your mind session this morning, he knows you will be later than usual to show your sister around.

"Then Mistress Kayte and Mistress Isis will share your time this afternoon. Don't forget to see Master Graham before our evening meal. Oh and inform Plyke to tell the others that I've invited you all to dine with me tonight."

Rilla nodded and opened the door for her grandfather before Shuut could say a word. She closed it gently behind him and then turned to face the inevitable onslaught of questions.

"What's going on here? Who is Master Aurelius? What testing am I undertaking and how can I possibly start training when I haven't enough money to even pay for this room? I mean, just look at it!" Shuut barely stopped for breath.

"I'll explain on the way. Just let me tell Plyke about tonight before I forget," Rilla told her as she ushered her out of the room and walked down the hall to their cousin's room. She had to knock on the door twice before she heard him coming.

He was still rubbing his eyes when he opened the door and saw the two of them standing in the hall. Without warning, he threw his arms around both of them and dragged them into a tight embrace for a few seconds before holding them out at arm's length.

"I'm so glad you're both alive! But Rilla, if you *ever* run off without listening to the rest of us again, I'll kill you myself," he scolded his cousin.

"Still causing trouble, I see," Shuut smirked.

"Well, if I had listened to them all, she might have killed you without giving anyone the chance to rescue you," Rilla defended herself hotly. "Anyway, that's not why I'm here. Lord Aaron has invited us all to dine with him tonight. I don't have time to tell the others so can you let them know? Master Reuben will have to bring Arishen in and out of the castle for that and Tika might need to scrub up a bit."

"What are you doing that makes you so busy you can't tell them yourself?" Plyke's interested was aroused.

"I have to show Shuut around and then take her to Master Aurelius for her testing all before my own training."

Plyke practically bounced in excitement. "Who have you got today? I'm finally getting a break from Jorg and will get to work with Kayte this morning and Aurelius this afternoon."

"About time too! I've got Reuben this morning, then Kayte and Isis this afternoon," she tried to suppress a smile. "They're going to test me today to see if I can join group lessons for healing and fire tomorrow."

"Fantastic news! Graham is ready to let me join the group lessons for communication tomorrow morning, but I probably have a long way to go for the others. Can you ask Reuben in your lesson if he can tell Arishen about tonight? I doubt I'll see him today."

Shuut interrupted their conversation with a hint of irritation. Rilla knew she had no idea what they were talking about. "Right, well, as fun as this all sounds, I'm starving. Can we get some food now?"

Rilla nodded and waved a quick farewell to Plyke before leading Shuut to the nearest stairwell to the dining hall. "I'm ravenous. We were so busy last night I didn't get a chance to eat."

"What were you so busy with?" Shuut asked curiously. Rilla suddenly remembered what she'd been doing and the fact that she couldn't tell anyone about it. How had it come about that a secret being revealed to three people caused her to keep even more secrets from everyone else in her life?

"I just had to tell them everything I could remember about what happened yesterday afternoon and go over all the attacks in the Outworld so that they could try to piece together what Lishe might do next." It wasn't exactly a lie, but she made certain to shield all her thoughts so that a stray one could not betray her.

Rilla spent the early morning showing Shuut around. Their first port of call was the dining hall where they both ate their fill. Afterwards, she gave her sister a quick tour of the castle grounds and then escorted her to Master Aurelius' own training room, the now familiar symbol etched into the door showing her which one to knock on.

Master Aurelius opened the door and welcomed Shuut inside. Rilla caught his eye as her sister walked confidently into the room. She could see the pain in his eyes, for not being able to keep their secret safe for longer than a week. Before he could question her further on what took place after he'd left Lukys' chambers, she risked a quick *I'm fine* to his mind before turning to the other training rooms for her first lesson with Master Reuben.

* * *

It had been the early hours of the morning when Eliséo broke off his link with Rilla. They'd discussed many more things than just Lishe. It wasn't often that the rulers of Illaria and Silvaren were in the same place together. Most of the time, they had to make do with sending messages through Eliséo. Having the rare opportunity to speak directly to each other, there were a vast array of topics they had wanted to discuss.

The link itself had not been exhausting for Eliséo, but he still hadn't completely recovered from his adventures in the Outworld over the past few months. All he'd wanted was a few days to rest in Silvaren with Elessa, so that he would be completely refreshed for whatever task his queen next set for him. It was a luxury he feared would not be afforded to him.

He'd barely slept a few hours when Elessa alerted him to Kora's presence. Eléna and Ensil had managed to convince her not to join them after she had run to fetch them the night before, but they knew she couldn't be kept in the dark for much longer. The elves agreed that she could be told Rilla was bound to his tree if she agreed to return to Illaria, if for no other reason than she would guess the truth herself the first time she saw Rilla's eyes glow. It was now on Eliséo's shoulders to convince her, with King Lukys' words, to return. It was a task he did not relish.

"Good morning, Lady Kora," he greeted the lintep as she walked into the common area of his tree.

"I believe I stopped being *Lady* Kora the day I left Illaria."

There was an edge of bitterness in her voice that surprised Eliséo. Not wanting to press her on the matter, he simply motioned her to sit and braced himself for the conversation ahead of him.

"I spoke to your uncle last night. He and your father were pleased to know that you are alive and well, considering the fate of your sister and the most recent events with Lishe." Without pausing to let her ask the question on the tip of her tongue, he continued. "King Lukys asked me to let you know that he would be most interested to learn what you discovered about Ophélie's work and would appreciate it if you would do him the honour of calling on him in Illaria at your earliest possible convenience."

"How can you possibly have spoken with him last night?" Kora's eyes narrowed suspiciously.

"I am not permitted to tell you unless you give me your word that you will return to Illaria."

The lintep stared at him for a time. He knew she was sorely tempted to use her powers to attempt to read his mind, even though it was the very thing she had taught her son never to do.

"Assuming I believe you, what good could possibly come of me returning to Illaria?"

"I've already told you that you would be welcomed by your entire family and that most of them are keen to help you in your quest, the rest is for you to decide."

"Can you promise me that my son will still be there when I arrive if I leave today?"

A smile spread across Eliséo's face. "*That* I can promise. Plyke was quite excited to begin his lessons. His power is strong, but raw. He has much to learn and, from what I've seen, he has the discipline to apply himself to his studies. By the time you get there, he should be coming along quite nicely."

"It *would* be nice to see him properly trained," she admitted, with half a smile. "But I want to know what happened with Lishe before I agree."

"She attacked Rilla and her half-sister – I believe you know her as the banwep who took your son and the others out of your Paradise."

"That banwep is my niece?" At a nod from Eliséo, she mused aloud. "So my son and my two nieces are now in Illaria. Was the attack successful?"

"Not as successful as Lishe hoped it would be, but it caused a great deal of trouble nonetheless. She burned both girls, Shadow quite badly, and put a mind snare on each of their minds. Lord Aaron managed to find a way to get the mind snares off, though I'm unclear on those particular details. Lishe fled from Illaria. No one knows where she is, but it's safe to assume she is not in the castle grounds."

Kora sat leaned back and crossed her arms. "So you somehow spoke to Uncle Lukys last night and he told you all of this?"

"Have you decided to return to Illaria?" Eliséo waited in silence while Kora thought the proposition through. He knew she'd left Illaria over twenty years ago and did not want to return. She had such different views to most lintep in the first place that it would be difficult for her to fit in, especially after such a long time away.

"I will return, but I can't promise that I will stay there." It was the best Kora could offer and Eliséo appreciated it.

"There was an incident when the Paradisians visited Silvaren. I took them for a tour around our home and showed them how they could create a flower or a leaf for the trees that belonged to no elves. The boys all did that with no incident," he paused, not knowing how to explain what had happened. "Rilla … well it was my fault really, I suggested she place her hand on my tree. I had no idea that Elessa would create a bond with the girl."

Kora stared at him in shock. "You mean that Rilla is bound to your tree?" He only nodded.

"Then you saw everything she saw last night and you spoke with Uncle Lukys and father through that bond. And I suppose her friends have no idea what happened?"

"We were in enough danger as it was in the Outworld," he shrugged his shoulders uncomfortably. "Now that she's in Illaria, and the danger with Lishe is at least partly over, it should be safer for Rilla. However, I don't know how the lintep or her friends will take the news, so she's been instructed not to tell anyone unless absolutely necessary."

"I can certainly think of a few lintep who would try to exploit that situation and others who might be jealous of the increased power the girl might now possess. From what little I saw, she was already quite powerful in our Paradise."

"You noticed that, did you? From what I've seen, she is possibly more powerful than Nyssa," Eliséo admitted easily. "I'm not sure what you saw in the Paradise, but the poor girl didn't even know she was a lintep until after they'd left."

Kora started at the news and shook her head. "How could Nyssa be so very stupid? I admit I probably should have taken my boy to Illaria, or at least sent him there somehow in safety, but at least I told him what he was and trained him to contain his power."

"That's probably why you didn't realise how powerful he is. You taught him to build such a magnificent wall that his power never had a chance to shine until it peaked. Had we been any further delayed, Plyke would not have lived to see Illaria."

Seeing the pain in Kora's eyes, Eliséo was quick to reassure her so that she wouldn't change her mind about returning to Illaria. "He's fine now and Lord Aaron is providing for him just as he has always done for his family. I doubt he will hold any grudges towards you once he realises why you left in the first place."

"I'll make arrangements to leave today then. It will take me weeks to get there, assuming I remember the way," Kora said, quietly avoiding any further speculation as to how her son would react when he saw her. Eliséo knew that one thought was the main reason she didn't want to go back, and the main reason she'd finally relented.

"I can speed your journey," Eliséo offered. "King Lukys lent me a horse from his own stables on my departure. It would only be right for you to return Fleuris to him. If you follow the coast and then continue due east when the shore curves away, it will lead you directly to Illaria. Trust me on this, you can't ever forget the way home – no matter how long you've been away. "

Kora smiled sadly and thanked Eliséo, assuring him that Lukys would greatly appreciate the swift return of one of his prize mounts. The elf watched as she left his tree.

Are you going to tell Rilla that Kora is on her way? Elessa had, as always, been listening to every word of their conversation.

I don't think we should. Eliséo replied. *The temptation for her to tell Plyke will be too great for her to resist.*

She will scold you on Kora's arrival.

From the looks of things, she will be too busy to notice. Eliséo mused as he watched Rilla's lesson through Elessa's view. *Her lessons are keeping her quite well occupied.*

Chapter Eighteen – Tests and Decisions

Plyke returned to his room to get ready for the day ahead. He'd been in Illaria over a week now. Lord Aaron had taken all of them for a visit to his favourite tailor and the clothes had arrived just a few days ago. He'd had to negotiate with Rilla to get at least one dress and had allowed her to choose the rest of her clothes. Plyke smiled at the memory. She'd worn more practical clothes since leaving their Paradise and she wasn't keen to be forced back into frivolous ones.

Even Tika and Arishen had been gifted with one set of fine clothes each. Plyke was certain it was only because his grandfather didn't want them dining in his private chambers in grubby clothes. He wondered what would happen now. Would Tika and Arishen be paid during their apprenticeships and look after themselves or would Edric provide for Tika, and Arishen's carpenter master provide for him? It was possible Master Reuben would provide for Arishen because the seer was now living under his roof, but since Master Reuben had gone to the trouble of finding Arishen a willing carpenter, Timothée, to take him under his wing, that wasn't likely.

Pushing these thoughts aside, Plyke quickly dressed in his favourite set of clothes. The brown and green hues brought out the colour of his eyes. He finally felt safe enough to show that he was different and was pleased that people could instantly tell he was Lord Aaron's grandson by the resemblance.

He rushed down to the dining hall where Tika was already waiting for him at their usual table. It was the first day that Arishen wasn't there to meet them. He would have eaten with Master Reuben's staff before being escorted to Timothée's workshop.

"Lord Aaron has invited us all to his chambers for the evening meal," Plyke told his Partner through mouthfuls of food. Tika hid a smile behind a chunk of bread.

"Don't you think you should start calling him 'grandfather' rather than Lord Aaron? Or even just by his name, like you did with Kora?"

Plyke stared at him incredulously.

"He *is* your grandfather after all, not your teacher or your lord or king. For that matter, I wonder if you should be calling the king Uncle Lukys instead of King Lukys."

"I couldn't possibly … they wouldn't like it …" Plyke started and stopped. Tika grinned openly.

"True, King Lukys might not appreciate it, but I can guarantee you that Lord Aaron would. After all, the three of you are his only grandchildren so he's never had the pleasure of anyone calling him that before. I doubt Shuut ever will and Rilla, well, I can never quite tell how she'll react to people."

Desperate to change the topic, Plyke turned to Tika's apprenticeship and avoided the issue.

"Is Edric still getting you to muck out stables all day or have you progressed to something else?"

"Generally, mucking out all of the stables takes about half the day, so once I finish cleaning all the tack, Edric has started to allow me to rub down the horses after their daily exercises." With a proud smile, he added, "I think he's pleased with how I handle them. The other stablehands tell me that it took them longer before they were allowed to have any contact with horses."

A shadow of concern crossed Plyke's face. The other stablehands had to know by now that Tika was a human. *Will his touch with the horses endear him to them or make them jealous?*

"Don't worry, Plyke. I know how to endear myself to people as well as animals," Tika reassured him, understanding exactly what was passing through his mind. "The other stablehands all know that I'm human but are happy to share their quarters with me because I love the horses as much as they do."

Plyke smiled. He still couldn't believe their luck now that they were both safe and happy. The same probably couldn't be said for Arishen or even Rilla. The seer would now start feeling the isolation he had predicted and they would have to do everything they could to keep their friendship going. As for Rilla, she was certainly happy to be learning more about her power with teachers who could teach her everything she wanted to know, but her mother's death and Lishe's attack had certainly taken their toll on her.

Eager not to be late for his lessons, nor for Tika to be missing long from the stables, Plyke finished eating as quickly as he could and walked with Tika to the hall outside the dining hall. Tika left with a promise to clean himself up before dining with them that evening.

Plyke watched him hurry towards the stables with a spring in his step before turning to run up the stairs, two at a time. He didn't stop until he'd reached the sandstone hallway where they'd first had their testing with Master Aurelius. He could sense the master inside, still waiting for Shuut. He walked quickly past the library and around the corner to the row of classrooms where he waited for Mistress Kayte to arrive.

"Good morning, young Plyke," she greeted him as she emerged from the twisting stairwell, a young boy in tow. "We're in the second room today."

Plyke took the hint and opened the door for the Mistress, closing it behind the three of them. He watched her gathering a few tools from the far chest of drawers and bring them to a small table in front of some wooden chairs. She'd chosen the ones nearest the window so they could enjoy the crisp autumn breeze. He joined her at the table, not entirely sure what they were going to do in their lesson, nor why the boy was with them, sitting quietly in a corner. His glossy black hair and brown eyes reminded him of some of the younger elves he'd seen in Silvaren.

"I understand you haven't tried your hand at healing yet. Is that correct?"
Plyke nodded, turning his attention back to the mistress. "Then we shall
have to start with the basics. As you may have noticed, travelling with Rilla,
everything with healing is a matter of balance. If you heal someone, you will
automatically harm yourself, but *how* you heal them will determine how
much you hurt yourself."

Plyke stared at her, amazement mingled with fear as she took a small
knife and nicked his arm with it, then placed her hand over the scratch and
instantly healed it.

"Now, can you tell me what I did?"

"You cut me and healed me," Plyke answered, not understanding the
question.

"In a little more detail," Kayte smiled kindly. "Did you notice anything
more than just that?" He shook his head. "Did Rilla ever heal you in the
Outworld or was it just your companions?"

"Yes, once," Plyke replied, trying to recall the incident. "I'd been hit on the
back of the head. I don't remember anything after that until Rilla started
healing me. All I know is that my head hurt a lot beforehand and not so very
much afterwards."

"In that case, I'm going to cut you again and this time I need you to pay
attention to what I'm doing. I know your skills lie in empathy, especially
through skin contact, so I need you to use those skills to tell me exactly what
I'm doing."

Without waiting for a reply, she picked up the same knife and nicked his
other arm. He felt her place one smooth hand over the cut and tried to pay
close attention to what she was doing, but all he could feel was pain seeping
from his body into hers.

"You're focussing too much on the pain, Plyke," she reprimanded him.
"It's only a small cut. Focus on what I'm doing with the cut or it will be over
before you realise it."

Plyke tore his mind away from the pain, blocking it out of his wall. Instead,
he focussed on the cut itself and Mistress Kayte's gentle hand. He felt, more
than saw, the cut getting smaller by the second. Watching more closely, he
noticed that the skin was mending itself at an incredible rate.

"How did you do that?" he asked her, curiosity getting the better of him.

"Dorian, can you tell him?" Kayte motioned for the younger boy to sit with
them at the table.

"Mistress Kayte took away some of your pain and spread it around her own
body," Dorian answered obediently. "She then used her lintep healing ability
to speed up your own healing process."

Plyke listened carefully to Dorian, doubt and confusion at war within him.
"I don't think that's what Rilla's been doing."

"Yes," Kayte answered carefully. "Well, Rilla is quite advanced in what she's currently doing. You need to start from the beginning because you don't know what you're doing."

"Neither did she the first time she healed someone, nor any other time after that," Plyke protested, knowing that his teacher was purposely keeping something from him.

"I feel you will find this task difficult enough for your first lesson, Plyke. Now, Dorian is here to help us, but will want to practise his own skills at the same time. So I'd like you to take turns in cutting and healing each other. Ask me any questions you like along the way, but I won't do any more healing myself the rest of this lesson, so make sure they are tiny cuts."

"You're turn first," Dorian held out the knife to a flabbergasted Plyke, who just stared at it. *Do they honestly expect me to cut another student? Is this one of the reasons Kora left?*

"Take the knife, Plyke, and be glad you aren't as advanced as Rilla or there would be much more pain involved."

Plyke swallowed nervously and took the knife from Dorian, as Kayte leaned back in her chair to watch. He couldn't believe he was about to do this. He was tempted to close his eyes as he nicked the boy, but reasoned that he didn't want to cause any more damage than necessary.

He took a deep breath and made the tiniest cut. Working as quickly as he could, he placed the knife down on the table with one hand and covered the cut with his other hand, doing his best to follow Dorian's instructions on how to heal him.

As soon as he made skin contact, he immediately felt Dorian's excitement at being allowed to work with Lord Aaron's own grandson. Before Dorian accidentally felt or heard anything else, Plyke quickly pulled back all his excess power behind his wall.

After an hour or so, Plyke finally grasped the concept and managed to heal Dorian's cut in a reasonable amount of time. Kayte saw the smiles spread across both their faces as their skin contact made Dorian feel the pride of Plyke's achievement.

"That's enough for today, I think," she told them as Plyke pulled his hand away from Dorian. "Plyke, if you don't take offence to it, I'd like you to join my group lessons for beginners. Dorian's class would be perfect for your level and you may find yourself progressing faster than the rest of the class in time. What say you?"

"Really?" Plyke asked, amazed. "Group healing lessons? That would be wonderful!"

Kayte was taken aback by his enthusiasm. She'd expected him to be disgruntled at being put in a class with younger students, but he didn't seem to care at all. It appeared as though learning to use his magic in a group was all that he wanted.

"Very well," she looked over to the younger lintep. "Dorian, can you show Plyke where to join us for our lesson tomorrow afternoon? That will be all for this morning."

The boys stood up, thanked her and walked out the door. Kayte sat for a while longer thinking about Rilla. Plyke was right. She certainly was an interesting case. Without any training whatsoever, she had figured out how to heal a wound and not just by passing on her healing abilities to speed the process – she was actually mending muscles and flesh herself. All she really needed to do was learn how to pass on her healing abilities and she'd be able to join Kayte's most advanced healing class. The question was whether she should allow the girl to join them.

She sent a tendril of her power questing towards Lord Aaron's rooms. He was there and, with a quick message to him, was now awaiting her. With a sigh, she stood up and walked up the stairs and through the sandstone halls to his room. He was standing in the open doorway when she arrived.

"What can I do for you, Mistress Kayte?" the old lord smiled pleasantly, welcoming her into his ante chamber. She waited until he'd shut the door behind her before speaking.

"How much do you know of Rilla's … experience with healing?"

Lord Aaron sighed and showed her to a chaise.

"I was wondering when we'd have this conversation. At least we can say she takes more pride in her skills than her mother did. I know she has tried more things than any lintep should have by her age, especially with healing.

"From the sounds of it, her second attempt left her almost dead herself, but she appears to have learnt quite a lot from that and never placed herself in as much danger again, only healing the bare minimum that she could each time."

"I know the choice is mine alone, as she'll be in my class, but would you approve of the decision to include her in my most advanced class at such a young age?" Kayte sorely wanted him to deny the girl that privilege. It was probably too dangerous to let her into an advanced class, but the girl was just too skilful not to give her the opportunity.

"Let's be honest, Kayte, I think the danger would come more in placing her in an intermediate class, making her bored and reckless. I don't know if she's entirely ready for the advanced class, but if she isn't at least that's one area where she will be forced to focus her energy and attention to distract her from any other sorts of experiments."

"I have a feeling Isis will not be putting her in a beginner class, despite her lack of experience. In just a few short lessons, Rilla has already mastered the simpler techniques with her," Kayte confided in him.

"Can you be certain she will retain her skill once she passes through her classes?" Aaron asked in concern. "I know Nyssa was a different person, however …"

"All we can do is regularly test her on all the skills she has learnt without making her understand why," Kayte shrugged her shoulders. "If we do that for a few months or a year and know that she still retains skills she learnt this week, then I think we should be safe."

Aaron nodded. "Very well then. Let Isis and her other teachers know the plan so that Rilla doesn't suspect anything from the two of you."

Chapter Nineteen – Healing and Fire

Rilla arrived at her lesson later than she'd hoped. Master Reuben had clearly been advised that he would be waiting for her longer than usual. She found him seated on a padded wooden chair near the window, reading a leather-bound book.

"Tell me, what's the last sentence I read in this book?" He didn't even glance up as she closed the door behind her. Rilla closed her eyes and saw a swirl of thoughts. In amongst them, she saw an image of the page he had just finished reading.

"Hence, the best way to train someone is to constantly test their limits," she opened her eyes and looked at the master. "But you don't appear to agree."

"Yes, Master Aurelius warned me you might do that." His sparkling light brown eyes matched his brown hair. "And you're quite right – I don't agree with the tactics this book employs. It was written many years ago in a time where lintep had to think quickly under pressure.

"I think it is just as important to see what lintep can do when they aren't facing dangerous situations, otherwise they may learn to only access their power through fear rather than in the normal course of a day."

"In that case, I think you may not be too impressed with my training so far," Rilla bit a corner of her lip in anticipation of his answer.

"On the contrary, I think the things that happened to you in the Outworld forced you to use your power to an extent that most young lintep are not asked to do until well into their training. If you hadn't done those things, I understand many people may have come to a nasty end and it made you practise your skills, meaning that you could last until reaching Illaria before your power peaked and became too much for you to handle."

Rilla said nothing as she stood before Master Reuben. She knew he had agreed to take Arishen under his wing to help him with his visions and that he wouldn't harm humans without compelling reasons. Other than that, she barely knew him at all. He was one of the lintep who rode out to find Nyssa and Shuut but she hadn't spoken to him since that day.

"You shield your thoughts well, young Rilla," Reuben motioned for her to sit. "What you need to do is stop yourself from prying into other minds without meaning to. I recall the day we met, you weren't at all surprised that someone was asked to look at Arishen's vision. In fact, I am fairly certain that the idea had already crossed your mind before the council meeting.

"In light of that, I am impressed you didn't actually do anything about it. Now all we need to do is make sure you don't keep accidentally listening to people's thoughts if they don't shield them from you. After that, you can join my group mind lessons."

After the shock wore off, a large smile spread across Rilla's face. She was almost bursting with excitement.

"I've managed to ask my power not to do it once before, with Masters Aurelius and Graham though I'm not certain if I can make that happen all the time."

"In that case, ask your power not to do it now and we'll take a little stroll around the castle and grounds so that we can see if you can do it for an extended period of time without constantly thinking about it." Rilla happily complied and followed Master Reuben out of the classroom.

* * *

The morning lesson with Reuben exhausted Rilla, especially after the traumatic events of the day before. She didn't know if she would have the energy to concentrate on her lessons that afternoon with Mistresses Kayte and Isis, let alone her daily lesson with Master Graham. That one always left her frustrated. She had made very little progress whatsoever in understanding the lintep whistle.

Consumed with her thoughts, Rilla barely noticed Plyke until he was sitting next to her in the dining hall. She looked up to see the beaming smile on his face. As usual, his mood was infectious and she couldn't help but smile despite her misgivings.

"So your lesson with Mistress Kayte went well, I presume?"

"It was fantastic!" he replied excitedly. "I don't mean to say that *I* was fantastic, but that I learnt so much. She told me I'd start with her group lessons tomorrow afternoon, in the beginner class."

"Group lessons, really?" Rilla tried to keep the bitterness out of her voice. This was already the second group class that Plyke was being allowed to join, including Master Graham's intermediate communication class. She was still waiting to be allowed into her first one.

"Don't be so down about it, Rilla," Plyke elbowed her playfully in the ribs. "You said yourself that Kayte and Isis will test you this afternoon for group lessons. I'll bet my dinner that if you pass their tests, you'll be put in a higher class than me. Anyway, how was your lesson with Master Reuben?"

"I struggled a bit," Rilla admitted quietly. "I don't know why, but I can still hear thoughts that I don't mean to hear unless I specifically tell my power not to do that. Like I did that time with Tika, you remember."

Plyke nodded his head slowly at the memory. Tika had said something and Rilla had heard him say something else but hadn't realised it was his thoughts and not his words that she'd heard until he told her so.

"So he won't let you into his group lessons until you learn to keep that under control?"

Rilla shook her head and played with the food on her plate. Plyke watched her silently for a while, eating his meal contemplatively.

"Do you always hear thoughts you don't mean to?" he asked her.

"What?" Rilla snapped out of her thoughts. "No, of course not."

"Then when does it happen?" he pressed her on the topic, making her actually think about it.

"Well, I suppose it's usually when I know someone is lying, or trying to hide something," a smile spread across her face as she realised the common thread. "Though I'm not certain that will help me."

"When do you see Master Reuben next?"

"Not for a few days now. He's got group lessons the rest of this week."

"Maybe we can ask him about it when he brings Arishen to the castle for our evening meal tonight. You never know," he smiled mischievously at her, "he might just be able to squeeze some time in for you somewhere like Master Graham does every evening."

Rilla nodded, smiling again. Somehow, her cousin always managed to boost her spirits and find solutions to the problems she couldn't work past.

They quickly finished their meal and took a short stroll around the manicured gardens together before parting ways for their afternoon lessons.

Mistresses Kayte and Isis were already waiting for Rilla in the classroom when she arrived, even though she herself was early. Off to the side was a boy Rilla didn't recognise. He looked up at her with big brown eyes as she entered and gave her a shy smile. Rilla was surprised to see Mistress Isis and the newcomer.

"Good afternoon," she greeted them warily. "I thought we were having separate lessons today."

"Oh, we are," Isis agreed amiably, "but I wanted to watch your healing test and Mistress Kayte was kind enough to oblige."

"Rilla, this is Dorian. He helped with Plyke's test this morning and has agreed to assist with your test, though he has been warned it may be quite a bit more painful than he imagines," Kayte looked meaningfully at the boy, seemingly to give him a last chance to withdraw. The excited smile on his face told her he would not recant his offer.

Rilla nodded uncertainly at the boy. She wasn't exactly sure how Mistress Kayte intended to test her, but it was bound to be unpleasant for whoever the subject was.

"Isn't there someone you can test me on who is already injured so we don't have to hurt anyone on purpose?"

"Rilla, if you prove to be as good a student in class lessons as I hope you will be, I will make it a point to let you work in our infirmary," Kayte promised her. "If that's something you feel you would like to do."

"But you don't want to let me near any of them yet because you don't know if I'll overextend myself and you want to test my skills in a controlled environment first," Rilla was almost too excited to speak.

She hadn't even thought of what she could do once she was fully trained. Perhaps she could still become a healer, just a different one from Rhanya. Tears stung her eyes at the thought of him. She blinked them away quickly and saw Mistress Kayte's eyes narrow at the sight. Her teacher didn't know about her plans in the Paradise and there had been no reason to tell her of Rhanya. Her teachers couldn't possibly understand how important the healing side of her powers were to her.

"I think it's time we start then," Mistress Kayte motioned for Dorian to sit beside Rilla on the chaise across from her and Isis. Rilla noticed, with a sudden lurch in her stomach, that there was a small knife on the table between them. She watched in disturbed fascination as her teacher picked up the knife and gave Dorian a small nick on the arm.

"Heal Dorian's arm."

Without hesitation, Rilla drew a deep breath and steadied herself. Now was not the time to panic. Who knew how many injuries she would be tested with? She would have to use the least amount of power that she could and take on as little pain as possible. Even a small cut could hurt her if she wasn't careful.

Releasing the breath, Rilla placed her hand gently on Dorian's arm and carefully stitched together the wound without taking any of his pain into herself. It took less than a minute. When she looked up, she saw the younger lintep's mouth hanging open. Confused, she raised an eyebrow at him until he realised he was gaping and closed his mouth. It wasn't quite the reaction she'd been prepared for.

"Did I do something wrong?" she turned towards Mistress Kayte uncertainly.

"No, Rilla," Kayte shook her head almost imperceptibly at Dorian, but Rilla caught it. "Your test is going to be different to Plyke's and Dorian was unprepared for that. Nothing more, nothing less."

"But she ..." Dorian spluttered before a sharp look from Mistress Kayte silenced him.

"She healed a tiny cut on your arm. I told you this test would be more painful. If you are not willing to be the subject, you are perfectly free to leave." Her tone was cold and steady.

"I'm sorry, Mistress Kayte," Dorian instantly apologised. "I'm ready for the next stage." He picked up the knife himself and handed it, hilt first, to the Mistress. She took it from him and cut deeper, down to the bone. Tears glistened in Dorian's eyes as he suppressed a gasp of pain.

Rilla watched in mounting discomfort as Mistress Kaye sat back in her seat and motioned for her to begin. Not knowing what their discussion had actually been about, Rilla tried to calm herself down.

Once again, she placed a hand on Dorian's arm, covering the wound, to assess the damage. The knife had gone straight through his muscles, but it was a clean cut, nowhere near as bad as what she'd had to deal with in the Outworld. She breathed a sigh of relief as she placed her free hand on his other arm to compare the muscles and repair the torn one.

In a few short minutes, the wound was healed. She'd managed to do it without causing herself any pain, but could feel her already tired body protesting slightly. It was bad timing for her tests to be the day after her attack. She was still tired from it, but needed to impress her teachers enough that they would let her into their class lessons.

Trying not to show how tired she already was, Rilla reopened her eyes, took her hands off Dorian's arms and sat back in her chair. She could feel Mistress Kayte studying her, but knew her wall was strong enough that she wouldn't be able to read her thoughts.

Suddenly, Dorian screamed out in pain. Rilla's head whipped around to look at him, her red curls flying around her shoulders.

"What happened?" she asked in confusion. "I didn't do anything."

"I did," Mistress Kayte told her calmly. "I broke one of Dorian's bones. You need to find it and mend it."

Before she'd finished speaking, Rilla had already sent out tiny tendrils of her power to see where his pain was coming from. It took her a few moments to locate the break. It was one of the bones in his left foot.

Rilla carefully took his shoe off, thanking her lucky stars that the boy was wearing soft shoes rather than the leather soled ones she and her companions had always worn. At least he was spared a small amount of pain there.

She touched the arch of his foot as lightly as she could. Pain threatened to engulf her but she held it at bay, taking only small bits at a time and spreading it around her own body.

For such a small break, there was already a substantial amount of inflammation in the muscles around it. Rilla looked around the room for an easy way to dispel the heat in the muscles. She couldn't see anything. Stamping her foot in frustration, she heard a small clink in her pockets. Immediately, she remembered her test with Master Aurelius where he got her to spread some heat into the stones. She hurried to take the pouch out of her pocket and poured the stones on the table.

Quickly and quietly she worked to draw the heat out of his wound and into the ten stones. She only stopped when she saw the hot air rippling above them in waves. Calmer than she felt, Rilla took his other shoe off and placed a hand over each foot, seeing the differences between the two bones, and began fusing the broken one together.

This time, she couldn't help it, the pain started to seep into her body. She was too tired and there was too much pain. Instead of finishing as quickly as she could, Rilla took her time and made sure to mend the broken bone correctly. It was just like the very first time she'd tried healing the fringa, but that had been so very long ago that she didn't want to make a mistake with a boy who had offered up his body just for her test.

Once she'd finished, she came to a decision. "I can't do any more today. I'm sorry if that means I don't pass the test to join your group lessons, but I'm too tired and I know each injury will get worse and I don't want Dorian to have to go through any more if I can't promise to help him."

"Congratulations Rilla," Mistress Kayte smiled at her. Rilla thought she spied a look of relief in her. "You just passed the test. You will join my advanced classes starting this week."

"What?" Rilla blurted out in confusion. "Why?"

"Dorian, tell Rilla why she passed the test."

The younger lintep looked at her in awe and smiled, despite the amount of pain he had just gone through. "You passed because you performed each task perfectly, but more importantly, you know your limits and won't compromise anyone's safety by pushing them too far."

"And why are you staring at me like that?" Rilla asked him, hoping Mistress Kayte would let him answer.

He looked at the older lintep then back at Rilla and shrugged his shoulders. "It was just amazing to see you at work is all."

You don't heal like anyone I've ever seen before.

Rilla heard his thoughts. Her eyes widened but she said nothing. Plyke was right, she only accidentally overheard thoughts when she knew someone was lying or hiding something.

She sat back in her chair, lost in thought as Dorian left the room. *Can I somehow tell my power not to take notice when someone lies? Would that even work? And what had he meant anyway? How many different ways are there to heal people?*

"Are you too tired for my test, Rilla?" Mistress Isis tapped Rilla on the knee to get her attention.

"Sorry?" Rilla's thoughts were still swirling around her mind. She shook her head and looked over to the youngest Mistress. "What did Dorian mean?"

"He didn't expect you to be so advanced with so little training," Kayte answered smoothly, before Isis had a chance to reply. Rilla eyed her suspiciously. She had answered too quickly, like she'd been prepared for the question.

"How many different ways are there to heal?" Rilla asked, lifting her chin defiantly. She was determined to get an answer.

"Two."

"And the way I'm healing is the least commonly used?"

Mistress Kayte sighed. "All lintep have a faster healing system than other creatures, including elves and karliki. *Most* lintep will begin their healing lessons by temporarily passing on that part of their power to the injured party, essentially, speeding up the healing process with their own natural ability.

"You, on the other hand, are actually mending the bones, muscles and skin yourself, without passing on any of your own power even temporarily. It's an unusual skill to possess. That isn't to say that no lintep can do it, but only the most advanced students ever even attempt it."

Rilla listened to the mistress carefully and thought back on her short amount of time with Ratchin. Which skill set had she used to heal the farmer's boy? She had certainly taken away some of his pain because the lines in his face had smoothed instantly at her touch. Then what had she done? His wound had become smaller, but Ratchin hadn't explained how that had happened. Rilla doubted it was as simple as passing on her healing powers.

"I think I do that when I'm not concentrating," her sudden declaration surprised the teachers. "When you pass on your healing ability, is that when you heal their wound at the same time as opening the wound on your own body? I mean, if it's a big one?"

"Yes," Mistress Kayte exchanged a glance with Mistress Isis. "Has that happened to you before?"

"When I healed Ensil," Rilla nodded, her eyes unfocussed as she thought back to that horrible day. "It sort of happened with the fringa, but only with the pain. His wing was broken at the shoulder and when I touched it, pain exploded in my shoulder, but I stopped that.

"It was worse with Master Ensil. I'd stabbed him with my sword, and we were too far away from everyone to wait for help. I was scared that he was going to die, so when I went to heal him, an identical wound opened up in my shoulder. I only healed him as much as I thought my own body could handle, and made his veins stop bleeding."

"Why didn't you tell me that before?" Mistress Kayte asked, her voice strangely gentle.

Rilla shook her in confusion. "I told you that I healed Master Ensil."

"But you didn't tell me how," Kayte corrected her. "Have you healed anyone like that since then?"

"Yes, but as I said, it's only when I'm tired and not concentrating," Rilla answered confidently. "After it happened that first time, I decided it couldn't be the best way to heal someone, so instead, I tried to spread the pain around my body rather than let it concentrate in that one spot where the person was injured and it seemed to help. I suppose it was just by accident that I thought about how to actually mend muscles and flesh – I only ever had to mend bones with the fringa's wing."

"What happens to you when you mend things, rather than when you aren't concentrating and the wound opens up in you?" Isis asked the question, intrigued by the sudden revelation.

"I suppose I just get tired," Rilla shrugged her shoulders. "It just seems to take energy from me, but doesn't actually hurt me, well not in the same way, anyhow."

Isis turned to Kayte. "So she uses her energy rather than her power, to fuel the ability to heal."

"Oh yes!" Rilla exclaimed "There was one time when there were too many people to heal and I didn't really know what I was doing yet. Eliséo told me he wanted to help, so after I'd spread out as much pain through my body as I could, I passed the rest through to him until he broke away from my touch. But I didn't realise he wouldn't be able to do the same thing, so a wound opened up on his arm too. I was so angry with him for not telling me that would happen."

Rilla lost herself in thought. So many things had happened since she'd left the Paradise. Everything seemed to happen by accident ever since she pieced together the fact that she was a lintep. It was an odd thing for her to deal with, but looking at Mistress Kayte, it must have been even stranger from an Illarian lintep's point of view.

The healing teacher said nothing, but only sat back in her chair and passed the testing over to Isis, who leaned forward excitedly. Rilla held back a smile at the younger teacher's constant enthusiasm.

"I won't spend too long testing you, Rilla. I know you're tired and I've already seen a lot of what you can do. I can see from your healing test that you know when you've reached your limit there, but we still need to prove you can do the same when it comes to fire and ice. Go and get a lantern."

Isis flicked her head to a corner of the room. Rilla obediently stood and walked over to a chest of drawers where an unlit oil lantern was the only adornment. She lifted it gingerly, not wanting to spill any of the oil on her hands. It would not be a pleasant test if her fingers caught fire at the same time as the lantern's wick. Once she'd placed the lantern on the table between herself and the mistresses, Rilla seated herself and looked over to Isis.

"I will be shadowing your every move," she warned the young lintep. "You will do everything I ask you to do, exactly the way I ask you to do it. Are we clear?"

Rilla nodded, clearing all thoughts from her mind. She knew she needed to be completely focussed for her next test. The fate that awaited her if she made a mistake was still clear in her memory.

"Light the lantern, using as little heat from your body as possible."

Rilla did as she was told. She'd had enough practice to know how little heat she actually needed for the task.

"Good. Now take back your heat and blow out the flame. This time I want you to draw the heat from as many of your stones as needed to light the lantern."

Rilla carefully drew the heat out of one stone, kept it at one end of her tendril and did the same with two other stones before she thought there was enough to light the lantern. Without drawing that heat into her body, it was difficult to tell how much it actually was. She led the tendril to the lantern and quickly pushed all the heat that had pooled at the end of it into the wick. The tiny flame that started there drew a smile of satisfaction from her.

"Well done," Isis encouraged her as she blew out the flame. "Now for last part of your test, I want you to try something that I think you haven't done before and I certainly haven't taught you. You will not fail the test if you can't perform the task. I just want to see what you can think of on your own.

"I want you to light the flame without using any of your own body heat or that which is still stored in the stones."

Isis, do you really think that's a good idea? The younger mistress heard Kayte's voice in her mind. *We should not be asking her to experiment in these tests. You know what Aaron's conditions were for us to put her in advanced classes.*

Hush, Kayte, Isis brushed aside the rebuke. *If I'm going to put her in one of my higher classes, I need her to earn that right. This is the same way I test all of them before they can advance themselves.*

Isis watched as Rilla thought through the problem. Neither she nor Kayte knew that Rilla had seen King Lukys, in a fit of anger, draw heat out of the air to create sparks before his eyes. Isis only realised the danger of what Rilla was doing once the air around her went cold.

"Rilla, that's too much!" Isis cried out a moment before the lantern exploded. Glass and flames flew out in all directions. She instinctively shielded herself from the shards with her power. Running to the windows, she pulled down the heavy drapes and covered the burning lantern, smothering the flames by stamping her feet.

Rilla unshielded herself and stared at the havoc she'd wreaked. None of them had escaped the shards of glass entirely, but at least there didn't seem to be any major damage. The lantern was, of course, ruined as were the drapes Isis had used to douse the flame.

"I'm sorry," she whispered.

"I told you not to test her like that," Kayte reprimanded Isis, not even deigning to acknowledge Rilla's apology.

"How could I be certain which class to put her in if I didn't test her the same way I test all the others?" Isis replied hotly.

"I wouldn't trust her in *any* of your classes."

"Then it's a good thing you won't be the one deciding that," Isis lifted her chin defiantly. "I may be the youngest mistress, but that does not mean you can tell me how to test my students or run my classes."

Kayte glared at the fire teacher before storming out of the room. Rilla clutched her tree pendant tightly as the mistresses fought. It was uncomfortably warm in her grip. How could she have been so clumsy and thoughtless? Her one action had hurt all three of them and was now a point of contention between her teachers. Isis let go of a deep breath as the door closed behind Kayte.

"She's never been one for taking chances. Don't worry Rilla, she'll be her usual charming self when you start your group classes with her."

"I'm sorry," Rilla repeated herself, not knowing what else to say.

"No need to apologise. Just help me clean up this mess and we'll call it even."

Rilla knelt down to help Isis place bits of the broken lantern in the folds of the drapes. "I suppose I've failed my test then."

"What makes you say that?" Isis asked, without looking at her. When Rilla didn't answer, she stopped what she was doing, placing one hand on the floor to steady herself.

"I asked you to do something and you did it. The fact that you didn't know how much heat to draw out of the air is something we can work on, but if you hadn't figured out how to gather heat from somewhere other than your own body, or the stone you knew had heat left in them, we'd be having a different discussion right now.

"I'd like to place you in my intermediate class until you learn to judge how much heat or cold to draw out of something. It should still be challenging enough to keep you occupied, but not dangerous enough for others to be injured through your lack of experience. Do you agree?"

"That … would be wonderful," Rilla stumbled over the words in surprise. She'd expected to be told that she could join the beginners until she stopped being so reckless with her powers. Isis surprised her. It was probably the first time that someone had acknowledged her quick thinking rather than reprimanding her for the consequences of her actions.

"Good, then I expect to see you bright and early in this room tomorrow morning. Make sure you get a good night's rest because your classmates will be keen to test your skills and match themselves against you."

Rilla smiled at the idea of a fire lesson with people at her own level rather than with Plyke who could barely move his stones around.

Chapter Twenty – Castle Library

Aurelius closed the door behind Rilla with a pang of guilt. He hadn't even had a chance to help keep her secret. With King Lukys in her mind, and seeing her eyes glow, there was little he could say to contradict the evidence.

Placing those thoughts safely behind his wall, he turned to Shuut. She was looking around the room suspiciously, as was to be expected from a banwep. Eventually, she found a chair where she felt comfortable and sat. Aurelius wasn't surprised to note that it put her back against the wall and offered her a view of both the door and the window.

"Rilla said you tested the two of them when they arrived." Shuut asked, as he sat in front of her, tapping her teeth together in what he was coming to think of as a family trait. "Well, what did you think of them?"

"That's not for me to tell you," Aurelius answered her bluntly. "My only task with you this morning is to test the limits of your skills. Did your mother teach you anything about your powers?"

Shuut raised an eyebrow at his direct response, but answered him nonetheless. "She taught me to read thoughts and hide my own."

"Let's start with that then," Aurelius suppressed a sigh. Each one of Lord Aaron's grandchildren was more difficult to test than the previous one.

At least he was confident of never having to test another lintep who had been burdened with another's powers and at such an age! Every Outworld lintep he'd had to test had been no more than sixteen years old. That was when their power peaked, so if they hadn't reached Illaria by then, either they died or their powers left them. It was as simple as that.

Shuut was a half caste, so her powers had never been great in the first place. A half caste's powers didn't peak like a full-blooded lintep. If the half caste had any control over their powers whatsoever, they kept them. So this banwep must have read and blocked thoughts her whole life to still have her power.

Now she would have to learn to deal with two conflicting powers in her body. Nyssa's power was obviously the more powerful of the two. It would be interesting to see if she could get them working together or if they would always be at odds with each other.

"First, I will think of a colour and you shall tell me what it is."

Aurelius fortified his walls in anticipation of the banwep's lack of control. He was surprised to feel only the barest awareness of her power before she retreated from his mind.

"Red," Shuut declared confidently. Aurelius barely gave her time to think before setting her next task.

"Very well, project a colour to my mind without cluttering the image with other thoughts." Again, he was surprised by the ease with which she carried out the task.

"Tell me, did you use your own power to project that grey to my mind, or your inherited power?"

"I believe I am using my own powers," she answered hesitatingly. "I think Nyssa's power is all still inside the wall everyone helped me build last night."

Aurelius hid his surprise at the statement. It would have made more sense to him if Nyssa's power was the dominant one, like the ones in the mind snare. He momentarily wondered if it made a difference that the power had been freely given – if that made it more tractable.

Without a word, he went to the chest of drawers in the far corner of the room and retrieved a green felt pouch and ten white stones. He walked back over to his student and handed the items to her.

"These stones are yours to keep, for training purposes," he explained as he did with every new student. "You must try not to lose them, for you will be hard pressed to find a master or mistress willing to replace them for you."

"What do I do with them?" Shuut asked, an eyebrow raised sceptically.

"For now, place one on the floor in front of you and lift it with your power before returning it back to its original place." He sat back and waited. Nothing happened. "You can begin when you're ready."

"No, I can't," Shuut answered. "I don't understand how to do what you've asked of me."

"Just send out a tendril of your power and lift the stone," he repeated the task, as if to a slow student.

"I heard what you said," Shuut replied coldly. "I don't know how to do that. Aren't you meant to teach me?"

"This isn't a lesson. I'm here to test you," Aurelius chose his words carefully. "Did Nyssa teach you anything other than to read and project thoughts?"

Shuut shook her head, suddenly feeling quite inadequate.

"Thank you, that will be all for today. I shall arrange for your lessons to begin tomorrow morning. I shall place you in beginner classes and let your teachers decide when you are ready to proceed to the next level.

"Master Reuben may be the only one to decide you should be put in intermediate mind classes, but he may choose to keep you in the beginner class until you learn to access Nyssa's power."

There was no point in continuing her testing. If the girl hadn't even been taught to use a tendril of her power, there was no chance she could possibly perform any other task in the test.

"That's all?" Shuut asked in annoyance. "From Rilla's account, the testing would take most of the morning. What am I to do the rest of the day if everyone else is occupied?"

"I would suggest making better acquaintance with your grandfather," Aurelius suggested gently. "He sorely missed your mother these many years and would be glad for the opportunity to get to know his granddaughter a little better. I can take you to his chambers if you are agreeably inclined."

"I am inclined to understand exactly what I'm meant to be doing here," the banwep failed to keep the impatience out of her voice. "I want to know why Lishe wants to stop the prophecy enough to try to kill Rilla. It's bad enough she's been stealing power from other lintep and leaving some of them dead, but at least there was a twisted reason behind that."

"I beg your pardon?" Aurelius leaned forward suddenly. "What was that about the prophecy?"

"Lishe wanted to kill Rilla to stop the prophecy," Shuut answered guardedly. "Getting Nyssa's power was fairly important to her and she would have liked to get her hands on Rilla's power, but both of those points were bonuses to her. What she really wanted was to kill Rilla. When she finds out that her mind snare didn't do the job, she'll be back to finish her off. I want to know what the plan is for when that happens."

"Come with me," Aurelius didn't wait to see if she was following before sending out tendrils of his power to ascertain where King Lukys was and heading straight for the throne room.

He walked briskly past one staircase and down a long sandstone hall and rounded a corner, past another staircase. The first door on the right was ajar and voice travelled to him from within.

Aurelius quickly assessed the situation as he pushed his way past the door. King Lukys was in the middle of a public audience with farmers and townspeople of Illaria.

Princess Aislen looked up at his sudden entrance. She saw the look in his eyes and motioned him to remain where he was. Unobtrusively, she excused herself from her father's side and walked down the side of the room towards the waiting Master.

"What's happened?" she asked him in a low voice.

"I need to speak with King Lukys – it's urgent," he twisted his robes in his hands impatiently.

"Master Aurelius, you know how important the public audience days are," Aislen kept her tone calm and firm. "Come with me and we can discuss what ails you until my father is free. He will know where to find us."

Without another word, Aislen ushered them out of the throne room into the empty hallway. Aurelius took the lead from there and escorted them back to the testing room. At least he knew they would not be disturbed there. Once inside, he explained the situation to Aislen.

"So Lishe is intent on stopping the prophecy," she mused aloud. "I can only see one reason for that, though I'd like to hear your opinion on the matter. But before we continue, are you certain we should discuss this in mixed company."

"She already knows the situation, Princess Aislen," Aurelius assured her. "Your cousin has felt the full effect of Lishe's power against her and knows her intentions better than others and travelled with both Rilla and Plyke. I doubt there is much we can say that she hasn't already deduced herself."

"Cousin?" Shuut asked in confusion. "What are you talking about?"

"Not now, Shuut," Aurelius attempted to silence her but Aislen intervened.

"My apologies, Shuut, we have not been properly introduced. Your arrival yesterday was so dramatic that I fear all the introductions you should have received were left by the wayside. I am Princess Aislen, daughter of King Lukys, who is the cousin of your grandfather, Lord Aaron, making us cousins."

Shuut's eyebrows shot up in surprise. "I thought Nyssa's family was all dead. All but Aunt Kora."

"That could be said of her brothers, sister and mother, but not of her extended family," Aislen smiled warmly. "I know even young Rilla and Plyke have not been properly introduced to them all, though they would have at least seen them at Nyssa's interment. I confess I've been too busy myself to meet with them."

"Nyssa's what?" Shuut in a panic.

"I thought you knew," Aislen turned to Aurelius to see him shake his head. "Nyssa was brought back the day before you arrived. Her body was placed in the crypt alongside her family just hours before Lishe attacked. Did no one tell you she had been found?"

"We were preoccupied with saving her life," Aurelius defended their actions from the day before. "Which brings me back to the matter at hand. I fear the only reason Lishe would want to stop the prophecy is to stall for time. She seems bent on taking power from as many lintep as she can. It's possible she thinks she can steal the power from each Paradise to add to her own. If she hasn't figured out a way to do that before the prophecy is fulfilled, then she will lose her chance to gain more power than she can dream of."

"No one even knows how they were created in the first place," Aislen pointed out. "Everyone who was present at their creation has long since died. How can we know how to destroy them if we don't know how they were made?"

"That's an interesting point, seeing as everyone, I suppose including me, thought that Rilla should just be able to do it because she's the prophecy child," Shuut voiced her opinion. "Do you know how the barriers around Illaria were created?"

Aurelius turned to her in confusion, not understanding the relevance of the question.

"I noticed the barriers around Illaria and the Paradise where I found Rilla, Plyke, Tika and Arishen felt a bit similar. I just thought if you knew how these ones were created, it might give you an idea of how the others were created," Shuut shrugged her shoulders uncomfortably.

"I ... don't think I've ever asked that question," Aislen admitted, looking towards Aurelius with raised eyebrows.

"Nor I," the Master admitted likewise, then turned to Shuut with a gleam in his eyes. "You were asking how to while away your time today. I think I've found the perfect task for you. Allow me to escort you to the castle library. You know your letters, don't you?"

"Yes," Shuut answered skeptically. "Why?"

"There should be documents somewhere of the histories of Illaria. Perhaps somewhere in those you can find the answers you're looking for."

Aislen smiled at the idea. "An excellent notion, Master Aurelius. Perhaps we can reconvene with my father and anyone else who should be included in a few days to see what you have discovered. Besides, I think it high time that our families dine together."

* * *

Shuut looked around the library in wonder. Her mother had taught her to read before they'd parted ways. But in all those years, through all the villages, towns and cities they'd passed through, never had Nyssa taken her into a library or any place that had more than a single shelf of books.

The castle library Aurelius had taken her to after their brief meeting with Princess Aislen held much more than a single shelf of books. Shuut looked around to see elaborately carved wooden shelves lining every wall except the one with the windows. There were ladders on wheels that could be dragged along the length of the shelves, making every book and scroll accessible no matter how high up.

A large, glass-enclosed fireplace was at a narrow end of the room. On a short set of shelves beside it were glass lanterns, presumably to light the way at the other end of the room once daylight dwindled away. A few armchairs were scattered in front of the fireplace with tables and chairs set up in orderly rows behind them.

Aside from the bookshelves lining the walls, there were freestanding bookshelves in rows down the length of the library. Those ones didn't reach the ceiling and had no ladders. Shuut spied a number of footstools in the aisles between shelves.

There were a few people in the library already that morning. Some were using the footstools as makeshift chairs as they leafed through pages of books before committing themselves to particular volumes and carrying them to the more comfortable seating arrangements near the unlit fireplace.

Closing her gaping mouth, Shuut walked to the nearest shelf and smiled as she breathed in the smell of dusty old books. She ran her fingers along the leather spines as she walked along the shelves. With no idea of where or what to look for, she strolled aimlessly around the library until she noticed an elderly lintep standing at a chest of drawers between two enormous windows, peering at her over the top of half-moon glasses.

"Can I be of some assistance to you, young lady?"

Shuut tried not to laugh. In all her years, no one had ever addressed her as "young lady". It was quite a step up from "banwep". Surprisingly, there had been no sarcasm in his question. Shuut squared her shoulders and walked over to the hunched man.

"I want to learn about the history of Illaria. Can you point me in the right direction?"

"Do you mean the history of our kings and queens, the castle or our entire stronghold?" he asked as he turned away from her and pointed to a number of drawers before selecting one and opening it. He looked up at her expectantly as she glanced past him to rows upon rows of stiff paper sitting in the drawers.

"I ... don't know," she replied, overwhelmed by the amount of topics this library must contain documents on. "I suppose whichever came first, the castle or the stronghold and I'll go from there."

"The castle it is then," he smiled at her and turned back to his catalogue. "It was built hundreds of years ago when there were fewer lintep clustered together and less threat from humans."

Shuut instantly knew that the castle itself would not be what she needed to research, but could not tell the old man without giving away her exact interest. She waited patiently for him to leaf through the papers in the drawers until he came across the one he was looking for.

He took the small, stiff sheet with him and led her through the maze of books to the clearly less-frequented part of the library. Here, there were fewer books than scrolls. Although they were in good condition, a layer of dust absent from other shelves covered them.

The old man raised his head to look at the higher shelves. In a matter of seconds, he had pulled a wooden ladder across to where he needed it and was already half way to the ceiling before Shuut thought to offer assistance. It was clear that he knew every inch of the library like the back of his hand. Every book, every scroll, every card, was exactly where he knew it would be.

Shuut watched as he selected two scrolls from one of the higher shelves and then held them close to his chest with one hand as he used the other to steady himself down the ladder.

"These should start you on your way," he said as he handed her the loosely rolled papers. "They are from our rarer collection, so I would appreciate it if you don't take them out of the library. If you wish to make a copy of anything within the pages, I will provide paper and ink for your convenience."

Shuut thanked him and followed the librarian back to the front of the library. She placed one scroll on a small table next to an armchair and sat down, curling her feet under her as she unfurled the other scroll to begin her research.

Chapter Twenty-One – Departure

It was late in the morning when Kora was ready to depart. Eliséo had organised things for himself and the lintep as soon as they'd parted ways earlier that day. He knew he shouldn't delay his departure longer than necessary. He'd made certain the chestnut mare he'd ridden from Illaria was saddled and ready to take her home.

Lady Eléna and Queen Liessa were standing among the tangled roots of Silva, assuring each other that the lintep had everything she would need for her journey. Eliséo suppressed a sigh at their attentions to her. He had made it in just five days, but he'd travelled as swiftly as only an elf could. There was no possibility of Kora reaching the lintep stronghold in less than a week herself, but she would be fine.

He had organised for her saddlebags to be filled with all the provisions she would need. Much as he grew quite tired of travelling rations after a few days of travelling, he made certain to give her as many of his as he could spare. Soon after his return to Silvaren, he'd requested they be made ready in preparation for whatever journey his queen chose to send him on next.

In reality, he'd already been fairly confident that he would be sent to Goraburg, but last night's conversation meant that he was now also bound to visit the Drakos Mountains, if he could not find a suitable messenger from among the Karliki to summon the leader of the crystal dragons, Celtan, to Illaria for him.

It was one of the things King Lukys had been quite insistent on in the end. He'd explained how Lord Aaron and Master Jorg had rescued Shadow and Rilla from the mind snare, but the fact that the two rogue powers were buried in a chest in their crypt weighed heavily on his mind. If any lintep, or in fact Lishe herself, discovered what they had done, it would only be a matter of time before they dug up the chest to recover the lost power. If the dragons had a way to release the power the way they should have been when they were forced out of their respective lintep, then they might be the only ones who could help them now.

Lady Eléna and Queen Liessa laboured over their farewells to both himself and Lady Kora before allowing the lintep to mount her horse. As soon as her feet were in the stirrups, Eliséo took the reins, to expedite her departure.

He led her through the amazing and unique array of trees that always signified he was home. Nowhere else in the Outworld was there a forest of smooth black trunks with such varied colours and shapes of leaves and flowers. He smiled bitterly at the thought that he would be leaving his home so soon after arriving.

Upon reaching Elessa, he patted his pocket to make sure the crystal heart was safely hidden. He stopped for a moment to double check the contents of his rucksack before shouldering it once more and fondly stroking Elessa's lowest branch. A gasp from behind reminded him that Kora hadn't spent very much time in Silvaren at all.

Elessa had just caused hundreds of silver buds to burst into bloom with darker silver leaves sprouting all over her. It was her way to bid him a fond farewell, even though they would always be with each other in their minds. He was surprised, almost to the point of anger, when he saw a single twisted red bloom fall to the floor with a number of silver ones.

Ask Kora to bring these to Rilla, Elessa told him before he could chastise her. *Her lessons will be difficult and I know how alone she still feels. These blooms will keep like the leaves your mother gave her from Silva. She will appreciate the gift and it might ease her into a closer relationship with her aunt.*

Eliséo nodded and bent to scoop up the flowers. He ran up to his common area, with Kora waiting curiously below, and found a spare piece of cloth to wrap them in. When he reemerged, she raised a questioning eyebrow to him.

"Lady Kora, if you would be so kind as to bestow this gift to young Rilla, I think you will automatically be in her good graces," he was surprised at the lump in his throat as he spoke of the lintep bound to his tree. "I would be grateful if you could give it to her when you are alone and tell her you found us both in good health. Tell her they will keep as well as her leaves from Silva. She will know what that means."

Kora took the precious parcel and placed it gently on top of the contents in her saddlebag. She couldn't possibly understand the full significance of it, but Eliséo knew his description of Rilla's reaction would prove to be true.

Eliséo took hold of the reins once more and led the Fleuris out to the thin strip of sand that was now underwater. It was high tide, but they did not have the luxury of waiting until low tide to cross over. The horse had been trained well and did not resist when Eliséo led her into the water. For himself, his clothing was made of such fine material that it would dry quickly. He only took off his boots and held them aloft, knowing from experience that the water would reach just above his knees and soak his boots on the inside if he wasn't careful.

Once on the mainland, he donned his shoes and pointed the graceful mare in the right direction, but before he could send her on her way, Kora's voice found him.

"You're certain he won't be irrationally angry with me?" Even without her mentioning his name, Eliséo knew exactly who she was talking about.

"Kora, Plyke will be so overjoyed to see you alive that he will likely forget any grudges he has held against you," Eliséo smiled in reassurance. "You'll have pleased more people than you can imagine by your return. Shadow spent her early years trudging through the Outworld with Nyssa in an effort to find you. Lord Aaron will be elated to have his entire family safe and sound within his reach. Rilla, Tika and Plyke will be excited to see you each for their own reasons. I can assure you, this is the best decision you can make."

Kora smiled, though Eliséo knew it was more to give herself encouragement than because she believed him. She waved a quick farewell then spurred her horse off along the coast. He looked after her for a few moments before turning north towards Goraburg and the Drakos Mountains.

As he would undoubtedly travel swifter than any lintep from Illaria, and with more discretion, it had been agreed that he could first pass through Goraburg to pledge whatever assistance might be required in their current political climate and then take a message to the Crystal Dragons.

It had been debated how best to send their message, but in the end it had been decided to tell them of Nyssa's fate and the safe arrival of Shadow to the stronghold. King Lukys had judged it best, much to Rilla's relief, to keep the prophecy child's own arrival hidden from them. If Celtan deemed it necessary to fly to Illaria and assist them with their problem, he would be told upon his arrival.

With these thoughts swirling through his mind, Eliséo set out at a swift pace towards Goraburg. He did not know when he would next see his home, but did not torture himself by taking a backward glance at the beautiful, shimmering forest.

* * *

Plyke smiled as he and Rilla walked back to the castle after their midday stroll through the gardens. He couldn't imagine his life being any better than it was. Reunited with a grandfather he never knew existed, a wonderful room in a castle adorned with the most beautiful tapestries and paintings he had ever seen, finer clothes than he'd ever had in his life, and probably best of all, lessons to teach him how to use his lintep powers properly. All of this freely and willingly provided by his grandfather without a hint of repayment.

He waved his cousin farewell as they headed towards different stairwells for their lessons. She was off to Mistress Kayte and Mistress Isis for testing and he was finally on his way to his first practical lesson with Master Aurelius. As he climbed the stairs, two by two, he fervently hoped that he would be able to control his power without letting it flood out of him again. He sprung from the open stairwell and almost collided with Mistress Kayte, Mistress Isis and Dorian.

"Hello Dorian," he smiled at the younger boy. "Are you going to help with Rilla's testing too?"

Dorian started in shock, probably that his name had been remembered, then quickly closed his gaping mouth and nodded excitedly. Mistress Kayte smiled as she hurried the young boy along. Plyke watched them for a moment then turned his attention back to the doors on his right hand side.

Plyke knew Aurelius was a master of the practical side of lintep power. That meant he was looking for a door with that symbol carved on it. Rilla had told him it was the one with a cross inside a circle. He studied each of the symbols as he walked past the doors.

The only carving he noticed was missing on this stretch of hallway was the one with musical symbols. It was quite possible that there was only one room specifically set aside for communication or possibly a single master who was skilled enough in that art to need more rooms. There were a number of rooms with a flame and a few with a staff with intertwining serpents on it. The latter was the symbol for healing, which was carved on the door where he'd met Mistress Kayte earlier that day, but her room was around the corner.

Finally he came upon a door with a cross inside a circle. Rilla had told him that Master Aurelius' room was between a flame and a triwave symbol. He knocked hesitantly at the door, hoping he hadn't got the wrong room, and was relieved to hear "Enter" in Master Aurelius' voice.

He pushed the door open and closed it behind him before looking around the room. It was much like every other training or testing room he'd been in previously. He idly wondered if there were really any differences between them or if it was just easier for the masters and mistresses to be assigned their own room for their specialty to make it easier for their students to find them.

"Good afternoon, young Plyke," Aurelius motioned him to the chair across the small table from him. "If you would begin by taking out your white stones and placing them on the table."

Plyke immediately obeyed and took the green velvet pouch out of his pocket. He found that he never went anywhere without them anymore. Not that he used them often in his lessons, but they were a constant reminder that he was finally where he was meant to be, training the same way as his mother and the rest of her family had always done. Carefully, he emptied the contents on the table in front of him and looked up at the master.

"Let's start at the beginning, shall we?" It was a rhetorical question, but Plyke nodded anyway. "Lift a single stone to eye level, like we did in your test that first day."

Trying not to dwell on the unfortunate lack of control he'd arrived in Illaria with, Plyke settled down into the lesson by focussing his entire attention on the task at hand. Master Jorg, harsh as he had initially been, had taught him how to pull his power from behind his wall and place it back there in safety. He'd only had to keep his power outside his wall with Master Graham so far, but that had gone relatively well.

Determined to be as cautious as possible, Plyke pulled out the thinnest tendril he thought he would require and carefully directed it towards the stones on the table. Choosing the one closest to him, he wrapped the tendril of power around the smooth white surface and lifted it off the table to eye level and immediately replaced it, drawing the tendril back inside his wall before looking up at Master Aurelius with a proud spark in his eyes.

"A week with Master Jorg and look what you've accomplished!" the old lintep exclaimed happily. "You haven't even broken a sweat. I'm quite impressed, Plyke."

Plyke was grinning from ear to ear. During his lessons with Nyssa, he'd never imagined that he would actually be able to complete the task without danger to himself.

"Now, let's not get ahead of ourselves. I want you to do it again, with a thicker tendril of power. Once we know you can handle keeping a decent amount of power outside your walls, I'll consider asking you to lift multiple stones, but let's just wait and see. So, again if you please."

Once again, Plyke did as he was told. He pulled out a tendril twice as thick as the previous one and used it to lift the stone. Amazed at the fact that his power wasn't trying to instantly get away from him, he carefully led it back inside his wall before Master Aurelius urged him to do it again.

The sky was already tinged with orange by the time Master Aurelius called a halt to the lesson. By that point, Plyke was able to keep two tendrils of his power out for extended periods, not needing to place them back behind the safety of his walls between tasks.

"You're doing quite well, young Plyke. I am pleased that you aren't fighting with your power anymore. It's plain to see that all you need now is practice, and a lot of it."

"So, more private lessons then?" he asked, trying to mask his disappointment.

"No," the answer was quick and firm. "I think the sooner you join beginner classes, the better. I know many of the students will be quite a lot younger than you, but it's the best place for you to practice your skills until you are ready to advance to the intermediate lessons. You can begin the day after tomorrow, in my afternoon class."

Plyke was silent for a minute. Aurelius almost misinterpreted it as annoyance at being put in so many beginner classes, until the young lintep finally spoke.

"Why is Rilla having so much more trouble than I am in joining group lessons? I mean, I know I'm only being placed in beginner classes for all but communication, but I would have thought that she would be placed in all the advanced or intermediate classes right from the beginning."

Aurelius sat back in his chair and studied the boy silently. It wasn't the reaction he'd been expecting. How much could he safely tell the boy? How much had he already figured out by himself?

"Rilla is a unique case, Plyke. She can perform more advanced tasks than you without even thinking about it. Quite possibly because of that, and her lack of formal training and the dangers you were both placed in during your journey through the Outworld, she doesn't understand the dangers she puts herself and the people around her in. She doesn't know her limits.

"You heard yourself at your combined training with Master Graham that she has foolishly been taught how to control other lintep, without their consent, if she catches them unawares. Because of all these reasons, her teachers need to be certain that their other students will be safe in a class with Rilla and that she won't accidentally teach them things that only masters and mistresses should know."

Plyke's eyes widened. He knew Nyssa had taught her how to cover them both with her power, the same way Master Jorg and Lord Aaron had worked together in his first lesson. He'd listened to Master Graham's explanation of it in their one and only lesson together, but hadn't quite understood the serious implications.

"But surely, even if she accidentally tells other students what she's done, they wouldn't attempt to do it themselves, knowing what it could do to their friends," he doubted it even as he said the words. "What she did with me and Nyssa, is that the only dangerous thing she knows how to do? I mean, I don't think she did anything else in the Outworld that was dangerous to anyone but herself."

"Oh young Plyke, that's only because you know as little about your power as Rilla," Master Aurelius sighed heavily. "There are things Rilla did by accident, or even sometime intentionally, that she had no idea the significance of but she did them because she had no other choice.

"I can already name a handful of lintep, without putting much thought behind it, who would not hold back from using their powers in the extraordinary ways Rilla has, if they only knew of the possibilities."

Plyke stared at the old Master in shock but his face transformed into one of horrified understanding. "You mean, the type of lintep who would come into a Paradise and use their powers to completely control an isolated human village, don't you? Like Erton." Aurelius nodded sadly.

"So what happens now? To Rilla, I mean. Will she just be kept away from all students or will she have to keep secrets again? It's unfair she has to keep so many secrets. Do you have any idea how many secrets she had to keep in our Paradise, from her own father, to keep everyone safe? It's not fair!"

Aurelius touched his arm lightly, exuding calm. Plyke could feel what he was doing, now that he knew what to look for. Perhaps because of that fact, it didn't work. Instead of calming him, Master Aurelius had only succeeded in angering him. With flinty eyes, he took the master's hand from his arm and dropped it defiantly.

"I understand now why Rilla doesn't want anyone here touching her skin. You just tried to do it to me again. What you've all been doing to me without telling me, without even asking my permission, like you have every right to do it. You have no right to try to change my feelings. They are mine and I won't have you changing them to suit your will," his chest heaved as his heart beat an angry tattoo. Without another word, he stood up and left his lesson, leaving a bewildered master behind him.

Chapter Twenty-Two – Discoveries

Shuut sat in the library, surrounded by scrolls and books. She'd asked the librarian, Guiscard, for more documents as soon as she'd finished the first two scrolls. Far from being daunted by the enormous task before her, she found herself completely fascinated with the histories and devoured the knowledge hungrily.

Eventually, Guiscard had helped her move a small desk to the back of the library, supplied her with ink and fresh parchment, and brought her a glass lantern to help her see in the dark corner. She found herself strangely pleased that he kept her company most of the afternoon, helping her find scrolls and eventually books that took her through the history of Illaria from before it was a castle stronghold to the beginning of the royal family.

Shuut felt guilty about deceiving him, but decided it was best he thought she was researching her family history. He had been surprised to hear that she was a granddaughter of Lord Aaron, but when he took a closer look at her, over his half-moon glasses, she saw him suddenly smile.

"I should have looked closer when you first walked in," he shook his head in disbelief. "You're more your mother than that redhead I saw at the interment yesterday. Everyone's been talking about the prophecy girl, Lord Aaron's granddaughter. If you ask me, she looks more like Princess Rilla than Lady Nyssa, but you, you have your mother's eyes and hair, even if it is shorn off."

With a confused smile, Shuut tried to get more information from Guiscard. "Did my mother visit the library often when she lived here?"

"Oh no, my lady, she rarely visited. Lady Kora, on the other hand, spent hours here every day for months before vanishing into the Outworld. At least she said her farewell to me before she left," he smiled sadly. "I hear she was at odds with so many people towards the end that she barely said a word to anyone before leaving."

Shuut finally asked what she'd been wanting to know the whole afternoon. "Do you know what she was researching?"

Guiscard cocked his head to the side, pensively. "She started out the same way as you, though she didn't go so far back. She wanted to know about her grandmother and her siblings, Ophélie and Edamo. After that," he waved a hand through the air, "she stopped asking for my help to source documents and kept her findings to herself.

"One day she ran out of here in such a hurry, I thought she must be sick. She returned the following day to replace all the scrolls and books she had borrowed, putting them all in their rightful places by herself. I remember that day clearly, because she looked around the library, as if to make certain she was alone. Then she bade me farewell and looked like she would request a boon from me, but she never did. She simply thanked me for my help and told me she was going into the Outworld and doubted she would ever be back again. That was nigh on twenty years ago."

Shuut barely breathed as he told her Kora's story. "Can you show me some of those books and scrolls? Do you know which one she was reading the day she ran out?"

"I do," he answered warily.

"Can you show me?" Shuut couldn't understand why he was holding back. "Please, Guiscard. Master Aurelius and Princess Aislen asked me to research these topics. I'm sure it would help if you could let me see what Kora was researching."

"Perhaps another day, Shuut," he said patting her hand, kindly. "Perhaps another day. Come, the light is dwindling. I must tidy up the library for the evening and I'm sure you've somewhere else you need to be by now."

Shuut nodded dejectedly. What was he so afraid of her reading? She knew she should mention this to Master Aurelius and Princess Aislen, but something in Guiscard's manner left her doubting whether she would. Thanking him for his help, she climbed the ladder nearest her to return the books and scrolls she'd been reading to their rightful places on the shelves.

When she was ready to leave, she waved dry the parchment she'd made notes on as she walked, helping Guiscard carry the small desk with her other hand back to the front of the library.

"Shall I see you again?" he asked, almost hesitantly, as Shuut placed her hand on the brass door handle. She stopped and looked back at him, confused by his refusal to help her and his hope that she would return to the library again. She didn't quite know how to answer him.

"You shall, but I may not come often if you won't tell me what you know or suspect."

She closed the door behind her and leant back on it. *What is Guiscard afraid of? That I'll discover something that I shouldn't know? Perhaps something that could scare or disturb me? Did he know what Kora was really researching and the reason that she'd left?*

Trying to push the thoughts from her mind, Shuut recalled her tour with Rilla that morning and retraced her steps back to their chambers. She didn't know where Lord Aaron's chambers were, but they were bound to be on the top floor as well. She climbed the half open twisting stairwell, breathing in the evening air as she leaned over the sandstone railing to see the empty inner courtyard below. It was truly an amazing building. She hadn't quite noticed it from the hallways, but all of the windows facing the inner courtyard were arched, some pointed and ornately decorated, others plain and round.

She'd never seen anything like this castle in the Outworld. Her travels had taken her to towns, villages and cities. But even the largest of those had no single structure as spectacular as this.

As she reached the top floor, she walked slowly down the thick carpet lining the sandstone floor. She knew if she took off her heavy travelling boots, her feet would sink into the woolen threads. The temptation was almost too much to resist. Almost.

Voices in the distance brought her back to the present moment. She raced around the corner to catch up with her old companions who sounded like they were fighting. They were muffled behind a door, but the tone was clear. Without hesitating, she pushed open the door to the chambers she would now share with Rilla only to find the cousins staring angrily at each other with Tika between them, holding his hands out to keep them separated.

"What's going on?" she asked as she closed the door firmly behind her.

"I wouldn't talk to her if I were you," Plyke pointed angrily at Rilla as he turned to address Shuut. "Especially not if you're going to have lessons like the two of us. The less you know about your lintep powers from her, the better you'll get along."

"Plyke, that isn't fair and you know it!" Tika protested, trying to keep the peace as usual. "You were just as angry as she was when you finally figured it out yourself. No need to get angry with Rilla over it."

"Would one of you just tell me what happened?" Shuut kept her voice as calm as possible. Clearly, the Paradisians hadn't grown up as much as she'd thought they had in the Outworld.

"Apparently, I've been disrupting too many traditions and breaking more rules than I follow," Rilla replied sarcastically, not taking her eyes off Plyke. "Or maybe I just take after Kora more than you do. Does that means you take after Nyssa? How many classes have you been allowed into now? Will you just breeze through them all without actually taking the time to hone your skills?"

"Rilla, don't make it worse," Tika pleaded with her. "Plyke, just calm down. Why don't we go back to your room until Arishen gets here? Then we can all go to Lord Aaron's chambers together."

"Fine," Plyke mumbled angrily. He stalked out with Tika close on his heels looking apologetically at the girls before closing the door gently behind him.

"What was that all about?" Shuut asked without giving Rilla a chance to walk away from her. "You were both so happy and excited this morning. What changed?"

"Plyke finally pieced together something I figured out as soon as we arrived and he's angry with me because now he knows," Rilla replied as she slumped into a chaise. "I think he's really just angry with how the lintep use their powers but he doesn't want to be angry with them so he's taking it out on me."

"And would this something be something you're likely to tell me about or are you going to wait and see if I figure it out myself?"

Rilla tapped her teeth together, in exactly the same manner as Shuut herself.

"There's actually a lot of things I've figured out, but most of them are not common knowledge amongst the students. Even some of the master and mistresses don't know about them, but because Nyssa was taught them with Lishe when they were advanced students, well … Nyssa taught me one of them in particular that is quite dangerous. The teachers who know what I did in the Outworld, *all* of what I did, don't want me telling any of the other students."

"Your day is starting to sound just as strange and frustrating as mine," Shuut replied. At Rilla's raised eyebrow, Shuut told her about her test and subsequent meeting with Princess Aislen and her research task. When she told her Guiscard's reaction before she left the library, she watched Rilla's eyes narrow in concentration.

"Do you think Kora was researching something about the Paradises? I know it had something to do with Ophélie, whatever it was she was researching. That matches what Guiscard told you."

"How do you know that if you haven't even been to the library yet?" Shuut asked, suddenly suspicious.

"I … don't think I'm allowed to tell you," Rilla shied away from the question.

"Not allowed to tell me," Shuut leaned on the chaise beside Rilla. "Is that because you're not meant to know or *I'm* not meant to know?"

"I can't do this anymore!" Shuut quickly lifted her hands out of the way as Rilla flung her head down in her lap and burst into tears. Without understanding what had just happened, and disturbed by the crack in the strong-willed girl, she stroked her long red curls.

Burning with curiosity, she almost fell back to her old habits of trying to read minds, but immediately thought better of it. Obviously Rilla had some secrets that she simply wasn't allowed to tell. In the Outworld, keeping some of those secrets had saved their lives. Shuut remembered, with a pang of guilt of how angry she'd been that Rilla had kept her own identity a secret. She'd seen no reason for it herself, but in hindsight they all realised it was a good idea when they figured out Lishe had only started sending people to attack them once she'd realised Rilla was with them. If this secret was anything like that, it would be unfair of her to push the matter.

"I'm sorry, Rilla," she whispered as she stroked her hair. "I should know better than most people that your secrets often save lives, even if they annoy everyone around you. I won't ask you what you know or how you know it. If you'd like to help me with my research, I can show you what I've found so far and maybe you can guide me to a better area if you think it would help."

Rilla went still under her fingers, then slowly lifted her head and wiped away the tears from her wet cheeks. She smiled sadly and threw her arms around Shuut. "Thank you," she whispered in her ear. Eventually, Shuut drew her away and held her shoulders firmly.

"By the same token, if it does come to the point that you want to reveal your secrets, you know you can trust me, right? I meant what I said in the Outworld. I know you saved my life more times than anyone should have had to and I know you could have left me behind any time you wanted to and didn't. You will always have my complete support if you need it."

Rilla gave her a strange look and closed her eyes briefly. When she reopened them, they were glowing a bright green. Shuut drew back from her in shock.

"It's not possible," Shuut whispered, putting a hand to her mouth. "We were barely there a few days and you spent most of that time around Silva. When did it happen?"

"One of the only times I wasn't around Silva," Rilla told her quietly. "I tried to keep it a secret for as long as possible, but it's getting more and more difficult. We told Master Aurelius when we arrived and then King Lukys found out by accident last night and told Lord Aaron."

"Now it makes sense that he was summoned away so urgently when I was still building my wall," Shuut nodded to herself. "So now what?"

"I don't know. King Lukys wants to keep using me to talk to Queen Liessa, but that only works if the elf is in Silvaren as well."

"And the only elf we both know who isn't always in Silvaren would be the ambassador," Shuut almost laughed with incredulity. "Oh, what a mess you're in! Do the boys know?"

Rilla shook her head. "It's probably best that as few people know as possible. Besides, with the state Plyke is in at the moment, I think this would only make him angrier."

"Thank you for telling me then."

Shuut knew what it meant that Rilla had chosen to reveal this secret to her, though she wasn't ever likely to betray her. They shared a room now and it would take too much effort to keep it from her.

"Why don't we go to Lord Aaron's room? We don't have to go together with the boys and maybe it will give Plyke a chance to calm down a bit."

Rilla nodded and led the way out of their room, down the long hallway and around the corner to their grandfather's chambers. She knocked twice and stepped back, waiting with Shuut for the door to open. When it did, they both stared in confusion.

In front of them was Lord Aaron's long table, laid out with fine silver cutlery and exquisite glasses. But that wasn't what grabbed their attention. Already seated at the table were nine other lintep they hadn't really met properly. Before they could say anything, Plyke, Arishen and Tika came up behind them and nudged them through the door, not knowing why they were still standing outside it. It was only when Lord Aaron closed the door behind them and Shuut moved aside that the boys realised they weren't the only guests that night.

Chapter Twenty-Three – Introductions

"What's she doing here?" Rilla asked angrily, looking straight at Marilisa.

"Rilla, mind your manners," Lord Aaron chastised her. "Marilisa is your cousin and I thought it high time you met all of your family."

"Mind my manners?" Rilla asked incredulously, turning towards her grandfather while pointing a finger at her cousin. "*She's* the one who attacked us outside the boundary of Illaria."

"I saw you as a threat to the stronghold," Marilisa defended her actions with a shrug. "How was I to know that the Council of Masters would break the first rule of Illaria just to get you two upstarts to stay?"

"That's enough," King Lukys said. Everyone turned at the sound of command in his voice. "The decision was mine. I will not have my family fighting with one another. It's bad enough to argue in front of your family, but I had better not hear of either of you fighting in front of others and most especially not during your lessons."

"Well that's hardly likely to happen, is it? They'll be in all the beginner classes anyway," replied Marilisa smugly.

"As it so happens, Rilla will be joining your advanced healing class. Mistress Kayte is rather impressed with her skills and she will be joining you there before the week is out," Lord Aaron informed her, somewhat smugly himself. Rilla had to suppress a smile at the angry look on Marilisa's face.

"Now, before we all go hungry, let me make proper introductions. You've already seen Rilla and Plyke. This is my oldest granddaughter, Shuut. Over here we have Plyke's Partner, Tika and their friend, Arishen."

Turning to face them, Lord Aaron continued the introductions. "Most of you have already met my cousin Luyks and this is his daughter Aislen. Here is my cousin Kynon, his sons Daegan and Braedan. Braden's wife, Luisella, and their children, Ulf and Umi. Marilisa, who you clearly already know, is Daegan's daughter."

Once he'd finished the introductions, Lord Aaron walked to the silver handle beside his door and pulled down twice on it before returning to his seat at the far end of the room. Rilla recalled that meant he was calling for food to be brought to his room.

Not knowing what was expected of them, Rilla stayed near the door with the others. She recognised all of her cousins from Nyssa's interment, but she hadn't spoken a single word to them that day.

"Plyke, come and sit across from Braedan," Luisella smiled, revealing a dimple in her left cheek. "I would love to get to know you. Kora and I shared many classes when we were younger, just as Braedan and Nyssa did."

At the mention of her mother's name, Rilla looked towards Braedan. She instantly took in his short brown, wavy hair and grey eyes. If she hadn't been told they were cousins, she would have immediately assumed Braedan was Nyssa's brother instead. She desperately wanted to know more about Nyssa from people who knew her best when she was younger, but Tika was already following Plyke to sit beside Braedan.

Keen not to be left sitting anywhere near Marilisa, Rilla walked alongside Aaron, who sat at the far head of the table. She sat by his left hand side, across from King Lukys. He wasn't exactly her preferred choice, given what had happened the previous night, but anyone was better than Marilisa or Kynon.

Shuut sat across from Aislen. Rilla saw them share a look as though they were continuing a conversation. What had she done today that caused her to speak with Princess Aislen? Rilla had been in Illaria over a week and only seen a glimpse of the princess once, at the interment.

Rilla's attention was soon diverted from that thought by Arishen. He hesitated in going towards his seat. The only one free was between Shuut and Tika. Unfortunately, it was across from Lord Kynon – the least amenable to humans in the entire royal family. Arishen squared his shoulders and walked confidently to sit across from the lord.

"You're looking quite self-assured for a human amongst the most powerful lintep in Illaria."

Arishen's cheeks flushed a deep red. Rilla cringed against the inevitable retaliation, but was surprised when Arishen answered quite coolly in the suddenly silent room.

"I was assured no harm would come to me while I am here. Master Reuben's entire household has taken me in willingly and I have already started my apprenticeship as a carpenter with Timothée. They all know I am a human seer and seem to have no problem welcoming me into their lives."

"Well, perhaps that's because they haven't had enough dealings with humans to know better."

"Kynon, that's enough," King Lukys came to Arishen's rescue. "I will not have my decision to allow humans into Illaria questioned and I expect you to make them feel welcome as friends of your cousins. This is the last time I want to have to talk to you or anyone in your family about this matter. Do I make myself understood?"

"You don't have to worry about us, Uncle Lukys," Ulf called out in a happy voice, his blonde hair sticking out at odd ends.

"Yes, we're excited to meet our new cousins and their friends," Umi chimed in, her identical blond hair pulled back into a more restrained plait. "There aren't enough people our age in the castle and Mari thinks she's too old to even talk to us if she's with her friends."

Her last remark earned Umi a scowl from Marilisa, but the older lintep held her tongue. Rilla smiled at the familiar banter between them. It was nice to know she wasn't the only one who had a problem with their older cousin.

"Will we be in any lessons together?" Plyke turned to his ask them at the same time that Tika called out, "Are you two twins?"

"Yes!" the dimpled siblings answered simultaneously, as Marilisa rolled her eyes and Luisella and Braedan laughed fondly.

"Yes to which?" Tika asked in confusion.

"Yes to both," Umi replied. "We're twins and ..."

"We're in Plyke's lessons with Kayte and Rilla's lessons with Graham."

"My lessons with Graham?" Rilla asked, hearing her name from the opposite end of the table. "I'm not in his group lessons yet."

"You will be from now onwards. He told us to bring you to our next class with him. It's the day after tomorrow," Ulf happily informed her then heard Marilisa snigger beside him. "Don't worry Mari, Plyke will be in *your* class with Master Graham."

"What?" Marilisa choked and spluttered over her glass of water. "But they haven't been trained yet. How can either of them be in a class with me? This is unheard of – I must be at least two years older than both of them!"

"You should know better, Marilisa," Daegan chided his daughter. "How many times have I told you that our entire family has the most powerful and skilled lintep in all of Illaria? Just because they lived in the Outworld until now, does not mean that they did not inherit power from the same family as you." Marilisa, finally chastised, bit back any further retort.

At the other end of the table, Rilla turned from the excited chattering between Plyke, Tika and the twins. She was too far away to contribute to it in any meaningful way.

"So, Shuut, I understand from your erstwhile companions that you had quite an interesting journey with them," Lord Aaron tried his best to spark a conversation. Half of the table turned their attention to her in expectation. Shuut swallowed, suddenly uncertain, and hesitated. Rilla found her half-sister's hand under the table and squeezed it reassuringly.

"I suppose interesting is one way to put it," Shuut began hesitantly. "I woke one day, after a rather unpleasant incident the evening before, to find myself in their Paradise. A lovely old healer..."

"Rhanya," Rilla supplied the name, swallowing a sudden lump in her throat.

"Yes, Rhanya, took care of me in more ways than one. He showed me around a bit and introduced me to Rilla."

Rilla knew she was leaving out chunks of the story and was thankful for that fact.

"Let's just say, a few unfortunate things happened after that and Rilla managed to convince me to take four untrained Paradisians into the Outworld with me. I still don't know how she did it, but I guess I'm glad she did."

"So are we," Arishen said quietly. Rilla glanced over but couldn't catch his eye.

"After that, I had a fine job trying to teach them the ways of a banwep and how to fight and survive in the Outworld, so that I could leave them at the first opportunity. You have to understand I didn't know who they were and saw them as a burden I needed to rid myself of as quickly as possible.

"But it seemed that Rilla found a way at every turn to make sure that I didn't abandon them. She even saved my life once or twice. So we visited the elves, the karliki and the crystal dragons, though I was unconscious for most of the last two. Then, well, we parted ways and Lishe caught up with us."

At the mention of the rogue lintep's name, there was a heavy silence. No one had forgotten the events of the day before and they knew at least part of what had happened beforehand.

"So, it really was Lishe?" Kynon asked, temporarily forgetting to be obnoxious and arrogant.

"That's who Nyssa said she was," Shuut shrugged. "All I can tell you is that she had long straight black hair, pale blue eyes and black tattoos on her arms."

"Black tattoos? Of what?" Princess Aislen asked curiously.

"The same tattoos the masters have," Rilla answered, knowing Shuut couldn't have understood. "I saw them yesterday, but like Shuut said, they were black instead of blue. She must have done them herself."

"It makes sense. After all, she was denied the right to even take the test," Lukys told them. "The Council called me in for my advice on the matter, years ago, and we all agreed that someone like Lishe should not be given the right to become a mistress. She was already too dangerous as a student – imagine how much worse she would be if she knew all that her teachers knew."

A sharp rap at the door announced the arrival of their food. Lord Aaron rose from his seat and opened the door. Servants came in bearing trays of roast herb potatoes, parboiled vegetables dressed with a rich buttery sauce, fragrant bowls of rice, plates of flat bread and platters of fruit.

Umi and Ulf didn't even wait for the servants to leave before serving themselves and passing the dishes around the table. Rilla smiled at their enthusiasm for food and followed their example. Soon, every plate and mouth was full of food. Conversation came to an instant standstill as they all ate their fill and then turned to much lighter topics to fill the rest of the evening.

Eventually, Lord Aaron bid his extended family farewell as they left to find their own rooms. Lord Braedan offered to escort Arishen back to Master Reuben's house and Tika back to the stables. Luisella took his arm and together, they walked out in front of the boys and their own children.

Aaron was left alone with his grandchildren. He had heard their shouted conversation, muffled down the hall, earlier that evening. The disquieting feeling was reinforced when Plyke bid him goodnight, but pointedly ignored Rilla.

"I think we should sort this out, young Plyke," Lord Aaron told him before he reached the door. "It's bad enough Rilla and Marilisa being on such bad terms. I can't stand the thought of the two of you fighting as well. What happened?"

"Nothing," Plyke immediately replied.

"Liar!" Shuut rounded on him. "You were at each other's throats by the time I returned from the library. Rilla won't tell us what happened and she seems to have been on the receiving end of your anger, so start talking now or I'll give you a weapon lesson tomorrow you won't soon forget."

Aaron's eyebrows shot up at the tone and content of Shuut's threat. He had resolved to sort out the matter diplomatically, but she had completely derailed his efforts. Amazingly, she had got the result he was hoping for.

"She should tell me when she figures things out. Especially if she knows I won't like it," Plyke mumbled. "How was I supposed to know what they were doing? What Kora was warning me of? She should have just told me. They *both* should have told me."

"I've been in so much trouble for breaking traditions I don't even know exist that I didn't know if I was allowed to tell you," Rilla retorted in an exasperated voice. "I didn't want to get you in as much trouble as me."

"You still should have told me," Plyke's anger had lost its edge, but was still there.

"Exactly what are you both talking about?" Aaron finally asked them, not understanding at all. "What did you both figure out and how has it gotten either of you in trouble?"

The cousins shared a look. Without a word, Rilla placed a hand on his arm and exuded anger and resentment. As soon as his feelings began to change, she exuded calm instead. There was a dramatic shift in his feelings before she withdrew her hand.

"*That's* what I figured out and didn't tell Plyke. He figured it out today with Master Aurelius and now he's angry with me for not telling him about it as soon as I realised what was happening. But Masters Aurelius and Graham both told me that I shouldn't upset too many of their traditions before I've even been here a month.

"Mistress Isis was the only one who didn't get angry with me, but even she didn't exactly want me to spread the news. She said it usually takes most students as least a few months, if not more, before they figure that out and it's so natural to all of you that you don't think anything of it.

"Well, I'm telling you, we don't like it. We were raised in a Paradise, not the lintep stronghold and we don't want anyone doing anything like that to us – ever!"

Aaron was speechless. He hadn't expected either of them to figure it out so quickly and then to react so badly to it. It only took him a moment to remember that it was one of the things Kora hated that the lintep did, especially to humans, so she would have instilled that idea in Plyke. Rilla clearly didn't want anyone toying with her life or her mind, understandably with the amount of things that had happened which were completely out of her control.

"I see," he said quietly, backing down from the argument.

"Well, *I* don't see," Shuut replied hotly. "Clearly the three of you are sharing something and leaving me out of it."

"I believe Rilla was correct not to say anything," Aaron told them all. "It would probably be best not to disrupt Shuut's lessons before they've even begun. I'm sorry, but that's my final word on the matter. Plyke, you've figured it out yourself and you are truly your mother's son in this matter, but don't lay your anger at Rilla's feet for something she had no control over herself.

"It's been a long evening and I think you should all rest before your lessons tomorrow. Shuut, I believe you will have a lesson with Mistress Vika in the morning and Mistress Kayte in the afternoon. Come to my room when you've eaten and I'll show you to your first classroom. Good night to you all."

Without another word, he walked to his outer door, opened it and waited for them to walk through before closing it behind them. He leaned back on the dark oak and closed his eyes. *What a mess my daughters made of my grandchildren!*

Chapter Twenty-Four – Group Lessons

Plyke rose early in the morning with a knot in his stomach. He had been so excited to start group lessons, but now his joy was tinged with apprehension. *Will I start to flinch away from a simple touch as Rilla always does?*

In the Paradise and the Outworld, he has always noticed that she shied away from it but never understood why. Now, she had a reason and he completely understood how she felt – he didn't particularly want anyone toying with his feelings either. At least there was little chance of him getting so frustrated in today's lessons that a master or mistress would feel the need to calm him down. He could not say the same for his cousin.

Reluctantly, he got out of bed and pulled on some of his new tailor-made clothing. No matter what anyone said, he still felt a twinge of guilt every time he dressed himself for the day, knowing that Tika would be spending the day in smelly old brown clothes that were passed down to every new stablehand in the castle. The only consolation was that his Partner had never been happier in his life than he currently was. Edryc seemed to be impressed with the small human and Tika had already made firm friends with a number of the other stablehands.

Smiling at the ease with which Tika made friends, Plyke opened the door and walked quickly down to the dining hall. He loved sharing the first meal of the day with his Partner and knew he would miss Tika if he didn't hurry. The horses woke at dawn and Tika was allowed a quick break in the morning only once they had been fed. Edryc would not allow any of his stablehands to eat before the horses and since the morning was the busiest time of day, they were not allowed much time to themselves.

Everyone in the stables knew Tika was Plyke's Partner and did not begrudge him their time together. Tika had told him they were in awe of his relationship with "Lord Aaron's grandson" and hoped that their friendship with him might bring them to the attention of the royal family.

"So, what are your lessons today?" Tika asked Plyke between mouthfuls of food. "Will you be with any of your cousins?"

"Communication this morning with Marilisa, which should be… interesting," Plyke, chewed a piece of bread thoughtfully. He still wasn't certain how he felt about Marilisa. It was clear she didn't approve of humans, but he was fairly certain she'd never met one, so he was curious to know exactly where her disapproval of them stemmed from.

"This afternoon will be a beginner healing class with Umi, Ulf and Dorian, the boy who helped with my testing yesterday morning."

"That one should be quite fun. I like Umi and Ulf," Tika waved a spoon towards them as they entered the hall. Now they knew what the twins looked like, Plyke realised they'd seen the twins most mornings since their arrival.

With identical dimpled smiles, the twins waved and quickly filled their plates with food before going to join the Partners.

"I can't wait for this afternoon's lesson. You're so lucky to get Mistress Kayte with us. She's got to be one of the best healers in Illaria," Umi was still swinging her legs over the bench as she spoke.

"Yes, and Dorian told us all about your test yesterday," Ulf's enthusiasm easily matched his sister's. "It will be so much fun for the four of us to work together."

"How long have you been in Mistress Kayte's lessons?" Tika asked curiously. Plyke found himself just as curious as his Partner for once. The way that lintep learnt how to use their powers hadn't quite been explained properly and he was keen to talk to anyone who would answer his questions.

"Did you have lots of private lessons first or are there group lessons for children?"

"Well most lintep, us included, are trained by their parents in the basics for years before they start group lessons. A lot of things are taught to us as we grow up, just part of our normal life. It's different for each lintep, but mostly we start group lessons when we reach our twelfth birthday," Umi explained.

"Yes," Ulf agreed with his sister. "Then you are usually put in beginner classes for everything and generally don't move up to intermediate until your power peaks because you just can't perform many of the tasks without a great deal of power.

"Sometimes, they'll switch your masters over every year if you don't progress after that point, but mostly you'll stay with the same one if you work well with them. Mistress Kayte is so much in demand by parents that sometimes they have to switch students out of her class every year just to give others a chance to learn from her."

"She sounds pretty amazing," Tika's eyes widened in awe. "I wonder if I'll ever get a chance to see her in action." Umi and Ulf looked at Tika, puzzled.

"Tika loves magic," Plyke hastened to explain, "and we saw Rilla and Nyssa do some pretty amazing things in the Outworld…"

"So I would love to see what else is possible if Nyssa barely finished her training and Rilla was completely untrained in the first place," Tika fairly bounced in excitement. "It must be amazing to know that one day you'll be able to do anything like that."

"Yes, um," Ulf exchanged a look with Umi before turning towards Plyke. "Dorian told us you mentioned something strange about Rilla in your healing test."

Plyke instantly withdrew, hunching his shoulders to look smaller, instinctively dislodging the hair from behind his ear to cover his blue eye and hanging his head down to avoid eye contact.

He knew Tika noticed the change but thankfully he said nothing. Plyke hadn't had time to explain every detail of his days to him since they'd come to the castle. He found it difficult to know there were parts of his life that would always be separate now.

"Tika, isn't it time you headed back to the stables?" Plyke deflected, standing away from the wooden table. "I'll walk you there." Without protesting, Tika made his farewells to the twins and caught up with Plyke as he walked quickly from the dining hall.

"What was that about?" he asked when they were walking through the empty manicured gardens. "What did you say to Dorian that got Umi and Ulf so curious?"

"I didn't know I was saying anything wrong at the time," Plyke defended himself. "Somehow, Rilla seems to be getting me in trouble in all of my lessons without even being there."

"Do you think she's getting herself into just as much trouble, or more?"

"From the sounds of it, probably more," Plyke admitted as he lowered his voice. "She can already do things that lintep aren't even usually taught. It's quite likely some masters or mistresses don't even know they are possible. Our teachers are scared of what she can do or what she could show other students that they can do if they have enough power."

"Well, why is that so bad?"

"Erton was a lintep who wasn't taught those things and Lishe was refused the right to take the test to become a mistress and gain that knowledge," Plyke left his answer at that and let the implications settle into Tika's mind.

"Oh," Tika put his arm around Plyke's shoulders. "Well, it may be best not to mention Rilla in your lessons anymore then. Just pretend you don't know anything is possible unless your teachers tell you they are and you should be fine."

Plyke nodded reluctantly. He wished this hadn't happened. He wished his new home was a place where he could freely be himself without having to hide anything, without having to keep secrets yet again. Once they neared the stables, Tika squeezed his shoulder before drawing slightly away from him. Lintep didn't quite understand the Partnership bond and didn't necessarily know how close he and Plyke actually were. Besides, it probably wouldn't do to have Lord Aaron's grandson stinking like the stables during his lessons.

Plyke offered up a quick farewell as Tika ran back to his duties, promising to meet him in the dining hall that evening. He watched until the newest stablehand disappeared into the stables before turning back to the enormous sandstone castle. Had it been made of any other stone, he probably would have found it oppressive, but the dawn light made the walls glow a warm yellow, brightening his mood no matter how dejected he felt.

He suddenly felt a pang of guilt for yelling at Rilla the night before. Lord Aaron had been right when he said they shouldn't tell Shuut. How much easier would his own training now be if he didn't already know how his teachers could change his feelings by simply touching his skin? The only reason he was going to have to hide things in his lessons was because he'd found out something from Rilla that she should have kept hidden. How stupid he had been to ever reprimand her for doing just that.

Running up the stairs two at a time, Plyke skidded to a halt on the top level. Barely pausing to catch his breath, he walked quickly to Rilla's room and knocked twice on her heavy wooden door. After a few moments, Shuut opened it.

"Is Rilla still here?" he asked without greeting her.

She raised an eyebrow and turned to call out to her sister. "Plyke's here for you." She only waited until Rilla had appeared from their bed chamber before walking out past Plyke. "Lord Aaron is taking me to my lessons today. I'll see you two later."

"Are you here to yell at me again?" Rilla asked as she placed her pouch of white stones in the pocket of her loose grey pants. "Because if you are, I don't think I can bear that with my lessons today."

Plyke scratched behind his ear. "Actually, I'm here to apologise. I wasn't really angry with you. I was angry with the lintep, with the way they just assume they can toy with our minds. Kora would never forgive that behaviour in me."

"Not so surprising now to think how she could possibly leave this place," Rilla agreed with a grimace, completely brushing aside his apology. "At least she grew up here. It must have been a fairly common part of her life if just the past few days are anything to go by."

"Yes, well, I guess we're going to have to make sure it isn't part of our daily lives without making any other students aware of what we know. How will we do it?"

"No idea," Rilla shrugged. "I guess Master Aurelius, Master Graham and Mistress Isis will tell the others not to try that in any of our classes so the other students don't get suspicious when we flinch away from them. Other than that, there isn't really much we can do unless we stay well away from everyone and that's not really going to be possible, especially in our healing classes."

Together, they walked down two flights of stairs to the classrooms. It was still early enough that the teachers weren't in their rooms yet. Rilla left Plyke milling awkwardly around Master Graham's room, not knowing whether or not to enter without the master there. She walked around the corner to find all the classroom doors closed with students chattering quietly in the hallway. A few glanced up at her approach, but most ignored her to continue their conversations.

Rilla found Mistress Isis' room next to Mistress Kayte's room. The only external difference between them was the image carved into the door. The flame was clearly for the fire teacher. She walked over to a large sandstone windowsill and seated herself on one end of it, furthest away from the other students. They appeared to be mostly older than her, though she spied at least a few who looked the same age as her.

Unlike in their Paradise where people were happy to ignore her, here she couldn't just fade into the background unless she really did disappear and she had been warned off doing that outside of lessons. It was going to be a long day. She was not to show students that she could use her powers so easily. She was not to accidentally teach them anything they shouldn't know. She was not to show them there were different ways to use their power.

So many restrictions! she thought as she closed her eyes and leaned her head back against the sandstone wall.

Just be yourself, Eliséo's voice sounded in her mind. She smiled, and fell into his comforting embrace. *You're a quiet, observant girl. You study everything and everyone around you. Listen to your teachers and do as they ask. Try to do only as they ask and they cannot fault you.*

The elf and his tree wrapped her in their mind embrace for only a moment before breaking contact, but it was all she needed. She opened her eyes to find a tall, muscular boy sitting across the hall, watching her closely. He looked a little older than she was. Suddenly, he held out a hand to her.

"I'm Réne," he introduced himself in a confident voice. Going against all her instincts to not let anyone touch her, Rilla reached out her own hand and grasped his firmly, letting go as swiftly as possible.

"Rilla."

"I thought so," Réne said, leaning back against the thick glass of the window. "I remember seeing you walk up to Lord Aaron at Nyssa's interment. I figured you must be his granddaughter."

There wasn't anything Rilla could think to say. Thankfully, she was saved from replying by Mistress Isis' arrival. A handful of students moved out of the way as she appeared, waving her keys around in the air as she looked for the one to her classroom. She unlocked the door and ushered her students inside. Rilla followed after Réne, not certain whether she wanted to be in the same class as him or not.

As the students scattered around the room to find any available chair, Isis closed the door behind them and clasped her hands behind her back, waiting for silence.

"We have an addition to our intermediate class today. Please make Rilla feel as welcome as you were made in your first lesson."

Rilla stood beside Isis, painfully aware that the mistress had gone to lead her in by her arm before settling for placing a hand on her clothed shoulder instead. She hoped none of the other students had noticed. Most of them were too busy murmuring to each other about her name – the prophecy child's name.

"Rilla, why don't you take a seat beside Réne. He is probably the closest to moving up a level in his studies. You will learn a lot from him."

Réne flicked the hair out of his face, trying not to show how proud he was to be singled out for praise. Rilla walked over and sat on the free chair across from the confident boy – his bright blue eyes a contrast to his light brown hair.

"For today's lesson, we will need one lantern per pair of students and one glass of water, quickly now," Mistress Isis clapped her hands to get the students moving.

Belatedly, Rilla realised that each pair of students had immediately split up to get the required equipment for the lesson. Réne had gone straight to the lanterns in the far corner of the room. Rilla, feeling like the sheep she had never been in her Paradise, followed the other half of the students to a cabinet filled with glasses. She took one and waited her turn to fill it with water from the only tap in the room. Eventually, she returned back to her seat and placed the full glass beside the unlit lantern.

"Now, decide between yourselves who will go first," she waited a moment for silence to fall again. "Listen to the whole set of instructions before you begin. First group, using a small amount of your own heat, light the lantern and recover your heat. Second group, transfer that heat to the water, leaving no flame behind. First group, transfer the heat from the water to one of your white stones. Second group, transfer it back to the lantern.

"Let me stress, as I'm sure you're tired of hearing from me every lesson – this is not a race or a contest. I will not be looking to see which pair can complete the task the quickest, but which pair performs the task as perfectly as possible with the minimum of heat lost between transfers and the fewest accidents. I do not want any glass lanterns exploding, water boiling over to burn you or stones left with heat enough to singe your clothes at the end of the lesson. Do you understand?"

Rilla nodded along with the rest of the students, seeing more than just herself turning bright red at the warning. She smiled at the thought that at least she wasn't the only one to have caused any such accidents.

"Do you want to start?" Réne asked her, hands clasped behind his head with his elbows stretched out. "I don't know what level your skills are at, but I assume you're at least capable of lighting the lantern if Mistress Isis let you in this class."

Rilla bit back a sharp retort. He, along with most of the students, probably thought she was barely adequate in her skills. Stories of their adventures through the Outworld clearly hadn't spread yet. Mistress Isis caught her eye and sent a mental caution to her. *Keep your temper and show him what you're made of.*

Rilla turned away from her teacher and smiled innocently at her partner before turning her attention to the lantern between them. Focussing her anger at a point just between her eyes, she drew the small amount of heat she needed out in a tendril and pushed it quickly towards the lantern's wick. In just a moment, it had gone from a tiny spark to a steady flame. Réne raised an appraising eyebrow as Rilla withdrew the small amount of heat she had lost from her own body.

"Your turn," she said sweetly, as she watched his every move. Knowing she shouldn't actually try it, she couldn't help but hear his thoughts as he worked through his part of the task. He transferred the heat from the flame to the water in exactly the same way she had done back in the karlik tunnels of Goraburg. The only difference was Réne had clearly performed that task hundreds of times and wasn't in a life threatening situation. She idly wondered whether he would be able to do it under pressure or not.

Once the water was steaming and the flame had disappeared from the fire, Rilla withdrew her pouch and retrieved a small white stone from it. She placed it on the table next to the glass and guided a tendril of her power to the glass, hovering over the water, and over to the stone. Once the tendril was in place, she dipped it into the glass and transferred the heat through it over to the stone, careful not to let any of the heat come the other way back up the tendril into her body.

Réne had gone still and silent by this point. He was watching her intently, heedless of the fact that she knew his attention was completely focussed on her. It was only when she sat back in her chair that he quickly performed the final, most difficult task, of withdrawing all the heat from the stone and lighting the lantern without shattering the glass. As soon as the task was complete, he returned his penetrating gaze to her.

Uncomfortable with his scrutiny, Rilla made sure her mind tower was secure and kept only the bare minimum of her power milling around outside it. She caught Isis glance over to her and returned the teacher's infectious smile, despite her discomfort with Réne.

"Once each pair finishes that task, I want you to swap roles. Second person now goes first, so that you both get a turn at all the tasks," Isis instructed the class.

"Let's see how well you do with the other side of things," Réne muttered, just barely loud enough for Rilla to hear it. He wasted little time in blowing out the flame and lighting it again.

Rilla took her cue from him. He had passed a tendril through the fire and into the water. She copied his method exactly. It wasn't so different to passing the heat from the water into the stone. Once he saw the water steaming, Réne immediately transferred the heat into the stone as though it was second nature.

With the next task, Rilla took her time. This was where she had gone wrong in her test. She didn't want to shatter the glass again. Carefully she directed a tendril of her power over the stone, placing her hand near it so she could judge how much heat was still left in it, and led the tendril over to the wick of the lantern. Instead of pushing all of the heat as quickly as she could, she chose to transfer a small portion of the heat as quickly as she could to ignite the flame. Then, very carefully, she transferred the rest of the heat from the stone to the lantern, making sure to never let the flame grow too big or too fast.

Finally, she sat back with a self-satisfied smile, until she caught the suspicious look on Réne's face and noticed the fact that the two of them were the only ones who had completed their second task. Quite a few pairs of students were still at the end of their first task.

"I want you to keep swapping this task between yourselves until I call a halt," Mistress Isis instructed her class. "See if you can find new ways of transferring the heat or learn to do it faster and more efficiently. By the end of this lessons, I want you to be able to do it even if you were blindfolded."

By silent agreement, it became a contest between Rilla and Réne. They were both so far ahead of the other students that they weren't competing against the other pairs, only against each other. Rilla varied the way she lit the flame initially. Sometimes she turned anger into fire, other times, she drew on her own body heat and then recovered it back from the flame. Only once did she consider trying to draw heat out of the air, but when she caught Mistress Isis' eye she changed her mind. Réne saw her hesitation at that point and followed her gaze to their teacher. He knew something had passed between them, but Rilla was refraining herself from any conversation with him.

At the end of the lesson, all the other students quickly filed out to rush to the dining hall. Mistress Isis' lesson had left them all famished. Rilla had been hoping to ask her teacher when, if ever, she would be allowed to try King Lukys' way of lighting a fire, but Réne's presence stopped her.

"Réne, that was well done," Mistress Isis clapped him on the shoulder. "I noticed Rilla learnt a lot from you this morning. Thank you for that."

The tall lintep stood up, towering over his teacher, though there was nothing menacing about his stance. "I didn't teach her anything. She didn't ask a single question, but performed every task you set her with increasing ease."

"Clearly she deduced what you had done and copied you," Mistress Isis' smile was thin and brittle. "You'd better run off to the dining hall with the others before your next lesson begins. Well done on your first formal lesson, Rilla. I'll see you back here three afternoons from now."

Trying to hide her disappointment, Rilla simply nodded and smiled before walking out of the classroom. She rounded the corner as quickly as possible and ran down towards Master Graham's class, hoping to find Plyke and get away from Réne.

The class was already empty when she reached it. She paused, hearing footsteps approaching, but quickly turned towards the spiral stairway and walked determinedly away. It didn't deter her pursuer.

"Rilla, wait for me," Réne's voice was close behind her. There was no way she could feign that she didn't hear him, so she stopped and turned to face him with a raised eyebrow. "That was your first lesson?"

"No, that was my first *classroom* lesson," Rilla corrected him as she turned to walk down the stairs. Maybe if she got them to a more crowded area, he would stop questioning her.

"So you had a lot of private lessons before coming to Illaria, then?"

"A few," she admitted, hoping that her impromptu lessons with Nyssa counted.

"You can't have had many private lessons with Mistress Isis. You haven't been here long enough," he pointed out as he followed her down the stairs. When Rilla didn't reply, he pressed her. "Well?"

"Well what?" she asked.

"Well, how do you come to be in an intermediate fire class when you've barely had any lessons at all?" he asked in frustration.

"I don't see how that's any of your business," Rilla quickened her step, forcing Réne to hurry behind her. She barely paused as she walked into the dining hall. Plyke, Umi and Ulf were seated together and waved her over to them. She tried to shake off Réne, but he followed her to the food table, where they both filled their plates, and walked over to the bench where her cousins were waiting for her.

"I'm not leaving until you answer," the blue-eyed boy told her as he sat across from her.

"Then you'll be sitting here all day, won't you," she told him as she adopted Tika's manner of eating and started shovelling food into her mouth. Her cousins looked on in confusion. Rilla did not enlighten them.

"So...the lesson went well then, did it?" Plyke asked nonchalantly.

Rilla nodded. "How was yours?"

Thankfully, Plyke knew her well enough to understand he wasn't going to get anything further out of her with the newcomer here.

"We listened to a few new whistles but Master Graham spent the rest of the lesson teaching us how to actually do a lintep whistle, as opposed to just a normal one. Not many of us managed it, but Marilisa did."

"Why does that not surprise me?" Rilla sighed. "Well, at least I won't be in a lesson with her until the day after tomorrow."

"Wait, wait, wait," Réne put his knife and fork down heavily. "Marilisa is older than me. You mean to tell me that both of you are in intermediate classes?"

"No, Rilla's in an advanced class with Marilisa. Mistress Kayte's, isn't it?" a dimpled Umi happily supplied the information she'd heard the night before. Rilla sighed inwardly at the gasp from Réne.

"But you said you've barely had any lessons," he spluttered. "How can you possibly be in an advanced class, a healing one no less?"

"Thanks for that Umi. Now he really won't stop following me," Rilla turned sarcastically towards the grey-eyed girl. "I'm off to find Master Reuben. Won't it be fun to see if he'll let me into any of his group lessons?"

She left her half-finished plate in front of her and stood up from the bench. Réne tried to stop her, but thankfully Umi and Ulf detained him with questions about his lesson with Rilla. He had no choice but to stay where he was and let Rilla disappear into the castle.

Chapter Twenty-Five – Shuut's First Lessons

Shuut descended the spiral stairway, basking in the dawn sunlight that crept through into it. Despite the arduous journey she'd endured, she couldn't believe her luck that she was finally in Illaria – the place she'd been searching for most of her life. To find that she was actually part of the royal family was unbelievable. Nyssa had never mentioned anything about her family, except for Aunt Kora. As she walked through to the dining hall, she wondered if she would ever get used to the idea.

It was still early enough in the day that barely anyone was in the dining hall. She filled her plate with food and sat in a corner, picking at it slowly as she took in everything around her. She could easily identify the servants in their plain, but serviceable, clothing, the students with either eager or anxious looks on their faces, and the masters and mistresses with their robes on, or slung over their arms to reveal their blue tattoos. She shuddered at the sight of the tattoos. Lishe's ones were black, but had been otherwise identical. Shuut hoped her teachers would be nothing like the rogue lintep.

Mistress Vika was to be her first teacher. Neither Rilla nor Plyke had mentioned her before. Perhaps they weren't her students. Shuut quickly finished her meal and walked up the long winding stairs to the top level. Rilla and Plyke had long since departed. The halls were empty. She padded slowly over to Lord Aaron's door and knocked. A few moments later, it was opened by the old lintep. She caught a flash of uncertainty on his face before he closed the door behind him and walked out into the hallway.

"I'll take you to your lesson," he told her as he led her back down the hallway, holding her hand over his arm. Shuut searched his face for a moment before breaking her silence.

"What are you worried about?"

"Nothing dear child," he patted her hand affectionately without looking at her.

"Why don't I believe you?" Shuut came to a halt, gently jerking Lord Aaron back as she did so. "You're worried about something and I want to know what it is. I think there are already enough secrets being kept around me."

Her grandfather looked at her sadly and sighed. "I don't know how to say this any other way, but I would have wished for almost any other teacher than Mistress Vika for you. She is not fond of humans and your background…well she may not be very forgiving in your lessons."

"So the fact that I'm a half-caste is going to be a problem," she said, arching her eyebrow and ran a hand through her short brown hair. "I assume being a banwep will only make matters worse, though I have no desire to hide who or what I am."

Lord Aaron scratched his stubbly chin thoughtfully. "That's what I'm worried about. Would you prefer me to organise private lessons for you? Or to take on your training myself?"

Shuut shook her head immediately. If she was going to live here then she wasn't going to start by being treated differently to every other lintep, including her sister and her cousins.

"Very well then," he sighed and continued leading her to the classrooms. Most of the lessons had already begun by the time they reached the second level. Shuut noticed a carving of a cross within a circle on the door that they stopped in front of. It reminded her of part of the tattoo on Lishe's arm. She suppressed another shudder as Lord Aaron knocked on the door.

"Enter," a stern voice called from within. Lord Aaron opened the door and walked in, Shuut trailing close behind him.

"Mistress Vika, I have a new student for your beginner class. This is my oldest granddaughter, Shuut," he motioned her forward. "Master Aurelius informs me that you know the history of her powers. I trust there will be no problems."

Shuut noticed his tone turn to warning at the last. She caught the glint of anger in Mistress Vika's eyes before he turned to depart. No doubt his concerns about her lessons had not been exaggerated.

"Sit down and take out your stones," Vika instructed her as soon as the door had closed. Shuut looked around the room. Unlike the one Master Aurelius had tested her in, this one had rows of wooden benches going down the length of the room with small round tables in front of each. There were two lintep to a bench and few very empty spots. She chose one at random, not really caring where she sat.

"As I was saying, most of you are in the beginner class because your power has not yet peaked so you don't have enough power to achieve the skill level required for the intermediate lessons. A select few of you are here because you simply haven't been trained properly. I shall remedy that as quickly as possible.

"There will be no shirking of your lessons. Any attempt to do so will end in your experiencing why you should master the practical skills as quickly as possible. If you are late," here she paused to glance at Shuut, "you will be duly punished. Do I make myself clear?"

"Yes, Mistress Vika," a chorus went up around the room. Shuut raised a skeptical eyebrow at the children around her but joined in only a second later nonetheless.

"We have a number of new students joining us today. How many of you already know how to use the practical side of your powers at all?"

A handful of students raised their hands. Mistress Vika quickly repositioned them with the more experienced students at the back of the class, closer to the window. She got them started on their task for the morning and returned to the front of the class.

"For the rest of you, our initial lessons will focus on using tendrils of your power. For the moment, I want you to get acquainted with your power. If you have never attempted anything practical, then these will be the most important lessons of your entire student life. Watch carefully as I demonstrate."

Shuut leaned forward as did her fellow students. They watched as Mistress Vika placed some of her white stones on the table in front of her and poured some black powder, probably ash, into a wooden bowl. Mistress Vika explained as she worked that she was pulling a tendril of her power from the main source in her body and placing it in the ash.

Shuut smiled as she realised what the Mistress was doing. In placing the tendril into the bowl of ash, the black powder attached itself to her power so they could follow her every move. She continued to move the tendril around, shaping it appropriately to pick up one of the stones.

Mistress Vika demonstrated various skills with her tendril before she pulled it back inside her. Because of the ash, Shuut could clearly see that the tendril had come from her forehead.

"Does the tendril always come from your forehead?" Shuut asked, amidst gasps from her classmates. She looked at them in confusion until she turned back to find a stormy look on Mistress Vika's face.

"You will not speak without permission in my class. You will raise your hand and wait to be called upon, do you understand?"

Shuut bit her tongue and nodded. She was twice as old as most of the students and did not like the fact that she was being treated like a child. In mock innocence, she raised her hand and waited for permission to speak.

"Mistress Vika, can tendrils come from any part of your body or only your forehead?" Shuut asked in her sweetest voice. The sarcasm was not lost on her teacher.

"The tendrils can come from anywhere, but the easiest place to start is from your head, which is where I assume everyone has built a wall."

The students all nodded their heads. Even Shuut understood the truth of what she said. All of the skills she had mastered were to do with her mind powers so it made sense that her power would initially be concentrated there.

Another student raised his hand and waited to for a nod from his teacher before uttering a sound. "Mistress Vika, how do we pull out a tendril in the first place?"

"That is something you must figure out yourself," Vika spoke to him less harshly than with Shuut. "You must learn to feel your power within you and stretch out a tiny portion of it and bend it to your will."

Shuut listened on curiously. She knew for a fact that wasn't how Rilla worked with her magic. After they had crossed the Bramble River and she was teaching Nyssa how to shape her power into a vessel to hold water, it had nothing to do with bending it to her will. She simply asked and worked with her power to achieve what she needed.

Not wishing for an argument with the teacher on her first lesson, Shuut kept her thoughts to herself, resolving to ask Rilla about it when they were next alone. She returned her attention to the stones in front of her, as did every other student in the class as Mistress Isis watched them all from the front of the room.

She closed her eyes and felt for the wall she had painstakingly built and rebuilt over the past week. All of Nyssa's power was locked up tightly inside. If she concentrated, she could feel it, not quite struggling, within her wall. Her own power was behind a wall to the side of that monstrosity. She was only a half-caste so her power was never going to be great. Her wall was built more so that people couldn't hear her thoughts rather than to keep her power inside.

Thinking back to her test, she had been able to tell what colour Master Aurelius was thinking of and could project a colour into his mind. In fact, she knew she was much more capable than that with mind powers, but had never actually thought about how she did it.

She pretended she was going to read the boy's mind sitting next to her and watched carefully to see what was actually happening with her power. Before she let it reach his head, she noticed her tendrils reaching out to him. She instantly brought them to a halt and studied them closely. They did indeed come from her mind, but rather than being one thicker tendril, like Mistress Vika's, there were dozens of tiny thin ones.

Instead of trying to merge them into one, she opened her eyes and redirected her tendrils towards the stones, using as many as she needed to lift one and place it back on the table.

"How did you do that?" the boy beside her whispered, clearly hoping not to catch the attention of Mistress Vika. His hopes were futile. The teacher had caught his whisper and walked determinedly towards their table.

"That's just what I would like to know," she said, placing the bowl of ash on the table in front of Shuut. "Do that again, but first pass your tendril through the ash so I can see it clearly."

Shuut obeyed, but with a knot in the pit of her stomach. She was certain the teacher was not going to approve of her method. A few moments later, she managed to direct the tendrils into the bowl of ash and let them slither back out and towards the smooth, white stone. As she had felt for herself, there were dozens of thin tendrils, now all covered in ash, surrounding the stone and lifting it off the table.

Only once she had replaced the stone on the table did she raise her grey eyes to meet Mistress Vika's dark brown ones. Curiosity was masked by something else. Was it anger or jealousy? Shuut couldn't quite tell. What was there to be angry or jealous about anyway. It couldn't have been such a strange occurrence, could it?

"You will refrain from experimenting in my class, banwep. If I use one thick tendril, you fill follow that example exactly. Do I make myself understood?"

Her icy voice sent a chill down Shuut's spine. She ground her teeth together as she nodded her head though every part of her wanted to scream out that she'd only done as she'd been told to do and couldn't see anything wrong with that.

Mistress Vika stared at her a moment longer, almost daring her to rebel against the decree, before turning on her heel and walking over to the other students.

Shuut was almost shaking with fury by the time Mistress Vika had left her. She turned her attention back to the task in front of her and noticed the boy sitting next to her was staring agog. Shuut could tell he was dying to ask her a thousand questions but dared not utter a word for fear that he too would be reprimanded by the teacher. Instead, he watched as Shuut tried to merge her thin tendrils into one thick one. She wasn't having much success with it. By the end of the lesson, she had managed to twist all of them together so that they resembled a single tendril, but a close examination would show exactly what she had done.

There were a few audible sighs of relief as Mistress Vika called a halt to the lesson for the day. "I will see you all back here in four days for an afternoon lesson. Don't be late."

* * *

Shuut passed Rilla in the hallway on her way to the dining hall. Her sister barely acknowledged her with a nod before storming off. Not knowing what had caused her anger, Shuut debated whether to follow her or not, but the temptation of eating after such a difficult class was too strong.

She walked into the dining hall to find her younger cousins and a newcomer sitting in their usual place. Before she'd even half-filled her plate, Umi and Ulf were already motioning her over to them. She smiled at their enthusiasm for everything and wondered how their parents coped with such energetic children.

"Anyone would think you hadn't seen me in months," she grinned at them as she sat down on the recently vacated seat. Turning to the newcomer, she asked bluntly, "Who are you?"

"I'm Réne. Who are you?" the tall, muscular lintep returned.

"She's our other cousin, Shuut," Umi eagerly replied. "Rilla's sister."

"Then maybe *you* can tell me how Rilla comes to be in intermediate and advanced lessons almost as soon as she arrives in Illaria," he peered at her curiously. "Are you in any of her lessons?"

Shuut raised an eyebrow, irritably. "Well, now I know why she was in such

223

a bad mood when I saw her outside. How would you like it if you had to leave your home, travel through the Outworld where people are constantly trying to kill you and then arrive in a place you should be able to call home only to be the object of curiosity and possibly ridicule?"

Réne stared at her in shock. "I didn't..."

"You didn't think about it that way. You just wanted to know how a girl descendant from the most powerful royal family could have more skill or power than most students," Shuut knew she was being harsher than she needed to, but she instinctively felt the need to protect her sister from the student. "Next time, try putting yourself in someone else's shoes before you hound them for answers they clearly don't want to give you."

Without another word, Shuut tucked into her meal leaving Umi and Ulf to carry on the conversation with Réne. Plyke had subsided into silence before she'd even arrived. She wondered how his lesson with Marilisa had gone that morning. It couldn't have been any worse than being Mistress Vika's least favourite student.

Walk in the courtyard? she threw the question to his mind, not knowing if he would hear it.

Yes! the eager reply was instant. She smiled at the way his face didn't move a muscle though his thought was projected so emphatically. She quickly finished the rest of her food and announced she was going to stretch her legs before their next class. Plyke joined her with a promise to meet the twins outside Mistress Kayte's room before class started.

Together, they walked under the massive archways through to the outer courtyard. Shuut was still in awe of such a fantastic display of flower gardens, constantly shaped into perfection by a team of gardeners.

"So, who was that?" she asked him without preamble.

"Réne? Apparently, he's a rather talented student from Rilla's class with Mistress Isis and doesn't like being equally matched, or bested, by her," Plyke explained.

"She seems to run into trouble everywhere, doesn't she?"

"Well, can't say it's been much fun for me either the past few days," Plyke replied grumpily. "Aside from that thing last night, I have to keep pretending that I've never seen her use her magic before otherwise it will get me into trouble and create suspicion amongst the other students."

"Yes," Shuut said slowly, "I noticed that this morning. My tongue is sore from how many times I bit it to keep from protesting."

Kicking up a tuft of dirt, Plyke walked on. "It will just get worse, trust me. You've only had a practical lesson. Wait until our lesson with Mistress Kayte. You'll have bitten off your tongue completely by the end of that.

"No matter what Rilla's can do with any other of her powers, I think her real skill is with healing. She was right to want to train under Rhanya in our Paradise."

"What about you?" Shuut asked him, turning the conversation away from Rilla. "Where do you think your skill lies or have you not figured it out yet?"

Plyke didn't hesitate for a moment. "Communication and mind powers. Well, the empathy side of mind powers anyhow. As soon as I learn to do it safely without touching someone's skin, then that will probably be my best skill." He smiled at the thought.

"How was your first lesson anyway? Does Mistress Vika know what happened, you know, with Nyssa and Lishe and all?"

Shuut shrugged. "I don't know. I think she might. Lord Aaron made some mention of it, but not in any detail."

"Is it more difficult to use your power now?"

Shuut knew what he really wanted to ask. Was she was using Nyssa's power as well as her own?

"No more difficult than it ever was," Shuut answered guardedly. "I'm just learning to do new things with it that Nyssa never showed me. Anything I got from her has been safely locked away and will never be used if I can help it."

Plyke nodded in understanding. She'd answered his unasked question as best as she could. She wondered if they would ever be able to get Nyssa's power safely out of her or if she would eventually need to learn to use it, like every other lintep. It was something that the masters and Lord Aaron would need to figure out at some point. It was too important to leave alone.

"You haven't met Dorian yet, have you?" Plyke asked, as she let him lead her back towards the castle, to Mistress Kayte's classroom. Shuut shook her head.

"He's the boy who helped Rilla and I with our healing tests. He must have figured out something was odd about Rilla from my careless words and her own actions. Mistress Kayte tried to brush his questions aside by making him assume he didn't know what he was talking about because he's a beginner student, but I don't know how long that misconception will last."

"I have a feeling I'll be wanting a chat with Master Aurelius about all of this," Shuut sighed. "I know Rilla's a bit different, but would it really be that bad if other students realise all the other things that are possible with their power? I mean, I did something just slightly different in my class with Mistress Vika and nearly had my head bitten off."

"I don't think you need to talk to Master Aurelius to figure that out, Shuut," Plyke stopped her before they got to the castle. "Just think for a moment about what Erton did with his *limited* knowledge and think what Lishe did with just a bit more knowledge than him. Do you really want every lintep in Illaria to have the chance to become like either of them if that's their nature?"

Shuut shivered, despite the warmth of the day. Both of those lintep had held her life in their hands and it was not a position she would wish to be in again or wish upon anyone else.

Before the bell tolled to summon them to their next lesson, they were already waiting outside Mistress Kayte's classroom. Plyke pointed out the symbol of the serpent entwined around a staff. Umi and Ulf joined them soon after the bell stopped ringing, with Dorian and a number of other students slowly gathering to mill around in the hallway.

Mistress Kayte emerged from the stairwell, her green and red dress swirling around her ankles as she walked through the students. The difference between the teachers was immediately visible. Whereas the students had been in complete silence for fear of Mistress Vika, they greeted Mistress Kayte with a respectful silence and even a few shy smiles. Those who were brave enough had their smiles returned graciously before she found the key to unlock her door.

Once they were inside, Umi immediately grabbed Shuut's arm and dragged her off to one of the pairs of chairs scattered throughout the room. Feeling a little at a loss, she searched for Plyke who was likewise being led by Ulf to a pair of chairs, next to his twin. Dorian, who had been pointed out to her in the hall, found a partner and made sure to sit as close to them as possible.

Mistress Kayte closed the door once all of her students had entered and walked over to Shuut and Plyke as the rest of them found their seats.

"Class, we have two additions to our number today. Plyke and Shuut have recently arrived in Illaria. To dispel any rumours before they begin – yes, they are Lord Aaron's grandchildren. Plyke lived in a Paradise and Shuut in the Outworld for most of their lives. Both had a difficult journey to get here with very little formal training.

"I want everyone to help them. I'm sure they are ready and eager to increase their skills in every way possible. But for now, I want you to carry on with what you were doing last lesson so that I can induct your new classmates. The twins, as you can see, have laid claim to their first lesson."

A chuckle ran through the class at the last remark. It was such a different introduction to the one she'd had in Mistress Vika's class that Shuut instantly relaxed. It was going to be a good lesson. She watched as Mistress Kayte knelt between Plyke and Ulf.

"Ulf, Plyke had his testing with Dorian's help yesterday. Do you mind swapping partners with him just for this lesson so that he can settle into the class properly?" Ulf looked completely crushed, but stood up to swap places with his classmate as his teacher walked over to his twin sister.

"Umi, Shuut hasn't been tested in this area. It appears she was only taught to use her mind powers. So, can I count on your courage while she fumbles her way through the initial steps?"

"Oh, it can't be any worse than what Ulf did to me the first few lessons," she replied with a laugh.

"You weren't any better!" Ulf retorted from his new seat. "Left me bleeding for almost an hour before you figured it out."

Half the children stifled their laughs. Jovial outbursts like this were quite common from the twins and their classmates were well accustomed to them. Shuut, however, was not diverted by their laughter. All she'd heard was that it could be painful and dangerous.

"Mistress Kayte, I don't mean to speak out of turn, but I really don't want to hurt Umi because I don't know what I'm doing."

Kayte put a hand on Shuut's arm and exuded calm into her, pleased that she didn't attempt to flinch away the same way Rilla had. "Don't worry, I will stay with the two of you until you are well on your way."

She flicked a knife out of her sleeve and went to cut Shuut's arm. The banwep flew into action, hitting her wrist so swiftly with the edge of her hand that the knife dropped to the floor. In an instant, her arms were pinned behind her back by the banwep. The entire class had turned to watch as she cried out in shock and pain. It only took a few moments for Shuut to fall, in confusion, to the stone floor.

Once Kayte was free from the banwep's grip, she turned to the class and bid them return to their lesson. Grudgingly, they did as they were told. Plyke turned away slower than the others, his face ashen. Kayte knew he'd understood what had happened – after all, Rilla had almost done the same thing with him in the Outworld.

She turned her attention to Umi. The young girl's grey eyes were firmly fixed on her cousin. Only the post powerful lintep could even think to attempt what she had done, let alone react as quickly and perfectly as she had. Kayte regretted the flagrant display in front of her entire beginner class, but she didn't know any other way to free herself from the banwep's grip.

"Umi, come and sit next to your cousin. We may as well not waste this opportunity to test your skills."

"Yes, Mistress Kayte," the young lintep leapt off her seat and instantly sat on the floor, cradling her limp cousin's head in her lap.

"Shuut, please don't panic," Mistress Kayte spoke directly to the fallen girl. "I'd forgotten you were a banwep. I should have warned you that I was going to nick you with the knife so we could begin our lesson. I don't usually warn students as it takes the sting out of it a bit if they are caught unawares."

She added a private mental message to the girl, not wanting the rest of the class to know what she had done if they hadn't already figured it out. *I had to take some of your strength to protect myself. I will now pass that strength to Umi and she will try to pass it into you. I need you not to attack me when you have your energy back. Can you do that?*

Yes, Shuut's reply was weak. Mistress Kayte nodded and set to work quickly to restore the banwep to her full strength. She was annoyed with herself for having put them both in such an awkward position in her first lesson. The girl must already be so wary of lintep since being captured and tortured by Lishe. It wasn't quite the start Kayte had been hoping for.

She crouched beside the young lintep and spoke as quietly as she could, cursing the fact that Umi's mind skills were not yet good enough to speak mind to mind.

"Umi, place your hand on Shuut's chest. Can you feel her lack of energy?" Umi nodded silently.

"Good, now take my hand. I will keep a ball of energy there. See if you can transfer that energy into her. You should be able to do it the same way as you transfer your healing power to someone. Do you think you can do that?" Another nod.

"Very well, then see if you can feel when she is back to full strength before I am forced to sever our skin contact."

Umi took her teacher's hand nervously. Now that she had seen what she was capable of, she stood in awe of her even more than ever. She was fairly certain Mistress Kayte would never intentionally hurt her but, then again, a few minutes ago she had also been certain none of the students would be intentionally hurt in their class aside from their own normal learning experiences.

She placed her free hand on her cousin's chest, laying skin against skin. Feeling the ball of energy in Mistress Kayte's hand, she tried to place a tendril of her power next to the ball and draw the energy away, but that didn't work. Next, she tried to wrap a tendril around the ball, to draw it away from her teacher but to no avail. Nothing she tried was working. It was completely different to passing on her own healing power. Eventually, she brought both hands back to stroke Shuut's hair.

"I can't do it," she said softly, her lowered head hiding the tears that stung her grey eyes.

"That's fine, Umi," said Mistress Kayte. "It's more of an intermediate or advanced skill. I just wanted to give you the opportunity to try. I'll quickly fix this little situation to bring Shuut back to her full strength, then we can continue our lesson from there."

Umi looked on curiously as Mistress Kayte placed a hand on Shuut's chest and closed her eyes in concentration. Less than a minute later, Shuut began to stir and Mistress Kayte pulled back from her, creating some small distance between them. The entire class tried not to show that they were watching as Shuut sat up and eyed Mistress Kayte warily.

"Eyes on your work please," Mistress Kayte told her students as Umi and Shuut returned to their seats. Guiltily, the students turned away and resumed their lessons. Kayte pulled up a free chair and sat with Umi and Shuut, the latter shifting her weight ever so slightly away from her as she bent to pick up the fallen knife.

"What exactly are you planning on doing with that?" Shuut asked before anything else could happen.

"I need to cut you so that Umi can heal you and you can start to learn how to do it yourself. Or you could cut yourself," she offered as she held the knife, handle first, towards the banwep. She watched as Shuut struggled with herself and was surprised to see her offer up her arm rather than take the knife. Without giving her a chance to reconsider, Mistress Kayte nicked the flesh just above her wrist and withdrew the knife.

Umi immediately flew into action. She placed her hand over the broken skin and explained what she was doing to Shuut, as though she were the teacher herself. It was the same process Plyke had undergone the day before, but whereas he had been healed by Rilla before, Shuut had never had that experience. It took Umi a number of times healing her before the banwep started to understand the process and agreed to try it for herself.

The bell tolled for the end of the lesson. Everyone finished up the task they were working on and started to file out of the room. Shuut flopped back in her chair, exhausted. She had just barely managed to pass some of her healing power through to Umi to heal a tiny cut on her arm but it was still taking much longer than it should to heal. It was much more difficult to learn the healing skills than the practical skills. For a moment, she wondered if her exhaustion was because of how the lesson began, but then dismissed that with a shake of her head. Mistress Kayte had given back all the energy she'd stolen from her. That wasn't the reason she was exhausted.

Shuut saw Plyke waving Umi, Ulf and Dorian ahead of them, telling them he would catch up to them in the dining hall later that evening. Once they had left, he closed the door and turned back to her.

"I know what happened," he told Shuut as she raised her eyebrow at him. Mistress Kayte kept her distance, working very slowly to pack away all the instruments from the lesson, but they knew she was listening closely to the conversation.

"Rilla did that to me accidentally, when we crossed under the Bramble River."

"So, that's another reason she's in the advance healing class then, aside from what she did with Tika."

"I'd say aside from what she did with most of us," Plyke corrected her. "Anyway, this is exactly why I told you our healing class would be difficult for both of us – because we know what can be done. But we can't do it ourselves or let any of the others know about it. I know the way we're learning to heal now isn't at all what Rilla does, but everyone needs to learn the basics."

Shuut listened to Plyke's words, seeing the truth of them, but she needed more. She turned to Mistress Kayte and waited for her to leave what she was doing to join them.

"I understand that we need to learn the basics, and I can see that I'm not going to learn it quickly, but I need to you promise that you will teach me how to steal someone's energy like you did to me today. Before you protest," Shuut cut her off before she could interrupt, "understand that Lishe is still out there and still bent on killing Rilla to stop the prophecy. *When* she returns, I do not want to be left defenceless against her. If I've managed to master any skills, I want to be taught everything that I will need to keep my sister safe from her. Do you understand?"

"Shuut, that decision cannot be mine alone," Mistress Kayte spread her hands out helplessly. "That is a decision that the Council of Masters, and quite possibly King Lukys, will need to deliberate when the time comes. I assume Rilla will request such training as well, but it will be more a matter of honing the skills she seems to have instinctively learnt to keep herself and her companions safe. There is more chance of the Council agreeing to let us train her than to teach you, but I promise I will do what I can to persuade them if I think it wise at the time."

It wasn't the assurance she wanted, but Shuut was clever enough to understand that was the most the mistress could offer her for now. As she got up from her chair, she noticed her teacher move to avoid any skin contact between them. She laughed at the irony of it but said nothing. Together with her cousin, she left her first healing lesson behind her.

Chapter Twenty-Six – Master Reuben

Rilla left the dining hall in a fluster, angry with herself for showing what she was capable of, even if that was only a fraction of what she knew was possible. But mostly, she was angry with Réne for pestering her when she had made it perfectly clear that she didn't want to talk to him.

She didn't take any notice of where she was going until she found herself at the door to the library. She paused, fingers on the handle for a moment, before pushing one half of the massive double wooden door open. Despite her mood, she smiled at the sight. Shuut had described it to her, but seeing it for herself was like walking into a dream. Without anyone trying to touch her, she instantly felt a wave of calm rush over her.

Closing the door behind her, Rilla walked over to an elderly lintep with half-moon glasses. "You must be Guiscard," she said as he looked up. "My sister described you to me last night."

"Good day to you, young Rilla," Guiscard nodded affably. "Are you here to continue your sister's research?"

Rilla began to shake her head but thought better of it. "I don't think we're looking for the same thing, Shuut and I. From what I understand, she's reading up on the history of Illaria. Is that correct?"

"More or less," the old man answered cautiously.

"I'm looking for something a little more specific than that. Do you have any books written by Princess Ophélie?"

The sudden change that came over the librarian was chilling. Rilla tapped her teeth together, suddenly realising she should have spoken to King Lukys before she started making any enquiries. She resisted the urge to back away from Guiscard and stood her ground, pulling all her stray thoughts back into her tower. This was one lintep who possibly knew exactly what she and Shuut were looking for and who seemed not to want to help her.

Eventually, he answered her. "I may have one or two volumes, but they would take a while to find. No one has wanted to look at them for over twenty years."

"That's about as long as Kora's been gone, isn't it?"

If Eliséo and Elessa weren't afraid of the librarian knowing of their existence, she was certain they would both be reprimanding her and pulling her away from this conversation.

"I couldn't say," he answered expressionlessly.

"You know, Plyke is Kora's son," Rilla continued conversationally. "She was living in our Paradise but we're fairly certain she left a little while after us. I wonder what she was doing in a Paradise when she could live here. You wouldn't happen to know, would you?"

Guiscard looked around to make sure no other lintep were around. The library was empty. At this time of day, most of the scholars were in the dining hall.

"I think you would break your grandfather's heart if you start down the same path as Lady Kora," he folded his arms and looked at her sternly over his glasses. "He lost almost his entire family to the Outworld one way or another. Don't make him lose his grandchildren as well."

Rilla was surprised by the tears that stung her eyes. She knew what it was to be heartbroken and recoiled from causing her grandfather that pain. "If the prophecy goes the way everyone expects it to, I'll have to leave Illaria at some point to destroy the Paradises, won't I?"

"That's not for me to say," his face softened at her glistening eyes. "I know it meant so much to Lady Kora that she researched as much as she could about the Paradises just before she left."

"Do you know why she left? Do you know which books she looked at before she left?" Rilla asked, almost in a whisper. She almost missed his imperceptible nod. It was so slight that she wasn't certain she'd seen it.

"Can you tell me?" The bell tolled for the start of the next lesson. Rilla jumped involuntarily at the sound.

"Come back tomorrow, and bring your sister with you," Guiscard turned away from Rilla and walked back over to his desk, paying her no more attention. She was torn between asking him for more information and getting to her lesson on time. Her fear of being late for Master Reuben made up her mind.

"Tomorrow then," she nodded. "We'll come after our morning lesson."

Rilla swiftly left the library and walked through the castle without noticing anything or anyone around her. Finally she would get some answers! Whatever Kora had been researching in the library had to do with Ophélie and the Paradises. Lukys knew why she had left. He'd practically said as much when he was talking through her to Eliséo. It almost seemed as though he had sent her on some sort of quest, but he was staying tight lipped about it. The one thing that puzzled her was why it had all been kept a secret, even from her grandfather.

Surely Lord Aaron would be angry with Lukys if he really had sent his daughter into the Outworld when she had barely finished her training, knowing what had happened to the rest of her family. She felt his imagined anger rise in her and only noticed what had happened when her knuckles protested at the force she used to knock on Master Reuben's door.

"Enter," came the terse reply.

Rilla opened the door and peered in with a guilty face. "Sorry, Master Reuben, I didn't mean to knock so hard."

"That sort of temper is not going to work well for your mind powers," he rose irritably from his chair and walked over to her. "I think we need to get you out of the castle. You've been confined here for too long without even walking into the city."

"Is that safe?" Rilla asked, her heartbeat immediately quickening. "I mean, with Lishe and all…"

"Lishe would not dare attack you so soon after being thoroughly bested by Lord Aaron. Even if she somehow knows that you've made a full recovery."

Without allowing her time to protest again, the Master led her out of his classroom, down the winding stairwell to the outer courtyard. Rilla finally realised how scared she was of being attacked by Lishe again when they had walked through the gardens to the drawbridge. She stopped short of the castle wall and stared out across the stone bridge that spanned the moat.

Master Reuben noticed a few steps later that she wasn't with him and risked her fragile trust by taking her hand and wrapping it around his arm. When she didn't pull back from him, he patted her hand lightly and led her gently out of the castle. He felt her tense as they neared the marketplace – her eyes darting everywhere, searching for a sign of the rogue lintep.

He had to forcibly pull her away from the scorch marks on the opposite side of the square. From what he'd heard, Rilla had intended the fireball for Lishe, but the rogue lintep had redirected it to burn Shuut instead. The cobblestones had been scrubbed clean, but some of the stones remained singed.

It was only when they were streets away from the main square that the green-eyed girl started to calm down again. Reuben shook his head. He had hoped getting her out of the palace would help her relax and take her mind off everything. All he had succeeded in doing was frightening her, forcing her to retreat into herself. He tilted his head and cocked an eyebrow towards her. In fact, it may actually have had an unintended side effect.

"Rilla, have you heard any of my thoughts since we left the castle?" At the shake of her head, he smiled. "Then we have had some success. You've managed to keep your power close to you, not spreading out to touch other people. That's the first step you needed to master before I could put you in my class lessons."

"What's the next step?" Rilla asked, curious despite her trepidation.

"We have to see which level I put you in," he replied easily. "I have a feeling you won't be starting in my beginner class, but I need to see whether you have the skill for my advanced class."

Rilla didn't reply. She carefully kept her thoughts to herself and cringed inwardly. At first, she had been elated to be placed in intermediate and advanced classes right from the start. Now, after her first lesson alongside Réne, she wasn't certain it was what she wanted. How would the rest of her lessons go? Would other students be as jealous over her apparent ease in her lessons as he was? Would they try to best her in dangerous ways before her teachers realised what was happening? Would she be able to keep herself safe from them, especially Marilisa, without injuring anyone?

"Well done, Rilla," Master Reuben's proud voice found its way through to her. "I can clearly see that your mind is a swirl of thoughts, but you are doing quite well to keep each individual one from me. That simply confirms you would waste your time in my beginner lessons."

"Thank you," Rilla replied slowly, knowing that he really couldn't have heard any of her thoughts if he was congratulating her after what she'd just thought. Keen to steer the topic away from herself, she asked, "Where are we going?"

"To get Arishen from Timothée's workshop. I promised to give him a lesson this evening and thought I'd save myself the trip into town later and escort him into the castle now. Besides, testing your skills on a seer could be the perfect way to work out which level to place you in."

"Wait," Rilla pulled her hand away from Master Reuben's arm. "Exactly what are you going to ask me to do with Arishen? You do know he's already broken my nose once and stabbed me in the ribs another time, don't you?"

The shocked look on her teacher's face showed that he was completely unaware of those incidences. Rilla found herself holding her breath. She didn't want to test her powers against Arishen and was fairly certain he'd feel the same way.

"It will be a supervised test, Rilla," he tried to reassure her. "There will be no chance of either of you getting hurt. I promise."

"It's all very well *you* promising. Just make sure *he* promises too."

* * *

Arishen was sweeping shavings from a vacant workbench when they arrived.

"Where's your master, young Arishen?"

He heard Master Reuben's voice and looked up in surprise. He'd only been living under his roof for the past two nights, but usually, his guardian didn't come to fetch him so early in the day. Normally, it was well after the bell tolled for the end of the last lesson in the castle.

He almost dropped his dustpan in shock when he saw Rilla standing just behind Master Reuben. He hadn't really expected to see any of his old companions now that he was living out in the city. She didn't look all too pleased to see him, but that was nothing out of the ordinary.

"Uh, Master Timothée, is out at a customer's house this afternoon, fitting a cupboard," he stumbled over his words. "Is there something you need from him?"

"Yes, I need to take you back to the castle with me. Can you find me one of the senior journeymen?"

Arishen quickly finished tidying up the workbench in front of him before running off to the back of the workshop. A burly lintep, not much older than Mistress Isis, exchanged a few words with him before looking over to Master Reuben and nodding. The seer thanked him and walked back over to his visitors.

"Bastien will let Master Timothée know," he told them, hesitatingly. "I just need to finish cleaning the rest of the workbenches before I leave."

"Very well. We will wait for you across the street, at the baker. Come, Rilla," he said, turning to the girl. "I have a craving for one of their apple pastries. If we're in luck, they may still have one so late in the day."

Arishen waited until they'd left to continue his work. He was both happy and proud to be apprenticed to a master carpenter, but he felt absurdly ashamed that Rilla should see him at such menial tasks now that he knew she was part of the royal family. He knew it was normal for all apprentices to start at the bottom of the rung. For days, he had mucked out stables with Tika, so this was quite a step up in his mind, but somehow he felt Rilla would sneer at the work.

A few minutes later, Arishen had cleared all of the workbenches and put his dustpan away. He hung up his apron on a hook by the door and brushed the tiny wood shavings from his hands before walking out of Timothée's workshop. Blinking in the sunlight, Arishen walked across the street to the baker, where Master Reuben and Rilla were sharing a pastry. The younger lintep broke hers in half and offered some to him. Arishen blushed as he hurriedly took it and thanked her.

"Back to the castle, then?" he asked, purposely ignoring Master Reuben's raised eyebrow. Telon had been right, all those weeks ago in Silvaren. The elf had told Arishen that everyone had noticed his feelings for Rilla, except the girl herself.

"Indeed. Let us proceed."

Arishen breathed a silent sigh of relief as Rilla turned to follow Master Reuben. He ate the morsel Rilla had shared with him as they walked, savouring the tart apple filling and the rich, flaky pastry. He had become accustomed to the food in the great dining hall in the castle. Since starting his apprenticeship with Timothée, he'd been fed good but plain food. The only lavish meal was his evening one back at Master Reuben's house, but he was always so tired by the end of the day's work that he had little energy to appreciate it.

It didn't take them long to walk back to the castle. Reuben tried to keep level with his ward and his student. Arishen needed to be led across the boundary into the castle grounds but, judging from Rilla's previous comment, he wasn't at all certain the girl would volunteer to take him across herself. It would be a disaster for their afternoon session to begin with Arishen in a sour mood because he was left waiting at the other end of the stone bridge before either of the lintep realised he wasn't with them.

"Come on then," Rilla huffed as she took the seer's hand. Reuben looked on in shock. She had left it to the very last moment, when he had begun reaching out a hand himself to help the seer across, before taking Arishen's hand in her own.

Had she bothered looking at the seer as she led him across the bridge, she would have seen his face, up to the tips of his ears, burning bright red at her touch. As it was, the girl seemed completely unaware of the seer's affection towards her, which made sense in a strange way. After all, he had apparently injured her quite badly twice, possibly meaning to. So how could she know if she barely spoke to him otherwise?

Not wanting to spark any fights between them in such public surroundings, Reuben quickly led them into the castle and up the winding stairway to his classroom, closing the door hurriedly behind them. He took the unusual precaution of locking his door, suddenly uncertain about the decision he had made to test Rilla's skills with the seer.

"So, what's the test?" Rilla asked him as soon as he'd turned back to face them. She wasn't as excited as he thought she would be. There was more an air of resignation about her, which puzzled him. Ignoring her for the moment, he turned to Arishen.

"Did you dream last night?"

The seer nodded.

"Do you mind if I have a look for myself? Just close your eyes and remember your dream, like you did the first day we met."

Arishen hesitated. His dreams had always been his own private world. Since coming to Illaria, he'd twice had a lintep looking at them with their mind powers. He wasn't at all certain how he felt about that.

"It doesn't have to been last night's dream. It could be whichever dream you like. Just close your eyes and recall one of them."

Arishen clenched his jaw and closed his eyes. In the end, it wouldn't matter which dream he showed them. They'd mostly been of his Paradise of late. Although, there had been one, two nights ago, about Kora, but he didn't know if it was a vision or simply a dream. Without realising it, he began to focus on that dream instead of the ones from their Paradise.

"Thank you, Arishen," Master Reuben lightly touched his shoulder. Arishen's blue eyes opened wide as he realised his mistake. He hadn't meant to show that dream. It was something that had puzzled him and he hadn't yet decided whether to share it with anyone. Master Reuben missed the warning in his eyes as he turned to face Rilla.

"Now, Rilla, I know you've thought about doing what I just did and I'm impressed you've never tried it so far, but I want you to now. I've seen the dream myself, so will know if what you see is accurate or not."

Rilla tapped her teeth together. "Don't you think you ought to ask Arishen if he's happy for me to try that?"

"Arishen?" asked Master Reuben

"What? No!" Arishen spluttered out before he'd realised it. Rilla shook her head, leaning back against the wall.

"She won't hurt you," Master Reuben reached out a hand to try to calm him, but Arishen flinched away.

"That's got nothing to do with it. I don't want her in my mind."

Belatedly, Reuben realised the problem. Rilla wasn't trained and could potentially see anything in Arishen's mind whether he wanted her to or not. With his obvious affection for the girl, there was every danger of her seeing more than she should.

"Don't go thinking I'm keen on this idea," Rilla suddenly protested, crossing her arms over her chest. "It's not as though I want to give you another reason to punch or stab me."

"That's not what I meant," Arishen replied indignantly. "I wouldn't do that."

Master Reuben watched the seer and the student glaring at each other. This was not at all how he had pictured the afternoon. He led the seer to the furthest chair in the room and sat him down.

"I would like to help you develop your skills as a seer, but to do that, you have to be willing to let other lintep see your dreams. It may come to the point where I want a lintep constantly by your side, to leap into your mind as you have waking visions so that they can project the images to whoever needs to see them. If you can't even let someone you've known all your life into your mind, we're not going to get anywhere."

He noticed Arishen peer over his shoulder at the irate girl at the other end of the room.

"I know you saw me blush earlier and you must have realised she has no idea," Arishen whispered. "What if she strays from my dream or I accidentally start thinking about her instead? What then?"

"It will be a test of control for both of you," Master Reuben sighed. "Had I known the situation, I would not have suggested she test her powers on you. However, now that I have, don't you think she would find it strange for me to change my mind? Just do your best and concentrate on your dream. *Only your dream.*"

The seer finally nodded. Reuben motioned Rilla to join them, taking the tapping of her teeth for impatience.

"Rilla, Arishen will close his eyes and think of his dream. It should be easy enough for you to see it. He won't be projecting it, because only lintep can do that, but I don't think that should make a difference to you. From what I've noticed of your skills, it won't be any more difficult than reading another person's unguarded thoughts."

Rilla nodded and sat across from Arishen. She waited a few moments after he closed his eyes to send a tendril out to his mind. Prying into his mind was the last thing she wanted to do, so she gave him as much time as she could to bring the dream to the front of his mind before going in to find it.

Kora sat at the lake under Silva, talking to Eliséo.

"Lishe," Kora whispered the word in terror. "I was always scared of her in Illaria. The masters taught the three of us things that we shouldn't have been taught, all because Lishe wanted more and more knowledge. They should have known what kind of person she was by then. They shouldn't have taught us things like that."

"Things like what, Kora?" Eliséo asked her urgently. "We think Lishe is on her way to Illaria as we speak, to kill Rilla. What things were you taught? Could she use any of it to kill her?"

The vision shifted.

"I can't do it," Kora told him, tears in her eyes. "If Lishe is on her way there, I'll only be in danger too. She knows I had just as much power as Nyssa, but I had more control of it."

"So you'll leave your son and your niece in Lishe's line of sight, while you stay tucked away safely in the trees of Silvaren?"

The vision shifted again.

Eliséo fondly stroked a tree's lowest branch. Hundreds of silver buds burst into bloom with darker silver leaves sprouting all over. Among them was a single twisted red flower. Eliséo bent to scoop up the flowers. He ran up to his common area and found a spare piece of cloth to wrap them in. When he reemerged, he turned to Kora.

"Lady Kora, if you would be so kind as to bestow this gift to young Rilla, I think you will automatically be in her good graces. I would be grateful if you could give it to her when you are alone and tell her you found us both in good health. Tell her they will keep as well as her leaves from Silva. She will know what that means."

Kora took the small parcel as though it were the most precious gift and placed it gently on top of the contents in her saddlebag.

Rilla's pulled back her tendril and snapped open her eyes in fury. "When did you have that dream?"

"I don't know," Arishen replied, clearly confused by her sudden anger. "I think it was a night or two ago."

"Was it all one dream?"

"What difference does it make?"

"Rilla, what's the matter? What did you see?" Master Reuben attempted to take control of the situation. Rilla described the dream to her teacher, pointedly averting her gaze from the seer.

"I didn't mean to show you that last bit," Arishen interrupted when she got to the part about the tree.

"And indeed, you managed to keep that part from me," Master Reuben sighed discontentedly. "Well, answer her question then. Was it all part of the same dream? Or did you dream the different parts on different nights?"

"I dreamt the first bit a few nights ago," he mumbled in reply. "The last part, well, I dreamt the first bit again and then it went into that part, just last night."

"Have you told anyone about it?" Rilla demanded hotly.

"No. I wasn't even going to show you, but I didn't manage to stop the dream in time."

Rilla stood up and stared pacing. Arishen stared at her in confusion, but Master Reuben watched her closely, starting to piece together what might have happened.

"Rilla, by any chance, do you know if Kora actually went to Silvaren after she left your Paradise?" he asked her. Rilla nodded uncomfortably.

"I see, and do you know if what she said about Lishe and the lessons is true."

Another nod.

"As for the leaves and the flowers, I assume they have some significance to you that Arishen hasn't understood as yet?"

Another nod. The seer sat upright at that.

"What significance can they possibly have to you?" he asked inquisitively.

"It's none of your business," the girl replied hotly. "You should learn to keep your dreams away from people you know. It could cause more damage than you know."

"Oh right, so my visions about someone attacking the camp or you shooting fire out of your fingers, I should have just kept all of those to myself or tried not to have them at all?" Arishen's temper flared. "I saved all our lives those days."

"Let's not forget that because you didn't wake up quickly enough, I had to heal too many people the first time and almost died myself the second time."

"Silence!" Master Aurelius roared over the top of them. "You're behaving like children. Rilla, I'm certain you know Arishen's dreams were helpful because you told the Council of Masters so yourself.

"Arishen is a seer, an untrained one at that. He can't help what he has visions of. There's no point being angry with him for dreaming about Lady Kora and Ambassador Eliséo when they spoke about you. He tried his best to keep the information secret and you should be thankful for that."

Rilla flushed with anger, but she held her tongue. He'd started to piece together all of the information she'd given him and understood the root of her anger, but there was little to be done about that.

"*If* this dream was a vision, we can assume that Kora is on her way here," Rilla reasoned aloud. "I need to talk to King Lukys – probably Lord Aaron too."

"Then let's make that part of your test," Master Reuben smoothly brought her back to her current situation. "You've already more than proved you should be in my intermediate class. If you can locate King Lukys or Lord Aaron and convince them to join us, you'll fit in nicely with my advanced class."

He watched as Rilla fought some inner battle. If he could read her mind now without having to breach her wall, he would. What was she so afraid of about the advanced class that she was almost willing not to test herself?

He breathed a silent sigh of relief as her curiosity won over her fear. He watched anxiously as her eyes went unfocused and she sent out her tendrils to find both her grandfather and her uncle. It took her far less time than he'd assumed it would for her to find them. In just a few minutes, she focused her eyes and was back in the room with them.

"Lord Aaron is on his way here now. King Lukys is in a public audience but will hand over to Princess Aislen as soon as he can," Rilla said with a small smile.

"I think that settles it then. Advanced classes start bright and early, three mornings from now," Master Reuben watched Rilla's reaction closely. Her small smile remained, but a slight creasing of her forehead told him all he wanted to know. "Unless you'd rather I put you in the intermediate class instead."

"No," Rilla answered quickly. "I'd rather not be bored in my lessons if it's all the same to you."

They waited in silence for Lord Aaron to arrive. Rilla knew she'd made it a sufficiently urgent summoning. They didn't have long to wait. As he entered the room, Rilla noted that his fingertips were stained with ink. He hadn't even taken the trouble to wash his hands after writing at his desk before rushing to find them.

"What's the matter?" he asked as the door closed behind him.

"Kora is on her way to Illaria as we speak," Rilla led with the news he'd want to hear. She was going to wait for her uncle to find them before she delved into anything further.

"My little Kora? How do you know?" The old lintep's voice was full of hope. He followed Rilla's eyes to Arishen. "Have you had another vision of her?"

Arishen nodded. "She left Silvaren this morning."

"Was Ambassador Eliséo with her?" Lord Aaron asked Arishen, his eye skittered over towards Rilla. The question was really for her. She shrugged her shoulders almost imperceptibly, but Master Reuben caught the movement.

"I don't think so," Arishen answered for her. "From what he said to Kora, it sounded like they were heading to different places. She was riding a horse, so I suppose it shouldn't take her too long to get here. Well, I mean, not that I really know the distance because we seemed to have gone the long way around to get here from Silvaren ourselves."

The door suddenly burst open. King Lukys stormed in and headed straight for Rilla.

"You had better have a good reason for taking me away from a public audience!"

Rilla involuntarily took a step back.

"Kora is coming back," Lord Aaron's words stopped him mid stride. "My little girl is coming home."

"I see," Lukys visibly calmed. "Do we know what the circumstances are?"

"She was in Silvaren for at least a few days, I'm not really sure how long," Arishen told them. "It looks like Eliséo was trying to convince her to come back and told her about Lishe…"

"It would just be easier if you watched his vision," Rilla interrupted. At the shocked look on the seer's face, she tried to reassure him. "Don't worry, they both already know the bit you're worried about and they should see the rest, the bit about Lishe especially."

She caught Master Reuben's inquisitive look and risked sending a message to his mind alone with a tendril. After all, it was meant to be a mind test for her this afternoon.

Lord Aaron and King Lukys already know what you suspect. They found out the day Lishe attacked me.

From the raised eyebrow, she knew he'd heard her thoughts as he nodded. She waited patiently for the two old cousins to watch the seer's vision. Their reactions were quite different to her own.

"I take it the first parts of the vision were at least a few days ago?" King Lukys looked over to her. She squirmed uncomfortably. It looked like he wasn't going to let her keep completely silent about her bond with Eliséo.

"It must have been," she tried to answer evasively. "It wouldn't have taken him very long to get back to Silvaren with the horse you lent him."

"That's not important," Lord Aaron brushed aside the issue. "What we need to do is find out which teachers Kora and Nyssa had in common with Lishe and what it was they taught the girls. I think we need to call a meeting of the Council of Masters."

"I'm not certain that's a good idea," Master Reuben finally spoke up. "If there were some masters or mistresses who were unwise enough to teach their students things they shouldn't know back in Lishe's day, how do we know the same isn't true now? We could just be encouraging them to do it."

"I think we need to risk that," Lukys replied, rubbing his forehead. "We need to know what the girls were taught so we can better prepare ourselves for the next attack. Once Lishe realises that Rilla isn't dead, she will come back to finish her off. We need to know what she could be capable of before that time." Rilla tried to control her temper at how callously everyone kept mentioning the fact that Lishe would come back to kill her.

"Let's not rush it then," Lord Aaron suggested. "Let's send out a message to all Council members, current and past, calling them all to a meeting tomorrow afternoon. That way we are certain to have all the old teachers there as well so we can try to find out what really happened all those years ago and try to prevent it from happening again."

"I'll leave that in your capable hands," Lukys deftly delegated the task to his cousin. "I need to get back to the public audience."

Rilla debated telling Lukys about her odd talk with Guiscard but decided against it. She was going to see the librarian with Shuut the next day anyway. She could wait until after then to confront her uncle about whether or not he had sent Kora into the Outworld without her own father knowing about it.

Chapter Twenty-Seven – Swords and Secrets

Rilla impatiently followed her grandfather out of Master Reuben's room. Her test was over and there was no point going back to the library until the next day. She was at a loose end, not knowing what to do with herself the rest of the day.

"You could help me write letters for all the masters and mistresses," Lord Aaron suggested to her. She tried to hide her displeasure at that task, but clearly he could see through her.

"Or, I could arrange a sparring lesson for you. After all, I did promise I'd look into that when you first arrived."

Rilla instantly perked up. They arranged to meet at the guardhouse, on the opposite side of the outer courtyard to the stables. Without waiting for her grandfather to leave, Rilla ran up the stairs to her chambers two at a time. She rushed into her room and opened the chest at the foot of her bed where she and Shuut had both placed their weapons.

Careful not to let the swords slip out of their scabbards, she pulled them out and strapped them to her waist. As she descended the stairs a little slower, she deftly plaited her hair in one long line down her back. From her experience of sparring practice with Shuut and her companions in the Outworld, she did not want loose curls impairing her vision.

Once at the bottom of the stairs, Rilla turned towards a part of the outer courtyard she'd never had cause to visit. She noted that the gardens came to an abrupt halt on this side of the castle, with plenty of room for the guards to train. As she approached the guardhouse, she could see Lord Aaron already in discussion with one of the castle guards. The younger lintep didn't look very impressed with the conversation.

"I don't think it's a good idea, Lord Aaron," the guard was saying in a doubtful tone. "She's just an untrained child who wants to play with swords. I guarantee you that within five minutes, she would be covered with bruises and run to you with tears streaming down her pretty little face. You don't want that, do you?"

Rilla had not had an excuse to show Lord Aaron her skills, but if he'd listened well to Tika's description of all that happened in the Outworld, he'd know the guard was underestimating her. She watched carefully as he smiled blandly, pretending he was nothing more than a doting old grandfather.

"You're probably right. However, what can an old man do but try to please his grandchildren? I would see it as a personal favour if you would give her a lesson today. Maybe you'll be able to put her in her place and she won't ask for any more lessons. What do you say?"

The guard looked Rilla up and down as she slowed to stand next to her grandfather. He raised a sceptical eyebrow, turned back to the older lintep and shrugged.

"One lesson. I won't waste my time on more than that if she isn't worth it."

"Thank you. I appreciate it," Lord Aaron said as he gave Rilla a warning look. "I'll stay for the first five minutes, in case she does end up covered in bruises and runs to me in tears."

Rilla caught his smirk as he walked past her to a nearby bench. She had to force herself not to smile back at him. After all, she didn't want to give the guard any sort of warning that she could handle herself with her swords.

The guard sighed at his unwanted task. "Right, well, firstly I'll thank you to put your swords down over here and take a wooden sword. We don't need any unnecessary injuries."

Rilla followed his orders, feigning excitement to mask her disappointment. Without Eliséo and his thickened air around the blades, it probably was a good idea to use wooden weapons, but she had hoped to practice with her own weapons. The wooden ones might unbalance her enough to make her seem like the petulant child he thought she was. Masking these thoughts, she went to pick up two wooden swords from the stash in the corner of the training ground but was instructed to leave the second one behind.

"You need to master one sword before the second one can become useful to you," the guard pointed out as though to a child. Rilla smiled sweetly at him and walked to the centre of the training ground, making sure her grandfather had a good view of the two of them.

"Ready when you are," she said as she held her sword with both hands, letting her power flood out of her to completely encompass the weapon. Once more, the guard shook his head in exasperation as he walked to where she was waiting.

"Let's just start with a few simple drills. I'll attack you and you deflect my blade."

Rilla nodded enthusiastically, though she was almost screaming out in frustration before the lesson even began. Her power was just as eager as she was for the fight to begin.

As the first blow came from the guard, Rilla reacted instinctively to defend herself. She used just a bit too much force and almost overbalanced. The wooden sword was quite a bit lighter than the swords Ensil had given her. She adjusted her stance accordingly and deflected the next blow just as easily.

The guard creased his forehead in consternation and renewed his efforts, trying more elaborate moves, feigning randomly before actually attacking. After a few minutes, Rilla became frustrated with constantly having to defend herself. Knowing it wasn't at all what they had agreed to and hoping it wouldn't cause the guard go back on his offer to give her a lesson, Rilla counterattacked after deflecting his latest blow.

The move surprised the guard, but he was clearly well trained and instinctively defended himself. His eyes narrowed at how close her sudden attack had come to connecting with him. Without taking the time to reprimand her, he renewed his attack on her and was prepared for her consequent actions. Any time Rilla thought his wooden sword would break through her defences to hit her, she spun out of the way.

"Enough," the guard called out after a while and looked over Aaron with a raised eyebrow. "Lord Aaron, is there something you neglected to tell me about your granddaughter?"

"Only that she was given her swords and initial training from the elven weaponsmaster, Ensil, in Silvaren," Aaron smiled with a twinkle in his eye. "Though, admittedly, I've never actually seen her in action before."

"Trained by an elf!" the guard whistled in amazement.

"Oh, and a banwep. Sorry, I should have mentioned that," Aaron chuckled at the expression on the guard's face.

"An elf and a banwep," the guard turned back to Rilla. "My apologies, young Rilla. I had mistaken you for a spoilt royal child. Run and get another wooden sword. If you were used to fighting with two, and that's what the elven weaponsmaster gave you, then who am I to stop you from training like that?"

His youngest granddaughter smiled at the guard and quickly embraced Aaron before running to the stash of wooden swords. He was left staring at her in shock. It was the most affection the girl had shown for him. He quickly walked away, not wanting to show her how much importance he placed on her action.

She would do well in her lesson with the guards. Perhaps he should organise the same for Shuut and Plyke. Would they expect him to organise it for Tika and Arishen? Tika would be easy enough to organise. He could always fit it in after his daily chores in the stables. But what about the seer? Perhaps he should leave that decision with Master Reuben. After all, he was the boy's guardian now.

Without giving the matter further thought, Lord Aaron returned back to his chambers and started the long task of writing letters to all of the masters and mistresses currently residing in Illaria, hoping that their meeting on the morrow would provide the answers they were so desperately in need of.

* * *

By the time the bell tolled to signal the end of the afternoon lessons, Rilla was already soaking her sore muscles in the hot waters of her bath tub. Once the guard, Nicodemo, had established her skill level, he had pushed her relentlessly. He quickly realised that she was petrified of letting any of his attacks hit her, to the point where she made reckless decisions which put her in even greater danger. He made her relate the difficult journey she'd had to get to Illaria so that he understood why she was so afraid.

"Better to allow your attacker to give you a small wound than to open yourself up to a worse one," he had cautioned her. They'd spent most of the rest of the lesson making sure that she understood when it was best to stand her ground and receive a small blow and when to try a more difficult manoeuvre without endangering herself. She had ended up with a number of bruises, just as Nicodemo had predicted, but he was sporting a few himself.

Not long after the bell tolled, Rilla heard Shuut and Plyke enter the antechamber. From the tone of their voices, she could tell something had happened in their class with Mistress Kayte. Savouring her last few moments in the hot bath, Rilla finally pulled out the plug to let the water drain away. She quickly dried and dressed herself before going to find her sister and their cousin.

The two of them looked up at her entrance. Instantly, she knew something was wrong. "What happened?" Rilla asked, looking from one to the other.

Shuut proceeded to explain how Mistress Kayte hadn't warned her about the initial cut, so she'd defended herself and somehow ended up almost unconscious on the floor. Plyke filled in the missing details, explaining to Rilla that Mistress Kayte had purposely done what Rilla herself had accidentally done to him before they crossed the Bramble River.

Rilla felt the blood drain from her face, remembering all too well the amount of energy she had taken from Plyke without even realising it. She would never tell him the ashamed thrill she felt when all of that energy rushed into her body. The fact that Shuut had requested to learn that skill shocked her and she began to protest.

"Rilla, Lishe is still out there and once she realises we aren't dead she will come back. She wants to kill you and she wants to steal Nyssa's power from me," Shuut pointed out to her. "Any skill we can learn to defend ourselves against her may very well save our lives the next time."

Her words brought Rilla back to her discussion with Guiscard earlier that morning and the following one with Lord Aaron, King Lukys, Master Reuben and Arishen.

"There's something I need to tell you," she began, looking worriedly at Plyke. She hadn't intended to tell him about her bond with Eliséo. At least, not yet. But there didn't seem to be any way around it. "Plyke, how are you feeling today?"

The question stunned the boy. *Well, that's not surprising*, Rilla thought to herself, *when else have I ever asked him a simple question like that before?*

"I feel fine. Why?"

Rilla glanced at Shuut, hoping she'd understood the reason for the question.

"She means, are you as angry with her today as you were last night or have you had time to cool off?" Without giving Plyke the chance to answer and possibly ruin the evening, Shuut replied for him. "I think he's in as good a mood as you can expect at the moment. You're not going to get a better opportunity than this to tell him."

"Tell me what?" Plyke asked, looking between the two of them. Rilla led him to a chair, where Shuut sat beside him. She seated herself across from them, tapping her teeth together.

"There was a bit of an accident when we were in Silvaren. Do you remember the day when Eliséo let us all touch a tree to make a leaf or a flower?" she waited for Plyke to nod before continuing. "Well, if you remember, the tree I touched grew an entire branch with hundreds of leaves and flowers." Rilla paused, not quite knowing how to go on.

"And?" Plyke nudged her.

She took a deep breath and closed her eyes, hoping that if she couldn't see him, he couldn't possibly react badly.

"I didn't find out until later that it meant the tree had bound herself to me. But it wasn't just any elf's tree – it was Eliséo's," she spoke the words quickly and softly.

"I see," Plyke said slowly. "So that time I saw your eyes glowing and the time in Goraburg that Anya said the same thing, and you dismissed both incidents as the reflection of firelight – your eyes really were glowing."

Rilla nodded.

"And when we went under the Bramble River and every other time we walked with the mist bubble and Eliséo asked for your help rather than mine, it wasn't because he didn't think I had enough power, it was actually because you were bound to his tree so it would be easier to draw power from you."

Again, Rilla nodded. "The most important thing you probably don't know about the bond is that it means I can talk to Eliséo any time I want to," Rilla finally managed. Plyke stared at her, startled. Shuut gently kicked her under the table to get her talking again.

"Yes, well, I did say I have something I need to tell you," Rilla began. "Kora was in Silvaren when Eliséo arrived there a few days ago."

Rilla hunched in on herself because she thought Plyke would attack her. What she didn't expect was for him to remain completely motionless and silent. She looked at Shuut for an indication of what to do, but her sister simply shrugged her shoulders. She hadn't known that nugget of information, but it wasn't *her* mother. Rilla knew if she'd just told Shuut the same about Nyssa, her sister would be overjoyed. Plyke showed no emotion.

"The other thing is, we think she's on her way here," Rilla continued, hoping to get some sort of reaction from him – any sort of reaction.

"You think?" Shuut asked, when it was clear Plyke was going to remain silent.

"Yes, Arishen had a vision and it was part of my test to try to look at it," Rilla brushed aside that matter. "Anyway, the vision showed Eliséo and Kora arguing. He was trying to convince her to return to Illaria, but she was scared to death of Lishe.

"The two of them, with Nyssa, were apparently taught some things by their teachers that they shouldn't have been taught and this has caused most of the problems. A huge Council of Masters and Mistresses, old and current, is being organised for tomorrow to try to figure out what the girls were taught to find a way to protect everyone from Lishe.

"The other part of the vision showed Kora on a horse, King Lukys' horse, leaving Silvaren. Eliséo gave her something to give me, so I assume it means she's on her way here right now. I don't know how long it will take her to get here, but I'd say less than a week."

Plyke remained silent, staring at her blankly. Rilla exchanged looks with Shuut.

"Plyke? Did you hear me?"

"Yes," he replied in a detached voice.

"Are you upset I didn't tell you earlier that she was safe in Silvaren?"

"Why should I be?" he said as he got up and walked silently out of the room, leaving the two girls looking after him in confusion.

"What just happened?" Rilla asked her sister.

"Either he doesn't care about his mother at all, which is doubtful, or he cares about her so much he is anxious for her safety and is angry with her for some reason we don't know about," Shuut answered, a little uncertainly. She turned her attention back to Rilla. "Was that all you wanted to tell us?"

"I went to the library today, before my test with Master Reuben," Rilla explained. "I had an interesting discussion with Guiscard which ended with him telling me to go back there tomorrow, with you."

Chapter Twenty-Eight – Preparations

Aaron woke the next morning with a throbbing head. He'd spent most of the afternoon writing out the same letter for every master and mistress still living in Illaria. He wished Rilla had agreed to help him, but couldn't blame the girl for preferring a more enjoyable activity.

He smiled briefly at the memory of her hugging him. It had been such a long time since any of his own children had embraced him. There were his cousin's grandchildren but Marilisa was always so proud and aloof that it didn't even seem to occur to her that they were quite closely related. Umi and Ulf were sweet children, but they had loving parents who gave them everything they needed. It was only on the rare occasion he bestowed them with a gift or a praise that either of them thought to hug him. How he missed tight arms wrapped around his neck as though he was the most important person in someone's life.

He sighed and pushed away those thoughts as he rose from his bed. There was still so much preparation to be done for the day. The letters had been sent out late the evening before. There had been close to sixty of them in total. He had no idea there were so many lintep who had retired from teaching either because of their age or to help their family. He'd had to work with the Royal Secretary to find where they currently resided and had ordered a number of servants to deliver the letters to each and every one of them. He had summoned them as respectfully and urgently as possible without exactly giving them a reason for the sudden meeting. Even so, he wasn't certain whether to expect any responses nor had he any idea if they would all attend, but he would have to make his preparations assuming full attendance.

Afternoon lessons would have to be cancelled or postponed until later in the day, unless he could get some of the more advanced students supervising the younger students for the afternoon. Or perhaps he could convince Nicodemo to give sparring lessons to all of the students. He dismissed that idea with a shake of his head. That would never work. There were simply too many students, most of whom had probably never picked up a weapon in their lives.

Another idea struck him. *Could they all be set a research assignment?* He almost dismissed it out of hand, but what if each class was set to researching a particular topic to do with the history of the lintep or Illaria? None of the students, other than his grandchildren, knew the current situation so they wouldn't understand the significance of the task, nor whether they had uncovered the important missing link they were looking for. They could just hand in their assignments at the end of the afternoon. Then he, and a select few others, could go through them looking for anything of importance.

He quickly dressed and washed his face before heading over to his cousin's chambers. Hoping Lukys was already awake, he knocked softly on the door. There was a sudden silence. He hadn't noticed the voices until they'd stopped.

A familiar pair of footsteps came closer. Aaron stepped away from the door as it opened just wide enough for Lukys' curly brown ringlets to poke through. As soon as Lukys saw his cousin, he drew him into the room and shut the door swiftly behind him, making sure to lock it before walking back to his other guest.

The librarian was seated on one of the more lavish couches around the antechamber. He seemed a little uncomfortable in his current surroundings, but smiled at Aaron nonetheless.

"Guiscard, how lovely to see you old friend," Aaron greeted him amiably. The two of them had been quite good friends years ago, before his family had fallen apart and he became the reclusive lord most people now knew him as.

"How fortuitous to find you here. I have an idea that will require your assistance today if the two of you agree to my plan."

"What is this plan?" Guiscard asked with genuine curiosity.

"I'm certain it has come to your attention that we are calling a Council of Masters, current and past, this afternoon," he waited for the librarian to nod before continuing. "I thought it would be the perfect opportunity to set all the afternoon students to a research task in the library. Perhaps each class could be set a different topic. It could lead us to the answers we're searching for."

Aaron watched as Guiscard visibly paled. He turned to his cousin to see his features frozen in place.

"Have I suggested something so terrible?" He would have laughed at the absurdity of the question had their expressions not concerned him so much.

* * *

Rilla woke with a start. It was early morning and Shuut hadn't even begun to stir yet, but something had woken her. The young lintep closed her eyes and stretched out her power to see what was wrong. It didn't take her long to figure it out. While she was sleeping, her power had been freely roaming outside of her body and picked up on the conversation behind King Lukys' door.

Careful not to disturb her sister, Rilla slid out of her bed and found a robe to cover her night clothes. Silently, she padded out to the antechamber, opening and closing their door as quietly as she could. She ran along the carpeted halls, around to the other side of the castle, past Lord Aaron and Lord Zadoc's rooms, all the way to King Lukys' chambers. Stopping just short of the door, she knocked on the wood, just below the carved crown, interrupting the argument. The door was opened by a red faced Lukys, who looked at her with fire in his eyes.

"What do you want?" he asked her angrily.

Rilla instantly felt uncertain of herself. What right had she to eavesdrop on their conversation and then include herself in it? Should she tell him she'd overheard their conversation and had been planning to ask him about Kora?

"I…forgot to talk to you last night about the library," she decided on a half-truth. "Shuut and I were thinking of researching a bit around the prophecy there and wanted to ask your opinion on which areas it would be best to start with."

Well, that part was a complete fabrication, but it might just get her in the door. She knew her grandfather and the librarian were in there too and she didn't want to accuse Lukys in the hall where Lord Aaron's anger might wake the entire royal family in residence.

"I may be holding back from breaching your wall right now, but I'd rather you didn't lie to me," Lukys told her in a low voice.

"Who's there?" came Aaron's annoyed voice when Lukys still hadn't made a move to let her in. The king, with a scowl on his face, opened the door just wide enough for Rilla to enter. She went straight over to her grandfather.

"Your conversation woke me. I knew it had to do with Kora and the prophecy, so I came over as quickly as I could. And what I told you was true," she said, glancing over to Lukys. "I *did* want to talk to you about the library. I know Shuut has been researching something there, but I'm fairly certain it's not the area we need. I asked Guiscard yesterday if he knew what Kora was researching before she left and got the distinct impression from that, and our talk a few nights ago, that you both knew exactly what she was researching and *you* sent her into the Outworld to do something but wouldn't tell anyone about it."

"You did *what*?" roared Aaron. "How dare you send my child, my little Kora, into the Outworld when she had barely finished her training? How could you do that without even consulting me?"

Lukys glared at Rilla with fire in his eyes, but she held her chin high and met his gaze evenly.

"It was necessary," he answered quietly. "She read about Ophélie quite without my urging and wanted to know more. I gave Kora all the information I could, including some pages from a diary Ophélie had written that I judged it best to keep hidden. We then both realised why the prophecy had come about and what we needed to do to help ensure it came to pass."

Before Aaron could respond, Guiscard spoke up. "Forgive me, Lord Aaron. I, too, knew what your daughter was researching before she left and kept it from you."

"Did you have a hand in convincing her to leave her home and family?" Aaron asked him in a dangerous voice.

"No, of course not," he answered, holding his hands up in front of him. "I'm a librarian. I helped her with her research and that is all. But I do believe that the task King Lukys set her was an important one."

"I think I've figured it out," Rilla interrupted. "Kora didn't come to our Paradise by accident, did she? She was she trying to find all the Paradises and plot them out so that it would be easier to destroy them all once we figure out how?"

Lukys and Guiscard looked over to her in surprise. Rilla smiled ruefully. "When people ignore you for most of your life, you get pretty good at watching and listening to what's not actually being said," she shrugged her guess away. "I'm right though, aren't I?"

"You are," Lukys conceded. "I don't know how many she managed to find before finding herself stuck in your one, but I hope she still has all of that information when she arrives."

"In light of this new information, I now agree we should submit to Aaron's suggestion," Guiscard looked over at Lukys. "It's only reasonable to find out as much as possible before Kora arrives. I will hand out appropriate assignments for each class and guide them to the areas I think may help us.

"Rilla, don't bring your sister to see me today, just come along with the rest of the students this afternoon. We don't want to arouse any more suspicion than there might already be over today's unusual events."

Rilla nodded in agreement.

Aaron, still smouldering from the knowledge that his only remaining child had been sent into the outworld by his cousin, led his granddaughter to the door. With his hand on the brass handle, he stopped and kept his teary eyes averted. "I don't know how long ago you figured that out, but thank you for finding a way to make them tell me."

"I know what it feels like to have a broken heart too," she whispered to him as she reached out to cover his hand with her own. Without realising what she was doing, the poor girl brought forth the painful memory of Rhanya's death and everything surrounding it. It melded with Aaron's own loss of his children and wife. He looked up at her, shocked that she'd shown him such an intimate part of her life in such a vivid way.

When she jerked her hand away from his, he realised she hadn't meant to do that. It must have been one of her most intimate memories. Not wanting to force a conversation about it, he opened the door for her and watched as she fled down the hallway, back to her room.

He would have to make more time for her in the coming days, before Kora arrived. He wanted to get to know her, to find out more about her life in the Paradise and even afterwards. Although Tika had told him about their adventures since leaving the Paradise and their reasons for wanting or needing to leave it, he'd been strangely silent about Rilla. Either he knew very little about her, or he respected her desire for privacy.

The boys didn't really seem to have any secrets now that they were here.

They'd lived fairly normal lives in the Paradise, with Arishen and Plyke hiding their differences behind their Partnerships, and that had continued into the Outworld. Here, in Illaria, there was nothing they needed to hide so he'd already found out more about them than they probably realised. Rilla, and even Shuut, were different. He would have to make time for both of them after today's meeting.

He turned back to Lukys and Guiscard angrily. The only reason they hadn't told him about sending Kora off on her quest and allowing her to research everything to do with the creation of the Paradises, was because he would have tried to stop her. With a heavy heart, he realised the truth of that – she was probably the only lintep in Illaria at the time who cared enough about justice and equality for humans for Lukys to entrust her with this task that he clearly could not carry out himself.

It had always been his side of the family, he reflected, that had a soft spot for humans. Even after humans killed her mother, brothers and baby sister, Kora still had enough compassion for them to try to save those trapped in a Paradise. Just as his own mother had done.

It surprised him to find out about Ophélie, but then again, if Kynon simply latched onto the fact that humans killed Ophélie and blocked out all else from everyone, how was he meant to have known about her? The simple answer struck him – he could have researched about her just like his daughter had.

"Guiscard, I'll leave you in charge of the research topics for this afternoon," he walked back to the two waiting lintep. "You and Lukys obviously know more about what we need to find out in regards to the Paradises. Lukys and I will deal with the Lishe issue instead."

Understanding that he had been dismissed, the old librarian nodded silently and left King Lukys' chambers, leaving the cousins alone.

"Aaron, I…"

"I don't want to talk about it, Lukys," Aaron interrupted him. "Let's just figure out what we're going to do in the meeting this afternoon. How are we going to ask the questions we need the answers to without giving other masters and mistresses the idea to do such reckless things themselves?"

"Are you truly concerned that they would?" Lukys asked him.

"Let's just say, the likes of Vika and Jorg sometimes frighten me."

"Surely Jorg would never teach his students any dangerous methods," Lukys protested.

"It's interesting you don't say the same of Vika," Aaron noted, "and that's exactly my point. I *would* have thought it of Jorg until he saw Lishe in action. He was mortified by what she had done and clearly could not manage the situation alone. I cannot say the same for Vika. I still think she, and a number of other masters and mistresses, might teach their students methods we'd rather they didn't learn."

"You're suggesting we keep a certain amount of knowledge from our students, permanently?"

"It's already being done to a certain extent, so I think we should formalise the practice. I know you are afraid that means some skills could become lost to the lintep altogether, but if we allow these skills to be taught once students become masters or mistresses, then they won't be lost, just confined to a select few who we trust not to misuse them."

Lukys remained unconvinced. He understood the reasons behind what Aaron was suggesting, but couldn't bring himself to agree. The unspoken agreement that some teachers had of keeping certain knowledge secret from students until they became masters or mistresses was precisely the reason they were finding it so difficult to deal with Rilla, Lishe and the Paradises that Ophélie designed. Knowledge was being lost over the years and they might never get it back again.

"I think we need to talk to Aurelius about this, possibly Kayte and Isis too," Lukys said finally. "They're the only ones who really know anything about your grandchildren and the unconventional ways Rilla, in particular, has already started using her power."

"What about Jorg, Reuben and Graham?"

Lukys shook his head. "They've had minimal dealings with her, they probably haven't noticed anything so very different yet."

"I can guarantee you, Reuben and Graham have seen things they never imagined possible from Rilla, and Jorg has already seen what Lishe is capable of."

"Very well," Lukys conceded, as he walked over to the pull cord beside the door to the hallway. They didn't have much time to organise everything else for the meeting, so they would need to talk with these six teachers as soon as possible.

Chapter Twenty-Nine – Aurelius' Idea

Aurelius lived in the castle. He had no family to speak of and found it easier to lodge in one of the rooms set aside for masters rather than keep lodgings outside the castle walls and travel in each day. Over the years, the room had begun to mirror his personality, from the tapestries and paintings he displayed on his walls to the books he had scattered over his desk and shelves.

His bed was quite austere compared to the rest of the room. He'd never seen the point of piling on pillows and lavish covers when all he did was sleep there. That was the reason why his chaise was the complete opposite – the most comfortable and opulent he could afford – he spent most of his spare time sitting on it, reading his books. Aurelius and Guiscard had become quite close over the years with his frequent visits to the library.

When the runner knocked on his door, Aurelius was not at all surprised. Since the letter from Lord Aaron the night before, he had almost been expecting a summons of sorts. He quickly dressed and walked to King Lukys' private chambers, where he knew he would have to wait a good while for Master Reuben, Mistress Isis and Master Jorg to arrive. They all lived out in the city with their families.

Master Graham and Mistress Kayte caught up with him on the stairwell leading up to the royal apartments. None of them spoke a word. It would not be a stretch of his imagination to assume they'd already come to the same conclusion as he had in regards to the summons.

The door to King Lukys' antechamber was opened quietly and closed quickly behind them. They were offered tea and bread with jam to break their fast. Lord Aaron was already seated at the table, quietly sipping a cup of tea.

Aurelius sat alongside him, with Kayte and Graham across from them. Nibbling his bread and sipping his tea, Aurelius started to feel the tension rising in the continued silence. He almost suggested they ask Rilla to use her elven mist to ensure their meeting remained secret, but instantly thought better of it. Not everyone knew of her bond and she was keen to keep it that way.

Perhaps he could use his own lintep power in roughly the same way. *If I can use it as a shield around myself, can I use it as a shield around all of us? Will the others let me try or will they not trust me?* With a smile to himself, he admitted he wouldn't let any of them try it on him either. *Could we all try it together and create a sort of bubble around us?*

"Good grief," he suddenly exclaimed! "I think I know how they did it!"

"How who did what?" asked Graham as they looked at him in confusion.

Aurelius beamed at them, proudly. "How they created the Paradises. Or at least the theory behind how they did it. Let's just wait for the others to arrive before I say anything further."

Aurelius was now thinking furiously, trying to figure out as much as he could before Jorg, Reuben and Isis arrived. *Have I really figured it out because of Rilla?* He wouldn't know until they tried it, but even the possibility of it was intriguing and exciting.

He silently thought through and discarded a handful of ideas before settling on one that might just work. By the time the others had arrived, he'd decided on how to explain it to them, but couldn't figure out, from his theory, how the lintep creating the Paradises had survived the procedure.

"Are you going to sit there, proudly beaming like a student who has finally mastered a skill all day, or are you going to tell us what you've discovered?"

Graham's rough old voice broke through Aurelius' concentration, jovially. Aurelius smiled at his old friend. Most students didn't realise the kind and generous nature of the communication master because of his gruff manner and rough voice, but Aurelius had known Graham long enough to know him to be the truest friend anyone could hope to find in their lifetime.

"I have an idea of how the Paradises were created," Aurelius told them with a smile. "Mind you, none of us have ever been to one, so we have to rely on the information we've been given from Lord Aaron's grandchildren and their friends.

"From what I've understood, the boundary of a Paradises *feels* much the same as the boundary of Illaria itself. I realise we aren't all guardians of the border, but most of you would have at least touched the boundary before.

"The main difference between our boundary and that of the Paradises is that humans can walk through those others, albeit only once in their lifetime if we listen to legends. I'm not certain how to make that possible, but I have an idea of how the boundary of Illaria *may* have been created, and so some sort of idea of how the Paradises may have been created.

"I suddenly thought back to a conversation I once had with Ambassador Eliséo. He didn't want us to be overheard, so he called up some sort of mist around us. I wondered if we lintep can use our power in the same way as that, create some sort bubble around ourselves. It should be possible, like creating a shield of sorts. But the more difficult part would be to see if a few of us could create one together, by letting our power touch one another's in a circle. That should work, if we're willing to try, but it would never be permanent unless we left that part of our power where it was."

The other lintep stared at him in silence. He scanned the faces carefully. King Lukys was completely unreadable, as usual. Kayte tried to be expressionless, but he could see horror flickering behind the calm façade. Lord Aaron and Reuben were curious. Isis looked as excited as Graham was intrigued. It surprised him to note Jorg's fear though, it did make a king of sense – Jorg and Kayte would both have understood what he hadn't said.

To make it a permanent barrier, they would have to leave part of their power in the barrier. To a lintep like Lishe, this was easily done because she had stolen so much power that she could just leave behind an entire lintep's power without feeling much difference. For everyone else, it would mean either giving their lives with their power or living half lives if their power wasn't too great in the first place.

"Should we try it?" he asked them, eager to test his theory.

"I think not," King Lukys spoke in a soft, but commanding, voice. "We have enough on our plate for one day. Let's not add any more to it right now. What we need to discuss is rather more urgent."

"I believe it is important to figure out this piece of the puzzle," Aurelius defended his idea, almost angrily.

"It is indeed important, Aurelius," Lukys placated him, "but what we have to discuss is more urgent because we need to have an answer before this afternoon's Council meeting.

"Aaron is convinced we need to confine certain skills to master and mistresses, however, I am unconvinced of this. I believe this is exactly the reason we don't know how to deal with Lishe and why many of you have already had trouble with your new students, Rilla in particular. What are your thoughts on the matter?"

"Until a few days ago, I might have agreed with you, King Lukys," Kayte found her voice, "but I feel that it may be more prudent to restrict certain knowledge from students. Rilla has already learnt or discovered certain skills that are both dangerous to herself and those around her. If we teach all of our students the same skills, we could very well create more lintep like Lishe and then where would we be?"

"Not every lintep would be like Lishe," Reuben pointed out. "Many would choose to protect and defend rather than attack. Imagine if all of our students had been taught what Lishe knows – we'd have a properly trained army capable of defending Illaria."

"We wouldn't need an army to defend us like that if students weren't taught these skills in the first place," Jorg pointed out. "The only reason we're in any sort of trouble at the moment is because Lishe *was* taught these things."

"So were Nyssa and Kora," Lukys pointed out, "but they were never a threat to Illaria."

"I know I am currently only teaching students their communication skills, but that doesn't mean any of my other skills have gone to waste," Graham spoke softly. "Rilla is already capable of controlling other lintep if the desire took her. From what I've heard, she also knows how to steal their energy, if not their power, and a good deal more. Most of this has been self taught, or figured out by a mere description of the feat. She was visibly horrified at how those skills could be used against anyone, lintep or otherwise.

"I think you need to redefine your question, Lukys. It shouldn't be whether we should teach students or only masters and mistresses such skills. Without a doubt, I think it should be taught to students, but only those we know the true nature of. Only those who would never use their power the way Lishe does. And *that* is where you will run into trouble. How will you know for certain which lintep to trust with such knowledge?"

"The masters and mistresses at the time knew Lishe well enough not to make her a mistress," Aaron pointed out. "Even though she was skilful to pass the test, they didn't afford her the title. However, someone still taught her dangerous skills. This is my point – only master and mistresses should be taught."

"I still disagree," Mistress Kayte ventured. "I've been asked by *your* oldest granddaughter to teach her the skills that Rilla knows and, if she doesn't access Nyssa's power, she will be among the weakest lintep in Illaria. This means she would never qualify to become a mistress in the first place, but I do not think we should deny her the knowledge, to defend herself and her sister, just because she doesn't have much power."

"I agree," Isis finally gathered the courage to speak. "I may be the youngest mistress, but I've already had to deal with Rilla and her eclectic set of skills. It's amazing what she can already do. She's been quite lucky not to have killed herself yet. From the stories I've heard, she could have died or badly hurt others a number of times had other people not been there to help or stop her.

"If other students figure it out by themselves or see Rilla doing things and decide to experiment on their own, we could have a lot of injuries or deaths. I think it would be safer to teach students about these skills. We should probably restrict them to the intermediate or advanced classes, as we do with certain skills already, but I don't think knowledge of these skills should be restricted to masters and mistresses."

"Well said, Mistress Isis," Lukys clapped her on the back as the young mistress reddened from the compliment. "Well Aaron, can you refute such an argument?"

Aaron shook his head, whether in regret or defeat Aurelius couldn't tell. All they needed to do now was find out exactly which set of advanced skills Lishe, Nyssa and Kora had been taught so they could be ready for the rogue lintep the next time she attacked.

Chapter Thirty – Library Research

As the bells tolled for the afternoon lessons, students started heading towards the library. They'd been told in their morning lessons about the change of plans. Guiscard knew a few rumours would have spread by now and knew he would have to make a conscious effort not to allow new ones to begin.

He could hear the students gathering in the hall outside the library. These walls had not seen so many people at one time in many years. His assistants had been warned and were as ready as possible for the onslaught.

"So, is this ridiculous mess of an afternoon anything to do with the three of you?" Réne asked Rilla, as she appeared in the hall outside the library.

"I thought I warned you yesterday to keep your distance from my sister," Shuut immediately stood between her sister and the tall, muscular lintep. He raised a cynical eyebrow at her. She felt herself blush at the scrutiny of his gaze.

"Before you ask," she said, "yes, I am a banwep trained in all manner of defence so perhaps you should think twice before attacking me, my sister or my cousins."

"It was just a question," he said, raising his hands in mock defeat. "I wouldn't dare incur the wrath of a banwep, even if she is only an untrained half-caste."

Shuut managed to contain her anger at the tone of Réne's voice as he called her a half-caste, which was more than could be said of her sister. In a manner of seconds, Rilla had pushed her aside and punched the startled boy in the nose. Blood instantly covered his lips and chin.

At the sudden cries of outrage and surprise, Guiscard opened the library doors to find a ring of students around Rilla, Shuut and another lintep, the latter with a hand to his face, trying to stem the stream of blood running from his nose. The banwep had a hand on Rilla's chest, forcing her away from the boy.

"Silence!" he roared. Every student instantly made way for the furious librarian storming past them. He walked towards the sisters and the boy, whom he did not recognise. "What is the meaning of this?"

"She punched me!" the boy replied indignantly, pointing a finger towards the red-headed lintep.

"I can see that," Guiscard replied stonily. "What did you do to cause such an action?"

"I didn't do anything," he answered, affronted by the accusation.

"You called her a half-caste in that *voice*," Rilla shook with anger. "You think you're better than her just because her father was a human."

"*All* full-blooded lintep are better than her. She will *never* have as much power as we do and all the time her teachers waste on her is time taken from other students who would benefit more from their lessons. That's no reason for you to punch me."

"She's capable of much more than just punching you, as her sister just did, young lintep. You're lucky you only ended up with a broken nose." Guiscard stole everyone's attention before Rilla could make the situation any worse by accidentally revealing that Nyssa's power now resided in Shuut. He placed a finger at the top of the boy's nose and healed it with barely a thought.

"Go and clean yourself up before entering my library. I won't have blood all over my floor and books. The rest of you, stop gawking and find a place to sit."

He ushered them all inside, keeping an eye out to ensure the bloodied boy did as he was instructed. As soon as he was certain the boy was gone, he held Rilla back.

"I applaud your loyalty to your sister, young Rilla, but I would appreciate it if you could try to keep your temper next time," he said, holding up a warning finger before she could protest. "I agree with your sentiments wholeheartedly, but there are many more in Illaria who disagree. Perhaps it would be wise to find a less confrontational way of pointing out your views on the matter. I doubt many of your teachers will treat this matter as lightly as I have."

He ushered her into the library and closed the doors as she seated herself on the floor between Shuut and Plyke. Many of the other students gave the three of them a wide berth. Guiscard went over to his intricately carved desk and sorted through a number of papers he had scattered over it. His assistants were standing by his desk, each one of them a number of years older than the most advanced students gathered in the room.

"I am well aware that most of you would rather be in your lessons than in a stuffy old library. However, here we are. To make this afternoon as painless as possible, you may choose to work alone or in pairs or groups as you see fit.

"Each class will be given a topic to research. Any interesting points you find on the matter should be written down and handed in when the bell tolls for the end of your lessons.

"As an incentive, for those who need one, there will be a special prize for the most interesting fact discovered about each topic. Prizes will be awarded by your teachers. I have it on good authority that some of these prizes will include excursions to places that are usually inaccessible to students, individual lessons and special privileges, amongst other things."

There was a murmur of pleasure from the students. Guiscard shook his head at their delight. No doubt there would have been no such joy derived from most of the students had there not been this extra incentive.

"If you would divide yourselves into your class groups, I shall distribute

the topics and then you are free to research with whomever you so desire.
I, and my assistant librarians, will be here if you need directions on how to
find the books you are searching for." The students quickly began to reshuffle
themselves into their classes and sat in lines along the floor.

Plyke looked around in confusion. He shared an uneasy glance with Shuut
before looking back over the shuffling lintep.

"What's the matter?" Umi asked.

"This was to be my first lesson with Master Aurelius, and Shuut's with
Master Reuben," Plyke answered in a whisper. "We don't know any of the
other students in our class."

"Shuut, you're with us," Umi answered easily and pushed her gently towards
Ulf. "Plyke, I think you may be in Dorian's class. Dorian!"

The young lintep turned at the sound of his name and sidestepped past a
number of students to reach them.

"What is it?" he asked more quietly than Umi.

"Are you in Master Aurelius' class this afternoon?" she asked, apparently
unaware of the commotion she was causing.

"Yes, why?"

"Great, Plyke is with you. Can you take him over to your class? He doesn't
know anyone but you yet."

Plyke didn't have time to react before Dorian took him by the hand. He
knew Dorian didn't notice him try to flinch away from the skin contact, but
pulled Plyke past seated students over to their class. Plyke instantly retreated
behind the walls of his mind, but he wasn't quick enough. Without meaning
to, he felt the embarrassed pride Dorian felt at having been singled out to
help one of Lord Aaron's grandchildren. Plyke smiled despite himself and sat
next to the young lintep.

Once the students had settled down into their class groups, Guiscard
addressed them once more.

"I will pass a topic, at random, to the head of each line. Please pass it back
along the line so that every student in your class gets to look at it. Once all
topics are passed around and you have decided on your groups, come to my
desk to get a sheet of parchment. There are quills and ink provided at each
desk in the library. If it turns out there aren't enough, I have spare sets at my
desk, so come and find me in that case."

Guiscard turned to his desk, shuffled some sheets of parchment over his
desk them scooped them up into a single pile. He walked along the head of
each line, handing out a single sheet to each student. There was a mixture of
murmurs from the students of surprise, pleasure and disappointment as the
topics were passed down the lines.

Rilla noticed Réne join the back of her line as she waited for their topic to be passed down. A tiny nudge from the mousy-haired girl next to her stole her attention back from the older boy. The quiet girl was holding out the topic to Rilla with the fingertips of both hands, her shoulders slightly cowed and eyes downcast. Rilla tried to catch her eye as she took the proffered piece of parchment. She looked at it with mild surprise before passing it to the lintep behind her. *Medicinal plants.* She wondered whether the lintep knew of more than the ones Rhanya had grown in their Paradise. At least she had an idea of where to start.

Once the topics had reached the back of the lines, students got to their feet and started dividing themselves into groups or pairs. Barely anyone was deciding to work alone. There was a greater chance of finding more interesting facts in a group and the prizes were certainly encouraging the students to take the task seriously. Rilla looked around and noticed most of her fellow classmates had already gathered into groups. She and the quiet girl beside her were the only two left unpaired.

"Would you like to work together today?" she asked, finally managing to catch the girl's eyes. They were light brown, just like her hair. The lintep looked at her with a mix of incredulity and happiness.

"That would be lovely. My name is Miette," she said, holding out her hand. Rilla's mind quickly rushed through the thought that this girl, Miette, couldn't possibly already know how to do what she was afraid of with skin contact, so she shook her hand with barely any hesitation.

"Rilla," she returned with a smile.

Miette laughed softly. "Yes, I think everyone knows who you are by now. Let's get some parchment before it's all gone."

Together, they walked over to Guiscard's desk. Rilla noticed Miette half hide behind her once she realised Réne was in front of them. As he turned away from the librarian's desk, parchment in hand, he sniggered at them with his group.

"Looks like our little black sheep has found her match," he laughed along with his friends as they shouldered their way past Miette, consciously giving Rilla a wider berth.

"What was that about?" Rilla asked curiously, as they moved closer to Guiscard's desk.

"All of them come from powerful families with masters or mistresses in their heritage," she explained in what Rilla was beginning to think was her usual quiet voice. "They don't really like the fact that I'm a bit younger than them and in the intermediate class without any powerful or well-known lintep in my family."

Rilla didn't reply. She'd punched Réne just a day after meeting him when he'd been jealous of her from the start. She could only imagine how Miette must feel having grown up with people like him around her all the time.

"Well, we'll just have to make sure to win the prize for our class. We should be off to a good start because I was to become an apprentice healer before we left our Paradise. I already know a few things about medicinal herbs, so I'm sure we'll be able to find our way to the more advanced books a little faster than the others, if even there are more people in their group."

She took a sheet of parchment from one of Guiscard's assistants and asked him for some guidance.

"I already know about herbs such as chamomile, sage and aloe. We'd rather spend our time on some lesser-known plants. Do you know which area of the library those sorts of books can be found?"

The assistant, a tall, lean lintep woman with angular features, looked down at the two of them with sharp eyes. Rilla was surprised when she suddenly broke into a smile.

"Such a pleasure to hear young lintep with such keen minds. Walk down the second row from the windows until you come to the third ladder on the left. Climb to the top shelf and there you should find what you're looking for," she said. Rilla and Miette thanked her with smiles and quickly ran off to find the books they needed.

Shuut watched Rilla start to befriend a young lintep. She still didn't know her sister as well as she would have liked, but knew enough to understand that Rilla didn't have any friends other than the old healer in their Paradise. Rilla had even taken quite a while to warm up to the boys in their travelling party. Shuut now understood, because of Rilla's bond with his tree, how her sister had come to be so close to the elf, but doubted they would have become such fast friends otherwise.

As for herself, friends were a luxury Shuut could ill afford in the Outworld. They were few and far between. Now, in Illaria, she was surrounded by family who seemed determined to entangle her in their lives. Umi and Ulf had brooked no opposition – the three of them were to team up in this challenge.

They had passed the topic to her with a delighted squeal. *Outworld customs.* Shuut was less than pleased with the topic. She had hoped to be able to continue her research on the history of Illaria and the royal family, particularly Princess Ophélie.

"Can't we have a different topic?" she asked Guiscard in a low voice. "I don't want to waste my time on the Outworld when I lived there almost my entire life."

"I shuffled the topics to keep them random," the librarian answered her as softly as he could. "Imagine what would happen if you found what you were looking for with the library full of students. Everyone would know and then we'd have to face King Lukys in the ensuing chaos."

Shuut grudgingly accepted his logic and traipsed off after her young cousins. They were eager to learn about a topic that was usually off limits to them because of Lord Kynon.

"Grandfather never lets us talk about humans," Umi whispered to Shuut as they walked in the direction Guiscard had pointed out to them. "It's because his mother, Princess Ophélie, was killed by them. We're barely even allowed to mention the Outworld around him. Of course, mother and father don't mind one bit if we talk about humans, so at least we know more than Mari."

Shuut was startled by the information. She knew whatever made Kora leave Illaria had something to do with Ophélie and Paradises, but this was news to her. Perhaps she would find out something interesting in this topic after all.

Plyke sat next to Dorian and waited patiently until their topic was passed down to him. *Paradises*. It was the last topic he wished to research. He'd lived almost sixteen years in a Paradise and most of that time had been spent trying to blend in, to hide from the leader, and to control his power to keep himself safe. There was little he could think to research about them that he didn't already know.

"Can we work together?" Dorian asked him, once their class had started shuffling into groups. "You lived in a Paradise, so we'd have a head start on the rest of our class. I'd love to know what kind of prize Master Aurelius would give us if we found the most interesting fact about Paradises."

"I think your interpretation of interesting and mine would be quite different in this case," Plyke pointed out sourly. "But we can work together if you like. I can tell you exactly what it's like to live in a Paradise, but if you want any more information than that, we'll have to ask one of the assistant librarians where to look."

"Well, we've got all afternoon," Dorian replied. "Why don't we find a quiet corner and write down the most interesting things you know and go from there. I'm sure once we have all of that, we'll know what else we can try to look for."

Plyke agreed with a shrug of his shoulders. Despondently, he followed Dorian toward Guiscard's desk for a sheet of parchment. Unlike the other students who had rushed towards the books, the two boys remained at the front of the library and found a cosy corner to sit and write.

Dorian asked Plyke a multitude of questions about the Paradises, writing down the things he found most interesting. Plyke found it interesting to note that Dorian's list included things that Shuut herself had found surprising when she'd arrived in his Paradise, such as the lack of money and personal possessions, the absence of locks and the isolation hut. Dorian was intrigued by Partnerships, but Plyke assured him it wasn't a practice unique to Paradises.

Eventually, they came to the topic of the boundary. Dorian was as amazed as Plyke himself had been to discover that the boundary kept the land in some sort of suspended reality from the Outworld so that you could walk over bare fields if you didn't manage to walk through the boundary into the Paradise itself.

The young lintep asked question after question until both of them realised something. It seemed easier for lintep to pass through the boundary than humans, from the amount of lintep who had found his Paradise just in the time he'd lived there. In total it had been Nyssa, Erton, Rilla, Shuut and Kora. That was five lintep he knew of for certain in sixteen years.

It made Plyke think about all the people Erton had murdered. Many of them had shown signs of strange powers. Had some of them been lintep too? Or could it be possible that the power Erton used on the humans had somehow rubbed off on them over the years so that more and more had been born with powers?

The thought sent him reeling. Had Erton helped to create the situation he was desperately trying to avoid? Plyke shook his head in frustration. The sooner they figured out a way to destroy the Paradises, the better.

"I think you've found out as much as you possibly can from me," Plyke said after a long moment of silence. "What I would like to know, if it's even in this library anywhere, is how the Paradises were built. Shuut told us some lintep created them as safe havens for humans, but that didn't go exactly to plan. I want to know how they managed to create them in the first place. Let's go and ask Guiscard about that."

Together, they approached the librarian. He turned to face them before they'd reached him.

"I was wondering how long it would take you to come asking about the Paradises," he said as he looked sharply at Plyke. "I can even guess what you want to know, but I don't have the answer for you. There is very limited knowledge about it. I can point you towards all the documents we have on the Paradises, but I doubt you will find what you are looking for."

Plyke tried to hide his disappointment. "Well, I've already told Dorian all I know about Paradises, so we may as well look in your books to see if they say anything different to what I know. You never know, we might end up finding out something interesting even if it isn't what I want to know."

Guiscard led the boys towards the books that Shuut had initially wanted, but had been too afraid to ask him about outright. He hoped Plyke had some luck there, but he knew that only the diary of Ophélie, which he was fairly certain Kora had taken with her, had the information he so desperately wanted. After Kora had left, Guiscard looked everywhere he could think of to find that book but it was no use. Either she had taken it with her or had hidden it so well that no one but herself would ever be able to find it again. He wondered if her son would have any better luck.

Chapter Thirty-One – Full Council of Masters and Mistresses

Kynon had not been a party to the preparations for the full council, nor did he know why the old masters and mistresses had all been summoned. A month ago, or even just a week ago, he would have been furious that he'd been left out and equally disgruntled that he had to appear at the council at all.

Since the attack on Nyssa, and subsequently on her two daughters, he'd finally understood the seriousness of the matter. He knew that Lukys and Aaron were more adept at organising such events and was pleased they had decided to involve him.

Nyssa had always been his favourite niece. She hadn't minded that he imparted such strong opinions against humans to his own children, though the rest of her siblings had been angry with him over that. He had, in fact, been mildly surprised when he realised Nyssa had managed to soften Braedan's view towards humans.

Both he and his son had been horrified to learn that Nyssa had been killed by a lintep who had just as strong views against humans as they themselves had. It had never occurred to them that a lintep would turn against another in the Outworld. If anything, they had assumed someone like Lishe would turn against humans.

Everything had changed in the past week or so. Eliséo had enlightened them about goings on in the Outworld, of which he had previously not taken an interest in at all. Humans were growing bolder in their attacks on the trees of the outskirts of Silvaren. Vladimir had tried to usurp his father's position as leader of the karliki. The crystal dragons had grown bolder in their manipulations of everyone around them. If that hadn't been enough, all lintep in Illaria, and indeed in the Outworld, were now in danger from Lishe.

Kynon had a strong feeling that this council meeting was somehow going to be about the rogue lintep. He walked down the hall from his chambers a good few minutes before he knew the bells for afternoon lessons were due to toll. Hesitating for only a moment, he knocked on Aaron's door. It was opened without any ceremony and Kynon was ushered inside.

"I know I don't usually take an interest in external politics," he began. Then he noticed Aaron's raised eyebrow. Kynon shifted uncomfortably under his gaze. "Well, not often in internal politics either, but I know this meeting is important to you and I can at least hazard a guess as to why. I should have asked earlier, but is there anything you need me to do before it? Or during it? Anything at all?"

Aaron stared at him. Kynon would be the first to admit that he had never been one to offer help of any sort when it came to running the palace, managing Illaria or any external situations, so it was hardly surprising that Aaron was startled.

"I could use your help to cool tempers in the meeting, if you think you can do that," Aaron gratefully suggested. "Considering the meeting Luyks and I had with a handful of the teachers this morning, I think we may be in for a rough afternoon."

"Cool tempers?" Kynon asked skeptically. "Exactly why will tempers need cooling and how do you expect me to do that?"

"I can't tell you beforehand and risk Lukys thinking I've influenced you. All I can ask is that you remember the situation we are all in now because of Lishe and Nyssa."

The bells tolled for the afternoon lesson. Kynon nodded his head gravely and followed his cousin out of the chambers and down the hall. Together, they descended the open stairwell to the council chambers. Lukys was already there when they arrived and had opened the doors to allow in the masters and mistresses who were gathered in the hallway. More were alighting from the stairs and walking down the halls. A few stray students risked curious glances at them as they ran down the hall towards the library.

Past and current masters and mistresses began filing into the council chambers. Extra chairs had been brought in earlier that day to accommodate them. As custom dictated, each one took off their robe to show their blue tattoos as they entered the room. It took some time for them to arrange themselves according to rank.

Eventually, they were all seated around the large rectangular table, double and triple rows of chairs going back. Kynon was seated at one end with Lukys and Aaron, close to the most skilled lintep. He noted that the palace cooks had been hard at work all morning preparing bite-sized sweet pastries and small savoury pies for the council. The table was laden with these delicacies in addition to teas of multiple varieties. Once everyone had settled down with a bite to eat and a cup of tea to warm their hands, the murmurs finally settled and all eyes turned towards their king.

"Masters and Mistresses, welcome," Lukys stood as he addressed them. "To begin with, I would like to thank you all for coming at such short notice. We realise many of you have retired from teaching and we apologise for disturbing your daily routine.

"For the current teachers, we thank those of you who have given up your free afternoon and extend our gratitude to those who will have to give out prizes to their students currently researching in the library. Guiscard will inform you by tomorrow afternoon who the lucky students are."

He paused, taking a sip of his tea to gather his thoughts before continuing. Exchanging a brief look with Aaron, he placed his cup back on the table and returned his attention to the members of the council.

"You will all know about the death of our beloved Nyssa and I'm certain by now that words has spread about the incident in the marketplace three days ago. Before any misleading rumours are spread, let me explain what happened."

Lukys carefully scanned the faces in the room as he related the events that ended with Lishe in the city, at the very entrance of the palace, trying to kill Rilla and steal Nyssa's power from Shuut. Those events, and the subsequent measures that were taken to free Aaron's granddaughters from the mind snare, were explained in more detail than anyone probably expected him to go into. Some of those gathered looked intrigued by the news, but most were horrified. He watched for signs of guilt or pleasure, but saw none. Perhaps the teacher they were looking for was not present.

An elderly master, with an impressive array of tattoos, coughed and half raised his hand once Lukys had finished speaking. "This is all quite disturbing news, my king, but I confess I don't understand why it warranted the sudden summons of all masters and mistresses in Illaria, whether they are still teaching or not."

There were a few murmurs of agreement around the table. Lukys was thankful he had always taken an active interest in the activities of the Council of Masters and Mistresses or he would be at a loss to recognise many of the faces before him.

"Master Elwood, it has come to my attention that we are in this situation because three students were taught skills which were withheld from other students. We have asked you here today for two reasons. Firstly, we need to know exactly what these students may have been taught and, secondly, we need to discuss how to proceed with lessons from now onwards.

"I am of the opinion that we are in this situation because too much knowledge has been restricted to masters and mistresses so we are ill-equipped to deal with Lishe. Lord Aaron is of the opinion that knowledge should remain restricted to masters and mistresses in the future to avoid similar situations. Of course, the two of us can't make this sort of decision on our own and we value the opinions of our most esteemed teachers."

There was a stunned silence around the room. Technically, the king could make decisions affecting every person in Illaria, but he usually let the Council remain autonomous. This was the first time he had ever hinted that he might change that.

"If I may," Aaron spoke up before the mood soured. "Our first aim is to find out who taught Lishe, Nyssa and Kora and exactly what sorts of advanced skills they were shown that was withheld from other students. We need to know exactly what we're dealing with so that we can be prepared the next time Lishe attacks.

"I realise it's not our usual practice, but could I please ask every master or mistress who remembers having any of them as a student to come with me to the other end of the room for a few moments? We can write down all the advanced skills you can remember teaching them so that we can see how

Lishe might have used those skills to develop her repertoire in the Outworld.

"For everyone else, King Lukys and Lord Kynon will pass around sets of white and black stones to everyone. If there is an empty chair behind you, please place a pair of stones there before passing on the rest. We won't take too long down the end here and then we can begin discussion on the second matter."

Earlier that day, Aaron had organised for an extra table with two chairs to be set up at the other end of the room. Some parchment, a quill and inkpot had also been placed there. A small wooden chest stood in one corner of the table with a round hole in the top for everyone to cast their vote with their stones when the time came.

A handful of elderly masters and a single mistress followed him to the small table. One by one, they sat down beside him and explained the more advanced skills the three girls had been taught. He tried to hide his dismay at not discovering what he was hoping for. Perhaps the master or mistress involved was keeping tight lipped about whatever it was they had taught the girls because they were afraid of reprisal. Perhaps they were no longer alive, or no longer living in Illaria. The possibilities were endless.

He thanked them all and walked back to his seat, trying to hide his disappointment. An almost imperceptible shake of his head told Lukys all he needed to know. He was beginning to understand exactly why Luyks didn't want knowledge restricted to just masters and mistresses. If every advanced student had been taught the same skills, they would know what dangers they faced with Lishe.

When everyone was seated again, Lukys held his hand up for silence. "Each of you has a pair of stones in front of you – one white and one black. At the end of our discussion, I would ask you to cast your votes with these stones. White is for divulging knowledge to advanced students. Black is for restricting knowledge to masters and mistresses. You know my opinion and that of Lord Aaron. I now open up the discussion to the Full Council."

Master Graham raised his hand to speak. Luyks nodded towards him.

"A number of the current masters and mistresses have had a few days to consider these issues. We did not know at the time that such a question would be put before us. I assume we each thought it would be left up to the individual teachers to decide what they would divulge to their students. In retrospect, I can see that's exactly what led us to this situation in the first place, so I would like to propose an alternative to the question posed to us.

"Lord Aaron, I understand your reasons for wanting to restrict knowledge of certain skills to masters and mistresses, but I think King Lukys is correct when he warns that too many skills may be lost that way. There are many people capable of taking the test to receive their tattoo who choose not to for one reason or another – you were one such person.

"Would you propose that you shouldn't be taught skills that could save your grandchildren simply because you are not a master? You possibly have more power and better control over it than every other lintep in Illaria, though few may remember that."

"What's your proposal, Master Graham?" Lord Kynon asked him, seeing the colour rise in his cousin's face.

"I propose that we do indeed teach students knowledge that could be considered dangerous, but not all students. We should be certain of their nature, just as we try to be when students ask for the right to earn their tattoos."

Graham lifted his cup of tea and sat back in his chair. There were a few murmurs along the table as some of the council spoke to those nearest them.

"I am willing to agree to those terms, Master Graham," King Lukys nodded, thoughtfully. "It would at least ensure that knowledge of these skills is more widespread than they are now."

"You saw what she did!" Jorg cried out suddenly. "You saw what Lishe did to Rilla, to Shuut. You saw all of that and you still think we should allow students to learn these skills. They're too dangerous!

"Rilla, because Nyssa was careless enough to teach her, already knows how to control another lintep, should the desire take her, or to steal their power. At the moment, she wouldn't dream of actually doing that, but who knows if that will remain the case in the future?

"Anything could happen to change her mind about that. What if we teach her even more skills and spread that knowledge around? We could easily have a hundred rogue lintep on our hands by the end of winter. Could any of you stand to have that on your conscience?"

"We all know what happened to Nyssa, and many of us saw the damage Lishe wreaked in the city," Kynon suddenly stepped in. Lukys looked over to him in surprise – he hadn't expected his younger cousin to join in the conversation.

"But just think, they were taught the same things by the same teachers, or so we assume. If that was actually the case, then Nyssa should have been able to defend herself against Lishe. Possibly the only reason she couldn't is because she didn't bother honing her skills the same way as her sister and Lishe did.

"Lishe was no match for Lord Aaron, even after she stole power from other lintep. I don't think it matters how much power a lintep has, as long as they are willing to work hard to increase their skill. Should we actually be restricting this knowledge just to advanced students?"

"I agree with Lord Kynon," Mistress Kayte instantly spoke up. "Shuut, even though she has had her mother's power thrust upon her, refuses to use anything other than her own power. Yet, she has asked me to teach her skills that could possibly save her life and that of her sister. Who am I to deny her that right, just because she will possibly never make it to my advanced class?"

The debate flew back and forth for hours, both sides wanting to be heard and expressing their opinions loudly and forcefully so as not to be ignored. Lukys sat back and watched it all with very few comments.

He silently counted how many parties there were on each side of the argument. A good portion of them appeared to be in favour of allowing students to learn dangerous skills. It was becoming more a debate of which students should be taught rather than if any of them should be.

It made Lukys feel a bit guilty to see Aaron withdraw into himself early in the debate. Aaron was badly outnumbered. All Lukys could hope was that whatever decision was made would not make his cousin permanently withdraw from society once more.

With the afternoon sun spilling orange and pink rays into the room, Lukys was surprised to see Aaron stand and hold his hand up for silence. Curious to see what his cousin would say, he made no move to stop him.

"I can see that most people have made up their mind. We should cast our votes and see what the outcome is. If the white stones win, which I admit is looking likely, I would like to make a suggestion."

"Agreed," said King Lukys, before another discussion could be started. "Could everyone please make their way to the wooden chest at the back of the room. Place a white for not restricting knowledge or a black stone for keeping knowledge restricted inside, as you see fit. When we have all done that, we shall count the stones in this room and see what the outcome is. All other stones will be collected before you leave, to avoid conflict over the decision outside of this room."

The masters and mistresses slowly stood and filed down to the back of the room where the extra table had been brought in. One by one, they placed one stone in the wooden chest and hid the other within the folds of their robes. Once everyone had returned to their seats, Lukys motioned to Aaron to bring the box to him. He knew it would be heavy and openly admitted that his cousin had more power than he could ever have hoped to have.

Aaron nodded almost imperceptibly and sent out a thick tendril of power to the back of the room to completely encompass the wooden chest. Seemingly, with barely any effort at all, he lifted it and directed it over the centre of the long rectangular table right to the edge in front of Lukys.

There was a low murmur throughout the room. Lukys reflected it was possible that some of them didn't believe Master Graham when he'd told them Aaron could have been a master himself had he chosen to take the test. With a final flourish, his cousin used a tiny tendril to reveal the key to the wooden chest from his own robes and unlocked the chest, flipping the lid back.

Lukys began to take out the stones. He placed the white ones on the left side of the chest and the black on the right side. In less than ten minutes, it was revealed that the whites had won the day.

Knowing how his cousin would be feeling, Lukys placed a calming hand on Aaron's arm. It surprised him to see Kynon's hand on Aaron's other arm. Kynon had grown in leaps and bounds over the past few days. It was only regrettable that it had taken such events for him to do so.

Finally, Aaron stood to address the Full Council. "The whites have won. This means most of you have decided that we should not restrict any potentially dangerous knowledge to masters and mistresses. As such, I would plead with you that we should still restrict the knowledge to students who understand the implications of what they are being taught.

"From your arguments, I can see this doesn't necessarily mean they will be advanced students, so I would like to suggest an alternate way to determine if they should be taught. We could have a panel of teachers and either King Lukys, Lord Kynon or myself examine each prospective student to see if we think they deserve to be taught these skills."

Lukys looked at him with pride. It was difficult to swallow one's pride in front of such a large gathering and still maintain enough composure to suggest such a reasonable compromise.

"I think that is a commendable idea," Lukys announced. "By open vote, all in favour of this course of actions, raise your hand."

Every single person in the room raised their hand. Lukys felt a small weight lift from his shoulders.

"It's unanimous. Let us begin from tomorrow. Any student who has already asked to be shown these skills or who has accidentally learnt some of them on their own should be assessed to see if they should be taught further. From then onwards, any student you think is a candidate for such knowledge should be taken aside and asked in private if they would like to ask for the privilege."

Master Aurelius raised his hand just before Lukys dismissed the Council. A nod from the king allowed him to speak.

"Now that this matter has been settled, I would like to ask for permission to help go through the skills the girls were taught to see if we can figure out what Lishe actually derived from them."

"Permission granted, Master Aurelius," Lukys nodded. "Are there any others who wish to work with Master Aurelius and Lord Aaron on this undertaking?"

Lukys noted with interest that the only mistress to have taught the three girls had raised her hand, along with Mistresses Kayte and Isis, Master Graham and Master Elwood.

"Very well, then. I will call a close to this meeting. If the six of you will remain behind for a few moments, you can discuss the finer details of your task with Lord Aaron.

"For the rest of you, I thank you all for giving up your time this afternoon. The palace staff have been advised that there may be quite a few extra mouths to feed in the dining hall tonight. You are all welcome to join us there."

Chapter Thirty-Two – Revelations

As the bell tolled, signalling the end of the afternoon lessons, students immediately began returning books to their shelves and handing in their parchments to Guiscard and his assistant librarians. Rilla was torn between commencing her research on a topic she actually wanted to or introducing Miette to her family. Guiscard made her mind up for her.

"Thank you for treating my books with care. I hope you all enjoyed yourself more than you expected to. Your teachers will announce the winners of this research assignment tomorrow in the courtyard just before your afternoon lessons. As such, the library will be closed this evening so that I can go through your answers."

Rilla caught Shuut's eye and smiled as her sister rolled her eyes at the news that they wouldn't be able to research anything further that day. While Miette went to hand in their parchment, Rilla quickly put the books away that they'd been looking at. She was amazed at the vast variety of medicinal plants the lintep knew of. If Rhanya had known about these, he would have given his right arm to get his hands on them.

She and Miette had written down a number of plants which had interesting medicinal properties including milk thistle which purged poisons from the body and comfrey which had several properties including healing weak or broken bones and severe burns and cuts. There were other interesting ones such as valerian, lemon balm and passionflower. All of these helped with insomnia and had various other properties.

However, Rilla's favourite remained the bitter oyster – a type of luminous mushroom which could staunch bleeding. It was hinted at, but not exactly specified, as the substance from which the ink of a master's tattoos was made from. They'd written down that suspicion in case it proved to be correct. Rilla had just finished putting away their last book when Miette returned.

"Thanks for working with me today," the shy girl said as she bowed her head and turned to walk away.

"Wait!" Rilla instantly called after her. Miette stopped and turned around slowly. "I don't know if you live in the palace or not, but if you're not busy tonight, do you want to sit with us in the dining hall?"

"That…would be lovely," the shy girl answered timidly. "I live in the palace during the week. It takes too long to travel in from my family's farm on the days we have lessons."

Guiscard watched the two girls from the corner of his eye. Miette was a particular favourite of his. She spent much of her free time in the library because many of the other students treated her with contempt. Jealousy was a horrible thing for children to deal with. None of the other students dared physically bully her because they feared her power, but their words cut her just as deeply as any other wound. He was glad she had found a powerful and influential friend. It would be good for her, even if the older students still ignored or taunted her.

He waited for all the students to leave before closing the doors behind them. Half of his assistants were walking down the rows of books, making sure everything had been put back in order. The rest of them were sorting through the sheets of parchment, placing them in groups.

"Will you be wanting help to decide on the winner for each topic?" one of the older assistants asked him dutifully. Normally, he would have jumped at the offer, but this was such a sensitive task that he waved it aside.

"Not this time. I have it on good authority there will be quite a feast in the dining hall tonight and you are all welcome to attend." The assistants failed to hide their anticipation of the feast as they hurried out of the library. Guiscard smiled at their excitement.

As soon as he was alone, Guiscard made sure all the lanterns except the one on his desk had been snuffed out, then stared at the sheets covering his desk. He closed his eyes and sent out a thin tendril of power out towards the council chambers. He needed to find either Lord Aaron or King Lukys and did not want to leave the research papers unattended. He found Lukys just leaving the room.

I need your help.

A few minutes later, the king knocked at his door. Guiscard opened it just wide enough for the slender lintep to enter and shut it quickly behind him, glancing quickly both ways down the hall to make sure they weren't observed.

"How did it go?" Lukys asked without any preamble.

"I don't want to hazard a guess just yet, but the random division of topics was far from what I'd hoped it would be. Young Plyke received Paradises, while Shuut worked on the Outworld. Both of them instantly went for areas of those topics that were stretching the limit. I couldn't keep my eye on everything, but had my assistants constantly updating me on any students who were going above and beyond what we expected them to research."

"You should have completely controlled it," Lukys chided him.

"Had I controlled it at all, they could easily have figured it out and spoilt our plans," Guiscard reminded him. "Imagine if the other students worked out that we were hoping for Aaron's grandchildren to find some information that we simply didn't have time to find ourselves. How do you think that would have gone?"

Lukys' face softened a bit. "Forgive me, Guiscard. You are right, of course. It's been a trying afternoon. Do you need help to sort through the papers?"

"I was hoping we could convince a few trusted teachers to help with the task," he replied hopefully. "Preferably ones who know the current situation."

"I can get Aurelius, Graham, Kayte and Isis. Possibly Elwood and

Chandrelle too, if you'll have them," Lukys added as an afterthought.

"It would be good to have all of them. Elwood, Chandrelle, Graham and Aurelius might actually remember some things from the research topics that the rest of us may have forgotten," Guiscard rubbed the stubble on his chin thoughtfully. "Will you and Lord Aaron be available as well, or shall I simply inform you of any important information we come across?"

"Unfortunately, we must be seen in the dining hall this evening or too many suspicions will be aroused. If you can make do with the others, I will send them to you and arrange for some food to be sent up from the banquet so you don't miss out on that."

* * *

By the time his helpers arrived, Guiscard had sorted the topics into those he wished to go through himself and those he was willing to delegate to others. He'd pulled some of the more comfortable chairs closer to the fireplace and was in the process of moving the small tables to their sides when there was a knock on his door. Guiscard abandoned his task to let in his guests. They quickly helped him rearrange the furniture and then stood a little awkwardly before him.

"We realise there is already a mountain of parchments to sort through," Aurelius told him eventually, "but we also have some notes from retired teachers that could help us in our current situation with Lishe."

"I see," Guiscard said as he quickly assessed the amount of work there was to be done. "Isis, do you want to go through the notes from retired teachers and see what you can piece together? The rest of us can start with the research topics and help Isis with the extra task later.

"I've sorted the topics into piles. Many of the students were interested in the topics because it meant they might get a prize from their teacher, but that did not inspire all of them. I think we should easily be able to sort the rubbish from the rest and then go from there."

Having been given their tasks, Isis took the notes from Aurelius and sat at the chair nearest the fireplace. She drew a small amount of heat from the blazing fire to light the lantern by her side and settled down to read. Guiscard marvelled at the ease with which she worked with fire. Even though she was the youngest lintep ever to attain a mistress status, he was still surprised by her skill level.

He led the other lintep to his desk and pointed out the ones they could start on. As he had predicted, it was easy to sort the useless information from what might potentially turn out to be important, or at least more interesting.

By the time the kitchen servants had arrived with food for them, they had sorted the completely irrelevant information from all seventeen topics. Guiscard had expected some of the topics he'd handed out to be completely useless, but they were required to sort through them to find a winner for each class nonetheless. They took a short break to eat the food before it became cold in the chill night air and then returned to their task.

"If you don't find very much of interest, try to keep aside at least the two best notes from each topic so that I can judge the winners. As soon as we've narrowed down the rest of the topics, I might go through them with Master Elwood and Mistress Chandrelle. The rest of you can then start helping Isis through the notes Lord Aaron took down during your meeting."

They worked long into the evening. King Lukys and Lord Aaron came to help them only after they could reasonably excuse themselves from the dining hall. The moon had already reached its zenith by the time they called it a night. The nine of them arranged to meet again in King Lukys' chambers the next morning to continue sorting through everything.

"I've requested rooms to be prepared for the three of you," Lord Aaron said to Isis, Elwood and Chandrelle, as they left the library. Guiscard thanked him with a nod. It had been a clever and generous arrangement as it was now too late for them to travel back into town and all because he had requested their help.

Guiscard reluctantly handed over the carefully sorted papers to Lukys to keep safe in his chambers that night and joined Graham, Aurelius and Kayte as they walked to their chambers.

* * *

Guiscard woke early the next morning with a sinking feeling. He hated not being able to perform his proper duties as a librarian. He rang for a servant and refreshed himself for the day before a young runner arrived. In a matter of minutes, he'd explained to her which of his assistants should be woken early to open the library for eager researchers.

He cursed the fact that he couldn't send a coded message with this runner to tell his assistants to keep an eye out for Shuut and Rilla in case they managed to slip in before or after their morning lessons. By the time he found himself knocking on King Lukys' door, Kayte and Isis had joined him in the hall.

"We can't help for too long this morning," Kayte informed him shortly. "We have lessons to teach and our students will get too suspicious if we cancel yet another class. Besides, it would be best that Rilla, Plyke and Shuut are kept well occupied this morning."

"Ah yes, that reminds me. I meant to have a word with you, Isis," Guiscard said as they walked through into King Lukys' antechamber. "There was a bit of a scuffle outside the library yesterday between two of your students."

"What happened?" Isis asked in surprise. "That class has always gotten along well enough, except for poor Miette I suppose."

276

"Miette wasn't involved. I am taken to understand that a certain young man insulted Shuut and Rilla broke his nose."

"Rilla did what?" Lord Aaron rose from his chair in shock. Guiscard turned to him in surprise. He hadn't seen Lord Aaron sitting there.

"She was defending her sister," he tried to placate the old lord. "There was no harm done really. I healed his nose instantly. I simply wanted to tell Isis in case she noticed anything odd in her next intermediate class. That's all."

"That would probably be Réne, then," Isis deducted. "He's powerful and skilful, but terribly proud of his heritage. He causes the most trouble for Miette and was immediately suspicious of Rilla because of her apparent skill with little to no training."

"Well, at least you shouldn't need to worry about Miette anymore," Guiscard informed her. "She and Rilla worked well together all afternoon. I was quite pleased to overhear Rilla extend an invitation to the young lintep to dine with her family last night. Réne will think twice before he approaches either of them again."

Isis smiled to herself until she caught Kayte's withering glance. Guiscard well knew the older mistress' opinion that teachers should not have any favourites. He didn't entirely agree with her in that respect, but he only had to deal with the students in the library. The odious ones, such as Réne never bothered to enter the library unless one of their teachers had set a research task. Others, humble as Miette, were so lovely and often found themselves walking through his halls. How could he possibly like them evenly?

"Let's get started," Lukys diverted their attention. "Aislen has agreed to perform my duties this morning, so I can spend that time here with you. Guiscard, I think it would be wise for myself, Aurelius and Graham to work with you on the research topics as we have more of an idea of what we're looking for than the others. We'll go into the next room so we can openly discuss them.

"Aaron, can you please send in Graham when he arrives, then you can stay with the others in this room and see if you can make any headway with what the retired masters and Mistress Chandrelle told you yesterday. See if you can't get Chandrelle to open up a bit more. She was there at the time – she might remember something."

Guiscard and Aurelius followed Lukys through to his inner chambers. Neither of them had never been into this room. It was larger than both of their own chambers combined and still wasn't the king's entire set of rooms. They exchanged a look of wonder as Lukys led them to the table where he'd set up the topics the night before.

"I had a bit of time this morning to make a start on the less important topics," Lukys said as he slumped into one of the four chairs arranged around the table. "I confess, I'm not as knowledgeable about literature as yourself, so you may need to choose the winner of that category yourself."

Guiscard took the small pile of parchments from Lukys. The students in that class had formed just four groups, clearly not wanting to tackle the task on their own.

"Now, Aurelius, I wanted to ask you, has Rilla ever seen your tattoo in the dark?" Lukys asked. Guiscard looked up curiously at the question.

"What an odd question," Aurelius remarked. "No, I don't think so. I don't generally remove my robe unless I'm in my own chamber or in the Council of Masters."

"In that case, we may already have a winner for the medicinal plants topic. Rilla and Miette have written down quite a few obscure plants and their uses, including a few common plants and their lesser known qualities.

"However, the reason I would give them the award is that they've found out about the bitter oyster mushroom. I doubt Rilla would have been in a state of mind to notice them in the crypt, but they've written down that they think it may be the substance used to make the ink for tattoos. The only thing they haven't figured out is that because the mushrooms glow in the dark, the ink made from them does as well."

"What did the class with the tattoo topic discover? Anything remotely similar?" Guiscard asked, listening to their conversation with one ear.

"I hadn't got to that class yet. I'll do that now. Aurelius, do you want to make a start with the Outworld?"

"That should prove to be interesting," Guiscard remarked offhand, as he skimmed through the literature parchment he was currently holding. "Shuut got that topic and I could have sworn I heard her talking to Umi and Ulf about Ophélie."

Aurelius immediately picked up the stack of parchment that Lukys pointed out to him and started reading through them intently. Most of them were completely useless. Many of the students knew nothing at all about the Outworld other than old stories that were passed down from any lintep who had actually left Illaria at one time or another. They hadn't looked very far for information and most of them had written down similar banalities to each other

One group had at least gone to the effort of finding out how and why banweps came about. He wasn't surprised to see that it wasn't Shuut's group. She did not see herself as an object of fascination, but surely she must have noticed that a lot of the lintep in Illaria openly stared at her short hair and worn traveller's clothes. If there was nothing else of interest, that group would win itself the prize for Master Reuben's class.

With some excitement, he picked up the last parchment in the pile. In the confident scrawl of a royal lintep, Umi, Ulf and Shuut had been written at the top of the sheet. He read it carefully. It had more to do with Paradises than the Outworld. Aurelius read on with interest. The three of them must have found some document that either Ophélie herself, or one of her close companions, wrote when they were first thinking of creating the Paradises. The parchment read:

Umi, Ulf and Shuut

Ophélie, along with a number of other lintep, discussed the problem left behind after the Great War. Rilla had impressed upon her younger sister that humans were to be cared for because they had no power of their own and the Outworld was becoming a dangerous place.

When Rilla died, Ophélie wanted to continue her work. She started with one group of humans who were willing to let her experiment with them. Together, they found a place nearby Illaria, where a running stream cut through empty lands. There they created the very first Paradise.

There is little information about how they did it, but there are suggestions that not all lintep survived the process and many of those who did seemed weaker to their friends and family and would not divulge the reasons.

Every Paradise created after that was done with close to a hundred lintep and different ones each time, though Ophélie oversaw them all. There were no more deaths recorded and little other information we could find about how those lintep fared afterwards.

As Aurelius read the parchment, his hands began to tremble. He re-read the parchment over and over again and started to mumble the words aloud. His odd behaviour was noticed by Graham as he walked through the door.

"How long has he been like that?" he asked Lukys and Guiscard, nodding towards Aurelius. The two lintep looked over to Aurelius. They had both been so absorbed in their own tasks that they hadn't even noticed him.

Graham nodded knowingly and walked quietly up to his old friend. With gentle movements, he placed a single finger on Aurelius' hand and exuded calm into him while at the same time taking the parchment from his slightly resisting hands.

"They found it!" Aurelius exclaimed as he let Graham take the parchment from him. "I don't know if it was one of Ophélie's diaries or some other document, but they found out about the first Paradise. We need them to show us where that document is!"

Graham quickly read the parchment and handed it to Lukys who read it and passed it straight to Guiscard. None of them reacted quite the same way as Aurelius.

"It doesn't tell us *how* they did it," Guiscard pointed out. "Nor does it tell us where that first one was located."

"I figured out how they did it yesterday morning," Aurelius told him excitedly, then cast an annoyed look at his king. "I was told it wasn't urgent that we try it for ourselves to see if I was correct, but from their description of that first Paradise, I'm almost certain I know how they did it."

Guiscard hadn't been at their meeting the morning before so Aurelius described to him exactly how he thought the Paradises could have been created by using a bit of power from each lintep involved to create a sort of permanent shield.

"We could try it now," Aurelius suggested excitedly.

"Exactly how do you expect us to be able to do that?" Graham asked him gruffly. "I don't exactly want to lose any of my power at my age!"

"Let's just try it, without making it permanent," Aurelius suggested with a shrug. "We would have to allow a certain amount of overlap or mingling of power to make sure there are no gaps. We should build it around ourselves, so that we are shielded within. Then, if we succeed, we could try to walk into the other room and see if anyone notices us. If they don't, then we know we have at least part of the answer to how Paradises were created."

Hesitantly, the others agreed. They stood with their backs touching each other's. Aurelius let a thick tendril of his power out, spreading it thinly until it touched Graham's on one side and Guiscard's on the other. It took some effort to make sure there were no gaps either at the top, on the sides or on the bottom. Once they were satisfied with the result, they began to walk to the other room.

* * *

Once Lukys, Guiscard and Aurelius had left them, Aaron started going through the notes with Isis and Kayte. It seemed like a hopeless task. They seemed very mundane extra skills to teach the girls – nothing that would cause Lishe to be able to do all she currently could do.

"I think we're going about this the wrong way," Isis said eventually, as a knock resounded at the door. "One of the things they were taught is how to help someone contain their power if they were losing control, like when a lintep's power peaks. It depends if the girls got to talking after that, either with that teacher or another, about what the implications of that are."

"I can answer that," Graham said, as Aaron closed the door behind him. "It depends how and why they were taught this skill. Rilla was taught how to do that to Plyke by her mother, but she had no idea what could happen if she wanted to go further. I had to tell her what she could do because she offered to help me contain Plyke's power if it got out of control and I refused to let her help me and, once she realised the gravity of the situation, likewise refused to let me help her with that same task.

"It isn't a far stretch of the imagination that a similar conversation took place either with one of their teachers or when they decided to experiment on each other, because that probably happened too, even though we warn students not to experiment outside of class."

Aaron scratched his chin thoughtfully. "Could that mean that the mind snare, which took us so long to figure out, could have come from that same information? If the power was confined not just to the person, but to the mind itself, that would render a lintep powerless. It would only be a stretch for someone like Lishe to then use one of the lesser powers she had stolen to keep such a person permanently in that state, thus creating her mind snare."

Kayte nodded. "It does make sense, though I wouldn't want to be the one to test it to prove your theory."

"No, I don't think any of us should," Aaron replied gravely. He turned to Graham for a moment. "Lukys, Guiscard and Aurelius are waiting for you to join them, just through that door." He pointed toward the inner chamber and then turned back to his own task as the old master walked away.

Only a few minutes later, Master Elwood and Mistress Chandrelle knocked softly at the door. He let them in and explained what they were doing.

"Without one of the three of them, I think your task will be quite difficult," Chandrelle pointed out bluntly. "Nyssa is dead. Kora has been gone for years. It's doubtful she would come back just when you need her. And Lishe, well, even if you did get close enough to talk to her, she'd more likely attack you than answer your questions."

Aaron listened to her opinions in silence. He didn't want to tell her that Kora was indeed on her way back because that would raise even more questions that he did not want to answer.

"Chandrelle, pointing out the obvious is useless unless you have some other suggestion to make," Elwood chided her softly. Aaron could tell from the gentle tone that the two of them were old friends.

"We should ask your grandchildren what they saw Nyssa do and what she taught them. It seems to be the only reasonable option. It's possible she taught them many things that they don't even realise themselves."

"That's a fair point," Isis said. "We already know that she taught Rilla a dangerous and powerful skill without telling her what it could do."

"I suppose you're right," Aaron sighed. "I didn't want to disrupt their day, but it's probably for the best."

"I think not," Lukys said, as he suddenly appeared in the room. Beside him were Guiscard, Graham and Aurelius, the latter grinning like a child. Aaron stared at them in surprise.

"What are you doing?" he asked Lukys irritably. "Stop wasting your time going invisible."

"It worked!" Aurelius cried out in excitement.

"Any lintep child can go invisible, Aurelius!" Aaron half shouted in exasperation.

"Not the way we just did." His smile only grew larger as he explained what they had done and that he was almost certain the Paradises had been created in a similar way.

"But who would do that?" Chandrelle asked in mystified horror. "How could they have convinced hundreds of lintep to do that and never breath a word of it to anyone? Illaria simply doesn't have enough people for that to have happened. Leaving that aside, did could they even convince a lintep to do something like that for a human?"

"You forget, Chandrelle, that lintep didn't always hate humans as much as they do now," Elwood reminded her. "There was a time when the barriers around Illaria were often crossed by humans with their lintep friends. As for the hundreds of lintep, they didn't all necessarily come from Illaria.

"There are plenty of lintep living in the Outworld and though Illaria may be the largest city, it is by no means the *only* lintep settlement. It is quite possible that once some of the others heard about the creation of that first Paradise, many of the lintep in the Outworld volunteered to help."

The room fell silent, everyone trying to sort through the information they had learned that morning. Aurelius was amazed to hear that there were really other lintep settlements outside Illaria. Even as old as he was, this information was news to him, as it was to all of his acquaintances.

"How far away are these other settlements?" he asked suddenly. "Do they have barriers around their lands as we do?"

Elwood rubbed his temples with his long, bony fingers. "I don't know where they all are. I've only ever been to one of them, which was between Illaria and Silvaren. They told me about the other settlements. From the sounds of it, they were quite numerous at the time.

"I don't know how many of them still exist. It didn't have a barrier around it, but they were all peaceful people who practised their healing skills most often. No human would ever need to harm them."

"Just like Ratchin," Aurelius mused aloud. "No human in or around Turon would dare attack her because of the amount of humans who asked for and received her aid. Every one of those humans would seek retribution if she were harmed."

"In any case, that sounds like quite a while ago," Lukys pointed out. "It's possible they tried to create barriers once humans turned more violent and intolerant against magic of any sort."

'That's perfect then," Aurelius exclaimed. "We should find one of these settlements and find out exactly how they created their barrier. It's the easiest way to find out if we're right."

"What then?" Graham asked him, arms crossed against his chest. "So you find out where one of these settlements is and discover that your theory is correct. How is that going to help you figure out how to destroy the Paradises?"

"Destroy the Paradises?" Elwood and Chandrelle asked simultaneously.

"Well of course, destroy the Paradises," Graham glared at them as though they were dull witted students. "What did you think we were doing here?"

"We were under the impression that you were looking for ways to protect us against Lishe," Elwood answered, somewhat disgruntled. Graham instantly understood his mistake and said nothing further.

"And indeed we are," Lukys tried to smooth over Graham's blunder. "We have it on good authority that Lishe wants to kill Rilla because she doesn't want the prophecy to come to pass.

"If we've understood Lishe's character correctly, she intends to steal all the power in the Paradises for her own. So we need to figure out how to protect ourselves against her and how to destroy the Paradises before she does so herself."

By the shocked looks on Chandrelle and Elwood's faces, it was clear they hadn't put all the pieces together from the Council meeting the day before. Aurelius found himself holding his breath, waiting for their reaction.

Chapter Thirty-Three – Summons

"You want to destroy the Paradises yourselves?" Chandrelle asked in disbelief. "How can you even contemplate doing such a thing, after so many lintep apparently gave their power, and some even theirs lives, to create them? Besides that, what gives you the right to do such a thing? What if the humans like living there? They were created for them in the first place. You can't just destroy them."

Lukys shot another angry glance at Graham, who had the decency to look chastened. "There were some notes that Kora and I found years ago – notes that Ophélie wrote, about the Paradises. It wasn't too long after they were created that the prophecy came about of their destruction. Ophélie couldn't understand why that had happened and went to check on some of them.

"In each one, she found that the lintep left behind to make sure things ran smoothly for the first few weeks, had in fact stayed longer than they should have and many had already set themselves up as the leader of the Paradise.

"From what we've heard recently, things have only gone from bad to worse. Rilla's father, Erton, was their Paradise leader and was killing off any human who showed magical abilities, helped those who were defiant of his rule or who spoke out of turn."

"That doesn't mean every Paradise is like that," Chandrelle protested. "Just because one was, you can't assume they all are. You have no right to try to destroy them all before you've even asked them if that's what they want."

"It's going to happen one way or another," Aaron pointed out. "Either Lishe will do it one by one, stealing all that power as she goes, or we try to beat her to it and release that power somehow."

Lukys had been so intent on Chandrelle's protests that he'd practically forgotten about the others in his chambers. Elwood startled him as he cleared his throat.

"What I don't understand is why you're trying to do it all yourselves. The prophecy mentions a child from Paradise destroying the Paradises. Does that not mean at least one of your grandchildren should be involved in this process?" the old master asked bluntly.

The simple statement took Lukys by surprise. Of course, he assumed Rilla would be the one to destroy the Paradises because of the prophecy, but so far they'd barely involved her in the process at all.

"Yes, well, we know Rilla is meant to destroy them, but the child can't have any idea about how to begin," he tried to defend their actions.

"You give that girl too little credit," Aurelius told him boldly. "She's seen and done more than you would imagine of her. She also saw the mind snare's effect on Shuut and how it was taken away. That's the best clue we have so far as to how to destroy the Paradises. She even had Lishe's mind snare placed on herself so knows what it's like from that side too. You should really talk to her, to all three of your grandchildren," he said, turning suddenly to Aaron. "They could have the missing link that you just don't see."

"We've already spoken to Plyke about the mind snare," Aaron reminded him. He neglected to say that Eliséo had also told them about the crystal that had saved Shuut in Goraburg. It was still something he was a little uncertain about. His grandchildren were all quite tight lipped on that subject. Could that be the key to everything? Perhaps he should talk to Rilla after all so that she could contact Eliséo and ask for his assistance in the matter.

"However, you may be correct. Let's leave it here for today and I'll talk to them before their lessons begin. If you'll excuse me."

Aaron quickly walked out of the luxurious chambers, leaving Lukys to deal with the aftermath. Without really thinking what he was going to say to them, he headed towards Plyke's room. It was still early morning, long before their lessons were due to begin. He hoped to be able to talk to them quickly, without disturbing their lessons.

Without wanting to wake the entire floor by knocking loudly enough to wake his grandson, he instead sent a tendril of his power under the door and through to the bedchamber. He barely brushed Plyke's mind to alert him to his presence. Immediately, the boy jumped out of bed and ran to the door.

"Follow me," he said quietly, as the bewildered boy stood there in his bed clothes. Together, they walked down the hall to Rilla and Shuut's room. Aaron employed the same strategy to get the girls out of bed. To his relief, all three of his grandchildren were too concerned about his sudden arrival to be angry at his method for waking them.

He quickly ushered Plyke inside and was about to close the door behind them when Aurelius came hurrying up the hallway. Irritated, Aaron let him in before closing the door behind them all.

"What are you doing here?" he asked bluntly.

"I think I know what you're planning on doing and there's something about Rilla you don't quite know," Aurelius tried to placate him. "Just wait a moment before you decide whether to send me away."

Aurelius looked Rilla in the eye, willing her to be receptive to his thoughts. He sent out a thin tendril to her, asking that she create the same mist around them that he knew she could do.

They all know your secret and, if I'm correct in my guess at what your grandfather is planning, you're going to want to make certain no one can see or hear you.

Aurelius could feel her hesitation as she looked at her sister, cousin and grandfather. Under her breath, she muttered the few special words Elessa had taught her and a thick mist instant gathered around the five of them.

Plyke, Shuut and Aaron stared at her, open mouthed. Aurelius grinned at Rilla, pleased that she had let him send her a message without resistance and for trusting her family so easily now. She returned his smile with a blush.

"Now are you going to send me away or let me help you?" Aurelius demanded. "I heard as close to the unabridged version from all three of them as any of us were likely to get, so can already suggest a few things to you."

"It appears you have me in a tight position," Aaron replied almost angrily. "Stay if you must, but don't interrupt unless you need to. Now, which of you can tell me exactly how the mind snare was removed from Shuut in Goraburg."

Shuut shrugged her shoulders and shook her head. Rilla and Plyke shared an uncomfortable silence.

"We don't really know if we're allowed to tell you that," Plyke finally admitted. Rilla nodded her agreement in silence.

"Then, I suggest you ask Eliséo," Aaron turned to Rilla. "He's already told me part of how it was done but I need more information."

Rilla wondered how her life had become so complicated so quickly. A few short months ago, she'd been an isolated human in a Paradise. Now, she was a powerful, royal lintep bound to an elf's tree.

She took a deep breath and opened herself to her link with Elessa. From the look on everyone else's face, she knew her eyes were already glowing bright green.

For a moment, she watched through Eliséo's eyes, trying to ascertain if she could disturb him. He was running through a forest and from the sudden droops of his eyelids, it looked like he hadn't slept in days.

Eliséo, I need to ask your advice. She waited until she felt the brush of his mind against hers before continuing. *Lord Aaron said you told him a bit about how the mind snare was taken off Shuut, but he wants more details. We don't know if we're allowed to tell him.*

Can you find out why he wants to know? he asked. Rilla could feel his trepidation about revealing too much.

They've been having a lot of meetings lately. Do you want to talk to him yourself?

That might make it easier. Get them all to touch your hands or your arms, that way we don't need to repeat anything. Aurelius already knows so much we may as well tell him the rest if we have to tell Aaron too.

Her eyes still glowing, she made sure the door to her tower was firmly shut and then asked Plyke, Shuut, Aaron and Aurelius to place their hand on her arms. They did as they were bid, all but Aaron not understanding what was happening.

Lord Aaron, why do you want to know more about the mind snare? Eliséo asked once they were all linked up. Rilla felt the sudden gripping of her arm.

but she couldn't tell who had been so stunned to react that way.

We have reason to believe the same concept is used to create Paradises so, if we know exactly how you got rid of the mind snare in Goraburg, we can try to employ the same technique, Lord Aaron replied a little evasively.

I was under the impression you had already found a way to do that by saving Rilla and Shuut, Eliséo replied shortly. *What is it you're trying not to tell me? And I'd appreciate a quick conversation as you may imagine it isn't easy to travel quickly and talk to you at the same time. My vision is slightly clouded.*

Aurelius saw that Aaron was hesitating and didn't want to lose this rare opportunity of speaking with the elf.

We did manage to free the girls, but we couldn't find a way to release the power Lishe used to put the mind snare on them. It's currently…safely locked away until we figure out what to do.

I see, Eliséo replied thoughtfully. *I can't actually help you with that. It's between the crystal dragons and the karliki. I'm on my way to Goraburg as we speak. If I can convince any of them to help you, I will let you know.*

Their connection with Eliséo was suddenly severed. Rilla, eyes no longer glowing, was quick to shrug away the hands on her arms. Aurelius was staring down an angry glare from Aaron.

"What do you mean the power is safely locked away?" Rilla asked.

"Does this have anything to do with the chest I saw the two of you and King Lukys carry out of the room while you were healing the girls?" Plyke asked at the same time.

"Yes," Aurelius answered, despite a stormy look from Lord Aaron. "Don't bother looking at me like that, Aaron. We never would have figured out even half of what we know if it wasn't for the three of them. What's the point of keeping them in the dark?"

"For their own saftey," Lord Aaron replied icily.

"Oh, what rot! Together, they're capable of defending themselves quite well now. It's time you started to treat them as more than mere children you want to coddle. They aren't your children. They know the dangers of the Outworld and how to deal with humans. The only person they need to protect themselves from is Lishe and they won't be able to do that if you start keeping secrets from them."

"You forget yourself, Aurelius. I am not some farmer out on the lands. I am Lord Aaron, son of Princess Rilla and I will not have a master speak to me like that in front of my grandchildren. Kindly leave."

"No!" Rilla called out instantly. "Master Aurelius held our lives in his hands when we first arrived. He's the one who decided to let *you* see your grandchildren before letting them just die. I trust his instincts and reactions."

"Rilla…" Aaron tried to interrupt her.

"And don't forget who told you about Kora and Lukys in the first place.

How would you like it if I had kept that secret or if Plyke hadn't told you all he could about the mind snare in the first place?" Rilla forged on ahead. Despite the circumstance, Aurelius was intrigued that Shuut and Plyke were torn between smiling and trying to look grave. As one, they stood on either side of Rilla in defiance of their grandfather.

"Tell them what you will," Aaron said to Aurelius with a wave of his hand. Rilla dissipated the mist just in time for him to walk away. The four of them stood in silence and watched as he closed the door behind them.

"Your grandfather is a proud man," Aurelius told them. "You'll need to somehow make it up to him, even though I thank you for standing up for me."

"Will you tell us what really happened when they tried to remove the mind snare from us?" Shuut asked him skeptically.

Aurelius took her skepticism in his stride. He knew these three lintep were the key to their success and if it meant involving them in things that might be best to be kept secret, then so be it.

"Rilla, if you will." He waited until the mist had completely surrounded them before continuing. "It appears as though, because Lishe stole a lot of power from different lintep and merged it all in herself, the stolen power now doesn't like being alone. Even just the two sets of power together wasn't enough. Both kept trying to attach to another lintep.

"Aaron was really the only one with enough power to safely contain them and he couldn't do that forever. So we got a chest, and I helped him put the powers in there and contain them inside that until we could get to the crypt. No one has the keys to the crypt except for Lukys so we thought it would be the safest place. We buried the chest as deep as we thought necessary for the power to be trapped there.

"The problem is that if anyone finds out that it's there and digs it up, the power will instantly attach itself to them and they will either become a lesser version of Lishe or be trapped in a mind snare. So we need to find a way to release that power the same way as when a lintep dies."

His explanation was met with stunned silence.

"The dragons won't be able to help," Rilla said suddenly. "Even if they know how to release the power, they won't be able to fit into the crypt and, unless you want to risk everyone seeing what you're doing, you won't want to bring the chest out again. Eliséo is going to have to convince the karliki to come instead."

"It would take them weeks to travel here alone," Shuut pointed out. "It would be better if Eliséo could convince both the karliki and a crystal dragon to come. Then they could fly here together and if the crystal doesn't work, then we still have the dragons as an alternative."

"Then, if Kora gets here before they leave, she can tell us what it was that Lukys sent her out to do with the Paradises so many years ago. It might help us find one a little closer than our one to try to destroy," Rilla added.

"Do you really think it will work?" Plyke asked doubtfully. "Any of it? What if it's more difficult to destroy the Paradises than to release just a set of two powers from a chest or remove Lishe's mind snare? What if you need a whole flight of dragons for each Paradise? You might only be able to work on a single lintep's power at a time."

Aurelius marvelled at the questions and insights these young lintep had. There had been a king, a lord and six teachers trying to solve the same puzzle, yet none of them had come up with any of these ideas. How could Aaron justify trying to keep secrets from them?

"Rilla, do you think you could relay that to Eliséo? If he could convince the karliki to go to the Drakos Mountains with him and fly here with one of the dragons, that would be quite helpful."

Rilla nodded and closed her eyes out of habit. She saw Elessa as soon as her lids were shut and reached out to both her tree and her elf.

We talked a bit more with Master Aurelius and it's probably best you bring the karliki and a dragon if you can manage it. Rilla told them as she quickly showed them both the memory of her last conversation.

I'll try Rilla, Eliséo replied hastily. *But with Vladimir possibly still lurking around the Lessa Mountains somewhere, it might not be the best idea for Mikhail, Kazimir and Anya to leave Goraburg all at once.*

Chapter Thirty-Four – Prizes

Kayte and Isis stayed with Guiscard for as long as they could, to help
determine the winners of the research task, but there were still at least five
topics to go through by the time the bell tolled for the morning lessons.
Together, they walked down the two flights of stairs to the classrooms and
were overwhelmed by the amount of students already gathered in the halls.
It seemed few of them had slept the night before in anticipation of the
announcement of the prizes.

It was an arduous time for everyone. The teachers found the morning
lessons almost as unbearable as the students. Everyone was jittery with
excitement and making careless mistakes. Masters and mistresses resorted to
making students practice only the most basic skills in their area so as to avoid
disastrous accidents which could easily occur under these circumstances.
Teachers and students alike heaved a sigh of relief when the bell tolled for the
end of the morning lesson.

The dining hall was busier than usual for the midday meal. Students were
squashing together on benches to make room for everyone. Even masters
and mistresses, who usually would have eaten in their own chambers to avoid
students, were making an exception so as not to be late to the courtyard.
Students didn't linger after eating their fill as they normally did. Every single
one of them walked straight to the inner courtyard when they were finished.

Rilla found Miette as she was walking out of the dining hall and called
out to her to join them. The mousey-haired girl shyly walked over to join
her and Shuut. Plyke was walking a step behind them with Dorian, Umi and
Ulf. Together, the seven of them found a patch of grass to sit on. They talked
together quietly as the courtyard filled up with other students. Much to Rilla's
relief, Marilisa and Réne both made a conscious decision not to sit anywhere
near them.

By the time the teachers and Guiscard walked into the courtyard,
every student, whether they had been assigned a research task the day
before or not, was waiting to hear the prize announcements. This was an
unprecedented occasion and they didn't want to miss out on it.

"Good afternoon, young students," Guiscard's voice rang out clearly
through the courtyard. He waved a handful of parchment above his head. "I
have here the winners of each topic. When I hand them out to your teachers,
they will name the winners and announce the prize.

"For the most part, I was quite happy with your research and I encourage
you to visit the library more often. For the rest of you, I hope the sting of
seeing your fellow students take their prizes is enough to push you to apply
yourselves more to your studies in the future."

He motioned forward a mistress that Rilla didn't recognise. Long, black curls blowing in the wind, she walked over to him, took the parchment that was offered to her and raised an eyebrow.

"For seers and prophecies, the winners are Dezra, Kalydron and Sheridan for discovering that many of the most important prophecies in the past have come from humans. Your reward will be to talk with a human seer and ask him about his visions." A murmur of surprise rippled through the students. Rilla exchanged a worried glance with Plyke. The only human seer in Illaria was Arishen and they doubted he had been asked about this reward before it was announced. Before they could discuss it, Mistress Vika had moved to take her parchment.

"For powerful lintep throughout the history of Illaria, the winners are Wilhem and Verté for noting that there have been many powerful lintep who are not at all connected with the royal family. Your reward will be to watch one of the most powerful, non-royal lintep in Illaria perform feats you could only hope to accomplish."

From her seat, Rilla noticed Marilisa bridle both at the fact that she didn't win, and that someone other than her family would be showing off their skills to students. Rilla noticed Miette's quiet smile as she watched the proceedings. Perhaps the shy girl was just as pleased as she was that Marilisa had been put in her place.

Her thoughts were interrupted by Aurelius stepping forward and taking his parchment from Guiscard. "For Paradises, the winners are Dorian and Plyke for the astounding amount of information they managed to write down in one afternoon. Your reward will be a day long reprieve from your lessons to ride horses around the magnificent expanse of Illaria in the company of our stable master, Edric, and one of his stablehands."

Plyke felt his cheeks burn with pride and embarrassment before looking down to see Dorian clutching his arm excitedly. Once he'd disentangled himself from his classmate, he was surprised to notice those feelings were actually his own and had simply been reinforced by Dorian's.

An entire day to just have fun and see more of Illaria than he had so far was a magnificent prize in his eyes. He wondered if there would be any way to convince Edric to take Tika as the stablehand. The two of them hadn't spent an entire day together since their time in the Outworld.

He was nudged excitedly by Umi as Master Reuben walked up to the librarian. This was their topic and she was confident of winning. The young mind master took his parchment from Guiscard and looked at it in surprise. "For the Outworld, the winners are Azura, Iliana, Mahlia and Serafyna, for disocvering the most about banweps. Your reward will be a short journey outside the borders of Illaria."

Plyke tried not to laugh as Umi and Ulf protested, with Shuut holding them both back. He didn't know what they had discovered, but from their outburst, it must have been significant enough for them to feel cheated out of their victory.

"We barely even stayed on topic," Shuut pointed out to them.

"Who cares?" Ulf replied sourly.

"We still found out some pretty extraordinary information," Umi pouted. He could tell they were about to start complaining even louder when Isis walked over and took her parchment from Guiscard.

"For medicinal plants, the winners are Rilla and Miette, for the discovery of a number of potent plants including the luminous bitter oyster, which is used both to staunch bleeding and to create the ink for our tattoos. Your reward will be an extra lesson with me."

"A private lesson!" Umi whistled. "I wonder if she's already decided what to teach you or if you get to ask for a particular skill."

"You should ask to learn how to make it look like your hand is on fire without it burning," Ulf immediately suggested. Miette laughingly shook her head at him.

"What about juggling balls of fire?" Umi asked.

"What about shooting fire out of your fingers?" Dorian suggested, not noticing Rilla pale at the thought. Plyke noticed it and quickly turned the course of the conversation.

"No, it should be something practical, like how to recover heat in different ways in case you use too much of your own. Or how to light a flame without using any of your own body heat."

This sparked a whole new debate amongst his friends. They became completely consumed by the thought of what might be involved in a private lesson that they didn't bother paying attention to the rest of the announcements. It was only when the bell tolled for the afternoon lesson that they realised the courtyard was already half empty.

Rilla hurriedly organised to meet up with Miette after class to find Isis and ask about their prize. She ran up the stairs two at a time, eager for her lesson with Master Aurelius. This was to be her first practical lesson and she didn't want to be late for it. In her haste, she bumped into the last student who was walking into the classroom. Her heart sank as she recognised Réne turning to face her.

"Watch where you're walking," he scowled at her. "Just because you won a prize with that little crumb is no reason to…"

"Réne, Rilla, to your seats," Aurelius called out to them before Réne could finish his sentence. Rilla quickly scanned the room as Réne went to sit with his friends. She didn't see anyone she recognised. Aurelius came to her rescue. "You can work with Kalydron today."

Rilla took her seat beside the hazel eyed lintep. "Didn't you win the prize for seers and prophecies?" she asked quietly. He nodded, smiling, his dark hair falling to half cover his eyes.

"I guess the seer we're going to talk to is one of your friends. There aren't any other humans in Illaria that I know of," he whispered back to her conspiratorially.

Rilla only shrugged in reply. She knew Arishen was the only human seer in Illaria but was fairly certain he wasn't going to like this situation. Hopefully either she or Plyke would get a chance to talk to him about it before it was too late.

Before she could dwell on the problem any longer, her attention was stolen away by Master Aurelius, who had closed the door firmly and was ready to begin the lesson.

"I know we have a newcomer to the class, but I see that as no reason to deviate from our current lesson plan. Today, you will continue to work in pairs to toss two stones back and forth with your power. Each of you will take out one of your stones and surround it with your power. You will then pass it to your partner, who will pass it back to you. In this way, you will learn to work with another lintep and their power, while doing two tasks at once."

Rilla looked around her in confusion as every student took out a white stone. She hurriedly fumbled in her pocket for her green velvet pouch, the same one that every other student in the class had. She pulled out a smooth white stone and placed it on the small table between herself and Kalydron.

"Don't worry, we'll take it slowly," Kalydron told her as he brushed the hair from his face. "If you want, we can start with one stone until you work out what to do, and then we can add the other one in."

Rilla nodded in agreement. Had she been partnered with Réne, she would have felt insulted by the suggestion, yet with Kalydron, she found herself astonished by the lack of condescension in his voice.

She quickly sent out a tiny tendril of her power and lifted her stone to eye level. Carefully, she pushed it towards her partner, but as soon as she felt his power touch hers, she immediately retreated and dropped the stone. She marvelled at his quick reflexes as he managed to catch the stone with his power before it fell to the ground.

"Uh, have you ever had to work with another lintep like this before?" he asked.

Rilla shook her head. It wasn't quite true, but she didn't want to tell him the only times she had touched another lintep's power was when Nyssa's asked for her help to contain Plyke's power and when she had actually borrowed some of Plyke's power to create a stronger mist under water.

"Well, you know there's nothing to be afraid of, right? My power isn't going to hurt you just by touching yours. When you feel our powers touch, just gently drop the stone into mine, like you would pass it to me with your hand."

"But, what if I don't want your power touching mine?" Rilla asked, knowing he couldn't possibly know any of the reasons behind her aversion to that thought. At the same time, she sent out a tendril towards Master Aurelius, almost in a panic. He turned away from the students he was currently watching and walked straight over to her.

"How are you finding the task, young Rilla?" The question was just for show. Rilla knew he had felt her mood through the light touch of her power on his mind.

"This is generally the first time that students work with another's power in practical lessons. Beginners can't really handle that skill. In this class, students only started working with this skill in the last week or two. Why don't you try it while I stand here so I can guide you if need be?"

Rilla started to shake her head until she felt Réne's eyes on her. She didn't want him thinking that she wasn't capable of carrying out the task and assuming she shouldn't be in the intermediate class for this skill as well. With that thought at the back of her mind, she tried again.

Leaving her tower carefully locked, she kept a large portion of her power milling around the top of it in case she needed quick access to it. She wasn't going to leave herself unprotected, even with a student lintep. After taking a steadying breath, she sent out a thin tendril toward the stone Kalydron had replaced on the table and lifted it again. This time, when she felt his power around her tendril, she gently placed the stone on top of it, just as he had suggested to her.

Kalydron passed it in front of his face and moved it back over towards her. She quickly threw up a shield in front of herself when she saw the stone coming back and let her tendril out through it so that he wouldn't know what she had done. She shaped the tip of the tendril into a small bowl shape for him to place the stone into.

"Well done, Rilla," Aurelius said loudly, then dropped his voice so that only she could hear him, "but I think you had better lower that shield. No one in this class will hurt you."

"What if he tries to breach my wall?" Her past experiences gave her irrational fears fuel to burn.

"Aside from anything else, that skill isn't taught until advanced classes. You have nothing to fear," Aurelius whispered before walking over to some other students.

Rilla looked over to Kalydron to see him quietly working with the two stones by himself. She wondered if he had been able to hear their whispered conversation. From his actions, she doubted it. If Master Aurelius was right, then she really did have nothing to fear from a student like this.

She smiled to herself, lowered her shield and sent out a thin tendril once more to work with Kalydron. He looked over to her as soon as he felt her power touch his and passed her a stone. Together, they began swapping stones with each other, sometimes making more elaborate moves when they passed each one in front of their faces.

By the time the evening bell tolled, Rilla had become comfortable enough with the task that she could carry on a conversation with Kalydron while passing the two stones back and forth with him. The prize winner had told her that his family lived in the city. His father was a blacksmith and his mother and sisters helped him run the workshop while he attended lessons in the castle. His sisters had both finished their studies and were training to become blacksmiths themselves.

"Is that what you want to do too?" Rilla asked him, as they walked down the stairs towards the dining hall.

"Not really," he admitted to her. "I know that's what my parents want, but I've never really liked working at the forge. I want to use my skills on something other than metal and fire all day long. What about you? What do you want to do?"

"I was going to be a healer in our Paradise," she told him in a quiet voice, "but that life seems to have disappeared. I still want to learn everything I can about healing, but I don't know if that's what I want to do the rest of my life. Now that I've seen more, travelled the Outworld a bit and found Illaria, I know there are so many more things that I can do. I'd like to just learn as much as I can and see where my skills really lie."

Kalydron gave her a strange smile. "I have a feeling you'd be good at almost anything you try your hand at."

Rilla blushed and quickly turned her face away from him as they walked into the inner courtyard. She found Miette sitting under one of the archways, waiting for her. Waving farewell to Kalydron, she rushed over to the shy girl and together they ran back up the stairs to find Mistress Isis before she left the castle for the night.

Chapter Thirty-Five – The Dangers of Fire

"Mistress Isis!" two voices called out in unison as the sound of footsteps running through the hall became louder. Isis had been talking with Kayte in the deserted hall outside their rooms. She turned to see who was calling for her and quickly cut short the conversation when she realised who it was.

"Miette, Rilla, I take it you want to discuss your prize?" Isis asked them with a laugh. She turned to wave to her friend. "I'll see you tomorrow, Kayte. I doubt these two will leave me alone until they have all the information they want from me."

As Kayte walked away, Isis ushered the two young students into her room. The sun had already started to set and being on the south side of the castle, the room was rapidly losing light. She quickly sent out a small spark to the fireplace where it quickly spread to all the logs until there was a crackling fire to light the room.

She heard Miette gasp at the feat of magic. The young lintep had only recently moved to the intermediate class and had not seen her perform many difficult feats of magic. "Will you teach me to do that?" Miette asked, pointing to the fire. Isis turned to the fireplace then looked back at the young lintep in surprise.

"Miette, you probably already know how to do that yourself, you've just never tried it," she pointed out gently. "I did intend to let you choose your lesson, but I was hoping you'd have a little more imagination than that."

"Oh," her reply was soft and injured. Isis instantly realised her mistake.

"Of course, I'll teach you that as well. But I thought you might like to ask for something else."

"What are we allowed to ask for?" Rilla asked curiously. Miette looked up at the question, just as eager to hear the answer. Isis eyed them both intently.

"Nothing too dangerous," she replied. "I suppose anything within reason. What did you have in mind?"

"There were a lot of suggestions this afternoon, mainly from the twins, but I don't think you'd teach them to us," Miette ventured, careful to avoid Rilla's eyes. Isis noticed it, but carefully stepped around the issue.

"What did those two rascals suggest?" she asked, knowing the answer would be outrageous. Miette returned her smile with a half laugh.

"The most outrageous idea was to shoot fire from our hands. As if that's even possible!"

The sudden silence was eerie. Isis sat as still as a statue, watching as Rilla paled and Miette looked at them both in confusion.

"It's not really possible, is it?" Miette asked hesitantly. "I'm sure they were just joking."

"I don't want to learn how to do that," Rilla spoke quickly to fill the silence.

"I'd like to learn how to recover body heat if there is no fire around. Can you teach me that?"

Isis regarded them both thoughtfully. "I should have thought a bit more carefully before offering extra lessons as the prize. You'll forgive me, but I can't answer your questions right now. I need to talk to…a few other lintep before we decide on your exact lessons. And now if you'll excuse me, I need to walk home before the light fades entirely from the sky."

Without another word, Isis snuffed out the fire with barely a glance in that direction, shuffled the girls out of her classroom, locked the door and quickly walked away from them towards one of the open stairwells.

"I saw your face when the twins mentioned it today. I shouldn't have suggested it. I'm sorry," Miette said in a quiet voice. Her apology surprised Rilla. She made a quick decision and took Miette by the hand. Together, they walked up the darkening stairwell all the way to the top level of the castle.

Rilla heard Miette's gasp as she walked along the carpeted hall. It didn't occur to her that this would be the first time the young lintep had been to the royal chambers. Rilla hadn't seen the student rooms, but from the small spaces between the doors on that level, she could guess at how tiny the rooms were. In comparison, her room would be the height of luxury.

She quickly unlocked her door and pushed Miette into her room as the girl stared around, eyes wide in amazement. Not wanting to scare Miette before she'd even really started talking to her, Rilla opted not to light her fire the same was Isis had, but instead lit a lantern, hanging on the wall behind her. They'd all done that in her first lesson with Isis, so it wouldn't make Miette wary of her.

"Where are we?" the younger lintep asked in amazement.

"My room," Rilla answered.

"*This* is your room? All yours? Where's your bed?"

"No, I share the rooms with Shuut. The beds are in the next room, over there," Rilla hurriedly explained. "That's not why I brought you here."

"Your rooms must be bigger than my whole house!" Miette exclaimed, completely disregarding Rilla's tone.

"Miette, this is important," she persisted, gaining the girl's attention again. "I've been told there are rumours flying all around Illaria about me and my cousins, but I don't know what you've heard and I don't know if any of them are true.

"Umi and Ulf *were* just joking, but neither of them know that I actually did that once, accidentally. I don't need to be taught how to do it and I never want to do it again if I can help it – it almost killed me the first time. If Isis can teach me, or both of us, to recover heat when we've lost too much, that would be much more helpful. That way if anything like that happens again, I'll be able to save myself if there isn't anyone else around."

Miette stared at her in shock. Rilla shifted uncomfortably. She didn't know if she was right to be telling her this, but from what Mistress Isis said, it was possible Miette would be taught that skill and Rilla wanted her to know exactly how dangerous a skill it was to know.

"You…really did that?"

Rilla shrugged uncomfortably under Miette's gaze.

"Then surely you want Mistress Isis to teach you how to do it properly, so that you don't injure yourself if you ever need to do it again. Of course, it would be useful to know how to recover heat but if you learn how to do it properly in the first place, there's less chance of you messing it up."

Miette was right, and Rilla knew it, but she was too scared of her powers to want to try anything like that again so soon. The last time she'd experimented with her power, she'd made a lantern explode. Miette clearly had no idea how powerful she was and how little training she had.

"I'm still going to ask to learn something spectacular. I'm the only one in my family with this much power and I don't want Réne and his awful friends lording over me the rest of my time as a student. I want them to realise that I deserve to be in these classes as much as they do," Miette told her defiantly.

"You wouldn't use your powers on them, would you?" Rilla asked in a panic. Suddenly, all the fears that her masters and mistresses had voiced made sense to her. It was one thing for older lintep to learn certain skills because they had years of experience behind them, but for student lintep to learn these things could be catastrophic if they used them for the wrong reasons.

"Of course not!" Miette replied instantly. "It would just be nice to learn a skill that they don't know yet and won't learn for years to come."

Rilla wasn't entirely convinced, but she simply couldn't imagine this shy, mousey-haired girl would actually attack Réne with fire if Mistress Isis taught her how. She tapped her teeth together, trying to decide whether to try to talk Mistress Isis out of it or not, but she knew the decision wouldn't really be up to her. It would be decided by the other lintep Isis was going to see.

Without wanting to make the situation with Miette worse, Rilla suggested they go down to the dining hall before all the food was gone. Miette nodded happily at the idea, not realising the turmoil she had caused her new friend.

Chapter Thirty-Six – Goraburg

Eliséo had been running for days. He was miserable, travelling in the rapidly cooling season. His trip would have been so much faster had he been able to ride Fleuris, but he knew Kora needed the chestnut mare more than he did. With any luck, she would only be a day or two away from Illaria. The sooner she got there, the better. It sounded like they were inching closer to the answer of how to destroy the Paradises and Kora was the only one who knew where some of them were located.

His conversation with Rilla and the others had disturbed him. From what he had understood, they wouldn't be able to actually destroy the Paradises without help from either the crystal dragons or the karliki. It was going to be dangerous to take Lord Mikhail Alekseevich, Kazimir Sergeyevich and Anya Nikolaevna away from Goraburg. He'd have a better idea of the situation once he reached the tunnels, but he doubted they would have already found Vladimir Mikhailovich and executed him. Even if they had, enough of his followers had escaped to be able to seek revenge for his death.

Despite the reason for his journey to them, Eliséo was glad to be returning. In his fifty year exile from Goraburg, he'd missed his best friend terribly. He couldn't wait to see Ilya Mikhailovich again, even under these circumstance.

As night fell, he was already carefully winding his way through the ghost gums of Lesa forest, their pale bark reflecting in the moonlight. He kept a close eye out for the single old, twisted snow gum that was a different colour to the rest. It's brown and red stripes marked it as the entrance to Goraburg. As he had done many times in his life, he bent down to the tangled roots of that tree and felt around until he found the cold metal latch. Grasping it firmly, he turned it to alert the karliki of his presence.

Sitting on a twisted clump of roots, he thought back to the last time he'd watched the earth open between the trees. Grigori Nikolayevich had met him and led them all down through the tunnels. The descendant of Sascha Vladimirovich and Nadya Grigorevna, the two karliki who had created the crystal dragons, had been a member of Mikhail's council until Vladimir had forced him out. Eliséo wondered if all members who had been deposed by the would-be usurper had been reinstated to their old positions.

It wasn't long before his questions were answered. The earth opened up to reveal a set of steep, stone stairs and a young karlik with a short black beard walking up towards him.

"Dobrey den, messenger of the karliki," Eliséo greeted the young karlik. "I am Eliséo, Ambassador of the Elves and I wish to have a private audience with Lord Mikhail Alekseevich and his son, Ilya Mikhailovich."

"Dobrey den, Ambassador Eliséo. I am Anatoly Borisovich," the black-bearded karlik greeted him in return. "I have been given instructions to take you immediately to Ilya Mikhailovich whenever you return to Goraburg. Please follow me."

Eliséo's heart lifted at the news as he descended into the tunnels. Not only had he been given free access to Goraburg once more, but it seemed as though Mikhail had actually reversed a lot of the damage that Vladimir had caused.

During the long, winding journey through the tunnels, Eliséo refrained from asking Anatoly the questions that were burning inside of him. He knew the echoing walls had ears.

Rilla had saved both his and Ilya's life when a rebel karlik had attacked them. It had been a much faster journey without the Paradisians, but he couldn't deny that they had certainly kept him well diverted during their time together.

"Eliséo!"

His name echoing from the walls brought him back to the present moment. Anatoly had escorted him safely to Ilya's chambers where his best friend had come out to greet him.

"Ilyusha!" Eliséo smiled and ran to embrace the karlik. "It's so good to see you again, my friend."

"And you!" Ilya replied while ushering Eliséo inside. He paused to speak a few brief words to Anatoly before dismissing him with a wave of his hand and closing the door firmly behind them. "So much has happened since you left. Not only did Vladimir escape, but so did a number of his followers. We haven't been able to find them as yet, but there have been rumours drifting down to us that a number of karliki have been seen in human villages in the past few weeks."

"Is there any word of the rebels planning an attack?" Eliséo asked in concern. He didn't voice his fears that if Vladimir was consorting with humans, it was reasonable to assume that he might try to tempt some of them to become mercenaries with the promise of riches from the depths of Goraburg if they succeeded.

"No, we've heard nothing of the sort," Ilya shook his head. "Father is worried that we've heard very little about them. He feels certain they are planning something, but with no news, we are at a loss as to what to do. Did you hear anything on your way here?"

"I'm sorry, my friend, but I avoided all settlements in my travels. We were somewhat less than welcome the last time I passed through Thistlehall. Besides, speed was of the essence. I haven't stopped to rest these past four days."

"How remiss of me – I'd almost forgotten about your companions. Did they reach Illaria in time?"

Eliséo grimaced at the memory of both Rilla and Plyke falling in and out of consciousness as the Kryti carried them to the lintep stronghold. "By a matter of hours! As it turns out, they were both the grandchildren of Lord Aaron, which meant their power was so great they would have died had we delayed any longer."

Ilya looked carefully at the elf's face as they sat together on the cushions covering the rock floor of his chambers. "We've known each other a long time, Eliséo. I can tell when something is troubling you, or when you're hiding something. I knew there was something you weren't telling me when you were last here, but we weren't left alone long enough for me to ask you." He didn't specifically ask a question, but Eliséo knew he was hoping for an explanation.

He turned the thoughts over in his head quickly before replying. If Queen Liessa, King Lukys, Lord Aaron and Master Aurelius already all knew about his bond with Rilla, what could it hurt to tell Ilya and Mikhail? How else was he going to explain to them that the karliki were needed in Illaria?

I didn't tell you, but she's also told Shuut and Plyke, Elessa quickly told Eliséo, making his eye shine momentarily.

At this rate, everyone who meets us will know.

She had very little choice in the matter once some of the other lintep knew. She hasn't told them your heritage and is doing her best to keep it hidden from everyone who doesn't already know.

"There was…an incident when those children were in Silvaren."

"An *incident*?" Ilya furrowed his brow, making his red eyebrows touch each other.

"My stubborn old tree decided to bind that poor girl to herself. Because of that, I've seen some of the events that have taken place in Illaria since I left. However, I think we should wait for your father before I tell you that side of it."

"Never mind that side of it," Ilya interrupted impatiently. "What has this done to you? Is that why Rilla risked her own life to save the two of us when Stanislav attacked us? Does she think that if you die, she'll die? Is she right? If anything happens to her now, will the same happen to you?"

"I don't know," Eliséo shrugged helplessly in the face of all his questions. "She's been in a bit of trouble since that time, but I haven't felt any ill effects, though I'm honestly not certain if I would. I have a feeling it's more that Elessa would be wounded should anything happen to Rilla. The one branch she grew for the girl might die but I don't know how far the damage would spread."

"Surely Elessa knows," Ilya exclaimed.

Eliséo shook his head. "Nothing like this has ever happened before, so we can only guess at the full extent of the consequences."

They were interrupted by a soft rapping at the door. Anatoly had organised food for Eliséo before returning to his post at the entrance to Goraburg. The elf looked ravenously at the steaming platter of food being carefully placed on the stone table at the side of the chamber. He waited only until the servant karlik had departed again before sitting down to devour the exotic food. No matter how often he ate in the tunnels, he could never become accustomed to the types of food they could grow under the mountain. There was always a hearty helping of mushrooms but the rest of the food was completely unrecognisable to him, despite the fact that he was the most travelled elf in the Outworld.

Try as he might, Ilya could get no more out of him until all the food had disappeared and Mikhail had arrived. Eliséo noted with regret that the old clan leader had aged considerably in the few weeks since their last meeting.

"Dobrey den Eliséo. What news from above?"

"Dobrey den, Misha," Eliséo greeted him warmly. "Very little good news."

Mikhail's expression darkened. "I don't like the sound of that. What bad news do you have?"

"No rumours of Vladimir, I'm afraid," Eliséo told him. "Aside from that, there is a rogue lintep in the Outworld. She has already killed Lady Nyssa and we are fairly certain she has been murdering other lintep by stealing their power. It appears she was the one to put the mind snare on Shadow, or Shuut as the lintep call her, my companion who you helped the last time I was here.

"Unfortunately, she has done this twice more and the lintep are at a loss as to how to stop her. Currently, they've managed to remove the snare from Rilla and Shadow's minds, but they could not release the power as was done previously."

"This girl, Shuut, she had the mind snare cast on her twice?" Ilya asked, aghast.

"Worse than that, she was captured and tortured by Lishe, as was Lady Nyssa before she died."

"Never mind about that," Mikhail replied brusquely. "What about the mind snares. What did they do with the power if they couldn't release it?"

Eliséo shifted uncomfortably. He didn't like asking the karliki for help, especially with the situation they found themselves in, but he really had no choice in the matter.

"This is one of the reasons I've come to you. They've requested your assistance. Lord Aaron and Master Aurelius managed to contain the power in a wooden chest and bury it deep underground, but they know that is only a temporary solution. They think the crystal dragons can help them, but the chest is in a difficult area for such a large creature. It was also be dangerous to draw attention to what they're doing – at least until they know they can complete the task successfully."

The old karlik stroked his brown beard thoughtfully. "There's more to the story than this. What aren't you telling me?"

"We think Lishe is trying to stop Rilla from fulfilling the prophecy so that she can steal all the power in the Paradises for herself. The lintep are trying to find a way to destroy them all as quickly as they can so that she doesn't succeed. From what I've understood, they think they've found a way, but they need your help to be certain."

"When did this happen?"

"The attack was four days ago. The rest of it happened only this morning," Eliséo answered, knowing he would now have to tell Mikhail about his bond with Rilla. To avoid the multitude of questions he'd received from Ilya, Eliséo proceeded to explain as much about his bond with Rilla as he thought was safe to tell Mikhail. He impressed upon them both that the bond should be kept secret to ensure the safety of both himself and the young lintep.

"I see. If I understand you correctly, you want me to leave Goraburg at this dangerous time, with both Kazimir and Anya, to travel for weeks to Illaria for the sake of one rogue lintep who may or may not actually be planning on stealing power from Paradises," Mikhail replied gravely. "You want me to leave my clan in the hands of Ilya, to fend off any possible attacks from his brother for a lintep who poses no threat to the karliki."

"Yes," Eliséo replied, barely able to meet the Karlik's brown eyes. "However, if you'll agree to the second part of my plan, it won't be for weeks. It could be simply a matter of days, a week at the most."

"What's the rest of your plan then?" Mikhail asked, without much enthusiasm.

"To take the three of you with me to the Drakos Mountains and ask a crystal dragon to fly us to Illaria."

"Karliki flying on the backs of dragons! Have you completely lost your mind?" Mikhail cried out. "We belong under the ground, not up in the skies. Absolutely out of the question!"

"Father, be reasonable," Ilya tried to placate him. "A short journey through the skies to save you weeks of travel – it really is the best option. I don't want you to be absent from Goraburg any longer than necessary. What if your worst fears are realised and Vladimir does indeed attack while you're away? If you're back in a matter of days, you can still regain control. If not, he may have time to slaughter all of your most loyal supporters and will succeed in becoming the clan leader."

"Your words aren't as comforting as you may imagine. I don't think I should leave at all," Mikhail crossed his arms in front of his chest with a huff.

"Misha, please! If Lishe is left to her own devices without the lintep knowing how to defend themselves against her, Rilla is as good as dead. Even leaving aside my bond with her, she is a spectacular lintep with amazing powers. Her life shouldn't be thrown away so carelessly. She and her family could be the only people keeping the lintep of Illaria and the Outworld safe from this rogue lintep. They will be in constant danger from her without your help."

"I'll go," Ilya suddenly spoke, his brown eyes sparkling with excitement.

"Father, if you tell me the words to say, I'll go with Kazimir and Anya in your place. That way you can still be here to protect our people from Vladimir should he attack."

"No! Absolutely out of the question," Mikhail replied without pause. "I will not let my son and heir fly on the back of a crystal dragon to possibly fall to his death. What would happen if you were killed in the Outworld? Who would I train to take my place then? Be reasonable, Ilyusha."

"I am being reasonable, father," Ilya protested as calmly as he could. "How many times have the elves helped us? How close was our clan once with the crystal dragons? All of the magical races have always rallied to each other's causes when their need was great.

"If what Eliséo has told us about Lishe is true, then what's to stop her from trying to gain control of Goraburg, for the riches she would gather from the tunnels? She already sounds like a force to be reckoned with and we, without any magic of our own, would be powerless to stop her. We should be helping the lintep so that they can stop this rogue and destroy the Paradises before things get worse."

Ilya was correct, and he saw his father's expression soften as he listened, but that didn't make it any easier for Mikhail to accept the truth.

"If you can convince Kazimir and Anya to go with you, I will teach you the words to make the crystal heart work," he finally answered with a sigh. Ilya almost knocked Mikhail off his feet with a fierce embrace.

"Thank you, Misha," Eliséo said with a warm smile. "I promise to keep your son as safe as I am able."

"Don't thank me yet. You still need to convince two other karliki."

"These are troubling times," Kazimir muttered, once he and Anya had been told the situation. "I'm too old to be travelling the Outworld, much less on the back of a crystal dragon."

"Don't be such a mossback, Kazik," Anya nudged him playfully. "My ancestors created the crystal dragons and I've never even had a chance to lay eyes on them. Eliséo, I'd be happy to help you."

"Anushka, you won't be so happy when you're so far off the ground that trees look as small as emeralds," Kazimir insisted. "Can't we just teach the elf the words so that he can use the stone without us?"

"Aleksander was uncertain about whether the crystal heart would work with other races," Anya reminded him. "What if you teach him the words and he gets all the way to Illaria and then realises it won't work?"

"Surely there is another karlik we can entrust the words to," Kazimir persisted. "What about Grigori? Surely your brother would be just as eager as you to see the crystal dragons."

"That's true," Anya rubbed her chin thoughtfully, "but he is expecting the birth of his first child at any moment. I doubt you will be able to tempt him away from that, even with the lure of the crystal dragons."

"You're going to dismiss all of my suggestions, aren't you?" Kazimir eyed the young carpenter in annoyance. She only smiled in return, neither confirming nor denying his claim. "Very well then, on one condition. We test to see if any other race, including humans, can wield the power of the stone without the help of the karliki once we're in Illaria."

"Kazik, do you really think it wise to let so very many people know of the existence of the crystal heart?" Mikhail asked him with raised eyebrows.

"If they plan to use it the way we think they will, there won't be much point trying to hide the truth much longer," the old karlik shrugged in reply. "I suppose there isn't much point in delaying now that we've decided to help you. I suggest we depart for the Drakos Mountains tonight, that way we'll be there by morning.

"Anya, Ilya, gather anything you think will be helpful, but nothing more than will fit in a rucksack. Eliséo, you look like a ghost. Get some rest before we leave. We don't need you collapsing on the way."

It was all Eliséo could do to nod. He was not used to being spoken to like a child, but Kazimir was so commanding that he instantly obeyed. Once Kazimir and Anya had left Ilya's cavern, he lay down on a bed of blankets, closed his eyes and slipped into oblivion.

Chapter Thirty-Seven – Homecoming

They woke him when it was time to go. None of the karliki had ever travelled far from Goraburg before and had been uncertain about what to take with them. At Mikhail's insistence, they had each packed a small pouch of silver nuggets from the veins running through the caves, in case they needed to buy their way out of a difficult situation. Though he himself never left Silvaren without coins, Eliséo doubted they would have need of it where they were going, but it was always better to be cautious in these sorts of situations.

With bittersweet farewells to Mikhail, Eliséo followed the three karliki on their long journey through the maze of tunnels. Unhampered by Arishen's vision, they were able to take the most direct route towards the Drakos Mountains. Without the Paradisians and their poor night eyesight, they proceeded carefully without the aid of lanterns. It was safer this way – any rebel karlik lurking in the tunnels wouldn't have a flickering flame to identify them by.

Even with their change in circumstances from his last visit, it still took hours to travel through from the heart of Goraburg to the rarely used tunnels leading to the Drakos Mountains. Eliséo's eyes took in the amazing sight of stalagmites and stalactites reaching out to each other, sometimes meeting to create a malformed pillar in the tunnels. His breath was taken away, as ever, by the sight of the underground pools of water. Stones shone an iridescent light, causing the water to sparkle bright blue.

The colours reminded him of the crystal dragons. He tried to think what to say to them. Would he have to deal with Groldor or Loreli again? Would he be able to convince Celtan to come with them? The sapphire dragon was by far his favourite. That wasn't to say that he trusted the old beast, but he didn't seem to be quite as bad as the rest. Or so he had thought until he realised that it had been Celtan's idea to tell Nyssa and Shuut that the other was dead in order to further manipulate them.

He still wanted to save Rilla from their clutches, but he would almost certainly need to mention her name to convince any of the crystal dragons to help him. Hopefully, he had taught her enough in their time together that she wouldn't let them manipulate her, as they did with almost every other person who came across their paths.

Dawn was breaking by the time they left the tunnels. Eliséo was instantly alert, not wanting to be caught off guard by either rebel karliki or scouting crystal dragons. He warned the others to keep their eyes in the sky to search for odd ripples in the light. It wasn't long before Anya spotted one. She pointed the creature out to the others, Eliséo confirming her suspicion.

Seconds later, what had looked like a creature the size of a large bird slowly began to descend towards them. It grew rapidly until it blurred the sky from before their eyes. The sun shone through the clear crystal body, creating rainbow patterns over the ground.

Eliséo steeled himself for the meeting even as the karliki gaped in awe at the massive form of Loreli landing before them, wings spread so wide she would have eclipsed their view of the mountains behind her had she not been made of crystal.

"Haven't you caused enough trouble for one year, elf?" she growled threateningly.

"Nice to see you too, Loreli," Eliséo replied coolly. "It may surprise you to know that I'm not here to cause any trouble this time. I need to speak with Celtan."

Loreli rumbled with laughter. "You are the last creature Celtan wishes to speak to."

"Nevertheless, I have news of his prophecy child, so I assume he'll swallow his pride for that. Or is it *your* pride that was hurt the last time I was here?" he challenged her confidently. Having mentioned Rilla, he'd guaranteed himself the right to speak with Celtan, whether Loreli wanted to admit him to the Drakos Mountains or not.

Without another word, she took off into the sky, growling lowly. Her belly started glowing orange as she started belching out fire and roared. The karliki looked at Eliséo in confusion.

"She's summoned another crystal dragon to take us to Celtan," Eliséo explained as they waited. "Loreli is one of their scouts and can't neglect her duties for long."

"What do such massive creatures need scouts for?" Kazimir grumbled.

"It's true, I've never known them to come under attack," Eliséo admitted, "but they don't like to be taken by surprise with someone simply walking into their home. They've made more enemies than you can count!"

As he spoke, he noticed a crystal dragon appear over the lip of the Drakos Mountains. The fire opal shining in the sunlight instantly gave him away as Pyrid. Eliséo had dealt with this particular crystal dragon a few times over the years. Although he actually liked Pyrid more than most of his kind, he was never quite sure if it was because of his colouring.

Though no one had ever understood why, it appeared that particular colours in the crystal dragons evoked certain feelings in other beings. Whereas the clear crystal dragons always put Eliséo on edge, as though their transparent bodies were the opposite of their nature, the sapphire, emerald and fire opal dragons always seemed to put him more at ease. He didn't quite trust himself around them. He sighed, knowing that there was no choice in the matter now, especially if he wanted to keep Rilla, and possibly hundreds of lintep, safe.

"Eliséo, I had not thought to see you so soon after the disturbance you caused a few weeks back," Pyrid rumbled, as the dust settled around his massive form. "What brings you and your karliki companions here?"

"We need to talk with Celtan rather urgently," Eliséo told him, not giving away anything for fear that rebel karliki might be spying on them. Pyrid eyed him inquisitively but said nothing. Instead, he held out a massive claw for Eliséo and the karliki to step into. The fire opal dragon waited until they had all climbed into his claw before gently lifting them to the spikes on his back. The three karliki followed Eliséo's lead and sat between spikes, tightly holding the one in front of them. Without warning, Pyrid stretched his wings and beat them strongly until he was a hundred feet in the air. Eliséo held on tightly as Pyrid soared through the sky, flying higher and higher to crest the jagged peaks of the Drakos Mountains.

It didn't take them long to reach the flat land within the mountains where dozens of crystal dragons lay dozing on the valley floor. Pyrid descended smoothly and easily towards a bright, sapphire dragon. As they approached him, Celtan raised his head curiously.

"Eliséo, what tidings do you bring?" Celtan asked as soon as Eliséo had touched the ground.

"A little good, but mostly ill tidings, Celtan," Eliséo replied softly. "Though Shadow and the rest of Lord Aaron's grandchildren are now safely living in Illaria, Nyssa was not so fortunate. She was attacked by Lishe along the way and gave her life to save her daughters."

"No! My poor Nyssa," the sapphire dragon wept crystal tears, completely missing the reference to Rilla. "If only she had never left."

"If she hadn't, both of her daughters would now be dead," Eliséo pointed out a little coldly, "which really only became a problem in the first place because *you* tried to manipulate the prophecy around Rilla and told Nyssa and Shadow that the other was dead."

"Yes, Eliséo," Celtan growled. "I am well aware of that situation."

"Good, then let's have no more of that when I tell you that Rilla is alive and safe, for the moment, in Illaria," he barely paused as Celtan's jaw fell open in shock. "She has been attacked numerous times, along with most of her family, by Lishe. One of these times a mind snare was placed on Shadow. You might recall that she was healed in Goraburg with the help of the karliki.

"The next time, the sisters weren't quite so fortunate. They both battled for their lives and the lintep did the best they could to remove the mind snares from them but did not succeed in releasing the power altogether. We may need your help in Illaria for that, especially if the same method of releasing that power doesn't work again."

Pyrid had been listening closely, even though his task had been completed as soon as he'd brought the visitors to Celtan. "So, you want one of us to fly the four of you to Illaria?"

"Yes, but there's more to it than that." Eliséo was now treading dangerous ground. "A few of the lintep think they've discovered a way to destroy the Paradises. That's actually where you come into it. They may need your assistance. Are you willing to fly us to Illaria and then stay to help?"

"Oh, is that all?" Celtan replied sarcastically.

"Actually, no," Ilya ventured. "It would be appreciated if you could ask your scouts to keep an eye on Goraburg and alert the karliki to any rebel movements."

Celtan looked down at the young karlik, as though seeing him for the first time. "And who are you to ask such a favour of the crystal dragons?"

"This is Ilya Mikhailovic, heir of Mikhail Alekseevich, clan leader of the karliki," Anya replied, almost angrily, "and *I* am Anya Nikolaevna, descendant of Sascha Vladimirovich and Nadya Grigorevna. Perhaps you've heard of them? I believe they created the very first crystal dragons, which is why your kind are forever in our debt."

Celtan and Pyrid stared at the furious blonde-haired karlik in shock. The fire opal dragon recovered first and roared with laughter, clapping the sapphire dragon on his wing good naturedly.

"She has you there, Celtan," he said between fits of laughter. "Besides, I think it will be fun. Let's go together! Two crystal dragons are always better than one."

"And what of the extra scouts?" Celtan asked him. "Do you expect Loreli will be impressed when she hears about that?"

"Loreli and Groldor should already have started training the younger clear crystal dragons to be scouts. This is the perfect opportunity for them to do that. How difficult could it be for them to spot rebel karliki around Goraburg?"

"Very well," Celtan sighed, unhappily. "Stay here with our honoured guests while I organise everything."

* * *

Kora slowed her horse down to a walk once she had the border of Illaria in view. She had left her home over fifteen years ago. So many thoughts buzzed through her mind. *Will everything still be the same? Are lintep still as intolerant of humans as they were before I left? Will my father be so angry with me for leaving that he refuses to acknowledge my arrival? Worst of all, will Plyke forgive me for what I did to him?*

This last thought had plagued her since he'd left the Paradise. At the time, she could only hope that he somehow made it to Illaria himself or found another lintep along the way, like Ratchin, who helped lintep in the Outworld. She didn't know that Rilla and Shuut were her nieces. How could she possibly have guessed something like that? She was still shocked to know that Nyssa had actually come to the same Paradise as she'd found herself stuck in and neither of them had realised it.

How different would things have been if Nyssa had stayed? Would Erton still have become the Paradise leader and threatened anyone who showed even the slightest hint of magic or dissent? Would Nyssa and I, instead, have lived side by side in that false haven and raised our children the way they were meant to be raised?

It was pointless to dwell on these thoughts and she knew it. Nothing would change what had happened. At least she came bearing good tidings for King Lukys. She still had the precious map of Paradises he'd sent her out to plot all those years ago. It had taken her a long time, but she'd managed to find eleven before falling pregnant with Plyke and having to stop her search. It would have to be enough to start with. They didn't actually know how many Ophélie had organised to be created but Kora doubted it could have been much more than that.

As she neared the border, she dismounted from Fleuris and led her by the bridle through the magical barrier. Going through it, a chill ran down her spine. It was so similar to the Paradise boundaries. How had Ophélie managed to change it enough to let a few humans through when it came to those ghastly places? If only they could figure that out, they might have a chance of destroying them.

Kora tried to clear her mind as she mounted the chestnut mare once more and headed towards the castle where she suspected Rilla, at the very least, would be awaiting her arrival.

* * *

It took most of the day to fly from the Drakos Mountains to Illaria. Eliséo had not expected to reach the lintep stronghold so quickly. He wondered if Kora was already there, but reasoned that Rilla, or Elessa, was sure to have let him know by now.

Calm yourself, Elessa warned him as she felt his nerves get the better of him.

*You realise these four races, five if Tika and Arishen make an appearance, have not met since…*he trailed off, trying to remember the last time it had happened. *In fact, I'm not certain they have ever all met and worked together towards a single cause.*

Worrying about it won't change anything. Have you decided whether you're going to wait outside the border or see if the Celtan and Pyrid can fly through the barrier?

I don't think it will be my choice. We didn't speak about it before we left and I don't think Celtan would hear me if I yell now.

Eliséo suddenly stiffened as he realised they had flown over the top of the border to Illaria. Perhaps the magical barrier only extended around Illaria and not over the top of it. After all, who but the crystal dragons could possibly enter that way?

Kora looked up at the sudden shadow over her head. A large sapphire dragon and a slightly smaller fire opal dragon were flying side by side. She could just make out three small figures on the back of the fire opal one and a single figure on the back of the other.

The only reason the dragons would be here is if Eliséo brought them, she thought. With barely a second thought, she extended a thin tendril of her power all the way up to them. They were almost out of reach before she managed to brush against the elf's mind. She was fairly certain he'd have felt it, but didn't want to risk touching minds with one of the crystal dragons. With everything she'd heard about them, she didn't quite trust them enough to do that.

Eliséo felt Kora's mind brush against his. It was the slightest touch, but he recognised her nonetheless. He looked down and immediately spotted her on Fleuris. Everything might go more smoothly if they arrived together with Kora. Gripping the spike in front of him tightly, Eliséo reached out with his other hand and pulled as hard as he could on Celtan's wing. He didn't know if the sapphire dragon would feel anything, but it was all he could think to try.

His efforts were instantly rewarded by the dragon circling down towards the fields below, Pyrid following just a length behind him. Thankfully, Celtan remembered that most horses and oxen were not accustomed to large crystal dragons, nor loud noises as the horses in the Drakos Mountains were. They settled far enough from the farms to not create a disturbance.

"What is it?" Celtan asked, once they'd landed. Eliséo looked around them, ignoring the question. His face broke into a smile once he'd spotted her. He pointed out the lintep riding a skittish horse towards them.

"I thought we might like to arrive side by side with Kora."

"Kora?" Celtan asked incredulously. "Nyssa's little sister? The one she trudged half way through the Outworld trying to find before finally giving up! She's *here*?"

"She should have looked a bit harder before giving up," Eliséo told him. "The two of them were in the same Paradise for a few days before Nyssa decided to leave. If only she didn't have the lure of the crystal dragons to take her away from her daughter, she would have found her sister and nephew and, just possibly, they would both still be alive and may even have properly taught their children about their powers without putting them in so much danger."

Celtan didn't reply. Eliséo had driven his point home a number of times already. There was nothing more the sapphire dragon could say to defend his actions. Thankful to have silenced him, Eliséo waited patiently for Kora to reach them.

"Lady Kora, would you allow us the honour of escorting you home?" Eliséo asked with a smile, as he made a small bow to her.

Kora returned the smile and, for the first time in years, didn't protest against the use of her title. She was home now and, in Illaria, she *was* Lady Kora. No matter what happened with her father and her son, though she fervently hoped for the best, she had returned from the task that her king had set for her and she was proud to be able to serve Illaria in a way that no other lintep had before.